Praise for

THE LIGHTHOUSE AT THE END OF THE WORLD

"*The Lighthouse at the End of the World* is a charming portal-esque fantasy with gritty wit, taking its readers on a twisty adventure that is both mythic and mystic, at times violent, with dashes of whimsy, exploring familial trauma, wayfinding and learning to navigate the world, reclaiming control of a life that has always been dictated by others, finding courage, and discovering the power and strength of found families."

AI JIANG, Hugo-nominated author of *A Palace Near the Wind*

"Inventive, immersive worldbuilding."

CAITLIN ROZAKIS, bestselling author of *Dreadful*

"A quirky riot of a debut that will leave you in stitches. Suggars's delightful voice brings to life Dickensian characters in a magical London. Stunning and startling in equal measure."

T. L. HUCHU, Nommo award-winning author of *The Library of the Dead*

"Do you like steam-punk beetles? Old gods? And scamming tourists? You can find it all in a single hallucinogenic book. This debut has cemented Suggars as an author to watch out for."

GREER STOTHERS, author of *Apparently, Sir Cameron Needs to Die*

"*The Lighthouse at the End of the World* is gloriously unhinged in all the best ways, with Oyster McLellen as the kind of scrappy, street-smart protagonist you can't help but root for, even as he cons his way across realities. If you've ever wanted China Miéville and Scott Lynch to get into a bar fight over a manuscript, this is the book that crawls out of the wreckage."

HELEN MARSHALL, award-winning author of *The Lady, The Tiger and the Girl Who Loved Death*

"The creativity and imagination on display is breathtaking. The language employed by the characters is unique and complex, while the story immerses you in murky microcosms that will leave you astounded."
CHARLOTTE BOND, author of *The Watcher in the Woods*

"A vivid and boisterous portal fantasy with a bold, playful voice. I loved the inventive and daringly weird world, mixing dangerous London gangs with 17th century slang and pagan folklore with body horror that made me squirm— but never losing sight of the personal story at its core about found family and lost fathers. More, please!"
GV ANDERSON, World Fantasy award-winning author

"Fantastical other realities, great characters – a glorious world to dive into."
MARIE O'REGAN, editor of *In These Hallowed Halls*, *These Dreaming Spires*, author of *Celeste* and *The Last Ghost and Other Stories*

"A collision of the razor-sharp, grounded and urban, with the hugely imaginative and fantastical. A fish out of water genre tale with flashes of Burroughs, Ballard and Barker. You'll never look at a beetle the same way again…"
PAUL KANE, award-winning, #1 bestselling author of *Sherlock Holmes and the Servants of Hell* and *The Storm*

THE LIGHTHOUSE AT THE END OF THE WORLD

The Lighthouse at the End of the World
Print edition ISBN: 9781835412497
E-book edition ISBN: 9781835412503

Published by Titan Books
A division of Titan Publishing Group Ltd
144 Southwark Street, London SE1 0UP
www.titanbooks.com

First edition: April 2026
10 9 8 7 6 5 4 3 2 1

This is a work of fiction. All of the characters, organizations, and events portrayed in this novel are either products of the author's imagination or are used fictitiously. Any resemblance to actual persons, living or dead (except for satirical purposes), is entirely coincidental.

© Philip A. Suggars 2026.

Philip A. Suggars asserts the moral right to be identified as the author of this work.

No part of this publication may be reproduced, stored in a retrieval system, or transmitted, in any form or by any means without the prior written permission of the publisher, nor be otherwise circulated in any form of binding or cover other than that in which it is published and without a similar condition being imposed on the subsequent purchaser.

A CIP catalogue record for this title is available from the British Library.

EU RP (for authorities only)
eucomply OÜ, Pärnu mnt. 139b-14, 11317 Tallinn, Estonia
hello@eucompliancepartner.com, +3375690241

Designed and typeset in Adobe Garamond Pro by Richard Mason.

Printed and bound by CPI Group (UK) Ltd, Croydon, CR0 4YY.

For whom I stopped my zig-zagging:
Red, Boo and Little Lou.

THE LIGHTHOUSE AT THE END OF THE WORLD

by

PHILIP A. SUGGARS

TITAN BOOKS

PROLOGUE

*Two men sitting at the back of
Deb's café in Camberwell, 2007*

"Is it done?"
"Of course. Separated out into three so it doesn't go off prematurely. We're not like the rank amateurs that you insist upon employing. It's quite sweet really, your naïve reliance on intermediaries."

"Whatever. You and I are taking a big chance here. What if he doesn't find them? Or worse, what if he finds them but doesn't use them?"

"'To work mine end upon their senses that this airy charm is for.'"

"I hate it when you talk bollocks."

"By which, we mean they're glamoured, aren't they. They'll do the trick. It's up to you to leave them close enough at hand to be found. What's the matter? Getting cold feet."

"No."

"You sure? If you want to forfeit this go around, we could always just forgo—"

"No. For this to work, he has to find his own way. They always do."

PART ONE

ON THE BRIDGE

1
THREE CARD MONTE

Oyster emerged from the burnt-air stink of Westminster Underground station and trudged up the steps, avoiding the gum and cigarette butts that might ruin his white Airmax 97s. As he crested the steps, a chill breeze blew around his ears and his fingertips tingled with nervous energy. Directly across the road from the Tube's exit stood Big Ben. No matter how many times he came here, he was always surprised by the reality and size of London's most famous clock tower.

This part of the city always made him uneasy. It was possessed of an artificial sheen and a sort of theme park energy. Nothing like the bit of town he'd grown up in; the place where he had attended – at least some – schooling. He'd always assumed the sensation was caused by the fact that there were probably more feds around.

On this day, though, he pulled the collar of his puffer jacket up around his ears and squinted, his eyes watering from the cold. He'd already made out Broadsides, the crew's rangy twist of muscle, lurking on the other side of the road. He was propped up against the bridge's low wall, smoking. Oyster nodded at him. Broadsides fluttered an eyebrow, drew on his cigarette and played it cool. Oyster scanned the bridge for Baby Ed, their lookout, but he was nowhere to be seen.

He watched Deano, their inside man on the game, arrive.

He was late as usual. There was an inevitability about the way he moved, Oyster thought, like an oil tanker or a freight train, coasting along the pavement and coming to a slow halt just far enough from the other members of the crew. He dropped his plastic palette to the ground and adjusted it with his feet till he had it just the way he wanted. Then came the shallow cardboard gaming table. Finally, with a hydraulic sigh, he settled onto the crate.

Oyster yelped as he was struck on the ear.

"Wake up, wanker!" yelled Baby Ed, as he ran past.

The teenager dodged across the road through the buses and taxis, taking up position where he could watch for feds. Unlike Oyster, Ed had no compunction about pulling bag snatches on old ladies or posting flaming shit through letterboxes. While Oyster had little enthusiasm for these sorts of jobs, he understood they were a necessary part of the crew's business from time to time, but the more filthy or violent the task, the more it seemed to appeal to Baby Ed.

In his more generous moments, Oyster put this down to the fact that Ed had been doing this since the age of twelve, while Oyster was relatively late to crew life. But whatever the reason, there was no love lost between them. Less generously, he remembered being at school with kids like Ed. The ones that seemed to enjoy the kickings and the shamings, who revelled in the boredom and the battles. Some people were just shits. Oyster found himself thinking about his dad and shooed the thoughts away.

Deano, meanwhile, had pulled three playing cards out of his coat and placed them face up on the cardboard: a king of hearts, a four of diamonds and a queen of spades. King on the left, four on the right and queen of spades in the middle. The cards were old, with a waxy sheen to them. They curled on their backs where they lay.

"Game of chance is a sacred thing," he announced. "Once you been challenged you've got to see it through. So, come on! Be part of something sacred! Come and watch the black queen. She's going for a ride!"

In one fluid motion, he threw the queen face down onto the middle of the makeshift cardboard table. With his right hand he landed the four of diamonds to her left, scooping up the queen with his right hand before throwing down the king which had remained in his left. With a deliberate rhythm he continued this shuffle for two or three rounds, always ensuring one card remained in his hands and two lay on the table.

"Easy money, people. Easy money. Come on. Come on now. Follow the lady. Follow the queen of spades," he chanted as he ran the shuffle.

After a fourth round he threw the final card face down onto the cardboard, turning his large palms up to the sky.

"Now, people, where is the little lady?" he said.

Deano flipped over the centre card with his index finger. The queen of spades rocked back and forth, staring up at him.

"And there she blows!" he said. "Come on, people. This is easy money. Just tell me where she's gonna be."

With the punters hooked, Deano would run a couple of straight shuffles. If no one had thrown down cash by the third hand, it was Oyster's job to step in and lay down a fiver out of his float. The game was a typical outside man scam, in that once people saw Oyster betting, they assumed it was on the level and followed his lead.

Buses shuddered over the bridge, bringing a steady stream of tourists past the game. A young man wearing a baseball cap and a black windcheater watched Deano run his shuffle.

"Lay down some cash, my friend," said Deano, looking up at him and smiling toothily, "and walk away with plenty more."

The young man reached into his pocket and pulled out a fiver. Oyster could tell from the unfamiliar way he held it that he was a tourist; a child with Monopoly money. The kiddie folded the note over and placed it on the edge of the cardboard box. Deano pulled a clear plastic paperweight out of his pocket and placed it on top of the money.

"Let's go. Queenie's doing one," he said, waving the two cards in his hand at the tourist so he could see the queen of spades.

Oyster hung back, playing the casual bystander. He heard the almost inaudible double click of cards hitting each other as Deano surreptitiously dealt the king over the back of the queen. This throw, a hype, was the key to the scam.

It meant that, even though the rhythm and motion of the shuffle looked exactly the same as a straight deal, the card Deano's mark was following around the table wasn't the queen of spades at all.

As the shuffle progressed, a young couple in matching T-shirts arrived, followed by a man in a buttoned-up black shirt. Three tourists with actual cameras riding on their chests were the last to be hooked in. Oyster clocked each of them, assessing their cash potential.

"Here we go! Where is she, my man?" said Deano.

The kid bit his bottom lip and squinted at the board. He tapped the centre card. Deano flipped it over to reveal the king.

"She's a sneaky one that queen of spades," he said, shoving the cash into his coat pocket.

The kid looked bemused.

"Listen," said Deano scratching his chin. "You look like a nice guy. So let me give you the chance to win your money back. Why don't we say double or quits?"

The kid bit his lip again. He reached into his back pocket and pulled out a folded wad of money secured with a metal clip. Silently, he put a tenner down on the table. Again, Deano placed it under the paperweight and shuffled the cards. Again, the kid's face twisted in disappointment as Deano threw a perfect hype and collected his winnings.

"Guess you just need to warm up a little more, cuz," said Deano, stowing the money in his pocket and opening his hands.

"One more go?"

Oyster could see the kid was cooling, so he stepped forward.

"Count me in, mate," said Oyster, laying down a twenty. "Let's go."

"A twenty from boydem with the big balls here," said Deano, running a regular toss now Oyster was in play.

"Where is that lady?" said Deano at the end of the shuffle.

Oyster knocked at the rightmost card. Deano flipped it over and gave a pantomime "Oh!" as he revealed the queen of spades. He grimaced and counted out four tens to Oyster.

Seeing Oyster win hooked the mark in for twenty on the next round. By the time they'd finished with him he stumbled away, dazed and a hundred quid lighter.

Oyster watched their victim go. He ran his hand over the stubble on his head. The guy looked like he'd been hypnotised. And in a way he had. The part of Oyster that felt bad for him was answered by the part that told him everyone was fair game. Everything was a con, one way or another. Everyone got fooled, abandoned, chewed up, or shat out. What he was doing wasn't any different than what the coked-up-brace-wearing ding-dongs that ran the square mile did. And those guys were fucking heroes. Captains of Industry. The only difference between them was their patter.

For the rest of the day, Oyster watched as Deano leaned into his work. With a mark hooked, he would regulate the rhythm of wins carefully, leavening the fair hands with the hype throws. If it looked like their mark was going to spring before they could soak him, or if he started to get uppity, Oyster stepped in to keep them in the game. As a general rule, Deano was so fluid in his deals and so generous with his smiles that Broadsides hardly ever had to get involved.

As evening arrived, they'd had a good run and were almost three grand up. The tips of Deano's fingers were nicked from running the cards all day, and when he sat up Oyster heard the man's back crackle from being bent over the deck. The sun was setting and the traffic on the bridge cast long shadows onto the punters as they trudged along the pavement.

They took one more slick billy for a ton and Deano decided to call it a day. With a nod, Oyster melted back towards the wall of the bridge, his legs aching from being on his feet all day. As he turned to head home, a tall man wearing a trench coat materialised from a hustle of suited commuters.

Oyster's gaze was drawn to the man's face. He looked, at least superficially, handsome: his eyes were a resinous black, his nose heroic, his jaw set like some cop show detective. Certainly, Oyster read him as a fed at first. But at second glance, the man's features were all off; each unhappy at being parked on the same face. Taken together, they looked like they had been arranged by someone who had only ever read descriptions of what a human face should look like.

"Excuse me," said the man in an oddly unplaceable accent. He paused to take a long sniff. "We've been watching your game for a while. Would you mind if we offer you a wager?"

The man sniffed again.

"Well, we're just about done here, friend," said Deano, rubbing his back with a conclusive sigh.

"That is a shame," said the man.

He withdrew a gloved hand from his pocket, holding a fifty-pound note between his thumb and forefinger.

"We really would like to play."

The man's mouth creased into a smile. Oyster glanced down at his shoes; spotless brown brogues glistened in the sunset.

Deano looked him up and down, seemingly calculating the benefit of parting this mug from his money and weighing it against the odds that he was a plant from an Eastern European gang or a fed in need of some collars.

"Nah, you're alright, mate," he said, stowing his cards and standing.

"Very well," the man replied, his expression frozen in a rictus smile. He sniffed deeply once more, as though transported by the smell of something delicious.

He turned to Oyster. The man's eyes bored into him. Oyster's neck prickled. He'd been made.

"Maybe next time," said Deano, picking up his palette and table.

He turned his back and trudged towards Westminster Underground station. Oyster suppressed a shiver and walked in the opposite direction.

He glanced back to where Deano had stood. The man was still there, grinning at no one and nothing in the gathering dark. The prickling sensation trickled down Oyster's back. And there was something else, too, a peculiar sensation that maybe he'd seen this man before.

It was at times like this that the black weight of his dad's absence crept out of his stomach and pulled him into the ground. If Lucas had been there, Oyster thought, he could just run home and lie on his bed with the lights out. He could go back to being a son who did not measure up, but who nobody noticed.

He shook his head. *All this, I wish. I wish. I wish. So much whiny kiddy-think. I'm too old for this.*

Time to man up, he thought.

He checked his phone. Amongst the jumble of status updates was a message from Cécile asking him whether he was okay with fish fingers for dinner. He imagined them now, Cécile and his mum, Paris, sitting at the small dinner table, ignoring the space where his dad, Lucas, ought to be.

Oyster leaned over the stone balustrade and looked down at the oily waves below. A refuse barge shrugged its way upriver, facing into the current and the wind. Its struggle put him in mind of his own situation. Stepping up in the gang hadn't been part of his game plan, but with his dad out of the picture, you did what you had to, to put food on the table.

Sighing, he started walking towards the Tube. It was late and Paris would already be sitting in the dark, watching telly and smoking herself into oblivion. She would be there now, dreaming about a world where her man hadn't gone out one day and never come back.

Oyster was knackered when he got home, handing the fish fingers and a couple of tins of beans to Cécile. He offered to help prepare the meal, but was shooed into the cramped lounge. Slumping deliberately in the tatty green armchair that Lucas had liked the least, he stretched, his legs aching from being on his feet for most of the day.

Several of his dad's books had been removed from their home on a crowded shelf and piled beneath. Likely Cess's doing, since Paris didn't read. Lucas had collected loads of books on wackadoo subjects such as past life regression, UFOs and stone circles. Oyster eyed their lurid, dog-eared titles, wondering how the founder of a short-con crew could have been gullible enough to spend his time reading such obvious bullshit.

He'd tried to toss the books out when it had become clear that Lucas wasn't coming back, but Paris would have none of it. He wondered idly now, looking at the pile, if he could chuck the remaining ones onto it, set fire to them and claim some kind of accident. He felt an odd antagonism towards them, sitting there taking up space while their owner was, well, who knew where exactly?

Cécile placed a steaming plate of food on the dinner table. The meal was simple stuff, oven chips, fish fingers and beans, but Oyster had wolfed half of it by the time Cécile sat opposite him.

"Trying to make some space for my own," she said, nodding at the heap of Lucas's property between mouthfuls.

"Let me give you a hand," replied Oyster. Standing with a back-cracking stretch, he took great pleasure in turfing a few more of the books to the carpet.

"Easy," said Cécile. "We might be able to sell some of those."

Three leaves of yellowed paper fluttered to the floor like paper butterflies.

Oyster knelt and picked them up.

Drawn on each sheet, with a hand too delicate to be Lucas's, were looping, twisting shapes, containing what looked like hundreds of diamond points connected to each other with threads as thin as spider silk.

As he laid eyes on them time stopped. The patterns were mesmerising. Despite their irregular, undulating shapes, he was overwhelmed by a sudden sense of recognition. That the designs were trying to communicate something to him, he was sure;

he just didn't know what that might be. It was like trying to remember a word that was on the tip of your tongue. A word that was too long and broad to pronounce, along with a niggling sense of incompleteness.

"S'up, bro? Is it a map to where the old man kept his treasure?" said Cécile through a mouthful of beans.

Oyster shook his head and stood, folding the papers back up and slipping them delicately into his pocket.

"S'nothing," he replied. But he knew it wasn't.

2
BIG MICKEY

Big Mickey was the largest person Oyster had ever seen. Big enough that he even made his chief lieutenant, Deano, look small, and Deano was a henched-up wreck of muscle. Despite his size, Big Mickey was quiet and his hands were small, with fingers that on a less imposing frame would have been feminine.

Those hands fascinated Oyster. Wrapped in tattoos, they seemed at odds with a man who had come up through the ranks and who had used them to do things which even other crew members were reluctant to describe.

The tip of Big Mickey's left pinky was missing from the middle joint onwards, something that Oyster found both hypnotic and repellent in equal measure.

Mickey sat opposite Oyster in the red vinyl booth of Captain Cluck's, a fried chicken joint on Streatham High Street he used as an unofficial office, drinking coffee from a small paper cup. In an attempt to look bigger and broader than his twenty years, Oyster was dressed in an outsize grey Champion hoodie, black track-pants and his spotless Airmax. Over the hoodie he wore a black puffer vest.

"How's it going, youth?" Big Mickey said, clapping Oyster on the shoulder. The booth's upholstery wheezed in complaint.

Oyster nodded. There was a silence which he felt too intimidated to fill.

Big Mickey eyed him, and after what seemed like an eternity, he spoke.

There was a foreign lilt to his words. It protruded into his South London vowels the way an ancient shipwreck pokes through the silt at the bottom of the sea.

"Your old man was an excellent ginnals. Knew how to reel in the punters. Solid. Kept his trap shut and not averse to more choice work upon occasion."

Oyster shifted in his seat. When he'd joined the crew, Big Mickey had started him on the usual low-key stuff: drop-offs and pick-ups; ferrying messages on balled-up cigarette papers. His progress had been steady. Nothing as meteoric as Lucas, who had founded the crew, but then Oyster had none of his father's flair for strategy or raw appetite for business. Lucas had been gone for almost two years now, but his absence still blindsided him.

Lucas's disappearance had been at the root of why Oyster had joined the Urbans in the first place. He'd never wanted to step into his dad's line of business, and Lucas had never pressed him on it. But once he was gone, the family needed money and flipping burgers just hadn't cut it. Oyster had been surprised that, despite his reticence, he had discovered an unexpected solidarity in the crew. A sort of fucked-up brotherhood that he'd not known anywhere else. It was a feeling he'd never realised he wanted or needed until he found it.

Big Mickey took a sip from his cup and exhaled. The sour smell of coffee washed over Oyster. Big Mickey's grey eyes looked through him. They sat in silence, neither of them sure how to navigate their way out of the awkwardness.

"How you and…" He paused, waiting for Oyster to fill in the blank.

"Cécile," said Oyster.

"Yep," Big Mickey nodded his huge head, "your sis, Cécile. How you all holding up?"

"Good," grunted Oyster.

"Knew your mum, Paris, back in the day. She's a good woman. Here in her heart," said Big Mickey, pressing a manicured digit to his chest. "You got to give her time is all. You're her last man standing."

Oyster pressed his lips together and nodded. He couldn't maintain eye contact. His phone buzzed in his pocket, rattling the vinyl of the seat. He fumbled to switch it off.

"When I stepped up," continued Big Mickey, "was a few years younger than you and your old man was captain."

Big Mickey leaned closer as though imparting some choice information.

"Ever wonder why we're saddled with that name, 'Urban Camels'? Your dad told me way back, he named our crew after some old-school word for trickster."

Oyster nodded with an expression which, he hoped, gave the impression he hadn't heard this little nugget a hundred times before.

"So, Lucas took me on even though I wasn't local," Big Mickey continued, "but I got it into my head he hated me. Used to slap me down like he was my daddy. The crew had a bunch of games all over town and Lucas had his fingers in lots of pies. Too many pies. Had us playing every game there was and had us pushing bathtub crank all over the south, but seemed to me no matter what I did I never got any props.

"One day, I thought, screw you Lucas, I'm gonna get myself some glory and some green. So, I got me some flake and jellies and went on a mission over the water, up north. Long story short, didn't go so well. Someone put it about I was working off territory and three Polish paid me a visit. They worked me over proper. Baseball bats. The whole bit.

"Lucas turns up and I think I'm saved. I swear that man was swollen three times his normal size, like a fucking berserker. Shoos these kiddies away like flies, and you know what he does? He picks me up from the floor. Dusts me down, puts my pinky in his mouth and bites. Bites till he gets to bone and keeps on going. Spits this little bullet of blood and meat onto the floor in front of me. Before I pass out from the shock and pain, he says, all quiet like, 'You belong to me. If I decide to eat you and shit you out, then that's what will happen.'"

Big Mickey's eyes were grey glass. He reached over and pulled Oyster's hand towards him, kneading the fingers apart with his own.

He looked down at them.

Oyster was momentarily distracted by ink knitted across Mickey's fingers.

"Got a tat each time I got a bump, didn't I," said Mickey. He rocked from side to side as though to beats only he could hear. "Now, you got another month on the bridge as outside man. Learn. Watch how the game is played. I got face riding on you, bumping you up so quick. Do not disappoint. And then maybe you get a new mark, too."

He released Oyster's hand. Oyster nodded at him and rubbed his palm.

"You do good, then I got plans for you," said Big Mickey. He shifted in his chair. "Dunno if Deano has trued you up to this, but we're comin' under pressure. There are some new players over the river. Some new outfit pushing in on our games, kicking us off turf. Pressing on all our business, actually. I've reached out, but these fuckers are like ghosts. So, we gotta expand."

Oyster nodded.

"You do well on the bridge and I'm gonna set you up as inside man. On your own game."

Oyster was surprised. This was a big jump up.

"I don't got the skills," he replied.

Big Mickey raised a hand to silence him.

"We'll take care of the necessary. You got the makings of a proper crew captain." He tapped his chest. "Ain't never wrong. This new game is a smaller gig, you'll have no muscle and a float of half a gee. Baby Ed will be roper. You kick the float back to me plus two points each day. Keep anything else you make."

"Thanks, boss," said Oyster.

"One other thing," said Big Mickey, pursing his lips and looking down at his coffee. "I can trust you, can't I, cuz?"

"Course," replied Oyster.

Big Mickey leaned forward and licked his lips. He looked over Oyster's shoulder for a second then back at him.

"I got the feels that someone on the bridge crew isn't kicking back their full share. So maybe the bag man is skimming. Maybe your lookout is lifting from the float and making it up from your winnings. Whatevs. I got the sense it's to do with this new crew breathing down our neck, but I ain't sure. Maybe you see something. Maybe you see nothing."

Oyster nodded.

Big Mickey eyed Oyster with the air of a man about to reveal a secret.

A tinny rendition of "Ride of the Valkyries" blared from his pocket, killing the moment. He pulled out his phone and checked the number.

"Sorry, got to take this, you know how mothers can get," he said, and shooed Oyster away.

3
MARY'S BOY CHILD

At home that evening, Oyster lay on his bed with his shoes off and his legs crossed. The telly burbled in the lounge with some sort of reality show. He sensed Cécile in the room next to his, trucking through her homework. Sometimes he wished he'd made more of an effort at school himself. But then, even if he had, with Lucas skipping out and the benefit not stretching to support the whole family, it wouldn't have mattered. He would have always had to get a job.

He'd spent some time staring at the papers he'd rescued from Lucas's books. Thin as Rizlas and humming with some sort of hidden intelligence, he'd stared at them. There was information buried in them just out of reach, but after staring at them for what seemed like an age, he'd set them aside on his bedside table. He was missing something here, but he couldn't seem to forget about them.

He took a gulp of warm beer and put the bottle down on the side, washing the mouthful back and forth between his teeth before swallowing it.

"Hey, Mary's boy child."

It was Cécile leaning against the doorframe.

"Got a plug? My ears are all out." She waved the pair of over-the-ear cans he'd bought her for Christmas with a desolate expression. "No tuneage, no brainage, bro-bro."

Oyster nodded and rolled off the bed, opening his bedside cabinet and rummaging around until he found a charger. Standing to offer the plastic block to Cécile, he clipped the neck of the beer bottle and sent it spinning, spraying suds all over the deck.

"Fuck!"

Cécile and he dashed for kitchen roll and tea-towels, and between the two of them did the best job they could of mopping the liquid up.

It wasn't until he was ready to turn in that he thought of the papers he'd left on the bedside table. They had been soaked and were stuck together into a single sheet. For a second, he thought they were ruined, but then with a sharp intake of breath he saw that somehow they had been perfected.

Stuck together and translucent, each page's patterns wove together into something more than they were alone. Admittedly, Oyster had no idea what he was looking at or what it meant, but the pattern was complete. Whole. The moment he saw the design he knew that it belonged to him. Or perhaps that he belonged to it.

Mickey's words came back to him about getting some ink.

4
EMBANKMENT

Oyster had already learnt the rudiments of being a pickpocket, a skill the gang resorted to on the rare occasions a punter went one-up on the game and skipped out early. But being a whiz-man relied on getting away before your mark realised they'd been robbed. As inside man he'd need a different set of skills, and so, as Mickey had promised, Deano set aside thirty minutes at the end of each day to teach Oyster the rudiments of dealing.

Oyster was nervous about the bump up, but he had no real alternative other than to accept the possibility. Like it or not, the crew was his life now, Deano and Big M were both mixed up with the unarticulated loss he felt for his dad. Their presence hard to separate from Lucas's absence. And words had never been his forte. Easier to say nothing, to swallow the hurt like the black stone that it was than talk about it. Both he and Cécile were like twin survivors from a shipwreck, clinging to each other in the cold water, saying nothing to conserve energy. Of course, Paris was there too. But she was her own problem.

The first dealing technique Oyster had to master was picking up the king and the queen with one hand using his fingertips. Done right, it made it easy to deal either card without your mark knowing. The second was the steady patter that conditioned them to follow the card and not your hands. Finally, there was the hype move: throwing down the king rather than the queen.

After three weeks of intense practice, Oyster arrived on the bridge one day to find Deano waiting for him. The man stood and pressed Oyster into his place on the blue palette.

"You've got your cards. Got your chat. You're ready," he murmured.

Oyster tried to get up, but a glance from Deano rocked him back onto the palette. Before he could object, Deano was off, blending into the crowd to play outside man.

Oyster took a deep breath. *I got this.* The early morning sunlight streamed through the cut-outs in the bridge's low parapets. He unzipped the pocket in his coat and took out his cards. His tongue was fat and his mouth dry. He became aware of the buses as they throbbed over the road, hissing, rumbling and shaking the palette.

The cards were slippery. As he threw them onto the table a gust of wind caught the queen and flipped her over its edge. He swore and grabbed her. Swallowing, he put the other two cards down on their backs and they rocked in the breeze. He traced around the edge of the queen with his fingertips, praying to her for the words to come.

"Come on, ladies and gentlemen. It's a lovely day to play," he said, scooping up the other cards and laying them face down. His voice cracked and was carried away by the wind.

He ran a practice hand and the cards moving in his hands loosened him up. The rehearsed movements getting him out of his head and into his body. He cleared his throat and started again. This time he upped the volume and moved backwards and forwards as he ran the shuffle, doing what he'd seen Deano do a thousand times before.

As he relaxed into his role, the cards flew from his hands in a hypnotic parade.

"Let's go! Go! Go!" he shouted, surprising himself at how loud he sounded.

A couple turned towards him. Their neat hotel-ironed pastel outfits marked them as tourists. Probably here to look at Big Ben, peer at the Houses of Parliament – and here they were now at his own talking shop. He breathed deeply and licked the edge of his mouth.

"You look like the lucky type," he said.

The man turned to him and Oyster ran a few more straight shuffles.

Deano's hovering presence receded as Oyster reeled in his mark, snagging sixty quid from him before his girlfriend talked him into walking away. Even so, Oyster had passed the test.

More punters followed and he rolled and rolled for three hours solid, racking up a good six hundred quid. He felt the rhythm of the cards and the flow of his patter weaving together, netting the punters around him. He sensed Deano's distant pride in him as he worked. Hell, he was pretty proud of himself, too.

He took a break at noon and hoofed it over the bridge to get a burger for himself and a smoothie for Deano. On the way, he noticed Broadsides had found an unlocked service ladder and climbed down to the embankment. Remembering what Big Mickey had said about someone on the game being bent, Oyster bought an extra cheeseburger, wrapped it in paper napkins and shoved it into his jacket pocket.

After delivering the smoothie to Deano, he headed for the embankment. The tide was low and stones protruded from the river like black knuckles. Broadsides was skimming pebbles across the chocolate foam of the Thames as it slid by.

Oyster was mildly surprised to see him doing anything so normal. Perhaps it was part of maintaining a hard man image, but Oyster had never seen Broadsides eat anything, take a piss break, or even nip off for a cheeky smoke as he and all the other members of the crew did from time to time.

"S'up, geez," said Oyster as he picked his way across the carpet of stones and mud, doing his best to keep his trainers on fleek, while simultaneously ignoring the amount of grease the cheeseburger must be oozing into his jacket.

Broadsides turned and nodded. Up close, he was an imposing figure. Tattooed arms as thick as Oyster's thighs ballooned from his T-shirt. On his left arm, the name "Ida" was woven into a thicket of faux Celtic motifs that many of the Urbans favoured. His right arm was covered in a group of geometric shapes that orbited a central red eye. A cheap sliver link bracelet hung from his wrist, the words "brute force" engraved on it twinkled in the weak sun.

"Ida your woman?" asked Oyster, standing next to him.

Broadsides rocked back on his feet, laughing. It was a noise that Oyster felt rather than heard.

"What's so funny?" said Oyster, suppressing his annoyance at being the butt of some private joke.

He pulled the cheeseburger out of his pocket and passed it to Broadsides, who took the offering wordlessly, before dispatching most of it in two bites. He swallowed, but still didn't answer.

Oyster shrugged, turning to return up the strip of beach to the service ladder.

"Hope not," came Broadsides' reply.

"What?" Oyster called.

"Said, I sure hope not," replied Broadsides. "Ida's my aunt."

Oyster took a few steps back to him.

"She raised me, didn't she," said Broadsides, swallowing the last of his burger and whipping the balled paper out into the Thames.

It bobbed up and down on the murky water.

Oyster nodded slowly. He pointed at Broadsides' arm.

"That's some serious ink you got, bruv-bruv, you been on the inside?"

"Ain't a prison tat," said Broadsides, raising his right arm and displaying its black and red spirals. "Traditional, innit. Protection against the evil eye. Or something. From the old country."

"Where's that then?"

Oyster picked up a stone and skipped it out at the white ball of paper as it floated away from them.

Broadsides tapped his nose. "You might be on the way up, but you've got a big hooter."

"Just into my ink is all," Oyster replied, embarrassed at having been called on his curiosity, and as if in explanation, he flipped up layers of clothing to expose his latest tattoo: the pattern that he'd found amongst Lucas's books It had only been finished the week before and its intricacies were still traced in pink scabs. It covered half of Oyster's midriff, wrapping around the sides of his torso, clutching him in inky tendrils.

The tattooist had charged Oyster double and then some, but he had to admit the dude had done a bang-up job. The design wrapped around him in an uncanny way, giving the viewer the impression that it extended into Oyster's body. It had taken weeks and a fair amount of his disposables to complete the job, with long gaps between each session while he healed. He had gritted his teeth against the discomfort as the design became part of him, but the pain had been something real, something he could hold on to.

Broadsides whistled and nodded in approval as he took the tattoo in.

"Very nice. Well fucking trippy. Might have one of those myself next time I get marked up, know what I'm saying."

Broadsides offered Oyster a high five that he had to stand on tiptoes to return.

"And thanks for the feed, cuz, I needed that," he said.

He turned and offered Oyster his hand. Oyster shook it.

"There's some bad blood around here about you, but you're alright, mostly," he said.

"Mighty big of you," Oyster replied sarcastically.

Broadsides laughed and launched a stone the size of a baked potato into the river. It missed the balled-up burger wrapper, but kerplunked into the water with such energy it washed its target beneath the surface.

"Brutalist!" said Broadsides with a cackle.

5
TOOTING BEC

Oyster took the Tube home. It was stuffed with suits, tourists, students. Peak time. All people who had a direction, a sense of purpose in their lives. He counted the stations, feeling himself pass through them as though they were organs in a sprawling, subterranean body. He suspended himself from a yellow plastic handgrip, arse jutting outwards. He was like this train, he thought, chugging underground in the dark. Unsure of where he was headed.

An elbow pressed into his back and he twisted around, ready to cuss out whoever was behind him, but there stood Broadsides. Oyster clocked he was toting the vinyl sports bag they used to transport the day's takings over to Mickey.

"Where you steppin' off, bro?" Broadsides asked.

"Tooting," replied Oyster.

"I'll come with."

Oyster tried to make conversation, but all he got in return was grunts and grimaces.

They rode the escalator, Oyster scurrying to keep up with his taller companion.

"Don't want to talk down there. Can't trust it," said Broadsides, over his shoulder.

"Whatever," said Oyster. "It's your trip."

Broadsides stooped as he walked, but it wasn't the stoop of a tall man fitting into a world too small for him. Rather, it was the stoop of a man who didn't want to be noticed. Broadsides' gaze flicked from side to side, sizing up travellers descending on the other side of the escalator, expectant and wary.

When they hit the street, they crossed at the lights outside the station and headed up Garrat Lane. There was a series of beeps and chirps as Oyster's phone lit up with messages from Cécile.

"You use that thing too much," said Broadsides. "They're keeping an eye on you, wherever you are."

He extended his index and middle finger, pointed them at his own eyes then turned them towards Oyster in a gesture of surveillance.

"And who would 'they' be?" Oyster replied.

"Alexa? Siri? They're all the feds. You forgetting the business we're in, brother?"

Oyster nodded and stowed his phone in his pocket. Broadsides had a point. And Deano was always ragging on him for using it too much.

It was early evening. Pairs of yellow headlights ran past them, whipping up the acrid smell of exhaust. Oyster and Broadsides ambled through rows of terraced houses, takeaway joints and lurid newsagents that advertised phone unlocking services. Shabby as it was compared to Westminster, Oyster was at home here. Everything torn up, tossed up, and he kind of liked the lack of greenery.

After five minutes of walking in silence, Broadsides visibly relaxed and drew himself up to his full height. He reached into his pocket, took out a bent roll-up and clamped it between his lips. He lit the cigarette and puffed.

"Some weird shit going down in this crew, man," he said.

"What's that supposed to mean?" replied Oyster.

They crossed over the road again and Oyster led them past the low stone walls of Streatham Cemetery. The first patch of green they'd seen since emerging from the Tube. Broadsides sniffed and cracked his knuckles.

"Lot of men down, women too."

Oyster didn't want to invoke the spirit of Lucas. He remembered half-caught conversations that his dad had had with other crew families. *We're soldiers. It's a war*, he would say. But Oyster couldn't repeat the words. They stuck in his throat. Broadsides rolled on anyway.

"We're a short-con outfit. Ginals all. How come so many been fingered, done runners or worse?" He twitched his head from side to side and looked around. "No dis."

"None taken," Oyster replied.

He thought of the games of hide and seek that he, Cécile and Lucas would play around the flat when he was home from the crew. Lucas was too big and tall to hide anywhere really, and his trainered feet would always stick out from under the curtains, or his shoulders would bulge from behind a door. It had become a joke in itself after a while.

Oyster pursed his lips, his throat was tight. There were a lot of car fumes around here.

Broadsides snapped a twig from an overhanging tree, suddenly uncomfortable. He stripped the leaves from it one by one and discarded them.

"What you still doing here, then?" said Oyster, scratching his nose.

Broadsides cracked a wide smile. He took a leaf between thumb and forefinger and mimed rubbing money.

"Need the papes, don't I?" he said.

Oyster nodded.

"Don't we all? If you need money there are better ways of making it."

"Ain't into shifting." Broadsides shrugged. "Know my limitations. I'm good muscle for a game. But once you go narc you have to step it up, mate, know what I'm saying? Ain't ready to rain that sort of shit down on everyone I know."

Oyster nodded. It was true. He'd made much the same calculation himself. You could make a lot of money selling drugs, but your life expectancy decreased proportionately. He bit his lip. Big Mickey had told him to play this close, but he felt Broadsides was being straight with him.

"You in the know about this new mystery crew causing so much grief?"

Broadsides cast him a sideways glance.

"Why you asking?" he said.

Oyster shrugged.

"Big Mickey asked me to keep an eye out."

Broadsides nodded and the two of them walked for a hundred yards in silence as the sky purpled like a bruise.

"Don't know nothing about them. And that wouldn't be all that odd. 'Cepting no one does. From what I hear, they just show up out of nowhere and knock shit right over."

"Games?" said Oyster.

"Everything. They're sticking their fingers deep into deals. Pop out of nowhere and then ghost afterwards. They know shit, too. Almost like they got sources. Like they're hooked up with the feds. Or got peepage on the inside."

On the opposite side of the road, a car pulled out of the traffic and drew up to the kerb. There was the echo of a backfire and Broadsides' expression made it clear he thought he'd said too much.

"Fuck this, man, I'm creeping myself out." He looked around, hugging the football bag closer to his chest. "What you reckon. Through the Stretch?"

The thought of heading home through disputed territory made Oyster's stomach twinge. He'd sneaked through this shortcut, which edged into the Stick Up Kidz' turf, in the past, but those occasions had been in daylight on a weekday. And he hadn't been carrying a bagful of cash.

His anxiety was initially balanced by how proud he'd feel at having helped to ferry the bag to Big Mickey, and that in turn made him feel manipulated. The feelings all swirled into a kind of righteous anger directed at… life? Fuck this shit. It would give him something mildly braggable he could drop into his next chat with Big M, and if he got shanked up? Well, who would give a crap. Paris? A crow landed in one of the overhanging trees and eyed them both. A ribbon of pain flickered around his tattoo and was gone.

"What we standing here yapping for then, geez?" said Oyster, hopping over the amputated stumps of the cemetery railings and into the wet green of the graveyard. His feet whipped through the unkempt grass, beating a counterpoint rhythm to Broadsides' huge trainers as they did the same.

Oyster's spider-sense tingled. He glanced at Broadsides, whose hunched frame betrayed how he felt too. They were over halfway across the graveyard when Oyster saw them: a group of youths on the other side of cemetery keeping pace, but hanging back just enough to betray their intention of avoiding being made. A Stick Up Kidz crew.

Oyster's toes prickled and his mouth was dry. He'd only got into a couple of beefs since stepping up. Luckily he'd inherited Lucas's broad frame, which meant he looked like he could handle himself. But the batterings he'd been involved in had left him feeling initially giddy and then sick to his stomach. He tried to count their pursuers. Four, maybe five: bad odds. He reached into the front pocket of his jeans where his knife pressed against his leg. His fingers curled around its grip.

He and Broadsides were marching now, heads down, across the green, heading for a gate in the graveyard's far corner. If they could get to it before the others, they'd be able to sprint back into Urbans territory and relative safety.

A moment later and their silent game of chicken dissolved into them both running as fast as they could towards the gate. The Stick Ups on the other side of the wall broke into a whooping gallop.

Oyster leaned into the run, but it was too late. The Stick Ups had already made it to the gate. They crowded around it, blocking the exit. There were two mean-faced minnows about Ed's age, one henched-up type in a bomber jacket who was probably captain and one tubbier lad who hung back. Oyster pegged him as the brains. While all the other crew members had their aggro on, the boy's pinprick eyes regarded Oyster and Broadsides coldly.

There's no shame in doing a runner if the odds are against you. Represent your ends and all that, but not at the cost of doing a dirt dive.

Deano's words tumbled through his head. Fear squeezed his insides.

The cemetery wall was too high to vault over, even with a run-up. Plus, it would be easy for the Stick Ups to catch them on the other side.

"Game's up," said Bomber Jacket, "you batties are off base, slipping in the wrong place."

Oyster and Broadsides slowed to a saunter. They couldn't show they were frightened. Broadsides sniffed and wiped his nose with the back of his hand. Every bit of Oyster's body throbbed with adrenaline. He wanted to turn around and run back, but without some sort of advantage they were stuffed.

"Could say the same for you and Supersize here," replied Broadsides. "Last time I checked, Stick Men turf started thataways."

He nodded at the road on the other side of the wall.

"Supersize? Is that all you got, fat-shaming?" the fat kid responded. "Tell me, if I'm such a wasteman, how is that we've battered so many of your bros?" The boy's delivery glittered with barely concealed malice.

"Looky," said Broadsides, "we ain't looking for no mischief."

"Bit late for that, innit." The fat kid nodded at Oyster. "We know all about boydem here. His daddy did a runner. Now he comes here, all shook, weeping his old man tears all over our territory."

Oyster closed his eyes and bit his lip. His knuckles ached as his grip became ever tighter on his knife. Everyone here would be tooled up, no doubt. That's why he carried. That's why they all did. It was times like this that he wondered about the value of getting strapped, just for show. But then a gun drew its own kind of trouble.

"Come on now," said Broadsides, "no one's looking to misbehave." He laid a hand across Oyster's chest.

"Could've fooled me," Bomber Jacket's voice was a deep baritone, "steppin' all over our turf. Guaranteed upset. Way I hears it, you lot have been leanin' on us all over. Kickin' over our games. Hurting on our business. Enough is enough. Message needs to be sent."

Broadsides shook his head.

"I dunno where you wallads get your information, but it's all fucked. Things have been peaceable between us. For the most part."

Oyster took a step forward. The Stick Up Kidz issued a chorus of mocking hoots.

"Just trying to rile you," Broadsides hissed to Oyster.

Memories stirred and Oyster pushed them down deep. He released the knife and pulled his hands out of his pockets. He cracked his knuckles. He had to do something to save face. But maybe not what they wanted.

"Stay tight," he whispered to Broadsides, gently pushing his friend's restraining hand aside.

Oyster inhaled deeply, trying to push his anger away along with his memories. He lurched towards the gate and gave his knuckles another crack. Shoving one hand deep into his other pocket, he fished out four coins. A two-pence piece, a fifty-pence piece and two tens. It wasn't great, but would have to do.

For all his bravado, the fat kid flinched as Oyster approached. Bomber Jacket intercepted him, his arms folded.

"That's enough," he said.

Fat Kid recovered his composure. "What you got to say for yourself?"

Bomber Jacket retreated, but reached his hand into his pocket, no doubt fingering his own knife. Oyster took a breath and stepped through the gate. He shook his shoulders, felt the air rolling across his temples. The sun was setting. All across the city it was getting dark. He sensed its raw earth under his feet, felt the stars turning unseen overhead and took a breath. Everything – him, Broadsides, the Stick Ups, the rotting bones in the ground beneath his feet – were all part of the same thing; the same mechanism, like a clock that had been wound too tight.

He held the coins in a stack in the tips of his right hand, and with a practised movement used his right thumb to spread them so that each was held between adjacent fingertips. A four-coin flourish, Deano had called it.

"Watch," he said, voice cracking. He held up his hand, brandishing the coins. The yellow flicker of streetlights turned them to slivers of gold.

"Fool's going to tug us off with some David Blaine shit?" said the smallest of the Stick Ups. "You seeing this, Tanks?"

Oyster ignored him and dug in with his patter. This was the most dangerous moment. Bomber Jacket could stick him easy enough now, but if he kept the crew distracted, he and Broadsides might stand a chance of getting away.

Silently, Oyster performed the first two of the four sleight-of-hand tricks he knew: Coin through the Hand and a French Drop. The first was always a guaranteed way of getting attention, sending a couple of the coins tumbling though the back of his hand only to make them reappear from behind his ear, while Le Tourniquet or French Drop was one of the oldest tricks in the book. You held a coin by your fingertips, only to make it vanish with a twist of the fingers and a theatrical puff of breath. Oyster supercharged it using all the coins to hand. By the end of the second trick, he knew he had them. He could feel the temperature of the situation dropping, but he was running out of repertoire.

He went into another flourish and then into the setup for a Three into Two. He needed to get the muscle off guard. He tapped Bomber Jacket's hand to get him to put it out for the trick's finale. By now, the Stick Ups were engrossed in the illusion despite themselves. The boy complied without thinking, but Oyster caught Fat Kid's eye and he knew he'd been made.

Instantly, Oyster whipped his hand back and let the coins fly at Bomber Jacket's head, but Fat Kid pushed him out of the way before they made contact. Oyster spun around and ran. Broadsides' long legs had already carried him a quarter of the distance back the way they'd come. He galloped over gravestones like he was a prize steeple-jumper. Oyster didn't look back. He wasn't sure who, if anyone, was behind him, but his trick had given them a head start. He ran as fast as he could, bearing away from the gate at an oblique angle. The sound of his feet on the grass and his breathing were his world.

A memory came to him. Him and Lucas running across the park not far from here. It had been a Saturday. Lucas had come home from the crew with a football autographed by the entire Chelsea squad. Even then he had already learned not to ask how such a priceless artefact might have come into his dad's possession. Cécile had still been a toddler, young enough that she could only run a flurry of steps before toppling backwards onto her bum. She had sat in the grass and watched and clapped as he and Lucas had chipped and flicked the ball back and forth between them, using their jumpers as goal posts. Another jagged breath and the memory evaporated.

Bomber Jacket streaked past him on the right, heading straight for Broadsides. They were after the money, and fast as he was, the bag was slowing him down. Bomber Jacket was gaining ground. Oyster's lungs were at the top of his throat as he swung towards Broadsides' pursuer and pumped his arms as fast as he could.

A burst of muscle-burning speed and he was directly behind him. Bomber Jacket was already reaching a hand out towards Broadsides. Oyster gulped in a final breath of air and dived at Bomber Jacket's ankles in a flailing, desperate rugby tackle. Bomber Jacket twisted in surprise and kicked back, but it was already too late. Oyster had him. He clung to his legs, wrapping himself around them, and closed his eyes. The two of them fell for what seemed like a long time and then there was a bright, sharp pain as a thick-soled trainer caught Oyster in the stomach.

They rolled to a stop. Oyster was breathless and paralysed. Shards of light flickered behind his clenched eyelids. He rolled to his knees, forced a breath into his rigid stomach, and then he was up and running again. He risked a glance back. Bomber Jacket lay sprawled among the grass. His temples were stained black in the yellow light. He must have head-butted a gravestone on the way down. The other members of his gang gave up the chase and turned back to check on their fallen comrade.

Oyster ran wide, heading to the gate furthest from them, but they'd no interest in him anymore. He caught sight of Fat Kid's face in the streetlight. The boy's expression was the face of a child, knitted with worry.

Broadsides caught up with him as he got back on their territory, out of breath but jubilant.

"Rep-res-ent." He offered a fist bump.

Oyster's hands were still shaking, but his breathing was returning to normal. He was elated at their escape. Something like pride unfurled in his chest. Then he remembered the boy's face. There was a *caw* from the nearest tree. With a flap of wings, the crow flapped up into the night.

It was dark now and they hurried deeper into home turf. Oyster felt the comfort of the neighbourhood wrapping around him as his shuddering breathing returned to normal. They walked a block in silence. After all the excitement Oyster was suddenly empty.

"Right," said Broadsides, patting the football bag. "Gotta skadoosh." He offered Oyster a fist bump, before turning and slouching into the city.

6
CEREMONY

Oyster dreamed he was being chased. The lifts in the block were out and he ran up the stairs, pursued by some sort of faceless dread. Hands trembling, he got the key into the lock, burst into his flat and slammed the door. It was then he was faced with the sickening certainty that whatever he'd been running from was already inside with him.

He raced to Paris's room and shut himself in a wardrobe, listening as the house was ransacked. Light seeped in around the doorframe. At his feet was a small enamel box. This was what his pursuer was after. He reached down to it and froze as he heard the sound of sniffs at the wardrobe door.

The thing outside wanted him to open the box, but he was seized by the certainty that its contents were more terrifying than what was searching for it. He dropped the box, held his breath and closed his eyes. Where was Paris? Why wouldn't she make all this go away?

The light went out and the sniffing stopped. Oyster waited for what seemed like an age and then opened the wardrobe door. He was in a wood. Blue light danced ahead of him through a thicket of naked branches.

Oyster pushed on towards the centre of the wood, skin crawling but drawn on by the flashes of lightning. The night was suddenly cold and his fingertips were numb. He pressed through a final clawing tangle of branches and into a broad clearing, dominated by a single oak.

On the muddy ground, centred on the tree, was a swirling symbol composed of three interlocking spirals which glowed with an unnatural fire. At the centre of each of these spirals stood a figure. The nearest, grasping a spear, had his back to Oyster. Lightning lanced down from the sky and danced around the weapon, energy coursing into the ground and illuminating the spiralled scrub in which he stood. The acrid smell of ozone stung Oyster's nostrils.

The second figure, on the far side of the tree, was tall, antlered and cloaked in shadow; the third, to Oyster's left, was a young woman. She looked to be a few years younger than he was and was barefoot, clad in a simple robe. The most disturbing thing about her was her face, which had been stained a shocking midnight blue. He felt as though he was witnessing something he shouldn't be, and as much as he wanted to keep out of sight, a feeling deep in his stomach compelled him to creep forward.

The antlered figure barked in a language Oyster couldn't understand, before emptying a leather purse at the foot of the tree; three coins glittered in the strobing darkness. As they hit the ground, some ancient circuit was completed and the spiralling symbol caught fire, crowning the antlered figure with a silvery halo. An ominous bass growl pressed in on them, so powerful that Oyster felt it in his chest.

The woman advanced stiffly like a doll and knelt before the tree. She scooped up the coins and stood. The low throbbing rose to a crescendo. Pausing for what seemed like an age, she stepped towards a terrified Oyster who, for a second, thought he'd been made. Panicking, he tried to hunker down into the foliage but found himself unable to move.

The woman was unseeing, though, totally tranced out. She faced the spear carrier and reached up. With a flash of metal, she pressed the coins to his forehead. The deep vibration became almost unbearable, making it hard for Oyster to think and shaking his lungs so much that it was difficult to breathe.

As the coins were placed, the man with the antlers threw up his arms and roared with hysterical laughter. Lightning came down again and again, striking the spear carrier, making him swell in size and strength. Then with a flash Oyster was knocked on his back again, staring up at the unfamiliar stars that gazed at him coldly.

7

THE BRIDGE

Cécile shook Oyster awake. He'd fallen asleep on the sofa.

"Come on bruv-bruv," she said. "Rise and shine an' all that."

She was dressed in her school uniform, her bag slung over her shoulder.

"You pull an all-nighter or something?" she said. Oyster's mouth was dry. Cécile pulled the curtains open, searing him with early morning sunshine. He grumbled and covered his eyes. The nightmare still had him in its grasp.

"You need a girlfriend," she said.

Oyster grunted.

"Or a boyfriend."

Oyster grunted again.

"Or any sort of friend at all. You need to get out of this house and get some sort of life. Other than work."

Oyster assumed what he hoped was a winning smile.

"What, and miss out on all this love and attention?"

Cécile rolled her eyes.

"I dunno what your malfunction is," she continued, "but you were dribbling all sorts of nonsense while you were asleep."

Oyster shrugged. Cécile shook her head in exasperation.

"Well, it is a *school* day, so you know, girl's gotta shift."

"Hey, hold it." He looked around to make sure that Paris

hadn't got up yet. He padded to his bedroom and returned with a thin roll of tens.

Cécile pocketed the money.

"I'll do a shop on the way home, we got nothing much in. Again," she said.

Oyster rubbed his eyes and nodded. Cécile snapped the front door shut behind her and was gone, leaving Oyster alone and uneasy. He felt small, as though he was being watched. Chalking it all up to the strange dream, he showered, dressed and ate in a trance, then made his way to the bridge.

The queasy, disembodied feeling haunted him all morning, throwing off his game so much that Deano stepped in for him and packed him off for an early lunch. Oyster improved a little when he came back, but the emptiness inside him had sucked up all of his patter and he couldn't get warm. He found himself turning the images from his dream over and over in his head: the ceremony, ritual or whatever it was; the tripped-out, stained face of the young woman.

He was jumpy, and every now and then he thought he saw the blue-faced woman: suited and booted and on her way to an office job; or as a uniformed attendant at the Underground turnstiles. A second look and she wasn't there. A breeze whistled across the bridge and Oyster pulled the zip of his puffer vest up higher around his throat. He leaned forward, flexing his toes in his trainers and lifting the arches of his feet off the floor to stop them going to sleep.

It was then that he spotted the shiny brogues and trench coat of the weird dude who had challenged Deano a few weeks ago. The coat was undone, revealing worn woollen trousers and an Ed Sheeran T-shirt that still showed the creases from its packaging. Oyster's stomach prickled and he realised the pain was coming from his tattoo. He scratched it with fingers that were suddenly numb.

Before he even opened his mouth, the wellspring of patter within him sputtered. He knew what was going to happen next. He realised that he'd felt like this before, on the night Lucas had disappeared. His mouth felt dry and there was a sickly sensation spinning around in his stomach. He shut his eyes and made a conscious effort to put it out of his mind.

He tried to picture something else. He thought of last Wednesday: he'd picked Cécile up after school, and flush with his earnings from the bridge they'd gone for Happy Meals. A ritual from an earlier, simpler life, they'd taken their time over the food and improvised a sweary puppet show with their crappy plastic toys as they fought over who got the last fruit bag.

His tattoo fizzed with pain, breaking him out of his reverie. The happy memory was chased away by an overpowering sense that he was falling; that there was an inevitability to everything that was about to happen and there was nothing he could do about it. The man pulled a crisp fifty from his pocket and laid it on the makeshift table. He sniffed loudly and a too-small tongue wet his lips. Several other people gathered around to watch the game.

"Now we've challenged," said the man, "you have to play. Those are the rules. After all, *a game of chance is a sacred thing.*"

Oyster wanted to refuse but he couldn't, not without blowing it entirely. He looked for Deano, hoping his captain would signal to tell him what to do, but he'd disappeared.

"Okay! People, let's go. Geez here wants to play. Let's see if he's got the juice!" shouted Oyster, but he knew he sounded forced and unconvincing.

Oyster dropped a stone over the fifty to hold it in place and the man nodded, moving in closer. A choking collection of smells emanated from him: cut grass and blood, plus the merest suggestion that he might have shat himself. Oyster winced.

He threw the cards down onto the deck and did his practice runs, calling out the black queen and flipping her over with his index finger.

"You still up for this, mister?" he said.

The man's almost-a-face creased into a lupine smile. Oyster did a quick scan for Deano, but there was still no sight of him. Broadsides' comforting bulk, however, lurked like an oak tree on the horizon.

Best to nip this one in the bud, thought Oyster.

He went in quick with a perfect hype pass and nodded to the man to choose where the queen lay.

"Well, let us see," he replied. "We're new to all this, but," he sniffed ostentatiously, "we think it may be this one." He touched the leftmost card. Oyster flicked it over. The queen stared back up at him. He couldn't believe what he was looking at. He'd made the hype and was sure the card should have been in the middle.

"That means we've won, doesn't it?" said the man, his maggot tongue poking through his lips again. His mouth twisted into a smile which failed to reach his unblinking, birdlike eyes.

For a second, Oyster was sure he saw something small and black emerge from the man's left ear and crawl into his hair. It was such a disconcerting sight, he looked away as he handed over the man's winnings.

"You're supposed to ask us if we want to play again," he sniffed. "Double or quits."

"Yeah. Yeah. That's it," said Oyster trying to recover. "Double or quits!"

The man put three hundred down in fifties. The crowd *ooh*ed in approval.

Oyster smiled mirthlessly and ran another perfect hype; the man picked the correct card again. And again. And again. Oyster felt sick. He was cleaned out. This wasn't supposed to happen.

"Cops!" screamed Broadsides, charging in and belatedly breaking up the game.

He scattered the crowd and kicked over the cardboard deck.

"Game over!" shouted Oyster, running past the end of the bridge for a few hundred yards, just for appearance's sake.

He stopped and looked back for the rest of the crew. The squat shape of Deano beckoned him to return. He ambled back, biting the inside of his mouth. His legs and lungs ached from the sudden exercise. Looking over Deano's head, he caught sight of the man heading west over the bridge, walking at a steady pace. It was late in the day and passersby threw long shadows onto the bridge's low parapets. Oyster shook his head and looked again, his brain unable to process what he was looking at. He squinted. It must be a trick of the light, but he was as certain as he could be that the retreating figure had a pair of shadowy antlers.

Oyster's confusion was interrupted by Deano's low whistle.

"You took your time," yelled Oyster, forgetting the man in his anger. "Where were you? I needed you to cool that mark down."

"Easy now. No need to go blaming me, young blood. You messed this one up good and proper all by your jackie-jones."

Oyster looked up at the sky and swallowed. He wanted to cry.

"This is a bad one, son. Bad. Sent Broadsides after your man, though. Let's see if he pulls your arse out the fire."

Oyster swallowed and wiped his eyes, trying to hide how upset he was. "Fucker picked right every time."

Deano wobbled his head from side to side.

"Maybe you just been clipped by a ringer from the Ukrainians or a Roma."

Oyster's chest was tight and his eyes throbbed. The inside of his mouth was wet from the bite he'd taken out of it.

"Listen. I'll try and straighten this out for you with Mickey. No need to pick it up with him. Whatever happens with Broadsides," said Deano clapping Oyster on the shoulder. "The Big Man knows everyone catches it in the shitter from time to time. Either way, you're on your own game from tomorrow."

Deano pulled out his phone and turned away. It was an ancient plastic lozenge the size of a brick. Binable and untraceable. He dialled a number and put it to his ear. He turned again, surprised to see Oyster still standing there. He waved him off.

"Go home," said Deano, "you're done."

PART TWO

LONDON UNSEEN

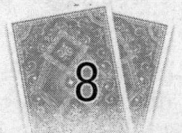

THE SERPENTINE

"This is Houdini's most deadly illusion, which I learned from him before his own mysterious death," said the old woman on the banks of the Serpentine. The crowd that had gathered around her tightened in anticipation.

She wore a tatty purple robe trimmed with gold lamé and a pair of black flip-flops. She took a drag from a roll-up she had cupped between yellowed fingers and spat into the water. A hessian sack lay at her feet. Next to it was a dented top hat containing a few pound coins.

Oyster stood nearby, holding his plastic palette and cardboard box. He shook his head in disbelief. This was a big day for him. After his fuck-up on the bridge he needed things to go well on the first day of his own game.

It was typical of his luck that he'd turned up to find some old relic squatting on the exact spot Big Mickey had chosen for their scam. With a sigh, he pushed his way to the front of the crowd and cleared his throat.

"This is my pitch," he shouted, rocking back on his feet as though the woman might take a chunk out of him.

She studiously ignored him.

He dropped the palette and box, kicking them both towards the top hat. He couldn't have this old lady soaking the crowd for their cash before he could. His stomach lurched as he considered what Big Mickey would do if any of this got back to him.

"Observe," she continued obliviously, leaning into her patter.

She picked up the chains coiled at her feet. Each was a yard long, ending in a manacle. The largest was attached to a padlock the size of Oyster's head.

"These chains and this lock belonged to none other than the great man himself, and were blessed and passed on to me, Madame Kaminsky, by Houdini's wife, Bess."

She held the links over her head and turned herself from side to side.

Oyster's phone throbbed in his tracky bottoms. The message was from Cécile, asking him to buy some milk. He needed to get this woman gone and fast.

"I said bounce," yelled Oyster.

Madame Kaminsky didn't bat an eyelid.

"Leave her alone," came a voice from the crowd.

"You, noisy man-baby, perhaps you would like to inspect?" said Madame Kaminsky, finally taking notice of him. She flicked the chains so they snaked around Oyster's feet.

"Leave it out!"

In a single motion Madame Kaminsky tossed away her roll-up and grabbed his chin in a spade-like hand.

"I will be gone soon enough and then you can get back to your grubby little con," she hissed in heavily accented English. She pushed him back onto his heels and dropped the chains to the floor.

"Now, this young gentleman will examine the aforementioned."

Kaminsky raised her hands theatrically and Oyster found himself picking up the chains and turning them over. Each link was the width of a finger and glistened coldly in the morning light.

"Yeah. These are on the up and up," he said at last. The sky was the same gunmetal grey as the chains. Beyond the park he sensed the city ticking away, a transaction here, a dodgy deal there, doing its business like an unexploded bomb.

"Please stop mumbling," said Madame Kaminsky, "people cannot hear you."

Oyster glared at her, but raised a thumb to indicate to the crowd that the chains were kosher.

Madame Kaminsky snorted and shrugged. She dropped her purple robe to the floor. Beneath it she wore a black swimsuit of the type favoured by old-time bathing beauties. The neckline of the suit was decorated with cream bands that crossed just below Kaminsky's throat. Its fabric legs reached to her knees, where they bloomed into similarly decorated puffballs.

Her arms were pale, but sturdy and stippled with cellulite. She was as thick as she was broad, and her belly hung proud and low. With her white arms and black hair coiled into a bun, she looked like a large penguin that had hopped out of the lake.

"So now, you restrain me with manacles, one here... and here... and here... here," she said, proffering each hand and foot in turn.

Oyster stepped forward, locking the metal bands and fastening their bolts.

Kaminsky gave a stage wink.

"Not to be worried, eh? No kinky stuffs!"

The audience chuckled. Despite his annoyance, Oyster had to admit that from a professional perspective this old woman knew how to work a crowd.

Madame Kaminsky stooped over once more and picked up a large metal key. She held it over her head.

"Observe! Key to the lock!"

She tossed it to Oyster. The key was so heavy he struggled to catch it.

Under Madame Kaminsky's direction he threaded the ends of each of the remaining three chains through the shackle of the padlock and clicked it shut. With all of them fastened, Kaminsky had to hunch over, bringing her head roughly level with Oyster's own.

"I am now bound with chains, which are locked tight with padlock and to which this gentleman has only key."

She looked Oyster in the eye.

"Do you wish to examine me to ensure I have no other key upon my person?"

"Not really," answered Oyster.

"Then how do you know I do not have one and same upon me when I get into sack?"

Oyster sighed again. Madame Kaminsky raised her hands as far as she could and performed a rotating shuffle. Oyster made a show of peering at her from all angles. He hoped his outside man, Baby Ed, wasn't standing in the crowd watching this panto.

To say he'd been upset when Oyster had been promoted into this game over his head was a supreme understatement. It was typical of Big Mickey that even though he knew they hated each other, he'd put them both on the same game anyway.

If Ed had seen any of this carry-on, then Oyster would catch a shit ton of heat. It was bad enough he'd lost his pitch, worse still now that he was shilling for this mad old goat.

"Yep. You're alright there," Oyster said, indicating to the crowd that Kaminsky had no key hidden anywhere.

"Speak up, please," she said.

"I don't see no keys, lady," he shouted.

Madame Kaminsky nodded and stepped into the sack. With surprising agility, she crouched down, springing back up with the sack pulled to her chin. Oyster fished his phone out of his pocket and pinged Ed a message. With all this going off it couldn't hurt to know where he was.

It was then that Oyster sensed a shift in the mood of the crowd. Panicking, he glanced around. He imagined it parting and Big Mickey emerging, eyes popping. He took a breath to steady his nerves. There was no way Mickey would be here. Then he caught a flash of blue uniform at the rear of the crowd. In an instant, he knew what was happening.

"Po-lice!" Oyster shouted and dashed away.

He pistoned his arms, fear in the pit of his belly as he sprinted, his phone jostling in his back pocket. This wasn't the first time he'd had to make a quick exit.

The words of his dad, Lucas, ran through his head: *Keep your head up and work out where they think you're going. Get indoors as soon as you can. Somewhere with lots of people, lots of lifts and lots of exits. Shopping malls are perfect. Plus, remember that coppers always come in pairs.*

Looking up, Oyster spotted a second officer, this one female, running around the far side of the Serpentine to cut off his escape. He doubled back, heading into the crowd.

Madame Kaminsky, meanwhile, had pulled the sack completely over her head and stood near the edge of the lake. As Oyster ran past her, she blindly hopped backwards, slamming straight into him. The impact knocked all the air out of Oyster's lungs and cannoned both of them into the lake.

He was aware of three things as his nose and throat filled with water. The first was his relief that it had been the cops and not Big Mickey who had bust up the crazy lady's escape act. The second was the sight of a crow wheeling overhead, cawing in a way that sounded like laughter. The third was that despite spending his youth dicking about on Wimbledon Park Lake, he had never actually learned to swim.

9
OLD WATER

Water burst up Oyster's nose and bubbled into his ears. Long fingers of weed wrapped themselves around his feet and his midriff, pulling him downward. The sack containing Madame Kaminsky rolled away to his left, illuminated by eerie glints of green from the light above.

Cold liquid eddied into Oyster's head, freezing his thoughts. The weight of the lake pressed on his chest and the fronds of weed tightened around his tattoo. He kicked his feet, but his waterlogged trainers felt full of concrete and pulled him down.

A strange impulse filled him. The urge to draw the green liquid into his lungs, to sink to the bottom and forget about everything, in this moment of in-between; in between the water and the land; in between the earth and the sky.

Emerald sunlight gleamed on the tombstone shapes of half-submerged breeze blocks and ancient shopping trolleys. Spectral plastic bags drifted in and out of undulating columns of weed. Bubbles of air trickled out of his ears and streamed upwards like stars. It would be so simple just to breathe in and leave this all behind.

He closed his eyes as his trainers were sucked into the mud at the bottom of the lake. The bubbling in his ears became silent. It was quiet and peaceful here in the dark. The ache in his lungs droned in every fibre of his body.

And that was when he knew that something was down here with him. In the black. In the dark. In the ice-ice-cold. The nape of his neck prickled and he sensed, rather than saw, that something was slithering towards him.

Panicking and suddenly desperate to breathe, he kicked his feet, but they were mired up to the ankles in the muck that sucked him down. He twisted and twisted, kicking and kicking, reaching down and pulling at his feet with numb fingers, all the while unable to escape the conviction that something silent and faceless was creeping towards him.

Oyster slipped one foot out of his unlaced shoes and then the other, and kicked his way up to the surface. His head filled with red flowers; his lungs ached. He broke the surface coughing, his arms flailing. Blinded and waterlogged, he doggy-paddled like a motherfucker, making for the lake's concrete bank. He spluttered and heaved air into his lungs, working his arms and legs as hard as he could to reach the shallows.

After a minute, he was able to touch the bottom with his feet. He did his best not to think of the used condoms, dead things and shit sliding between his toes. He reached the jutting lip of the bank and grabbed it with both hands. Taking a final deep breath, he hauled himself out and lay on his back. He shivered and his breath came in shuddering gasps. Water bled out of him, dripping over the concrete path, returning to the lake and the thing that lurked within it.

Part of his thawing brain told him to get up and run away from the police, but his legs and arms ached, and his head was pounding. Before he could act, two uniformed figures loomed over him.

You gotta realise two things about the law, Deano had said to Oyster once. *First up: the cops are all about property. You don't touch nothing belonging to no one else and they leave you be. Second: the law are just the biggest, baddest gunned-up crew out there, that's all.*

"Take it easy, sir," the officer said, "that was quite a dip you took, are you feeling okay?"

Oyster nodded and shivered at the same time. He clammed up

instinctively, his body tightening to keep the cops at a distance. He knew of enough kickings in custody to discount their friendly public-facing demeanour.

"Did you bang your head at all when you fell in?" asked the female officer.

Oyster shook his head and with help he struggled to his feet. He staggered under the unfamiliar weight of his wet clothes. His lips wouldn't move, and his teeth chattered as the wind cut through his soaked puffer vest. Pools of water formed at his feet.

"I'm Officer Peach," said the policeman and pointed at his partner, "and this is Officer MacDonald. We're with the Metropolitan Police. Can you tell us your name and address?"

"Ed," said Oyster thinking of the pale-faced man's T-shirt. "Ed Sheeran."

"Mr Ed Sheeran?" repeated Officer MacDonald, sighing and pulling a pad from her jacket pocket to write the details down. "Is that with one 'e' or two?"

Oyster tried to remember more about what Deano and Big Mickey had told him about getting pinched and what might happen next. Being part of the Urbans meant that being nicked was always a possibility, but it had never happened to Oyster before. There was a lot of bravado talked in the gang about getting arrested. Some of it whirled around his head now, but if he was honest, he was numb. The whole situation was so surreal it made it hard for him to think straight. Best idea he had was to stay schtum.

He ran his hand under his nose and blew a jet of pond water out of his nostrils onto Officer Peach's shiny boot cap. The copper arched an eyebrow and flicked the mixture of snot and green water from his shoe.

"How old are you?" he asked.

"Fifteen, last birthday," Oyster said.

The officer gave an even heavier sigh.

"Really, sir, this will all go a lot easier if you are straight with us."

"Oh yeah," said Oyster through chattering teeth, "easier for who?"

"Are you or your partner licensed to gamble here, Mr Sheeran?" said Officer MacDonald, deciding to change tack.

"Partner?" said Oyster.

He looked at the dark surface of the Serpentine. An empty sack floated there, its open mouth gaping at him. He shivered and looked away.

"Where is she?" said Oyster, nodding in its direction.

"We were hoping you could tell us that, sir," said MacDonald, her face officious and wan.

Oyster shook his head. Water still rumbled in his ears, imbuing everything with an air of unreality.

He looked down at the concrete and up at the sky. He shook his head and the water made a staccato stream of burps in his ear.

"Right," said MacDonald, scribbling a note, "have you had any trouble with the police before?"

Oyster shook his head.

"Let's drop the nonsense." Peach's demeanour hardened. "What crew are you with? Stick Ups, Westsides, Burger Bar Boys?"

"Dunno what you mean, officer." Oyster affected an innocent air. "What's this all about anyway?"

"Okay then, we'll play it this way if you like," said Peach. He stood a little taller, all pretence at friendliness gone. "Mr Sheeran, I am going to search you as I have reasonable suspicion to believe you may be carrying a weapon. Can I ask you to remove your jacket?"

The words were robotic, well-rehearsed. Steel toecap edged.

Oyster panicked for an instant, but then remembered he'd been in such a hurry to leave in the morning he'd forgotten his knife.

Peach made him lean against a nearby tree while he patted him down. Oyster reflected on Deano's words. The feds really were a gang just like the Urbans, loyal mostly to themselves, but with more muscle and the ultimate sanction of banging you up if they felt like it.

Peach pulled out Oyster's phone, which was sodden and dead. Meanwhile, MacDonald searched Oyster's jacket, finding his playing cards and the sopping roll of banknotes that had been his float. The cops grinned at each other. They had him.

"I'm afraid we'll need you to come with us to the station, then, Mr Sheeran," said Peach in a sing-song tone. "We'll need to ask you some questions about what you and your partner were up to today."

"She's not my partner," said Oyster. "I've never met the crazy-arse bint before this morning." He winced as he realised he'd been baited into giving Peach more information.

"You can tell us all about it at the station," said MacDonald. "And while you're about it, you can give us your real name as well, eh?"

Oyster rolled his eyes and shivered.

"I won't be needing these will I, sir?" said the Peach, tapping the handcuffs on his belt. They looked small and shiny compared to the enormous padlocks Kaminsky had heaved in his direction earlier that day.

Oyster shook his head.

"Are you okay to walk? You seem to have lost your shoes," said MacDonald.

It was only then that Oyster registered the loss of his trainers. He shuddered as he imagined whatever-it-was down there at the bottom of the water holding on to them.

A loose knot of bystanders had gathered around the police. At the edge of the crowd, Oyster caught sight of Baby Ed. The boy's elfin face was pinched into a perfect combination of contempt and glee.

The cops walked Oyster across the wet, grey concrete surrounding the lake and towards a waiting patrol car parked on a slip road. MacDonald opened the back door of the car and the radio within hissed. She pressed Oyster into the back seat, ducking his head beneath the doorframe in the exaggerated way he had seen in a thousand TV programmes.

The car was an estate that smelled of polish and vinyl. A wire mesh separated the back seat from the front. Oyster tried to muster some sense of outrage or even fear, but nothing came. He waited for the panic to arrive, but it didn't. The wheels spun in his bubbling head.

It was only when his thoughts turned to what Baby Ed might be saying to Big Mickey that anxiety gnawed at his gut. He wished they'd put him in a windowless bully van rather than a police car, at least then no one would see him.

Ed would waste no time in letting Big Mickey know he'd been nicked, and if Big Mickey came to the conclusion Oyster hadn't kept his trap shut, then things would get very messy indeed.

The police car coughed into life and reversed, before swinging around and out of the park. Oyster imagined what he must look like to the shoppers as they slid past him. He thought about Baby Ed's pleasure at seeing him collared, then pulled the sodden hood of his sweatshirt over his face and slumped back in the car.

10
HARRY GREGG'S SOCK

After collecting his possessions, Oyster was disgorged into the late afternoon daylight outside Marylebone police station. He blinked. The cops had charged him with unlawful gambling and bound him over to keep the peace until a court hearing.

After the fluorescent dungeon of the cells, he hadn't expected the sky to be so bright. He was unsteady on his feet, so disorientated and numb that he might suddenly float up into the cloudless blue. He thought about what he had sensed at the bottom of the lake, but he was less sure now that anything had really happened at all. It had all been in his head, he assured himself. A lack of oxygen; a crack on the skull on the way into the water. Whatever.

He inhaled deeply. A plane scudded across the sky. The slabbed concrete of the cop shop hunched behind him. He needed to get gone.

He looked down at his feet. The duty officer had pulled a pair of worn leather shoes a size too big for him from the lost and found. They smelled as raw as they looked. Wanting to let Cécile know where he was, he checked his phone, but his dip into the Serpentine had reduced it to a slab of black glass. He sighed. Okay, so it was going to be like that. Whatever else happened, he had to let Big M and the rest of the crew know he'd been pinched and that he'd kept his trap shut.

Oyster pulled his hoodie up and slunk down the road, looking at the pavement. Up ahead, a vintage car turned the corner in front of the police station and rattled up the road towards him. Oyster's peripheral city radar picked it up immediately as being out of place.

It had a wide, flat front with two round headlights, flanking a grille that was speckled with rust. It was low-slung, heavy looking and decorated with tarnished chrome trim. Oyster guessed it had probably been cream once but was now evenly coated in grime. It pulled up next to him and the passenger door creaked open.

"Get in," came a female voice that Oyster recognised only too well. Madame Kaminsky.

"Get lost, lady," he said, anger and disbelief rising in him in equal measure. "I just got collared 'cos of you and your bullshit. Don't you think you might have done enough for one day?"

"I have not even started, young man," she replied. "Now get in if you want to realise full potential."

"My potential, as you call it, is severely limited after your fuckwit antics this morning."

"Get *in* car," she replied.

Oyster turned away from her and began to run in the opposite direction. There was a crunch as Kaminsky put the car into reverse and followed him. The horns of oncoming traffic dopplered past as she pursued him.

"Leave me alone!" shouted Oyster.

His ill-fitting footwear slapped against the concrete in a way that made him feel like an escaped clown being pursued by an overzealous ringmaster.

As he ran, one of his unlaced shoes flicked from his foot and into the road, where it was crushed under the wheels of a passing car. Off-balance, he tripped over and hit the pavement sidelong. The car pulled up as he sprawled on the kerb.

For the second time that day a figure loomed over him. Oyster looked up. Madame Kaminsky was resplendent in a blonde wig and fur coat.

"It really will be easier if you just come with me," she said.

"Okay," said Oyster. He was tired and exasperated. He just wanted to be at home in front of the telly right now. As much as he didn't want to admit it, being hooked had left him shaken. He closed his eyes. For whatever reason, it seemed like there was no way to escape this mad old bag's attentions. Maybe he could just roll with it for now. He raised his hands in surrender. "I give in, alright. I give in."

"Good." Madame Kaminsky extended her hand.

Oyster slapped it away and stood unsteadily. He tested his weight on his naked foot and limped around to the passenger door.

"I don't suppose you got any crepz handy?" he said.

"Sorry, what is *crepz*?" Madame Kaminsky raised an eyebrow.

"Shoes," grunted Oyster, pointing at his foot.

She wrinkled her nose and shrugged.

"Yes. Am sure I can find something."

Oyster's stomach rumbled. He had eaten nothing more than a couple of Rich Tea biscuits at the station.

"Got any feed?" he said.

"Not so much, but I will buy lunch if you hear me out," she replied.

"Deal," said Oyster, settling into the car and looking for the safety belt. When he found it, the metal tongue which slotted into the lock was missing.

"Broken," said Madame Kaminsky, keeping her eyes on the road. "Golem snapped it."

"Who's he?" said Oyster.

Kaminsky shrugged gnomically.

Oyster tied both ends of the belt into a knot around him as Kaminsky kangarooed the car into the afternoon traffic. He crossed his arms and sat silently in the passenger seat. His stomach rumbled again, prompting Madame Kaminsky to lean across him and open the glove compartment. She reached inside and retrieved an ancient packet of Tic Tacs which she handed to him.

The mints had fused together into a solid white mass at the bottom of the container. Oyster shook it experimentally, but the contents refused to move.

"Jesus, lady, how old are these? Did they come with the car?"

"Do not be an idiot. Tic Tacs not for sale in 1960."

He tossed them back into the glove compartment, slammed it shut and folded his arms again, resting his bare foot on the dashboard.

"Just get me to my yard, yeah. I've had enough hospitality for today. I'm proper clappered."

Kaminsky nodded grimly.

Oyster gave her his address and she steered them erratically through the snakes of afternoon traffic. They slewed over lanes and weaved across Oxford Street. Then turned to lurch down Park Lane and through the ice-cream-block embassies of Belgravia, before heading south-west towards Wandsworth and his housing estate. They were taking a ridiculously circuitous route home.

Oyster wanted some air, but the nearside window handle was missing. He shook his head in exasperation and prepared to let Kaminsky know exactly what he thought of her shit-mobile. Before he could say a word, however, his head lolled forward and he was lying in bed, back home in his family flat. From the next room there was the muffled sound of raised voices. It was Paris and Lucas at it again, another one of the volcanic eruptions so typical of their relationship, of which frosty glances and curt responses were the only remnants the following day.

Tiny plaster stalactites of Artex dangling from the ceiling, ignoring the sickly sensation in his stomach. He knew this night. There it was: the dull thunder of furniture being overturned. He pulled the pillow over his head, but he still heard the muted impact of the front door slamming: Lucas leaving the flat. He'd dreamt this all before. He wanted to get up, run out of his room and tell his dad not to go, but the sound of the door closing had cauterised the wound forever.

He sat up in his bed, pulled back the curtains and looked out of his bedroom window. Pressing his face to the glass, he counted the streetlamps down below on Strathdon Drive as the windowpane cooled the tip of his nose. He listened to the sound of Paris sobbing, moving through the flat like a ghost. She knocked on his door and called his name. Oyster froze, pretending to be asleep, and she moved away.

He watched as Lucas emerged from the block, walking across the car park between Deeside and its sister building Blakemouth, and a sense of rising panic writhed in his gut. This man, who loomed so large in his life, looked tiny as he picked his way across the moon-silvered concrete. Oyster knew he was leaving them forever.

But there was something different about the memory this time. As he watched, Oyster realised that Lucas was not the only person in the car park. There was another figure down there, lurking amongst the dark green row of plastic bins at its far corner.

At first, he thought it was someone enjoying a joint or a smoke, but then he realised the figure was watching Lucas too. It slipped like a shadow between the bins, keeping him in view as he made his way across the tarmac.

There was something odd, both in the proportions of the figure and in the liquid way it moved. He wanted to bang on the window or call out and warn his dad, but he was too high up.

Then something even stranger happened. The shadowy figure stepped out from behind the bins and looked up, smiling.

In that instant, Oyster had the distinct impression that the figure was looking directly at him. The hairs on the back of his neck stood to attention and he ducked below the windowpane, his heart beating so loudly he could hear it in his ears. He crouched in the dark, frightened, but aware of how ridiculous it seemed. No one could have seen him from that distance. Yet he was sure the figure had been staring up at him and smiling. When he gathered the courage to look out of the window again, both Lucas and the figure were gone.

He was roused from the dream by Kaminsky shaking him by the shoulder.

"Mum?" he said, rubbing his wet eyes. "What's up?"

"We are here, Mummy's boy," replied Madame Kaminsky.

Oyster grunted, hiding his face behind his hands and wiping it dry. He hoped she hadn't seen the tears. The dream had left him with a feeling of despair, like he was marooned on an island with no hope of rescue. Lucas had abandoned them. Left them all to rot. He sniffed. The anger in him boiled up, making his fingertips tingle and dispelling the sadness and fear. At least there was a sort of restless life in getting vexed.

"Hey, aren't you forgetting something?" he said, pointing at his naked foot.

Kaminsky shrugged, rummaged in her coat pocket and brought out a thick red-and-white football sock.

"Here," she said, offering it to him.

Oyster pulled a face.

"A sock?" he said. "Is that it?"

"You really are ignorant toad, are you not?" she said. "I gave this sock to Harry Gregg in 1957."

"I don't give any shits about all of your oldy-worldy bollocks." Oyster could feel his temper rising. "You told me you had shoes."

Kaminsky rubbed her chin.

"Tell me, honestly, what sort of person would carry man-shoes around in back of car?" replied Kaminsky.

"I dunno," he retorted, "maybe the same sort of demented that would do an escape act in Hyde Park?"

Kaminsky shrugged. "Listen before you go. I have proposition for you."

Oyster grimaced.

"Not that sort of proposition, weasel-dick," she sniffed. "Put simply, I want you to be my assistant."

"Assistant?" said Oyster.

"Yes, is what they call entry level position. I am illusionist, amongst many other things. You have potential, would make an excellent assistant."

Oyster snorted.

"You're having me on," he said.

"I never joke about such things," she replied.

"Well, I think I can honestly say the chances of me prancing around in a sparkly leotard while you get your Merlin on are on the low side," he replied.

"Let me ask you one question at least," she said, pressing Oyster back down into his seat. "What happened to you in the water today, eh?"

Oyster shrugged.

"*She* wanted you to stay, hmm?" whispered Madam Kaminsky.

"What does that even mean?"

"It is old London, that lake. Always hungry. She came right up from clay beds in Roman times. They used to sacrifice to her, you know. Been there since they closed off return to Tyburn or Westbourne. I never remember which."

"Blah blah blah, lady." Oyster mimed a mouth with his hand, but the car was suddenly colder.

"She must have thought you were interesting." Kaminsky inspected one of her walnut-sized knuckles and looked Oyster over. "All appearances to contrary, that is."

She smiled, revealing an undisciplined array of grey teeth.

Oyster wanted to ask how she knew any of what had happened under the water, but he didn't want to buy into any of her crazy. He had enough on his plate already.

"You have air of someone who has seen something he shouldn't have," she said.

"For your info, I kept my eyes shut down there," said Oyster, immediately regretting his reply.

Kaminsky tapped her temple and nodded sagely.

"Indeed. Makes sense from one perspective, but if horizons are expanding, is keeping eyes shut so wise?" she replied, leaning into him. "More importantly, don't you want to know what happened to your father?" she said.

Oyster's insides became molten. How the fuck did she know this? Had he said something in his sleep? He climbed out of the car, his breath hissing through his nose, limbs tight with suppressed rage. Rage at her sticking her nose in, and the rage that was constant, directed at Lucas. Crackling, invisible, but always there like the electricity on a railway line. He leaned back through the door and grabbed the red-and-white football sock that Kaminsky held. He threw it away.

"Fuck your stupid fucking act. Fuck your bullshit and fuck you!" he shouted.

Kaminsky was unperturbed.

"So that's a 'no' then, is it?" she said, slipping a business card between the second and third fingers of his hand.

"Just in case you change your mind," she said. "It was pleasure to meet you."

Oyster flicked the card back at its owner and headed towards the block of flats. Behind him, Kaminsky's car bounced away into the early evening.

11
MESSAGE CENTRE

Oyster headed towards the main entrance of the Deeside tower block, still fuming. He picked his way past faded murals and a long-dry fountain filled with fag ends and crisp packets. His tattoo itched and he scratched it with cold fingers. The loss of his trainers and Madame Kaminsky's casual mention of Lucas boiled around his head. Who the fuck was she, and why was she so keen for him to become her butt-monkey?

He fished out his keys and let himself in. The lobby assaulted him with its usual scent of polish and piss. The door slammed behind him with a metallic echo.

The lifts were out and so he took the stairs, ticking off each of the floors as he slogged his way up. There was the boiled cabbage smell from the third floor where the old-timers whiled away their final days; the sub-bass throb from Voodoo Ray's party flat on four; and the black hole of dark and silence on seven that he always hurried past.

It didn't seem to matter how many times the caretakers changed the bulbs on that floor, come evening they'd always burned out. He shivered as he ran past it.

That said, he loved this building and its moods. He loved the way it cooled and heated to its own weird rhythm. When the weather was good the tower sat like an enormous block of ice, resolutely sweating in the sun. On cold days, it scalded its occupants with water that circulated in its pipes like boiling blood. He didn't even mind the inevitable walk up the stairs. He was safe inside its walls; protected. From here you could see right over the city's ragged arse, the lights stippling its concrete hide like fallen stars.

Before he returned to his flat, he had one more thing to do. He checked to make sure he wasn't being watched, then stepped into the shadows at the end of the corridor. He knelt and prised the cover away from an air-conditioning grille near the floor. Without needing to look, he reached inside and felt around, retrieving a rolled-up cigarette paper: a message from the Urbans. He replaced the grille and slipped the paper into his pocket. He wouldn't read it here.

Oyster tiptoed to his front door. He checked his watch, it was just past six. He unlocked and stepped in. The flat was small. It smelled of fish fingers and chips. *Love Island* blared from the TV. To the right, silhouetted in what remained of the daylight, his mother's vertical ponytail towered over the back of the sofa.

To his left, yellow light limned Cess's bedroom door. Beyond that was the darkened doorway of his own bedroom. The place he'd slept ever since he was a kid.

Oyster crept inside, slipped the lock over and eased the front door shut. He checked to see if he had disturbed Paris, but the telly was so loud he could have done a cartwheel and she wouldn't have noticed. He prodded at the mess of post that occupied their dinner table: a pile of unopened bills and a pack of nicotine gum.

He slipped past the bookshelves and the mixtapes beneath it, stacked up like plastic bricks and labelled with Lucas's uneven scrawl. They had always seemed impossibly exotic to Oyster, as much for their content as for the fact that they'd never had a cassette player in the house.

Back when Paris still talked to Oyster, their conversation had been threaded with the words *after your dad gets back*. As though he'd just nipped down to the shops and would return any minute. This particular elephant, pink as a rose and trumpeting loudly, galloped through all their discussions and was never acknowledged by anyone.

He ran a hand along the spines of Lucas's books, all back in their place again now. Paris's work no doubt. He fought the childish urge to send them tumbling from the shelf, and before he had the chance to stomp the notion found himself wondering where Lucas might be. He pushed the unhelpful thought away. Kaminsky must have got into his head. He slipped past Cécile's open door. He really wasn't in the mood for any of her shit.

"Mum wants to know where you've been, bruv-bruv," came his sister's voice, freezing him in his tracks.

Oyster sighed and stuck his head around the doorway. He blinked in the bright light of the room. Cess was lying on her stomach, on her bed with a notebook in front of her. Music played from a small stereo and she was humming along to it. The walls of her room were plastered with stickers and boy band posters. One of the shelves housed an array of Hello Kitty merchandise that Oyster had bought for her on various birthdays.

"What happened to you?" she said without acknowledging him. "You stink."

"Even more than usual?" he said.

She looked up.

"Even for you this is a new low, I reckon."

Oyster stepped into her room and shut the door behind him.

Cess mimed putting a clothes peg on her nose.

"Ended up in the drink today," he said.

"How does that even happen?" She sat up cross-legged.

"Biz."

Cess rolled her eyes.

"What's this racket?" Oyster nodded at the stereo and reached out to turn it down.

"Touch that and I drop you, beast," said Cess. It was Oyster's turn to roll his eyes.

Her gaze dropped to his naked feet.

"And what is up with that?"

"Alright, enough," said Oyster, putting his index finger to his lips. "Hush now."

"I will but not 'cos you're telling me to, *cousin*."

"I'm your brother, dingbat."

"Whatever. Dismissed," said Cess.

Oyster shook his head, laughing silently as he slid back into the dark of the flat. Paris remained bathed in the spectral TV light. It was easy for him to sidle into his room without being noticed.

He put his phone on the radiator in his bedroom. There was a chance it might dry out. Then he collapsed on his bed. He wasn't sure how he was going to tell Cécile he was in trouble with the law, on top of all the other shit that had already capsized the family in the last couple of years. He could already hear her rebuke: *What did you expect, dim-low?*

A little voice in the pit of his stomach wanted him to run to Paris and plead with her to it to make it right, but that wouldn't happen. *Button it*, he thought. That's what Broadsides or Deano would do. *Shut it up. Man it up.*

He undressed and chucked his clothes into a pile in the corner of his room. It was only then that he remembered the message. He pulled it out of his jeans' pocket, collapsed onto the bed and unrolled the paper. It contained a scrawled picture of a spiral wearing a crown and the number ten beneath.

It meant Mickey wanted to meet him at The Clip at ten a.m.

Anxiety wriggled in his stomach. Did Mickey figure him for a snitch? Probably not. If he had then he'd already be at the bottom of the Wandsworth. And what was he worried about? He hadn't done anything wrong. He'd kept his trap shut. Been a good soldier. The phrase filled him with a peculiar pride. The crew had been there for him, provided a sort of family. But Broadsides' words ran through his head:

We're a short-con outfit. Ginals all. How come so many been fingered, done runners or worse?

All Oyster knew was that he had no answer.

12

THE CLIP

Oyster was outside the rendezvous early. He couldn't risk annoying Big Mickey in any way, and he certainly didn't want to give his boss any sense at all that he might not be on the up and up.

He wandered back and forth on the cratered tarmac around the booze joint that the Urbans called The Clip: a big-arse shipping container stacked on two others at the edge of Wandsworth Enterprise Park. The sky was a powder-blue and the air was crisp. He shivered and pulled his puffer jacket tighter around himself.

The area smelled of old rubber from the abandoned tyre garage next door. The garage's roof had collapsed in on itself and its doors swung open onto a concrete courtyard that had cracked open as though giving birth to something long buried beneath. The garage's brick walls buckled under the slow, subtle assault of moss, saplings and bushes. The whole place gave him the creeps.

There was a figure in the shadows of the abandoned building, something looming and long. Someone watching him. A ribbon of anxiety uncoiled along his spine. He sucked in a breath, unable to move, then forced himself to look again. Relief flooded in from the edges. It was nothing, just a tree twisting in the shadow-tinged dark.

A car horn sounded. Oyster jumped. A black beamer with tinted windows slid around the corner like a shark. It cruised to the kerb where he stood.

The window rolled down.

"Inside, youth," commanded Big Mickey.

Oyster took a deep breath and climbed in. The car reeked of weed and Lynx. Taking up most of the rear seat was Big Mickey. The car looked like it might split apart at any moment, unequal to the task of containing him. Mickey gently tapped the cream leather of the seat with a manicured finger. He was expressionless. Once Oyster was inside, they pulled into the road without making a sound. Oyster sat back, feeling himself swallowed up by the car's luxury.

He cleared his throat; all clammed up. Being in Big Mickey's presence was always intimidating. The few words that he'd prepped in his head to explain what had happened on the bridge had fled the moment he'd got into the car. Streatham High Road slipped past them, one chain of shops following another. Oyster's hands were sweating as he held them flat against the car's leather interior. He cleared his throat again and swallowed.

When he gathered the nerve to look up, Big Mickey was staring at him, nodding gently.

"So, you got stiffed, young blood?" he said.

Oyster nodded.

"Yeah," he said. "Sorry, boss. I dunno what happened. I should have seen him coming."

"Yes, you should have," replied Mickey. His tone was neutral; unreadable. "And that will come with time. I get it. You're all juiced up. Keen to prove. Keen to earn. You gotta know when to cool it too, though." He prodded Oyster's midriff. Oyster winced as his tattoo squealed in pain.

"You got instincts, I know. I got 'em too. But I always listen to mine. I know when a play is bad; when shit is going down. When someone smells fed even when they look like they're hundred-percent. However close a grass might be, I always sniff them out. Where I come from, it's a talent. That's the diff between a captain and a soldier. Confidence in your talents."

Oyster looked at Mickey again and tried to hold his gaze. Mickey's grey eyes burrowed into him as though measuring his soul. Oyster had to look away, his cheeks burning. Mickey had a way of making you feel guilty even when you were innocent.

"Anything you need to tell me about while you were detained by the Five-O?" said Mickey, bringing his hands together and cracking his knuckles in a manner that Oyster found both menacing and strangely delicate.

"Kept it tight, didn't I?" he said. "Name, rank and serial number, just like you taught me."

Now it was Mickey's turn to look ahead. After a beat or two, he turned to Oyster, who smiled nervously. Mickey's face remained blank.

"So, have you learned anything else?" he said, the car interior sighing as he rearranged himself.

Oyster wasn't sure what Mickey could mean. Then he realised.

"Yes, yes. I mean, uh, no. I haven't found anything out about that mystery crew." He thought for a second. "Except, me and Broadsie had minor beef with the Stick Men the other day. They insisted that we've been painin' them all over."

Big Mickey grunted.

"Not so, cousin."

"Right," said Oyster, "so—"

"—so, you reckon they're feeling this new squad too?" Big Mickey said.

Oyster nodded. Keen to keep the subject of the conversation away from how things had gone during his arrest.

"It's gotta be this new lot, boss," he said.

Mickey cracked his knuckles again and nodded thoughtfully.

"Nice Sherlocking, youth. Right. This is your stop. You're running the graveyard shift tonight. You'll pick up the package from Cluck's at six, make the drop at seven. You can pick up your burner from Arthur's."

He reached across Oyster to open the car door. Big Mickey's bulk crushed him into the car seat. It was a suffocating mixture of sweat and aftershave.

"I don't need to tell you, do I," whispered Mickey, "that even though we're like family, you can't be junkin' shit up on the regular. That is a lesson that Lucas himself taught me. Up to me to pass it on now. Goin' soft ain't good for discipline, disciple. Comprende?"

Oyster nodded and tumbled out of the car. He drew in a deep breath of London air; after the fug of Mickey's ride, it tasted sweet.

"Be seeing you, young blood," Mickey said, as the car pulled into the traffic and back the way they had come.

13
DEAD DROP

Once a month, Big Mickey had one of the crew make a big money drop deep in Stick Up Kidz territory. Rumour had it the cash went to bent coppers, to keep them turning a blind eye to the crew's activities.

In any case, the Stick Ups had gotten wise to the money snaking through their turf and the drop was so prone to jacking that the rest of the Urbans, only half-jokingly, referred to it as the graveyard shift.

Being entrusted with any part of the drop was a step up, and Oyster knew Big Mickey was testing him by suggesting he carry it out. He prickled at the idea anyone might rate him as a snitch or yellow, but now he was on his way to pick up a burner, anxiety about the whole thing worked its way into the pit of his stomach.

I can do this, he told himself. Lucas had done it and so could he.

Arthur's was a nondescript phone repair shop on the High Road. It nestled between Rico's the Turkish Barber and Touch Frik, a Nigerian cafe where Oyster treated himself and Cécile to goat stew with eba whenever he had the spare. The sweet smell of the food made his stomach rumble as he approached. He caught sight of himself in Rico's shopfront and adjusted his beanie. The heartbeat of the town was close to the surface here: the smoky scent of paprika; the *snip-snip* of Rico's scissors; the rush of overlapping people and ways of being. This was what the city had always been to him. Oyster loved it and the sense that he was a tiny, integral part of it.

The Urbans slipped the shopkeeper – whose real name was Aahil – a bundle regularly to ensure they always had a ready supply of untraceable use-once-and-destroy phones. The shop was a narrow unit framed in jaunty yellow, its shopfront crammed with row upon row of used handsets. Two semi-deflated balloons hung from its doorway like stale grapes. Hangovers from the shop's opening "bonanza sale", they'd been there as long as Oyster could remember.

He stepped inside. Aahil's niece, Farida, was working the counter. Earphones in, she was nodding to some tunes and sucking on a cherry vape. She looked up and evaluated Oyster with a dead-eyed glance.

"Hang on," she said, ducking under the counter, to return with a brown paper bag which she slid across to him. She backed away as he approached, removing her earbuds and regarding him like some sort of escaped zoo specimen. Nice kids, good kids, usually did.

Oyster nodded, ignoring her attitude, and checked the bag. All on the up.

"Hey, can you throw in another burner?" he said. There was no reason not to replace his phone with a new one. It would be basic but could tide him over till he got around to a maxed-out replacement. Farida did as he asked.

"Much obliged," he said. "Tell your old man to stick this lot on Big M's tab."

Farida stayed where she was, looking at him with undisguised disdain. Oyster turned to leave.

"Why do you do it?" Farida blurted the words to his back.

Oyster turned to her and shrugged.

"Gang bangers. You give this place a bad name," she continued.

Oyster gave her a smile, determined not to look riled.

"Before you get too up on your righteous, it's the same reason your old man doesn't mind being an accessory after the fact." He rubbed his thumb and forefinger together, echoing Broadsides' "money" gesture from the other day.

He stepped out of the shop before she had a comeback. Farida's words had pissed him off. What he did was no different to what everyone else did. Everyone was on the make. Everyone was engaged in the same game. The whole city was just a collection of wins and losses; counted and paid for with money, tears and blood, sometimes all three. He was on the bottom of the pile right now. But maybe he was on the up. Unfair as it was, if there was another way of arranging the world he had yet to work out what it might be.

In any case, it wasn't like anyone gave a shit about what he thought. Right now, he was all set. As per Big M's instructions, he waltzed up to Cluck's where Deano sat in the window, trying and failing to fit into one of the restaurant's plastic bucket seats. He was holding court with Ed and a couple of kiddies that Oyster didn't recognise. New recruits, probably. Deano eyed him as he entered, nodding him on to the counter. Cluck's smelled of hot oil and spray clean, his stomach gurgled. He ordered himself a box of nuggets and sat at the back squinting under the fluorescent lights. The food arrived and he made short work of it. Deano sauntered over and winked at him. He disappeared through the swing doors that led to the loos, returning with a plastic bag which Oyster knew held a brick of money.

He sat across from Oyster, placing the package on the table, leaving one hand on top of it. He slid him a Rizla paper that contained an address written in Deano's simple block capitals.

"Know what to do, soldier?" His voice was low.

Oyster nodded.

Deano's face cracked into a smile.

"My baby's all grown up," he said, fanning himself as though overcome with emotion.

"Fuck off," replied Oyster good-naturedly.

He took the money and zipped it into a khaki backpack he'd brought along for that purpose, along with the burners he'd picked up at Arthur's. He looked at the address on the cigarette paper, memorised it and then tossed it into his mouth, chewing and swallowing. He rose, ready to leave.

"Hold up," said Deano, waving him back into his seat. He passed Oyster a second carrier bag under the table. He could tell immediately it was some kind of fucked-up knife: a machete or something even more brutal.

"Just in case you gotta carve out," he said. Then, nodding approvingly, he left Oyster to his business.

Oyster pulled his beanie down and flipped up his hoodie. He slipped the knife out of its bag and into a long pocket in his puffer. It was a hunting knife. A lot more serious than the sort thing he normally carried. Eight inches long, with a wound leather grip, its razor edge looked like it would cut the air itself. *I'll be lucky if I don't gut myself just carrying this thing*, he thought.

He walked out of Cluck's, his brain already churning through the permutations of public transport that could get him to the drop's address over in Tooting. He caught a rattling bus up to the nearest Underground, then hunkered down on the Tube with the backpack. He wanted some tunes to steady his nerves, but his phone was still dead and his new burner too basic. *Just as well*, he thought. *I should probably stay sharp.*

He trucked north from Tooting station and headed past the hunched brick houses of Links Road. He didn't like this street. It was long, monotonous and the railway line it paralleled to its south meant there were fewer turn-offs to evade pursuit.

At its mouth was a patch of scrub that stretched into an overgrown alleyway; one that curled around the houses' rear, and was bordered by uneven backyard fences. The passageway was lined by thin, circumspect trees and sparse muddy grass that revealed the city's chalky bones. He was staring down a tunnel that led into an alternate city, one composed of dirt and absence. He scratched at his tattoo and the nape of his neck prickled. He had the sense that something was coming this way, something he did not want to be around.

He double-stepped it, with his head down and spider-sense tingling, logging each house number with a sinking feeling. By his estimate he had to get most of the way down this bloody road to complete the drop-off. He pulled his unfastened jacket tighter around him; a zipped-up coat would make it harder to pull his shiv if he needed to.

His skin was proper crawling now and he had the unmistakeable sensation he was being eyeballed. Creepiest thing was he couldn't see anyone on his six. He pulled his hoodie up over his head and tried to fade as best he could. *I just have to haul my arse a little bit further and then I can bunk on a train and be home.*

Footsteps hammered behind him and he spun around. He had the blade half out of his jacket before he saw Broadsides grinning at him under the streetlights.

"Easy, killer," he said.

"Jesus," said Oyster. "I just shit myself a bit. What are you doing here?"

"Great to see you too," said Broadsides.

He was relieved to see his friend, but then considered that perhaps he had thought Oyster needed help.

"I don't need backup, my man."

"Nah, that's not it at all," said Broadsides. "You're looking tight. Heard you was on the run solo out here. Figured you might want some chat."

Oyster snorted, offering him a fist bump. Pride aside, he was glad to see him. They swaggered up the street together, Oyster trying to unwind. Streetlights wove their shadows into long-limbed monsters. They reminded Oyster of the stories Lucas used to tell him back when he was a kid. Tales of the time before people, when giants roamed the land, twatting each other with clubs and anything else that was to hand.

"You ever wonder what it would be like to jack this all in and go straight?" said Broadsides. He pulled a bent joint out of his pocket, waved it at Oyster.

"Not for me, mate," he replied, nodding at his backpack. "On duty, innit."

"Fair-zy square-zy," said Broadsides, lighting up anyway. The paper crackled as the weed caught, its tip glowing red in the dark like a dying star.

Oyster considered Broadsides' question. He hadn't been in the crew long, but he found it hard to imagine any way that he'd ever leave. It was like some sort of benign virus, he thought; it changed you, rewired you, made you a different person. He wasn't sure how suited he'd been to the Urbans' way of life at first, but these days he found it hard to imagine ever doing anything else.

"Nah," said Oyster, "not sure leaving the crew is even an option now. You?"

Broadsides dragged on the spliff and held the draw in his lungs for a moment before exhaling through his nose.

"Yeah, as a matter of fact, my man, I have."

He pulled out his phone, swiped though a couple of screens, and then waved it at Oyster.

Oyster reached out to steady Broadsides' outsized hand. He squinted at the display. It showed a fuck-off big boat in a showroom, probably somewhere near Chelsea Docks. He guessed it was a luxury yacht.

"I'm saving," said Broadsides. "Come the day, I'm stacking up all my green and gonna go in and buy that motherfucker. Then me and my aunt, we're gonna go sailing. Down the coast to Brighton, then on to France. See how those froggy fuckers live it up in Saint Tropez."

Broadsides looked wistful, younger, despite his bulk.

Oyster grinned. "Fuck it, man, never figured you for the nautical sort."

Broadsides laughed. "I got no fucking idea. But never too late to learn, blud."

Oyster mock-saluted. "Aye, aye, Cap'n Birdseye."

"You can scrub the decks, you cheeky fucking zero."

They were just a couple of doors from their destination. Oyster mentally rehearsed how he would drop the money off, text the number he'd memorised from the burner, walk to the park, strip the SIM, and toss it and the phone separately.

Then the low-level aggro from his tattoo flared white hot and he flinched. *I need to get this thing seen to*, he thought. When he looked up, Broadsides was a pace behind him, frozen in place, eyes wide. And that was the moment Oyster knew they were in big shit trouble.

14
THE MANNISH BOYS

Oyster was face down on the ground. Someone had pulled his feet out from under him, and he'd hit the pavement with his face. He was winded and confused. *Where had they come from?* His mouth flooded with pain and the copper taste of blood. In shock and anger he kicked out at his unseen assailants. The streetlamp above his head flickered like it was having a fit.

"Get off me, you fuckers," he shouted. He couldn't see Broadsides. He tried to get up, but before he could, someone sat astride him and his face was clamped to the pavement. The only thing visible to him was a low garden fence and the scraggly bush behind it. A lump of gum burrowed into his temple and grit gnawed his face. All he could smell was dust and shit. He tried to manoeuvre out from under them, but whoever had knocked him over had him locked in place. He couldn't move, could hardly even breathe. Whoever it was must be the size of Deano and Mickey put together.

"Cut the wrestling, kiddo, and this all goes easy," said a voice in his ear. It was melodic and throaty, so low it was almost a whisper.

Oyster was scared, but things were happening so fast, panic had yet to arrive. He struggled to get up again but was held fast. Who could it be? The Stick Ups? The Westies? In answer, cold metal pressed against the side of his throat.

"I said cool it, chitty. Wouldn't pay to pink that pretty visog, would it?" The knife dragged across the back of Oyster's neck, and then with a *pop* his backpack was cut from its straps.

"Hey, hey. Hold up, that loot there belongs to the Urbans," said Oyster. He opened his palms, laying them flat against the concrete. "Think this through. Let's say you pull this off. Nothing's going away. You make a run for it, we're still gonna hunt you and your crew down."

There was laughter. Oyster tried to move his head to see, but it was in a vice. Three voices, maybe four? It would be tough for him and Broadsides to turn this around.

"Glad you think it's funny." There was more raucous laughter. "You can't hide forever."

"We aren't hiding nothing here, dandyprat. Let the other kiddies in your clown troupe know your portable has been liberated by the Mannish Boys."

There was a quality in the voice that was unexpected.

Then it came to him.

"What a minute, are you… are you lot girls?" said Oyster.

Even more laughter this time. But Oyster was sure he was right.

"'*Are you lot girls?*'" repeated the woman mockingly. "We're no more girls than you're a man, arseworm."

Oyster felt the woman's breath on the back of his head. The knife's edge cut into the flesh beneath his earlobe. Oyster smelled rosemary and mould.

"What you reckon, Squeech? Should I give Mr Banditti here a memento? Sever his lug, chuck it in the river, see if he can hear the naiads sing?"

The threat gave Oyster a burst of adrenaline. It took all his strength, but with a twist and a shrug he rolled away from the knife, out and under from his attacker. The unexpected move caught his assailant off-balance and Oyster was able to scramble to his feet. Inexplicably, the Mannish were already gone.

Nearby, Broadsides sprawled on the concrete, his hands bound tight with cable-ties and his mouth gagged. Whoever they were, this Mannish lot were professionals. No doubt he'd just had a run-in with Big Mickey's mystery crew.

Hurriedly, Oyster released Broadsides, who stood unsteadily.

"You alright?" said Oyster.

"Leg's gone to sleep is all," replied Broadsides. "Had me trussed up proper."

"Am I right, were they all women?" said Oyster. He'd heard of such things: the Tetsies, the Tottenham Amazons, Forty Elephants, but an all-female crew was a rarity, at least in this neck of the woods.

"Yeah, yeah, yeah, who gives a toss about any of that. They got the package. Bounce! I'll catch you up." Broadsides pointed towards the end of the road.

Without a second thought, Oyster powered back the way they'd come. One hand held the bottom of his jacket to keep his knife from spearing him. The burner jangled in his tracky bottoms. He put what remained of his energy into sprinting. His legs throbbed and his lungs ached. He was running alright, but he wasn't sure exactly what he'd do when he caught up to the other gang.

Somehow the Mannish already had a good lead on him; four figures up ahead, the evening closing in around them. A streetlamp flared nearby, bright enough to give Oyster a headache.

"Come on!" he shouted back to Broadsides. Hopefully, between the two of them, they could come up with something. *Four to one is bad odds at the best of times.*

Ahead, the Mannish had already reached the end of the road. They had slowed to a walk, looking for something. Oyster glanced back. Broadsides was catching up. But now the Mannish were nowhere to be seen. *Fuck.* He had to find them and get the cash back. Anxiety crawled around in the pit of his stomach as he thought of the consequences if he didn't.

He reached the end of the road. Still no sign of them. The streetlights behind him jittered. Oyster had a sudden thought.

"Check up that way," he yelled at Broadsides, indicating the station. "I've got an idea."

Oyster turned tail, heading back to an alleyway he'd spotted earlier. The worry about what would happen if they didn't get the money back mixed with his anticipation of a ruck. *Why had Lucas left them?* If he'd stayed then Oyster wouldn't be here now, up to his neck in this fucking mess. And what would happen to Cess if he got banged up or iced? *Fuck. Fuck. Fuck. Fuck. Fuck. Fuck. Fuck. Fuck.* He couldn't breathe. His tattoo lit up with pain as though it had been cut into him. *Why was it so hard to breathe?* He felt himself sinking into the ground. He pressed his hand to a wall. The damp touch of the brick, the sense of being rooted, steadied him a little.

It was darker here, away from the strobing street light, but he sensed movement at the end of the alleyway. What should he do now? If he called out for Broadsides they would know he was there. How could he stop them?

Keeping low, he crept forward, pushing low branches out of his way and sticking to the shadows. Sweat tickled his armpits and stippled his forehead. He came to a high fence where the alley turned left. He heard voices.

"Ambidexter, where the dick you taking us to?"

"Shh, Banbarra," Ambidexter hissed. "You know the science. Squeech has to dowse the path."

Oyster recognised Ambidexter's voice at once as the person who had attacked him. She certainly didn't look all that henched up.

"I don't want to be marooned in this midden until the last trump sounds," Banbarra replied.

"Think I don't know that, you scabby tart? Give her a chance. Hurry it up, S."

A sliver of moon emerged from behind a cloud. With his eyes adjusted to the dark of the evening, Oyster could see they were dressed oddly. Each wore knee-length trousers and dirty stockings, with what looked like top-of-the-line trainers and long vintage jackets of varying cuts and colours. With the exception of the trainers, the clothes were tatty and falling to bits.

The third member of the gang, Squeech, walked around the others, mumbling to herself. She drew closer, and for an instant

Oyster thought he'd been made and he froze. But to his relief, the woman was blindfolded. Held up in front of her was a street map with the word *Paris* emblazoned on it in large white letters. He fingered the hunting knife. They seemed to be unarmed. Could he try to take them?

"The Beach is nearby, I can smell it," she muttered, "this map's warmed through."

"What's that?" said Banbarra.

Oyster held his breath. Footsteps approached at speed from behind.

"Stubble the gab," hissed Ambidexter.

With a yell, Broadsides flew past Oyster, shouting at the top of his lungs and spinning a rotten tree branch over his head as a makeshift club. He flew straight at the crew.

Charging first at Squeech, he aimed a blow at her forehead, but the blindfolded woman cartwheeled effortlessly out of harm's way. Banbarra, meanwhile, emerged from the darkness, dived headfirst onto her hands and windmilled her legs over her head in a close approximation of a breakdance airflare. Her feet connected with Broadsides' face in a vicious one-two. He dropped to the floor and crumpled into a ball, cradling his head. Oyster had to give this lot their due, they were hardcore.

Above them a second-storey window in one of the houses squealed open.

"It's the middle of the night," a posh voice yelled, "take your thuggery elsewhere!"

Oyster took advantage of the sudden distraction and lunged at Ambidexter's legs, wrapping himself around her, bringing her to the ground. She was heavier than she looked. Instinctively, she struck out at his face with a flat palm, an attack Oyster knew was intended to break his nose and drive the bone into his brain. More by luck than judgement, Oyster deflected the blow, grabbed her wrists and twisted himself over her chest, pinning her arms under his knees. It was all he could do to keep her still. He pressed his knife to Ambidexter's throat.

"Stand down or your captain bleeds out!" he shouted. The

other two members of the gang, who had started laying into the prone Broadsides, stopped and looked up.

It was the first chance he had to get a clear look at the woman's face. It was long, tight-lipped with narrow features and stained skull white. Her hair was skinhead short, her eyebrows shaved. Her eyes seemed overly large, filled with black pupils that drank in the light. A long scar knotted the length of her forehead and every inch of visible skin was tattooed with connected black curlicues that centred on a three-looped Celtic knot on her forehead. Oyster recognised the patterns immediately as being close cousins to the one he had around his midriff.

"Well, this is cosy." Ambidexter pouted and blew him a kiss. "Appreciate the interest, but you ain't exactly my type."

She punctuated the sentence with a violent twist that nearly toppled Oyster.

"Get your crew to hand back the green," Oyster said, "and we all go about our business."

"Look at you, playing the top knave when it's plain even to a poor sot like me you're nothing but an oversize boy with a hole in his heart."

Oyster swallowed. He pressed the blade into Ambidexter's pale skin.

"Whatevs. Negging on me ain't gonna save your ugly arse," he replied.

"You lack the fibre, welp," she spat. "I've been fucked over by the best of the worst."

Fixing Oyster with an intense, inky glare, she pressed her own throat against the knife. The edge of the blade slipped into her flesh as though it wasn't even there and blood ran onto the blade, black like oil under the streetlight.

"Leave it out, you crazy fucking witch," he said.

"Closer than you know, chitty," she replied.

For a long second, they regarded each other, Oyster determined not to give an inch, Ambidexter determined to call his bluff. The knife carved a welt the length of her throat.

Oyster eased the blade back a fraction. As soon as she sensed him relenting, Ambidexter was up, twisting and gaining enough momentum to smack her forehead into his nose. He fell onto the mud, stunned by the pain. Blood gushed from his nose and clogged his throat. Tears filled his eyes. He was ashamed and embarrassed at his own lack of resolve. What would he tell Big Mickey? Broadsides? Deano? This was what he deserved.

Ambidexter rolled to her feet, tipped an imaginary hat in his direction, before turning to meet Squeech, who already had her map out and was leading the way, stumbling deeper into the alley.

Police sirens sang in the distance. Despite the pain from his nose, Oyster noted ruefully how quickly the cops arrived in upscale neighbourhoods. Blue lights strobed across the walls. The siren squalled again, much nearer now.

The streetlamp beyond went into its on-off dance; the Mannish Boys were gone, Broadsides was curled and groaning. Oyster struggled to his feet. Everything was spinning. He was sick and weak. His tattoo was acting up again, too. He was vaguely aware of the police slamming car doors near to where they were. He wouldn't get collared again; couldn't afford to.

He stepped over to Broadsides to check on his friend. He was looking pretty banged up, but he would survive.

"Follow 'em, get the cash, or we're effed," Broadsides croaked.

Oyster nodded. He hawked and spat; then turned and ran into the darkness.

15

THE BEACH OF LOST THINGS

Oyster wiped the blood from his face with the back of his hand. The bleeding had stopped. He ran as quickly as he could, his feet slipping and sliding in the mud. He tried not to think of what his trainers would look like after this little adventure. He'd already lost one pair of shoes this week.

He found himself thinking of the time Lucas had taken them all to the seaside. It had probably been Camber Sands. He'd only been a kid. There were vague sensations of Paris roundly pregnant with Cécile. Him, kneeling in the sand with a bucket and spade; the waves rolling in, soaking his feet and drenching his kickers; washing away his sandcastle. Paris had dried his tears and hugged him, and he'd felt Cécile kicking away against his face; the promise of a life that would not be denied.

Police cars flickered behind him, rendering the alleyway in slivers of blue. He heard muffled cries and shouts from the cops; Broadsides must be making his getaway, too. Oyster needed to press on as fast as he could, he wouldn't have much time before they figured out where he'd gone. Panic made his knees feel like noodles. He couldn't think about what would happen if he didn't retrieve the money. He scratched at his tattoo.

His breath came in gasps. *Keep it together. Keep it together. Keep it together. Keep it together.* His fingertips were tingling. He was suddenly convinced he was going to die. Tears rolled down his face. For fuck's sake, why was he so useless at this?

Thin branches whipped his aching nose, but he stumbled onward, the alley becoming increasingly narrow. Where had the Mannish gone?

Shit. The solid wooden slats of a garden fence blocked his path. But Ambidexter and her crew hadn't doubled back. Tramping feet behind him told him he had been boxed in by the pursuing cops. He was vaguely aware they were shouting at him. Telling him to come quietly. Things were unfocused. He dropped to his knees feeling dizzy; there was a deep throbbing in his ears.

Oyster's midriff shimmered with acute pain, as though he was wrapped in a bale of barbed wire that was tightening around him. He yelped and dropped forward onto his hands. At the bottom of the fence he became aware of a pencil-thin strip of light, as though someone had cut a wide, narrow slice out of the wood. More than that, the light was... *daylight*?

He leaned forward, reaching towards it with his fingers. As he pressed into it, the gap widened into a broad mouth swallowing his hand and the wrist that followed it. The light became blinding. Despite his fear of what was happening, there was recognition here, too; a sense that he'd done this before. There were more shouts from the police behind him and so he pushed himself forward, managing to slip his head and neck into the gap before something on the other side grabbed him bodily and pulled him through.

An ice-cold kiss landed on Oyster's cheek. He twitched and scratched the spot, then he lurched awake, heart pounding. What had happened to him? Had he been unconscious?

He was lying on his back. There were patchy clouds overhead and the sky had an odd greenish hue. The icy sensation came again and again. He rubbed his face; his hand was coated with fragments of paper. Each piece was frayed around the edges and coated in ice like a snowflake. Each contained sequences of letters that weren't quite words.

He read ATHAL, SONDER and XTCH before the ice melted, turning the paper to mulch. Several more settled on him, sailing down out of the clear sky. He sat up.

He was on a broad beach of grey, damp sand. The snow was falling gently all around him, but failing to settle. Deano's knife was nowhere to be seen. The sea crested white in the distance to his right. Far to his left was an uneven black wall that stretched off to the horizon. A few hundred yards ahead of him was an enormous opening in the ground. He rubbed his eyes to make sure that he was seeing what he was seeing.

All round the hole lay wrecked vehicles: railway carriages, buses and cars piled one on top of another. Tube trains lay like great, silver worms rusting in the sand. A number 11 lay on its side like a felled animal, windows smashed, doors prised open. He staggered to his feet, swaying a little as he accustomed himself to standing and approached them. Fragmentary snowflakes pattered around him, flurrying into his eyes and fizzing as they hit the shallow pools of water nestling amongst the sand bars.

Picking his way around a nest of dead trains, he saw they were of differing shapes, sizes and ages. Each was a twisted metal tube with shattered windows. The nearest was composed of several carriages that snaked back to the enormous hole, as though it had emerged from it like some monolithic metal worm and then crashed back down onto the sand. The blue plush of its seats had been slit and the foam within removed. Anything of value had been taken from the wreckage long ago. Was this some sort of seaside junkyard?

Where the hell was he? And where were the Mannish?

It was as though he was in a dream. The sound of faraway waves lapped in his ears. Could you hear in dreams? Perhaps. But at the very least he didn't think you could smell, and he was struck by the way the dark sand eddied into pools of stinking black mud. *Hang on.* There were footprints around him, top-of-the-line trainers by the looks of them, leading away from the sea back towards the hunched mass of the wall. The Mannish must have come this way.

His tattoo burned with bee-sting glee. Then his whole torso flared into agony. He yelled, yanking off his jacket and hoodie and throwing them onto the beach. Gingerly, he prodded at his aching body. The tattoo's ink looked darker and its edges pulsed an angry red, as though trying to break free and leak into the rest of his skin. Each pulse generated a throb of pain – and then, as suddenly as it had started, it stopped. When he got back to his manor, he was going to have some serious words with the two-bit joint that inked him up.

But that was the least of his problems. He breathed in, trying to steady himself as he replaced his now damp clothing. Things were weird, but he wasn't going to wig out. *Okay*. Work this problem. Keep it simple. Where was he? He'd slipped through a fence with the cops in tow and then woken up on a beach somewhere else. He squinted at the dilapidated wall to his left. Perhaps this was one of those backward Kentish shitholes like Ramsgate or Folkstone? They were just names to him, but the names had enough power to calm him, make him feel like he was at least a little in charge of his fate.

How had he ended up here? Had the Mannish dosed him somehow; carted him out here and left him on the beach just for shits and giggles? What could they have mickeyed him with, though? He'd had a passing acquaintance with most Class A's in his time, including a very sticky patch with speed back in his teens, but what could they have given him that would take him out for so long? Ketamine? GHB? Maybe something more specialist.

Okay, so I know where I am and I've a rough idea of how I might have gotten here. Now, I just have to work out how to get back. Shit. With a sinking sensation, he remembered: the failed dead drop; the cash the Mannish had run off with. He was in it and deep.

But he couldn't do anything about that right now. With a sigh, he struck out towards the wall, following the Mannish's footprints. There were no seagulls, not even a single tourist, and apart from the distant lapping of the waves everything was quiet. He listened to the hypnotic sound of his feet as they squelched into the sand with each step, sometimes sinking so deep that he had to stop and pull them out. It was slow progress.

As he approached it, he saw that the sea wall was about twenty feet high and constructed from irregular bits of wood and concrete. Coated with thick black tar, its ramparts were decorated with curls of rusty barbed wire.

He hopped from one dry patch of sand to the next, avoiding water as much as possible. A flurry of snowflakes blew into his eyes and he shivered. The nearby mudflats were strewn with flotsam. There were the bleached metal bones of a pram, dead shoes and fragments of flatpack furniture which the action of the sea had worked into pieces of abstract sculpture.

He walked to a stretch of mud, boasting a mountain of old brick-sized mobiles, ancient printers and shattered laptops. As well as lifting the cash, the Mannish had also run off with the burners, so he was out of contact. He picked up a Nokia 3600, the same model Lucas had had back in the day. He held down the "On" button, but its LCD screen remained blank, so he let it tumble back onto the beach. His stomach gurgled and he winced in discomfort.

There were jumbles of footprints and what looked to be wheel tracks leading over the sand and back towards the wall. A whole bunch of people had been out here recently. Seemed like they had carts with them, or maybe had just dragged the heavier booty left on the beach back with them.

Oyster needed to pee. He stepped behind an unruly tower of office furniture and ragged bicycle frames, unzipped and let rip. The furniture looked like it had fallen straight from the sky rather than being washed up. Whoever had been combing the beach earlier had left this particular treasure. Or maybe it had washed up after they had left.

He finished and zipped up before kneeling to rinse his hands in a pool of sandy water. The snow had stopped. Looking out at the sea as the weather cleared, he saw a pair of long ladders out near the horizon. What was more, there were figures halfway up them. Squinting, they appeared to be painting clouds onto the sky. He looked again, but they were gone.

Then something large, moving out on the sea, caught his attention. At first, Oyster thought it was a boat; but the more he looked at it, the less it seemed like a vessel. For a start, it was the wrong shape, looking more like some sort of massive insect. And then there was the way it moved. It was wading *through* the waves on long legs rather than riding over them.

As he watched, the thing reached the horizon, then walked up into the sky. A circular window opened in the sky and the thing, whatever it was, disappeared into it, taking the hole with it.

Fuck. I must be seeing things. Whatever I was spiked with is still rattling around inside my head. For a second, the silence became more intense. Oyster swallowed. He needed to get back to civilisation, this beach was doing his nut in.

He sighed and returned to walking in the direction of the sea wall, listening to the rhythmic slurp of his feet in the muddy slurry of the beach. There was a chill breeze, and although he couldn't see the sun, the sky had reddened. It must be the late afternoon.

He had been walking like this for ten minutes or so – head down, lost in thought – when the silence was rent by a scream. He looked around for its source. Had it come from further along the wall? He heard the cry again, more urgent this time. Instinctively, he ran towards it, knowing it was probably the stupid thing to do but doing it anyway.

Further ahead, along the length of the great, tarred mass of the sea wall, he spotted movement. As he got closer, Oyster saw three people in the midst of some sort of ruck. Two men versus a woman. Of the men, one was tall and thin, the other short and stocky. They were dressed in matching black coats and three-quarter trews that resembled the Mannish Boys' outfits, but where that crew's gear had been all styled up, these were subdued black uniforms that made their wearers resemble paramilitary undertakers or priests. Either way, they reeked of authority.

Oyster bristled immediately. Whatever was going down was way off base.

Each man wore a thick belt from which hung metal tongs and a leather bag about the size of a deflated football. Both wielded ebony batons a couple of feet long. Their long jackets and skinny legs made Oyster think of a pair of ill-matched beetles.

The woman was the palest person he'd ever seen. She wore scarlet, side-buttoned trousers, black sixteen-hole Doc Martens and was wrapped in a shabby fake-fur coat.

The two men were trying to outflank the woman, who was crouched low, coiled with defensive energy. In one hand she held a long, tasty-looking bone-handled dagger. Oyster reached into his puffer jacket and slipped out his own blade. It flashed red in the afternoon light.

He sensed there was a standoff here; that his arrival would tip the balance one way or another. They felt it too. The tall man cocked his head to one side, taking in Oyster at a glance, his face as long and glum as a wet Sunday. A pair of thick crimson sunglasses perched on his pinched nose. A raw 'S' shape carved into his cheek told Oyster that not only was the knife the woman held pretty tasty-looking, but its owner was no slouch at using it either.

The man arranged his lips into a smile, eyes constantly flicking back to the woman, revealing a mouthful of missing and yellowed teeth. There was a studied air about him, masking an underlying anxiety. Oyster recognised it as the sort of jacked-up calm emitted when you were caught off your home turf.

"Good day," said the man in an oily voice. "I am Scudder and that is Collier. We are clerks, Section 586. This is City biz. So best be on your way, eh, chitling?"

Oyster nodded. He looked across at the woman. Her face was so pale it was almost translucent; her eyes were odd: the whites a fucked-up dark colour and her irises a colour that matched her hair as though they were both catastrophically bloodshot.

"S'up?" he called. Her gaze remained fixed on the clerks.

"Do as told, squirt, this ain't your affair," grunted the stockier man. There was something squat and doglike about him, his tone glinting with the threat of violence. An angry slash across his forehead dripped blood onto his own pair of sunglasses.

"What's all the heat about?" said Oyster. "You get booted out the *Matrix* triple-bill?"

"Do not press our patience, bantling," said Scudder. "Collier, here, will not require much excuse to detach your melon from its wheeze pipe."

"After I've given you a proper basting, gobshite," added Collier with a hiss.

"I dunno about that," said Oyster, "from what I see she's got the measure of you two spods. You might want to rethink your play—"

It all happened really fast then.

The woman leaped at Scudder, aiming a kick at the hand holding the truncheon. The clerk was caught off guard, the momentum of the blow spinning him off-balance and whipping the weapon out of his hand and into a pool of water, where it landed with a *kerplunk*.

Collier rushed to defend his partner, aiming a blow at the back of the woman's head. Somehow, she dodged out of its path, but lost her footing in the sand. Oyster charged into the fray, swinging wildly at Collier. His fist connected with the man's temple, knocking his glasses from his face. Twisting towards Oyster, Collier brought his truncheon down.

Oyster raised an arm to block the blow and lightning flashed up from his elbow. Dizzy, unthinking through the pain, he brought his knee up between the man's legs. *The finisher*, Deano had called it.

Collier dropped into the sand groaning, hands cupping his groin. Oyster aimed a couple of kicks at the man's head for good measure and then jumped over him, aiming to help the woman, but she had already recovered. Scudder retreated, hands raised. The woman feinted at the unarmed clerk's chest, driving him back towards the wall, near where Collier lay.

"Take yourself and this bottle-head cully back to the metropolis with you," she said, her voice lilting, musical; accents on all the wrong syllables.

"Very well, very well," replied Scudder with a supercilious smile. Collier staggered to his feet.

"But we will see you pretty buck-fitches again," he said.

"Yeah, and I won't forget you two shits neither," said Oyster. "Like the woman said, fuck off back to your crib." His fingertips fizzed and his hairline prickled with adrenaline.

The two scuttled to the wall. They ran along its length for a few yards then disappeared. There was the sound of a bolt being drawn and a door being slammed, and then they were gone.

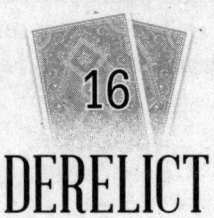

16
DERELICT

Once their assailants were gone, Oyster and the woman appraised each other. She stepped back, rising to her full height, several inches taller, observing him dispassionately. Despite the shabbiness of her clothes there was a regal tilt to her chin.

Oyster was amazed once more by just how pale her skin was, so light that he could see the purple veins beneath. There was something else, too, perhaps a very subtle tattoo of an ink he'd never seen, but it hinted at pulsating trails, like strings of fairy lights illuminating her face from within.

She reminded Oyster of some sort of deep-sea creature, comprised in equal parts of anemone and angler fish. Her eyes were a piercing, mesmeric red that was perhaps the result of the fight. A froth of vivid orange hair licked around her face. Her hands were in constant motion, sheathed in black patent leather gloves; they swayed like fronds of seaweed underwater.

"Nice shiv," he said.

She rolled her bloodshot eyes, gunslingered her dagger back inside her coat, then produced a blue scrunchy to tie her hair back into a tight ponytail.

She sniffed, turned, and set off towards the sea wall.

"Wait up," said Oyster, taking a few steps after her. He rubbed his numb arm where Collier had struck it. The feeling was gradually returning, but he would have a big-arse bruise on it tomorrow.

He was collecting injuries at a pretty high rate.

"Mille grazie for the assist and all," she said over her shoulder, "but I got vexes of my own with which to deal." That accent again. Wrong and right at the same time. Her voice was iron and salt, wind and sky.

"Can you at least tell me where I am?" he said. His voice sounded unfamiliar and small; keening. The unease, stowed away inside him ever since he'd woken up, detonated like a slow bomb. The childish fear of being lost surged over him. He couldn't breathe again; tears welled up in his eyes and he wiped the dried blood and snot from his sore nose with the back of his hand. He sniffed.

Mixed in with the feelings, there was an anger. Anger at what stupid bloody Lucas had done with his crew and his crimes and his need to be the biggest swinging dick in town. He and Cécile had never asked for any of it, yet they had paid. More than Paris. More than anyone. The anger fired him. Drove away the hurt. He sniffed and spat into the water. *Fuck this shit. Fuck them all.*

The woman was a few hundred yards away now.

"Wail all you like, Captain Hackam, but best bet is to steer out of the black sands double quick," she called over her shoulder. "Beach should be cheek by jowl right about now."

"Wasn't crying," said Oyster.

"Course you weren't, honey child."

"Name's Oyster," he called to her, running a few splashing steps through the mud to catch her up.

She nodded.

"Margate? Sheppey?" he said, nodding at the wall.

The woman glanced at him quizzically. "What the feckle is a shippee?"

"Where we are we?" he said. "Kent... by the sea? Or is it Southend? Why are you being so bloody mysterious?"

She stopped, straightened so she could look down on him.

"Talk a lot, don't you?"

Oyster shrugged.

"Look here, Royston, or whatever asinine moniker you've given yourself: being grateful for your abbetence does not obligate me to be your cully-wife. Plus, I'm getting a very fresh-off-the-beach vibe from you and can't be babysitting. Fam's in need, gotta speed, and so on."

She adopted the sort of posture minor members of the Royal Family might when meeting factory workers.

"Thank you. Kind regards. There we go good chap. Et cetera, et cetera, et cetera." She clapped Oyster on the shoulder with pantomime bonhomie and stormed away.

"Fuck me, you just sped right through the lights there, didn't you?" said Oyster, anger rising back up inside him. "I was just asking where the fuck we were and who the fuck you are."

They had reached the wall. Up close, Oyster could see it was a jumble of found objects piled one atop the other and fastened together with bolts, nails and anything else that had come into the hands of its builders. Here and there a few beams protruded, joined together and reinforced with brass couplings, but there was nothing about it that followed any sort of plan. It looked like it had been thrown together hastily, the result of an overwhelming terror of the world beyond it.

The sickly feeling that had been pursuing him for a long time finally materialised. The sticky whisper of fear told him what he had not wanted to accept: he wasn't anywhere that he knew. There was too much weird shit going on: the snow; the wall; the clerks; the woman; hell, even her eyes fed the creeping suspicion that he wasn't anywhere he'd ever been before. His head was doing a number on him. Perhaps he was lying in a ditch somewhere in a coma. Or in a car boot, tripping his tits off.

An ear-rending blast of sound from behind him interrupted his thoughts. The noise was so loud his lungs vibrated as though he was at a house party with an 8K rig. He spun around in terror. Out at sea, heaving around the curve of the great wall, was an enormous black-legged something. At first glance, it resembled a curved metal-and-glass skyscraper, slung upon its side and walking on elongated legs. It paused for a second, like a monolithic crane fly, and gave a second foghorn wail before spouting a plume of black smoke.

Oyster recalled the creature he'd seen climb up into the sky earlier. There were similarities, but this one seemed smaller. Even so, close up, this one was huge. It moved again, faster now, shaking the beach with each footfall and sending eddies of water over Oyster's feet. It was heading straight for them and closing with surprising speed, but his brain was bricked; he was frozen in place, paralysed by the impossibility of what he was seeing.

The woman bolted the remaining distance to the wall and scuttled up it fluidly, her silver skin seeming to prickle with actual light. The smell of the thing behind him hit Oyster: a cross between burning engine oil and stale dog; a stench so overpowering, it was a like a slap in the face. He regained control of his legs.

With a step and a hop, he grabbed the nearest of the joints with his left hand. The wood was damp, and his fingers dislodged a rain of salt crystals that peppered his eyes. His arms ached and his fingers were slipping. Swinging his arm up, he grabbed onto the beam with his other hand. Oyster's feet scrabbled for a foothold as he pulled himself up. He hung for a second from both hands until the tip of his left toe found a knothole which supported his weight. He felt around overhead for another handhold.

Above him, the woman had climbed almost to the top of the wall. She tugged open a small door and wriggled into it.

"Hey there," he shouted, but the woman had already disappeared as far as her knees.

Oyster fumbled for his next bit of purchase. He cursed. It was just out of reach. The woman was almost through the wall. If she shut the door behind her, he was royally fucked. He looked down and the ground welled up beneath him. He was sliding sideways. He closed his eyes and exhaled. Standing on tiptoes, he tried to lever himself up far enough to grab the next handhold with his fingertips. Above him, all he could see now was the woman's booted ankles.

There was nothing for it, thought Oyster: he'd have to do something desperate. He breathed in again and shut his eyes. Then, bracing himself as much as he could, he jumped up with his hands outstretched.

The fingers of one hand closed around another joist and he hung on for dear life. His feet swung like pendulums, scrabbling against the slick patch of wood beneath them. His fingers cracked and his stomach lurched as he glanced down.

Above, the woman's boots disappeared into the tunnel, kicking free a shower of pebbles that pelted him in the face. Behind him, the pursuing creature gave another cataclysmic bellow. The sound was so deafening he thought the creature must be on top of them. With a heave, he got his other hand onto the joist, and with a shoulder-cracking strain placed his feet on the protruding lip of a wooden beam. He sighed. The door above him was still open. He worked along the wooden ledge and tiptoed to another handhold before levering himself into the passageway.

He glanced back. From this higher vantage point, the creature looked like an office block had mated with a giant cockroach. Black smoke spouted from row upon row of tubes that curled from its flanks. Steam gushed into the sky from vertical slits, pulsing like gills near its head. He looked in vain for joints or bearings, anything that would give away how the legs worked or how it was propelled. In any event, its movement, a monolithic slow-motion scuttle, made him doubt that it was entirely mechanical or animal.

The beast hooted again and there was the sound of a whipcrack. The wall was pounded by a long, leathery tentacle, sending splinters of wood and rock flying in all directions. The thing was trying to shake them loose from the wall. Oyster slammed the trapdoor shut behind him and slithered deep into the safety of the passage, heart pounding.

"We need to shift," came the woman's voice. "Almost night."

Oyster started. He was surprised to see her still waiting there, her strange lights twinkling suddenly in the blackness.

"This really isn't Kent, is it," puffed Oyster between breaths.

In answer, she turned tail and crawled through the tunnel. Oyster followed, edging himself further into the wall's interior.

17

GREATER LONDON

The passage was narrow, about twenty feet long and full of an assortment of objects: protruding chair legs, tabletops and bicycle pedals. Far from being a part of the wall's original design, the tunnel appeared to have been hollowed out over a period of days, months or even years. It smelled like a rubbish tip, and he had to take care to avoid cuts and splinters from its uneven surface.

The pounding stopped. The creature had given up trying to catch them. In the silence, Oyster wondered what on earth he was doing. Assuming he could even catch up with the Mannish and get his things back, what would he do then? How would he get back to London?

Ahead of him, the woman opened a small wooden door and slipped over the passage's lip with practised ease. Oyster followed, blinking in the dim light. Almost plunging into thin air, he pulled himself back inside the tunnel with a yelp.

"Move it, lickyspit," hissed the girl from below. "Down's easier than up, innit. Shickle your arse."

Oyster poked his head out. She was right. Footholds and handholds protruded from all over the wall's surface. He swung his legs out over the edge and gasped.

Below him and beyond him stretched row after row of buildings in a giddy jumble of styles. Some were simple redbrick two-up two-downs that wouldn't have looked amiss in

Tooting, others were exotic concoctions of enormous bones and dried mud.

In the distance, an oily river snaked through the city's centre, crisscrossed by ramshackle bridges, each one piled high with structures in a confusion of styles and shapes. Some had lower storeys of wattle and daub, twisting upward into wild golden minarets. Others combined the sombre spires of churches with cranes and derricks that reached down to the river and the paddle boats that ploughed up and down it.

On the river's far side were buildings of enormous size in marble and gold. One had more monolithic Grecian columns than Oyster could count. Next to it was an enormous semi-spherical red-brick monument. Atop it sat a golden pyramid, a fire at its apex spouting white smoke. The building's true scale was only revealed when Oyster realised that the dots promenading along its outermost balcony were people.

Nearer his vantage point, the structures were distinctly worn down and built on a much more human scale. Many were constructed from reclaimed materials that Oyster presumed must have been collected from the beach. A nearby pub hung its sign from a repurposed television aerial, while a neighbouring cottage was built entirely from car doors and featured a roof thatched with plastic drinking straws.

"Where the hell am I?" asked Oyster. The question slipped out, not even consciously directed at his companion. This was not like any city he'd ever seen before. Fuck, this wasn't even like any *country* he'd ever seen before.

Clouds streaked the greenish-blue above his head, but there was something far too regular about them. It was only then that he realised what he was looking at was actually an enormous dome, decorated to look like the sky. It arched over the entire city, encompassing the beach and the sea beyond it. His head swam with vertigo, and he shut his eyes to steady himself. He felt dizzy and sick.

A cold red sun hung bloody and low on the artificial horizon. His body told him it was still only morning, but here inside the dome, he guessed, it could be any time. Oyster shivered. For an instant, he had the distinct sensation that the sun was looking back at him.

The woman clambered to the ground at speed. She looked like a moth in the dying light, her coat flapping about her like a pair of furry wings. Oyster followed her down.

As he neared the ground, a briny smell assaulted his nostrils. He coughed a little and spat, trying to rid himself of the city's taste.

Touching down at the bottom of the wall, the ground crackled underfoot. It was littered with thousands of fish bones, some whole, some just tiny skeletal fragments. The woman waited for him in the shadows.

She wrapped herself in her coat and pulled a battered-looking powdered wig over her hair. She stared at him with her marmalade eyes.

"New to Greater London, aren't you?" she said.

"But this isn't London." His words were a whisper.

The woman chuckled.

"Well, it's the one you happen to be in right now, so you may as well get used to it. Might want to stop walking around with your mouth open, as well."

Oyster nodded. He swallowed. Whatever had happened to him – crack on the head, drug-induced coma, whatever – he should just roll with it. If he played along with the whole thing, maybe he could pull his head out from between his own buttocks long enough to find a way back home.

"What was that thing, back there?" he said, taking a few crunching steps away from the wall.

"Company looüt," she replied. "A derelict, I reckon; crew long dead or worse. Looked like she was in heat, too. Probably what scared all the combers off the beach."

Oyster nodded again. He was trying his best not to freak out. If he was going to make any progress here, he would have to just accept what he saw.

"I thought I saw one of those things disappearing through a sort of hole earlier, in the sky."

"Yeah," said the woman. "That's where they go. Sailing on the outerside of the lid. Fishing trips. Merchanting. Commerce. Profiteering. Taking what they don't own and selling it for what they don't spend. Doing whatever turns a gelt out there in the black."

Oyster nodded, trying to absorb what she was saying while ignoring the lingering feeling that if he'd been a proper ginnals, like Lucas, he'd have taken this all in his stride. He missed Cécile, too. He was sure she'd have been much better at coping with all of this.

The woman gazed at him, unblinking.

"Alright, in any case, we're just about done for here and now." She gave him a mocking salute. "Wishing you a good night and all that." And she turned to walk away.

"Wait up," said Oyster, running after her. "You can't leave me here."

"You do like telling a woman what she can and can't do, don't you?"

Oyster reddened.

"It's not that. It's just... do you know where I can find the Mannish Boys?"

The woman turned back to him.

"That name's trouble and I'm just about up to my nubbin already, sweets."

"You owe me," said Oyster. "I helped you out. Back on the beach." He pointed back to the wall with his thumb. He knew it was a dick move, but as much as he didn't want to admit it, he was desperate. If this woman left him, he'd be totally untethered in this strange, new place.

She snorted.

"I see. That's how it's gonna be, is it?"

She leaned towards him and grabbed the neck of his T-shirt, pulling him towards her. Oyster was hypnotised for a moment by the traceries of golden light that trickled around her skin; they glowed brighter for a second.

"Look, Man-Friday," she continued in a whisper. "You and

I both know I could've basted that pair of jackdaws with or without your assist."

Oyster shrugged.

"I don't know how I got here," he replied. "I don't even know where 'here' is. For all I know, I'm lying in a bed somewhere with one of those beep-beep-beep machines in the corner and a pipe down my neck feeding me baby food."

The woman shook her head.

"That is both a sorry and totally incomprehensible story all at once. Even so, it's not my habit to be adopting opaque strays. Not my problem," she said.

"But I need to get home," said Oyster. "I gotta look out for my sis. I'm all she's got. Please."

The word didn't come naturally to Oyster. As soon as he said it, part of him despised himself for having to use it. He hated the notion of having to plead, of throwing himself on someone else's mercy.

The woman's cheeks and neck shimmered as though sewn with golden thread. She regarded him with a mixture of disdain and curiosity.

"Well, I suppose that is the magic word," she replied, thinking for a moment. "Lookee, I got errands to run, Man-Friday," she said, "but I suppose you can follow me into town."

The light from the sickening sun had faded now and Oyster followed her along the foot of the wall, past a row of darkened houses built from crumbling brick. The air was suddenly alive with the sound of hundreds of flapping wings, and Oyster looked up to see it throbbing with what looked like bats. He shivered. This place really was doing a number on him.

Everything had happened so quickly, his brain hadn't had time to catch up with the pace of events: the beach, the clerks, the creature. It was all so dreamlike and yet, as the pain in his arm and bruised face confirmed, all so undoubtedly real. And then there was his tattoo. The way it was acting up. It was all connected somehow. It had to be.

Night fell quickly, and he sensed rather than saw how they

were penned in on one side by the great black wall and a row of silent, deserted houses on the other. The woman led them to a stretch of scrub strewn with bushes. She bent down to pull at something and promptly disappeared.

Oyster ran after her, fearing she had deserted him once more, but the woman was perched on a rusted metal ladder leading down into a tunnel. She looked up at him with no great enthusiasm.

"What do you call yourself, anyway?" he said.

"Call me Nonesuch, Dry Bob," she replied before disappearing into the gloom.

18
POST OFFICE

Nonesuch emitted a low wattage trickle of fairy light, illuminating the way underground. Oyster was fascinated and, if he was honest, slightly repulsed by the way she was able to do this, but he'd already exceeded his quota of questions for the day.

Although there was just enough height for Oyster to stand in the passageway, Nonesuch had to hunch over for the duration of the journey. After an age, they climbed up a passage braced with barrel hoops and emerged into the darkness above. Nonesuch plugged the tunnel's mouth with a circular piece of tin and disguised it beneath a covering of rocks and fishbones.

They were in a deserted patch of scrubland surrounded by inverted, empty buildings whose unfurnished insides appeared to be on their outsides. The internal radar that helped him recognise and avoid threats was seriously on the fritz in this place.

He wondered idly about the drop money that he'd lost. Then he wondered about Broadsides, hoping his friend had made it away from the cops safe and sound. He pushed the thoughts away. *One problem at a time.*

And then he thought of Cécile. He hoped she wasn't fretting about him too much. She was used to him fading for a day or two occasionally, and she had enough green to keep things ticking over for a week or two, maybe more.

"Where is everybody?" he said.

"Curfew," answered Nonesuch.

They arrived at a modest brick building that superficially resembled the sort of dwelling often converted into post offices or corner shops back in Oyster's London. It even boasted a broad, wire-reinforced front window.

The house's walls were coated in overlapping fist-sized bumps. Each one a deep, glossy black, spiralled with blue and green petrol whorls. Oyster prodded one and jumped back with a yelp as it sprouted eight skeletal legs and a tiny red mouth, lined with rows of needle teeth. The creature's curved back cracked open and iridescent wings fluttered out.

As Oyster watched, two more of the animals descended to settle on the house's walls. These were the flying creatures he'd mistaken for bats. Nonesuch flicked back the lapel of her coat and exposed a white linen shirt and an expanse of gossamer shoulder beneath. At the top of her arm was a tiny black nipple. Her skin rippled with lightning and one of the creatures flew from its resting place on the wall to suckle at her shoulder. She cooed in response.

"Nuajin here are mostly retired, but this one's my boy, Bamyasi," she said, stroking the creature with her other hand. It crawled up to her throat and nuzzled against Nonesuch's ears.

She turned and whispered something to it that Oyster could not quite make out. The nuajin chittered in return and its wing casings flicked open. With a buzz it flew away into the dark.

"Did you just use that thing to send a message?" he said.

Nonesuch nodded. "Well, the lights are on in there after all, Dry Bob." She tapped his forehead. "Even if your skin's too thick and ugly to see."

"I guess it beats having to find three-bar coverage," Oyster said.

"My crib," said Nonesuch, pushing the door open and stepping inside.

She stooped, struck a match and lit an old brass lamp which she passed to Oyster. Long shadows leaped around the room. Rusted metal shelving ran along the walls that flanked the shop window, and at the rear was a counter which had clearly once hosted a cash register.

Nonesuch hustled them to an upstairs room. It was unfurnished except for an out-of-place dirty glass chandelier which hung crookedly from the ceiling. The walls were decorated with peeling, gold-striped wallpaper. An empty gilt frame hung from a far wall. It smelled of mould. Scattered around the carpet were a pair of bedrolls that had been unceremoniously upended and disembowelled, their contents spread across the floor like ersatz snow. In the corner stood a large jug surrounded by a mismatched set of mugs and chipped china cups.

Nonesuch sighed as she surveyed the mess.

"Apologies for the caca-fuego. Clerks have been here too," she said.

She picked her away across the rubbish-strewn floor to kneel in the corner of the room. She cleared some of the floorboards and whistled into a large knothole at the end of one of them. A staccato crackle came from beneath it. She pressed the end of the floorboard and it upended.

With a twitter, a larger nuajin emerged from under the floor.

"She's my bro's," said Nonesuch by way of explanation. "What they were after, but never found."

The beetle shone like polished coal. She flew up into the air, making straight for Oyster, who lost his footing and fell over backwards. The nuajin landed on his chest and scuttled towards his face. He yelled, trying to swipe her away.

"Step off," said Nonesuch. "Nothing to be scared of. And speaking frank, she's worth more to me than you are."

The nuajin scuttled under Oyster's elbow to rest beneath his right armpit.

"Get it off me," said Oyster, his voice rising in panic. The creature squirmed beneath his arm.

"Ease up," said Nonesuch. "Let her settle and I'll have her offa you in a blink."

Nonesuch reached under his arm and tugged gently at the creature. There was a stinging pain beneath his arm.

"It hurts!" he yelled.

"Ah. Fucksticks."

"That's not good, is it?" said Oyster, panicking anew. "What's happened?"

"I need you to keep yourself calm. But I think our ickle ink beetle here has taken a liking to you. Which is odd and an inconvenience."

Oyster wanted to yell, but held himself in check.

"Alright," he said, forcing a tone he did not feel. "And what does that mean?"

"Means she's bonding with you… somewhats, and so there'll be no getting her off you—"

"What the fuck!" yelled Oyster, his fake calm blown.

"—for now!" She held her hands out to calm him. "Sure, we can coax her out given an itsy time, but right now there's no way of removing her without taking a supper-sized portion of you with. More you make a fuss, more she'll dig in."

Oyster swallowed.

"Dig in?"

"Best thing you can do is relax. If you have any sort of inkling how to, that is."

Oyster bristled again.

"I'll have you know that when I'm not being fucked over by walking buildings, having my head stoved in by undertakers or armpit-shagged by beetles, I'm pretty fucking chill."

Nonesuch gave him a look that indicated she was unconvinced of his claim. He looked into her eyes and saw her irises, pulsing orange like car indicator lights. For the first time since Oyster had been picked up by the cops in the park, the anxiety at the pit of his stomach melted away. He tried to stand, but the blood rushed to his head and he staggered. "I got the helicopters," he said.

"Just a peck of glimmer to unwind you," said Nonesuch. "Your kind are susceptible. Shineheads out there would happily pay top guinea for that hit. You're all tensed up, chip. It'll pass."

Oyster swayed and sat back down in a heap. He knew now why the clerks wore sunglasses.

She turned and picked her way through the mess of the room, returning with a yellowed china teacup.

"Water," she said, offering it to Oyster.

He took an exploratory sip. The liquid was dark and tasted metallic, but he was suddenly thirsty and drank several cups without stopping.

"So then, what's the deal with your bruv?" he said, sitting up. The water had restored his spirits a little. "His beetle thingy's here, but he's not."

Nonesuch nodded.

"Motet was mixed up in something bad, well over his addle-pate," she said. "Last time I saw him, he's got all this coin and swagger on him. Tells me payday's coming and I should keep low 'cos something bigtime's gonna happen. That's why the clerks were freestyling on me at the beach. They thought I was in on his business."

Oyster considered what she'd said. The nuajin rearranged herself under his armpit. He thought for a second. He needed allies in this place. He was so out of his depth, he couldn't even see the bottom, let alone touch it on his tiptoes.

"How about this," he said finally. "I help you with your brother, Motet. You help me find this Mannish crew?"

Nonesuch looked at him. She flexed her fingers and Oyster's eyes were drawn to the lights that danced beneath her cheeks. She swallowed and they faded to black.

At last, she shook her head.

"Nothing personal, but there's enough mitts round my throat already."

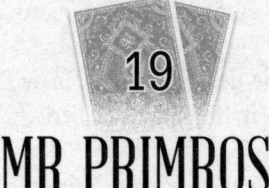

19

MR PRIMROSE

Nonesuch settled in the corner, bathing the room in a flaxen halo. The light caught in the empty gilt frame and for a second Oyster imagined what this room might have been like once, before the house had been deserted.

Opposite him, Nonesuch sat unnaturally still, ever watchful, her red eyes catching the embers of yellow light and turning them to gold. There was no sound. No bustling of cars. No rattling Tube trains beetling overground between subterranean stations. The silence was unbearable.

"So how do you do that?" Oyster said at last.

"Do what?" she said.

"The lights," he replied.

"How do you *not*?" she said.

Oyster rolled his eyes.

"What I mean is, where I come from people can't do that," he said.

"Ah ha. And where would that be then, Dry Bob?"

"Tooting – uh, London. I mean, England."

Nonesuch nodded slowly, digesting the information.

"Well then, all I can say is that your Tooting-uh-London-I-Mean-England must be one gloomy knothole."

"Now you sound like my sister," he said.

"Well, by rights, at least one of your circle must tote their wig on somethin' other than bone."

"Sticks and stones, glow-stick, sticks and stones."

"Very well," said Nonesuch with a sigh. "I'm a gebel. We make light. Is that good enough for you?"

Oyster nodded.

"So how did you wind up here?" she asked.

Oyster shrugged. "Just woke up here, didn't I? Honestly, if I had any clue as to how it happened, I'd go back home straight away."

"Hmm," said Nonesuch, "perhaps you possess the knack, but just aren't acquainted with it full-like. Now, zed-time. I'll keep watch over us and your new friend too, so we don't have any unexpected visitors."

Oyster didn't want to rest. He was still too buzzed from everything that had happened since he'd woken up on the beach. Or perhaps he was still up on whatever the Mannish had slipped him to put him there in the first place.

Riding alongside the physical sensation, he realised, was the fear that going to sleep here would somehow strand him in Greater London for good. A bit like that kiddie idea that dying in your dreams would kill you. If he slept here while in a dream or a coma, would he ever wake up? He chased the thought away. It was idiotic. With a sigh, he wrapped himself in what blankets he could find, lay on the floor, and fell into a deep sleep.

Oyster was at the foot of a great black tree whose branches dwindled to tendrils that wrapped around each other, forming an endless knot. Lucas was tangled motionless amongst the boughs. He sported sunglasses and a rictus smile. A spear had been thrust through his leg, pinning him to the tree's trunk. He was long dead and flies crowded around the swollen tongue protruding from his mouth.

"S'up, Smallweed?" the dead man whispered through blue lips. "Who'd have thought it, eh? The Horned One did me in."

Oyster opened his eyes with a jump. Nonesuch was leaning close over him. She smelled of salt and seaweed. Without thinking, he puckered up, then he realised one of her hands was under his jacket, exploring his armpit.

"Hey!" he shouted, suddenly awake, more embarrassed than angry. "Hands off!"

She backed away, her fingers spread wide in a gesture of innocence.

"Nothing to see here. Just trying to see if our friend had loosened up at all."

Oyster rubbed his eyes. The adrenaline that had woken him tingled through his fingers and toes. He was disappointed everything was just as it had been when he'd fallen asleep. He'd been hoping yesterday had been a dream.

The nuajin still wriggled beneath his arm. Maybe that was the reason for his nightmare. Couldn't be normal having a freaking beetle nesting under there. Keeping Nonesuch in sight, Oyster pulled the neck of his T-shirt back a little and peered down. The creature squeaked and retreated.

"And I suppose, once you'd got it, you were going to skidoosh and leave me for dead here?" he said indignantly.

Nonesuch shrugged.

"Nothing personal," she replied. "Said beforehand, got my own matters to arrange."

Oyster nodded.

"Big shame for you, then, that I've got your bro's beetle thingy, eh?" he replied. "I guess without it you're proper stuffed."

Nonesuch flickered.

Oyster's eyes were heavy with sleep. His hands and legs were cold and his stomach grumbled. The inside of his mouth felt like something had been camping there.

"Oh-kays," she said steepling her fingers. "Since Motet's nuajin has taken such a shine to you, Bobby, maybe we should be working together."

Oyster crawled out of his blankets and stood up.

"Okay. I'll think about it," he said regally. "Now where's your john?"

Nonesuch looked confused.

"House of office is upstairs, if that's what you're after," she replied, pointing back towards the landing. And you'll be needing this."

She held the lamp up to him. Oyster took it and picked his way down the corridor, passing a couple of deserted rooms with gaping doorways. He poked his nose into one but was rewarded with the smell of mildew and naked floorboards. Shadows swayed across the chess-pattern linoleum in the bathroom. There was a yellowed bathtub, a free-standing porcelain sink and a filthy toilet bowl. A cool breeze whipped around Oyster's cheeks, and he noticed the entire rear wall of the bathroom was missing.

Placing the lamp at his feet, he unzipped and peed into the dirty bowl. Lurid piss splashed from the unplumbed rear of the bowl and spiralled into the darkness. Cécile would have told him he needed to drink more water.

He wiped his hands on his jeans and stuck them in the pockets of his damp puffer. His fingers closed around the playing cards he'd been carrying since falling into the Serpentine. Had that been just a couple of days ago? Things had moved so quickly it was hard to tell. He pulled the cards out and examined them. It seemed odd he even had them anymore; they belonged to a different Oyster, not the one peeing into the darkness of some made-up city.

"Magnificent view, isn't it," whispered a voice in his ear.

Oyster yelled in surprise and spun around, lurching off-balance. There stood the man who had tricked him on the bridge. His mashed-up body odour washed over Oyster in a choking wave. As he tottered backwards, Oyster upset the lamp, spilling flaming oil onto the linoleum. He fell backwards into space, clawing the air in front of him for purchase. The man grabbed Oyster's chest, righting him with no effort whatsoever. He smiled an insincere smile.

"What the fuck!" said Oyster in shock.

"Not expecting us, blood?" said the man with a voice like a well-oiled door. This time, he was dressed in a faded Take That T-shirt pulled over a checked shirt. A battered trilby perched on the sheer ledge of his forehead.

"We would like to have a word with you." The man offered his hand. Oyster ignored it, still reeling from his sudden appearance.

"And just who the fuck are 'we'?" Oyster said, his mouth finally recovering.

"Well, that is a question and a conundrum all at once. But for your purposes… let's call us Mr Primrose," he said.

Primrose smiled, although the expression looked as though it had been assembled from a list of instructions.

"How are you even here? What do you want?" said Oyster, recovering his balance.

"Ah, the youth of today. Here we are spending our precious time clearing up other people's messes so everything goes to plan, and" – Primrose sniffed loudly – "this is the thanks we get. Back in our day you'd have to make an offering to receive answers to so many questions all one upon the other."

Primrose released him and patted Oyster on his puffer jacket. Oyster tried to edge past Primrose, away from the yawning darkness behind him, but the man blocked him.

"Messes?" he said.

"Well, not yours right now," Primrose replied. "But perhaps, if you stretch your mind back to our last meeting, you—"

"You've gotta be Po-po. Plainclothes. If that means dressing like a paedo on day release."

Primrose issued a staccato laugh that sounded more crow than human.

"We aren't the police," said Primrose, indulging in another luxurious sniff. "Perhaps we are, however, in a position to help you, given your current predicament. In return—"

"Fuck off," interrupted Oyster, steadying himself against the sink. Flames from the lamp crept along the floor and licked at a pile of rubbish next to the bath.

He wasn't sure that refusing the man's help was a good idea. But right now, he wasn't sure that he would even know what a good idea looked like. In any case, he was as certain as he could be that being in debt to Primrose was not smart.

"Are you sure you won't reconsider?" said Primrose, blocking his way.

Oyster shook his head. Primrose's scent of cut grass and horse manure was suffocating. He suppressed a gag.

"You can just owe us a *little* favour." Primrose indicated a tiny distance with his gloved finger and thumb.

Oyster shook his head and the fire grew, throwing wavering shapes on the yellowed bathroom tiles. A fishy breeze blew in from the city beyond.

"But in that case how will you find your way home?" His tone was icy and mocking. "And what's more, if you're not there, who can look after your sister?"

Oyster burst forward, grabbing Primrose by his collar, but the man was like a block of concrete, unmoving.

"*You* don't mention her!" Oyster shouted.

Primrose, unblinking, nodded at the growing fire.

"Should we put that out, blood?" he said.

Oyster suddenly felt weak and empty. The anger drained out of him. He was lost somewhere he didn't understand.

"Okay. Okay. You win. Just get me home, you prick," he said.

"Now, that's more like it," said Primrose. "That, we can work with."

He sniffed and gave Oyster a shove. Oyster fell backwards, end over end, cartwheeling into the Greater London night.

20

LONDON

The smell of burnt air. Car horns rippling. The screech of brakes. Two people talking smack about each other in loud, south-of-the-river accents. Before Oyster opened his eyes, he knew that he was back in *his* London. His head hurt and his clothes were wet. He opened his eyes, and when he sat up, his senses swirled around his skull.

He was in a nondescript alley, shivering. It was fucking cold. Drizzle drifted down from the sky, penetrating everything, and traffic sizzled as it slipped along a nearby main road. He rubbed his eyes and his nose throbbed in reply. *Ouch*. Rolling his sleeve back revealed a plum-sized bruise on his arm, already beginning to yellow. The souvenirs he'd collected while he was out cold were real enough, but he wasn't ready to believe that he'd really gone to Greater London any more than he was going to believe that Mr Tumnus lived inside his knackered Ikea wardrobe. If he'd been that much off his tits, anything might have happened.

He pressed his hand to his armpit, where Nonesuch's beetle-thing had been nestling. There was a sore lump there and it itched intensely, but of the creature itself there was no sign. That settled it, then. It had all been in his head.

He stood gingerly, bracing himself against the alley's damp brick. He drew strength from its solidity, from the knowledge that he was here again, back where he was supposed to be. *Shit*.

And then he remembered. He also had some explaining to do. How was he going to tell all of this to Big Mickey or Deano? *Sorry I lost your green, boss, but I got jumped by some skinhead chicks, then washed up on a beach with a walking building and a human Christmas tree.*

His best bet might be to check in with Broadsides. They could get their stories straight before turning themselves in to the rest of the gang to face whatever punishment Mickey deemed necessary. And Oyster was in no doubt that there would be punishment.

He breathed in deep, steadying himself, and picked his way to the end of the alleyway, stepping over fossilised dog turds and crisp packets.

Peering into the road beyond sank whatever initial relief he had felt at being in his London. One of the walls of the alley comprised the white plaster facade of a church on Mitcham Road near Amen Corner. This was Stick Ups territory. He pulled up his damp hood. He had to get out of here.

Keeping his head down, Oyster tried to fade as much as he could, heading for the nearest bus stop. His phone was dead, but he still had his wallet. He had no idea how much time he'd been out for, but there was daylight. Perhaps it was the day after he'd been jacked?

He hopped onto a semi-deserted bus that lurched down the street, lurking near the rear doors so he could bounce if he got scoped. His head lit up with a sudden flash of the enormous creature that he'd had encountered with Nonesuch in Greater London. For an instant, the bus seemed just as unlikely. He shook his head to clear it. The Mannish had probably given him years of flashbacks. Hunkering down, he tried to look as unnoticeable as possible, and spent the rest of the trip flicking on and off his phone in a vain effort to get the thing to wake.

He hopped off the bus near the Clip and slipped over the chain-link round the back of the old business park, hood up, head down. He didn't want anyone to see him coming. The wind picked up, cold with a hint of afternoon sleet from the concrete sky. The park was just a strip of tarmac with a few empty units scattered about it.

Overgrown bushes ran the length of the fence and so Oyster squatted, concealed. His hiding place afforded him a good rearside-on view of the Clip and anyone entering or leaving it. Sooner or later Broadsides or Mickey would turn up here, he was sure. He didn't want to explain what had happened to Mickey back at Captain Cluck's; there was too much face riding on it. Mickey would likely go hard and dust the living shit out of him in front of the rest of the crew. Smart thing was to catch up with him outside office hours. If Broadsides showed up first, they could get their act together before talking to the boss.

Oyster was sheltered from the wind and sleet now, but lurking as he was in the undergrowth, he started to get cold almost immediately. It leached up through his butt and feet; dulled the tips of his fingers. To make matters worse, the lump under his armpit itched and his tattoo throbbed like it was radioactive. He wanted to be home. He wanted his bed.

The container stack's rear was plastered with low-end graffiti tags, the result of kids with too much time on their hands and access to a couple of spray cans. One stood out, though: a smoky black silhouette. The figure was out of proportion, asymmetrical, tree-like, with a too-small head and limbs that ended in antlers. The outline of a crow perched on its slanted shoulders.

Oyster's eyes kept getting drawn back to it, its black so dense that it really might be a hole in the metal siding – one leading who knew where? The figure reminded him of the horned creature from his weird-arse dream.

There was a growl and a low-slung sports car slinked around the tarmacked lip of the business park, its headlights dipped in the dying afternoon light. Oyster recognised it immediately as Deano's. It pulled up at the container stack's rear and its engine died. Oyster wasn't sure what to do. Should he approach Deano first? Throw himself on his mercy and then get him to talk to Mickey? He froze, unsure of his play. The door opened and Deano squeezed himself out the car. *Fuck it, I should just stand up here, make myself known. Man up.* Whatever that meant.

But some instinct stopped him. There was something sus

about Deano's manner. Usually, he was a man who was hard to miss. He carried himself in a way that invited your inspection, that radiated about a gazillion megawatts of *I don't give a fuck what you think of me.*

But now he looked diminished, like he didn't want to be seen. A grey beanie was low over his brow, and he nestled his chin on his chest. He shifted his weight back and forth on the balls of his feet. Whatever he was up to, he was trying to keep it on the down low.

Something shifted at the rear of the Clip, and Oyster couldn't quite believe what he saw. Standing crooked like a sketch of a shadow in the rapidly gaining evening was Mr Primrose. Deano nodded and the man approached him. *What the actual fuck were these two doing together?*

Oyster felt very cold. There was some seriously bad-vibe shit going down in front of his eyes. The two men casually chatted to each other. He couldn't hear anything, but this clearly wasn't the first time they'd met. They were tight. His overwhelming urge was to creep back further under the cover of the foliage, but he didn't want to risk moving. If he was spotted it would be the end of him. He held his breath. After a lung-bursting age, the two of them finished their meeting and Deano took off. Primrose was nowhere to be seen.

Oyster's legs had gone to sleep and his stomach gurgled. He felt sick. He went over the scene he'd witnessed again and again, trapped in a loop of disbelief, unable to quite believe what he'd seen. After a long time, he stood and rubbed his numb legs until he could feel them.

His mind was locked up with a sort of sickly vertigo. When he'd been a kid, he'd gone on a school trip to St Paul's Cathedral and had become paralysed climbing one of the trellis stairwells inside it, unable to take his eyes away from the drop visible between his feet and unable to move a step further up or down.

It was exactly that sort of feeling that had him now. Everything he'd thought about the gang was wrong. He stumbled into the road and shuffled his way into the main road on legs like stilts.

In a trance, he made for home, unable to think straight or process what his next move should be. He stumbled on, the trails of the car lights like lazy ghosts flashing past him. It was a risk, but that didn't seem to matter anymore. He knew that he might get turned over by another crew, or (worse) picked up by his own. But that didn't seem to matter anymore either.

At the back of his head, he knew he needed to let Cécile know he was alright. That was the only thing that was important. And so, he staggered on through the night, walking across the south of the city towards the stacked lights of his block, cold beneath a colder moon.

21

"YOU DON'T DO THINGS BY HALVES, DO YOU?"

Oyster was still a shambling wreck when he reached Deeside. The tower block had been erected in the seventies, then been refurbed at some point in the eighties, which explained the prevalence of plastic red-and-blue fittings.

From outside, the building looked like someone had taken a cruise liner and driven it into the ground prow first. While he knew the place was a dump, the sight of it warmed him somewhere inside, beneath the accumulated crud of adulthood. He loved it; it was the only home he had ever known.

Nearing the building, his street-smarts came back online. It was fair to assume the rest of the Urbans were on the lookout for him now. For all they knew, he'd done a runner with a sack of Mickey's cash. And although Oyster fully intended to front up to his boss about what had happened, the only chance of being able to walk away from that conversation would be if it happened on his own terms. It was vital he wasn't brought in, and it was very possible that his block was being watched.

He took a route around to the south side of the building, one that led him to the unlit entrance of its parking underworld. Again, he crouched out of sight and waited, his breath turning to vapour trails. For the first time in a long while he was itching for a ciggie, just to give his frozen fingers something to do.

The building had been conceived as twin stacks of flats, known as East Tower and West Tower, that backed onto each other. Each half of the building had its own main entrance, lifts and stairs, but no communicating connections apart from a shared rooftop. Inevitably, this separation had led to endless confrontations with the kids from his tower's doppelgänger.

For the most part they had been relatively good natured, consisting mostly of chucking talc-filled condoms and waterbombs at each other. Conflicts that would always be forgotten when the Deesiders combined forces to get into it with the headbangers from the Coulston Estate on the south side of Streatham.

Truth was, Oyster had always been fascinated by his building's unknowable twin. Enthralled by the idea of the parallel lives unfolding a few centimetres from his own.

From where he was sat, he could observe both the East and West Tower entrances. Sickly yellow light spilled through the wired glass of their doorways, illuminating what looked to be the typical platoon of kids goofing off and tooting on some marijuana vape. He could smell its florid perfume from his hiding place.

At the edge of this knot of petty troublemakers stood taller figures, not really taking part. It was too far away to see for certain, but he had the feeling they might be Urbans, keeping an eye out for him.

"Ahoy, fuckwit."

Oyster spun around, heart drumming. There was Broadsides. Banged up as hell but larger than life and twice Oyster's size.

"Fuck!"

"I thought maybe..." said Broadsides.

Oyster shook his head.

"How is it someone as big as you is able to sneak up on me like that?"

Broadsides grinned and tapped Oyster's forehead. "Perhaps you just don't pay enough attention to your surroundings, padawan." His grin subsided. "Where did you get to, you munton? You closed on those women with the cheese, right? Everyone's on our backs. We've gotta get it back to the Big Man."

Oyster nodded.

"You're never gonna believe what's been happening to me."

Broadsides' expression darkened.

"It's nothing compared to what's gonna happen if you don't got that cash."

"Look, I'm really sorry, but they got away from me, right. You saw what they were like? All that Jackie Chan shit they were busting. They fucked me over, dosed me up and dropped me somewhere in Kent. Ghosted me, totals."

Broadsides shrank. He chewed the inside of his mouth.

"And that's not all."

Oyster flashed back to Primrose and Deano. It weighed like a stone in his belly. He needed to vent what he'd seen; to get all the toxic shit out of him. He described the clandestine meeting he'd witnessed. Broadsides turned pale.

"Fucking hell. Fucking hell! This is some seriously bad shit, disciple."

"I know, right?"

"What's the next move?"

Broadsides chewed at his thumb. It was obvious from his expression that he had an inkling as to what it was, he just didn't want to say.

"Mickey, innit," said Oyster. "But before that, I want to let Cécile know I'm alright and where my main stash is."

Broadsides cracked his knuckles and broke into a gallows-humour chuckle that sounded like water gurgling down a drain.

"Right. Well, if we're gonna go out, let's do it brutalist."

Oyster smiled. It was the first time he'd relaxed even a little bit in days.

He pointed to the East Tower entrance.

"See them?"

Broadsides peered into the distance.

"Yeah, couple of young guns are keeping the eye out for you, I figure."

Oyster nodded.

"They're probably looking out for you too, B."

"So, you want me to get their attention?" he replied.

"Exact."

Before the word was even out of his mouth, Broadsides was up, galloping across the rippled tarmac of the car park.

"If you need to get a message to me, go via my Aunt Ida at the Balham Sally Army shop," he yelled over his shoulder.

Oyster wanted to call him back, to tell him the rest of his plan, but Broadsides had already covered half the distance to the entrance. He had to hand it to his friend, he was brave. Hopefully it wouldn't cost him.

Broadsides got within twenty yards of the suspected Urbans, jumped up and down and waved his hands at the three kids standing by the door.

"Stick Ups rule, you fucking wastemen!"

The sentries wasted no time at all in chasing after Broadsides. Deano would have been proud of their wish to represent, but the ease with which they were lured away illustrated what many OGs complained of: that new recruits were as excitable as they were thick.

Once he was sure they were all gone, it was Oyster's turn. Trying to look unhurried, he waltzed up to the main entrance. He was nervous, but slipping inside, he was immediately at home. He figured there still might be other Urbans stationed in the building, so he avoided the mostly unreliable lifts and picked his way up the stairs instead. He needn't have worried; the stairwell was empty of everything other than a couple of friendly tweens, puffing on cigarettes and flicking through a stack of old comics.

He halted at the entrance to his floor, peeking through the whistling gap in the glass and wire-mesh fire doors. *No one.* He was home free. Getting out of Deeside might present another challenge, but he had a plan for that, too.

Unlocking the door, he slipped into the darkened flat and pressed his back against the wood once it was closed. He shut his eyes and drew in a deep breath: the sickly-sweet smell of weed, the fruity bass notes of a curry. Cécile must have sprung for a takeaway. For a second, the troubles of the last couple of days fell away.

Taking another breath, he slipped past his sister's bedroom door. The ghost light from within told him Cécile was up, but it was later than he'd realised. Better to get a night's sleep and then talk things through with her tomorrow, he figured.

He undressed and fell into his bed. The last couple of days had been too much. First the cops. Then the Kaminsky woman. And what had Deano been up to with that Primrose dude? The unease at the pit of his stomach quickened. If Primrose and Deano were working together, then were the Mannish Boys working for them? Did that mean he could no longer trust Deano? It seemed like his whole life had been upended.

He listened to the soothing noise of the traffic below. As a kid these sounds had always helped him get to sleep. Instead, he found himself wondering about Greater London and the woman he'd imagined there. Nonesuch, was it? The weirdness of the whole episode fizzed electrically at the edge of his mind. The twin aches of his armpit and his tattoo fenced him in. He needed to get them both checked out. He could already hear Cess's rebuke: *You were lucky you didn't get bummed in a skip, duff.* And then he was asleep.

Cécile was screaming. He leapt up and burst out of his room. For an instant he was blinded by harsh electric light. Cécile was standing by the front door in her pyjamas. Paris was nowhere to be seen, no doubt anaesthetised by the massive amount of dope she'd smoked.

Cécile's hands were at her mouth, transfixed by a twitching smear on the door mat. Oyster grabbed her from behind and pulled her away from the door. She kicked and struggled.

"It's me," he whispered. "It's me. It's okay."

Cécile elbowed him in the stomach and they both collapsed onto the floor.

"Let me go," she yelled.

Oyster released her and got to his feet. Cécile remained where she was, dissolving into heaving sobs.

He approached the thing on the door mat and looked down. Whatever it was that had been posted through the letterbox, it had been alive once. Only the stumps of wings gave a clue as to what it might have been. The bird's eyes had been gouged out and its beak torn off. Whoever had done this had taken great pleasure in it. As Oyster leaned over it, the bloody mess twitched. He yelped and jumped backwards.

"Go to your room," he said to Cécile.

"No way," she shuddered.

"Seriously."

"And where the hell have you been anyway? I've been worried sick," she replied.

"Long story. Go on."

Cécile glared at him but complied, slamming the door behind her.

This was clearly a message from the Urbans. But a stunt designed specifically to shit his family up. Make them come clean on his whereabouts, rather than something to smoke him out of a hiding place. Chances were, then, that they still didn't know he was home.

Oyster went to his room and pulled on some jeans, a black hoodie and a dark metallic puffer, surprised by how calm he felt. He found his second-best Air Max at the back of his cupboard and slipped them on. Prising up the carpet behind the door, he grabbed his knife and stowed it in his jeans' pocket.

He crossed to the kitchen and grabbed a bin bag from under the sink and some kitchen roll. Picking up the twitching bird-thing, he smothered it in paper and dropped it into the bin bag, trying not to flinch when it squirmed under his hands.

He dropped to his knees, scrabbled around in the darkness of the cupboard under the sink, finally locating what he wanted: a heavy vinyl bag that had belonged to Lucas, which he swung over his shoulder before standing.

He opened the cutlery drawer and selected a short steak knife, then yanked the drawer below off its runners and out of the cabinet completely. He tipped the collection of tea-towels it had contained into a pile on the floor and flipped the drawer over to reveal a blue polythene sandwich bag taped to its underside. Using the steak knife, he cut the bag free. He opened the packet and drew out a folded manila envelope, and reaching into it he withdrew a thick wad of twenty-pound notes secured with a rubber band.

He put the money to his nose and sniffed. The smell of used notes always reminded him of the city: a rich, earthy smell of brick dust and something slightly shitty. He wondered if he was smelling the cocaine which, rumour had it, coated every twenty in circulation.

He unfolded a dozen notes and slipped them into his tatty blue vinyl wallet, returning the remainder to the envelope. Replacing the knife and the tea-towels, he wobbled the drawer until it hopped back onto its runners. Then he addressed the envelope to Cécile and propped it up against her door. She would be up way before Paris in the morning, so there would be little chance of their mother finding the money first.

Oyster picked up the bin bag and gingerly released the latch on the front door so that it made as little sound as possible. He didn't think anyone would be outside waiting but it didn't make sense to take risks. He peered out. As far as he could tell, the corridor was deserted.

Behind him, light flooded into the hallway. Cécile stood at her door, holding the envelope in one hand.

"So, you were just going to run out on us then?" she said.

"It's complicated," he said.

Cécile looked at him in a way that opened up an abyss inside him.

"Is it something to do with Dad?" she whispered.

"Nah," said Oyster, bristling at hearing that name on her lips. "I'm in trouble."

"Who with?" she replied.

"Five-O. Mickey. Others," he said.

Cécile shook her head.

"You don't do things by halves, do you?"

Oyster shrugged.

"And how does any of this become simpler if you do a runner?"

She edged around him, putting her body between Oyster and the door.

He thought for a second.

"Come with me," he said.

Cécile rolled her eyes and tapped the side of his head.

"Is this thing even on? How would that work?"

"I dunno—"

"Exactly," said Cécile. "I've got school and stuff. Someone in this family should end up with a GCSE in something other than woodwork."

Oyster shook his head.

"I gotta go straighten this out".

"Stay," she said, "fix it here, with us."

He shook the bin bag.

"How do I fix this here? You'll be safer this way."

He ran his tongue around his lips, then he released the door lock and placed his own hand around Cécile's. The envelope she held in it trembled.

"This and the benefit should keep you ticking over till I'm back."

"And when will that be?" she replied.

"I dunno right now. I'll call you."

She didn't respond, but pushed him away with her other hand.

Oyster reached over her, pulling the door forward. It nudged Cécile's slight frame aside.

The thing in the bin bag twitched.

"I'm gonna find him... Lucas," Oyster said, nudging past her and out of the door. He wasn't entirely sure why he said it. Lucas was the last thing on his mind right now. "Lock this behind me."

After the door closed, he leaned on it in the dark corridor. Was this how Lucas had felt when he'd left? *I'm just another one of them*, he thought. *Another man who's walked out of this door never to return.*

22

THE DEESIDE SHUFFLE

Oyster walked to the end of the corridor, opened the rubbish chute, and tossed the bin bag down it. Pulling the drawstring on the vinyl bag tight over his shoulder, he dived up the stairwell, taking the stairs two at a time. He needed to lie low tonight and then see Big Mickey as quickly as he could tomorrow. Although he'd managed to get into the building without being seen, he now had to get out of it somehow without being nabbed. But he had a plan.

He got to the next floor up and the hairs on the back of his neck prickled. *Were those footsteps?* He leaned over the stairwell and looked up and down. The yellow light from above was swallowed by the darkness on seventh. All the while, the image of the mutilated bird replayed in his mind.

Keep it together. Keep. It. Together. There was a metallic smell as he hit the ninth-floor landing. He stopped once again. The steps behind him might have stopped an instant later. Or were they just echoes?

The tenth floor was a block of shadow. He stopped again and listened. The unsettling thing was that the noises didn't sound like footsteps, they were more like tree roots being played across concrete.

"Hey?" he called.

There was no response. He smelled mould but also the

unexpected, unmistakeable scent of cut grass. The sound came from above him again. *Someone is trying to fuck with me.*

"Who's there?" he called.

His voice echoed down the stairwell.

Oyster shook his head and ran upward into the buttery pools of light on the floors above. He kept his head down and focused on getting to the top of the block. Passing the last flat on the top floor, he scuttled up a final flight of stairs to the fire exit. He leaned into the horizontal bar lock that secured it and it clunked open. *So far so good.*

Emerging onto the roof of the East Tower, he was pelted by raindrops that flooded down from the sodium-bleached sky. The air was alive with the hoots of late-night traffic. He ran across the concrete rooftop, making for his maintenance exit's twin, the one for the West Tower, on the other side of the roof.

Pulling up his hood to protect himself from the wet weather, he dropped Lucas's bag from his shoulder and tipped out its contents. Three metal crowbars of varying sizes clanged onto the rain-slicked roof. Licking the water from his lips, he picked up the smallest and slipped its tip into the gap between the fire exit and the door jamb. He heaved at the bar, putting his weight on it and tugging as hard as he could. The frame splintered, but the door itself refused to give. Oyster tried again and again, alternately using his body weight to pull and push at the bar, in an effort to prise the door open, but it would not move. He couldn't be stuck up on this roof forever.

His frustration and anger boiled over and he yelled and kicked at the door. Why did this shit always happen to him? His entire plan for getting away undetected relied on him getting into the West Tower and sneaking out of its unguarded entrance. He threw the crowbar down and switched to one of the larger ones. While it prised away more of the door jamb, the door itself remained stubbornly in place. Panic fluttered in his chest and he stepped away from the door, backing into something.

There was a *crack* across Oyster's temple that sent him flying to the ground. Another blow and another. His hands came up to protect his head, but he was so surprised that he was only abstractly aware of the pounding he was getting.

Part of him already knew who it would be, coming in hard with no warning: it had to be the Urbans. Sure enough, Baby Ed's pointy features loomed over him in the city-glow and broke into a smile. Oyster had never noticed before, but there was a coy gap between the boy's two front teeth. He was carrying his prized possession, a metal baseball bat decorated with Panini football stickers he'd nicknamed Nora.

Now the pain arrived, and heavy waves flooded Oyster's skull, back and arms. He contracted into a pinprick surrounded by agony.

"You been spoken to, dim-low," Ed said, voice cracking up and down the syllables.

Oyster tried to sit up, but nothing happened. Baby Ed placed the bat down with a hollow ringing. He grabbed Oyster's wrists and dragged him towards the low perimeter wall that ran around the edge of the roof.

"This isn't personal," said Baby Ed, puffing from the effort. "But as it happens, I don't like you very much. Soz-not-soz."

Oyster tried to reply, but his tongue felt like a dishcloth. Baby Ed stepped back to the landing and retrieved the baseball bat. He tapped Oyster's right temple with it and Oyster flinched. The pain was everywhere now. He tasted blood in his mouth and his nose was spongey. He thought of the knife in his back pocket and he tried to twist around to grab it, but his arm hurt too much.

"Big Mickey's got beef with you, disciple. Proper vexed, so he is. Skipping out with his green? Not very smart. I always figured you to have more up top than that. At least, street enough not to come crawling back to your shitty crib after you'd done it. You and Broadsie both."

Oyster shook his head.

Ed grinned. "Yeah, we know all about your plan to split the cheddar."

"That's not it," said Oyster, his mouth bubbling blood.

"Don't you chat me," replied Ed. "I could give you another

sparking with Nora here, but Big Mickey says, 'Make it brutal, not fatal.'"

Oyster shut his eyes and turned his head away, instinctively trying to make sure Ed couldn't see him blub. When he opened them again, he was surprised to see water lapping around the boy's trainers.

"Sea?" said Oyster.

"No sea here, disciple," Baby Ed squeaked.

He knelt and tapped Oyster's head with Nora again.

"Something's wonky up here," he said. "I've spasticated you proper."

Oyster squinted. He saw Baby Ed, that was certain, but behind him was a wall made from mismatched bits of furniture and chunks of timber. He recognised it immediately as the one he'd scaled in Greater London. This was wrong, something must have come loose in his head, but the vision wouldn't go away.

The concrete beneath him was covered in black beads of volcanic sand. The white noise of waves splashed around him as they washed against the base of the bric-a-brac wall.

The cold water played over Oyster's feet. Behind Baby Ed, sitting on the top of the wall, was a figure. The man was dressed in a white T-shirt and baggy engineered jeans. His greying hair had been close cropped. He sported an immaculately trimmed salt-and-pepper goatee and a pair of Aviator shades.

"Dad?" said Oyster. The word slipped out of him before he could stop it. But no doubt, it was definitely Lucas.

"I'm your daddy now, pig," said Baby Ed.

Whatever it was that Oyster was looking at, he alone could see it. Baby Ed adjusted his jeans by tugging at his oversize belt buckle. He unzipped his flies and pulled out his cock.

"Don't look too close, you fucking wannabe," he cackled.

"Fuck off," said Oyster, trying to shuffle himself backward with his feet.

"Hold still, this is hard to do on demand," said Ed.

He whistled to conjure a yellow jet of piss which sprayed onto Oyster, who groaned and twisted away.

"I needed that," said Baby Ed, shaking himself off and doing up his flies. He wiped his hands on his jeans.

"Big Man wants you breathing, but what he doesn't know won't hurt. So, I reckon another love-tap from Nora here and I'll dump you off the roof. Lost your footing running away, innit? I can explain it all away. Proper tragic."

Grains of sand washed under Oyster's fingers and the smell of the sea assaulted his nostrils. Lucas looked down at him from the edge of the surf now, shaking his head. He removed his sunglasses. There were empty sockets where his eyes should have been.

Baby Ed raised his baseball bat, ready to swing it. All Oyster could do was raise his own arm in a feeble gesture of defence, but the blow never came.

23

THE GOOD OLD DAYS

Oyster thought there might have been a flash of light. But when he recalled it later, perhaps it had just been lightning. It seemed as though a lot of time had passed, but also that no time had passed at all. Lucas and the seawall were gone.

He tried to sit, but his head felt like an elephant had sat on it. Lying back again, he licked his lips and tasted blood, along with a harsh saltiness that he realised must be Baby Ed's piss. He spluttered and spat, trying to rid himself of the taste. At least his teeth were in one piece, he thought. His left temple had taken the brunt of Baby Ed's attack, and he probed it gently, crying out as pain lanced across his forehead.

"Oh, do stop whining," came a voice that Oyster immediately recognised as Primrose's. The man was sitting hunched on the low parapet that encircled the East Tower's roof, watching the storm break over the rest of the city.

"It's no Greater London, but this is still quite the view, isn't it?" the man continued.

Oyster managed to sit up this time. Primrose sat with his back to him, wearing a raincoat that boiled as though the body beneath was in constant roiling motion, like something that wasn't entirely fixed. Nearby, Baby Ed lay in a bloody knot.

"Fuck. What did you do?" said Oyster.

"You really are beginning to mount up a significant amount of debt on your account. We do hope you can pay it off."

"What did you do to him?" asked Oyster again.

Primrose cleared his throat.

"He's still alive. If you can call it living. Honestly, we do wonder how you lot stand it. Take all this *time* nonsense, for instance."

He held up a finger tipped with a grubby nail.

"One second. And another. And another. Like tiny rabbit turds all in a row. We cannot fathom how you are able to stand it. It's like ordering steak and chips and then the waiter brings the peas one at a time."

Oyster rolled over and stood to his feet. His head hurt catastrophically.

Primrose pointed at the prickle of city lights that ran to the horizon.

"The place was better in the good old days. What is *this* all about, anyway?" He waved at the other blocks on the estate. "All living on top of each other like insects in a hive. This *civilisation* of yours isn't right, anyone can see that."

Primrose turned away from him, addressing himself in a whispered monotone to the city:

"*The cloud-capp'd towers, the gorgeous palaces,*
The solemn temples, the great globe itself,
Yea, all which it inherit, shall dissolve."

"Very impressive." Oyster tried to shrug but his whole body ached. He gulped in a breath. Hurting as he was, he wasn't going to put up with Primrose's schtick. "So, you voted Brexit and now you're all sad about it. Who cares?"

Primrose looked at him, appearing genuinely crestfallen.

Oyster fought past the pain. He bent over, supporting himself by leaning on his legs. This was maybe a chance to get some answers himself.

"He was one of you lot, was he not? Shakespeare? So, you're not entirely clueless as a species—"

"What are you up to with Deano?" interrupted Oyster. He tested his left arm with his right hand. It was tender to the touch. He prodded his jaw; it was sore, but thankfully that seemed to be about it.

"Up to?" Primrose turned his hands palm upwards and assumed an innocent air. "Why, nothing. But since you mention it, you owe us twice over now. You really should come and work for us. There are things you need educating on, boyo."

"Absolutely not," said Oyster. "And don't call me *boy*, you plainclothes prick."

Primrose shrugged. "Uff, such language. *We* are not the po-po, as we've already said. Do try and pay attention. There are wonders and horrors that you are not capable of comprehending. At least in your currently reduced state."

"And what would they be?" said Oyster. He stood, shakily. His head throbbed and he was exhausted.

Primrose sniffed.

"The Hermeneutical Mysteries. How to get a high score on *Ghosts and Goblins*. Your father."

The vision he'd had when Baby Ed attacked him flashed into his head again. He leaned against the parapet and breathed in hard, steadying himself, riding out the aches all over his body. The concrete slabs at the base of the tower lurched and he wanted to puke. He breathed in to steady himself and stepped back from the edge. A gust of wind brought the sound of distant police sirens.

"People keep talking to me as though I know nothing about that man," Oyster said.

"But you don't, not even the first thing," said Primrose, turning back to look over the city.

Oyster swallowed. He'd kept his curiosity hostage for so long he had forgotten what it felt like; he'd buried that need to know beneath layers of concrete, locked it away in a room at the back of his head and thrown away the key. Now, it rose suddenly, zombie-like, in a way that overwhelmed him.

"Tell me this," he said, "if you're such a big, bad OG: why all this hide-and-seek nonsense?"

Primrose nodded. "Let's just say you aren't the only one in reduced circumstances at the moment. Ergo we are, at present, forced to work through intermediaries. But this state of affairs will not persist. The human cycle is closing again. We are growing in strength all the time. You will need to choose a side."

Primrose's words possessed an odd hypnotic quality.

"So what did you mean, 'working for you'?" Oyster said. The words had escaped from his mouth before he'd had time to think them through.

Primrose didn't move.

"Well, first off, you come with us," he replied.

"And...?" said Oyster.

"And then we tell you all about the *thing* you call Lucas McLellen."

His dad's name triggered a memory of the time he'd fallen into the Wandle near his nan's in Runnymeade as a kid. Lucas had fished him out. They'd caught the bus home and hadn't been able to get a seat, so he'd sat on Lucas's lap all the way home, soaking him through and through.

There was lightning somewhere over Tooting Common. The world was shifting under his feet. Going with Primrose made a sudden sense. The life he'd built up. His friends. The Urbans. That was all over now. As sure as shit was shit. But then he thought of Cess; this shifty fucker had threatened her.

"Nah, ain't happening. Get lost, creep-o."

"As you please," replied Primrose with another sigh, coat twitching in the wind. He slid over the parapet and into the nothing beyond.

Oyster lurched forward and peered over the edge in horror, but there was no sign of Primrose on the dark tarmac below. He shook his head in disbelief. Too much weird shit had happened to him in too short a space of time.

Nearby, Baby Ed groaned. So, Primrose hadn't lied, the boy was still alive. Oyster had to make himself scarce. Suppressing the very strong urge to go over and give him a kick in the teeth, he saw that the East Tower maintenance door was now open. Another dubious gift from Primrose? He scuttled across the roof and into the dark, echoing comfort of the stairwell. He slammed the door shut behind him. Ed didn't look like he'd be up and about anytime soon, but the door ought to keep him off Oyster's six. He tested his temple again; it hurt like fuck, and was already swollen, but remarkably nothing was broken. His head ached and his jaw throbbed, but he was still in one piece.

He picked his way down the stairs as quietly as he was able. The building filled him with an odd mixture of familiarity and difference. Everything about it was the same as his home tower, except that they were mirrored. It even smelled different as well. It was more antiseptic, cleaner somehow.

As he threaded down the stairs, he tried to work through his next move. He did his best to ignore the pain in his side and in his head, but each step jarred him, wounding him anew. He needed somewhere he could hole up for a bit. Given that the Urbans were out for his blood, his options were limited. He wanted to see Broadsides to warn him that he was on Mickey's shit list too, but that, he knew, would be a mistake.

The stairwell was deserted, and he was thankful for reaching the ground-floor fire exit without running into anyone. Peering through the door's mesh glass into its lobby, he could see only streetlights and the glistening black of the car park beyond. He slipped his hands into his pockets and his hand closed around an unfamiliar square of card. He pulled it out and caught sight of Kaminsky's business card. Hadn't he chucked this away?

It read:

On the reverse side was an address in St John's Wood.

24

LAMASERY

"Ach, my gods. What the fuck happened to you?" said Marya Petrovna to Oyster as he stood in the doorway of her top-floor flat. She was dressed in a scarlet dressing gown, decorated with what looked suspiciously like tiny yellow swastikas.

"Got dooked up," he mumbled without meeting her gaze.

"By the Ascended Ones. That smell!" she said, holding her lapel up to her nose and wrapping the robe more tightly around her. "You smell like goat has made water on you."

Oyster shrugged.

"Can we just get the humiliation bit of this out of the way? I need a place to crash for a few days, you down with that?"

"I need cigarette just to get rid of smell," she said and pulled her tobacco purse out of the robe. "But yes, of course, dear. You stay as long as you wish. Come in. Come in."

Marya Petrovna opened the door wide and turned down a cramped hallway. Oyster followed, hopping to catch up with her.

"Close the door," she shouted over her shoulder, "and take your shoes off."

"What's with the Hitler Youth chic, anyway?" he called after her.

Marya Petrovna tutted volubly from further down the hall.

"These are sauwastikas, ancient spiritual symbol. Those employed by the bohemian lieutenant and his thugs were rotated…" she made a spinning gesture with a blunt finger, "…laterally."

"Well, that told me," Oyster said with a sigh as he slipped off his Air Max. "I suppose there's no chance that you might be a Nazi with your nightie on inside out?"

Marya Petrovna hissed him quiet and shook her head.

"Do not joke about such things, young man. Especially when you have no idea of the burdens other people have shouldered."

Oyster shrugged.

A single yellow light bulb burned overhead. The walls of the flat had been painted a deep crimson. Every inch of them was covered with pictures and bric-a-brac. A hatstand stood next to the door. It hosted a stuffed python and a feather boa which hung from it like a long dead bird.

He kicked off his other shoe and squinted at one of the pictures. It was a tiny black-and-white lithograph contained in an ornate gilt frame that was at least twice its size.

The picture showed someone who bore a strong resemblance to Marya Petrovna, curtsying before an even older woman. Oyster knew his grasp of history was sketchy, but the older woman looked a lot like Queen Victoria.

He sniffed and his head throbbed. His entire face was swollen and his shoulder felt like it had been dislocated. For the most part, though, the pain had reduced to a dull background ache.

"Tea?" called Marya Petrovna.

"Yeah," shouted Oyster. "Milky with three sugars."

He followed Marya Petrovna into the bowels of the flat, passing an enormous potted plant and a pair of dingy painted portraits before entering a tiny kitchen.

"Sugar is poisonous to the humours," yelled Marya Petrovna. She stood at a stove and placed an enamel kettle on the gas hob.

A stainless-steel pedal bin, filled to overflowing, sat in one corner and a covered birdcage in the other. Dirty plates were piled high in the cracked sink. The kitchen had once been a cheery yellow, but years of neglect and cooking stains had left it a muddy orange.

"Fuck me, I thought our kitchen was a dive," Oyster said.

Marya Petrovna finished making his drink by squeezing the

used teabag into the sink and slinging it in the bin's general direction. The teabag ricocheted off the bin's open plastic lid and hit the wall next to it, coming to rest on the floor.

"By Almighty Yemama, such a stench," she muttered, pressing Oyster into a nearby chair and placing a chipped mug on the kitchen table in front of him.

"Drink, drink!" she said.

Oyster drew the mug to his mouth and took a long gulp. His nose told him there was something amiss with the pale brew, but it was too late. He hiccupped and tried to keep the foul-tasting liquid in his mouth, before spitting it copiously all over the black-and-white linoleum.

"It tastes like vomit," he said.

"Yak's milk… and something of my own origination that will aid healing. *De gustibus no est disputandem*," she said and threw a damp tea-towel in his direction. Oyster mopped up. "Now, tell me what happened to your face."

Oyster sighed. He really didn't want to spill his guts, but if he was going to doss on her floor, he realised he owed some explanation at least. Haltingly, he told her about the crew, about the business with the drop and how Baby Ed had worked him over.

"Nasty business you are into," she said, sucking air through her teeth. She prodded her chest with a large thumb. "Though Marya Petrovna has been in worse. In any case, first things first. Finish your tea, it will make you feel better."

She levered herself out of her chair and strode out of the kitchen.

Oyster heard a tap running. Marya Petrovna reappeared carrying a small green first-aid kit and a damp flannel. Humming tunelessly, she cleaned his face, dressed his wounds, handed him a couple of paracetamol, then fussed him into a cramped bathroom next to the kitchen.

"Wash. Wash," she commanded, closing the door behind him.

Oyster was relieved to see the bathroom was much cleaner than the kitchen. He peeled off his stinking clothes and showered.

Despite the fact that the water pressure was weak and the only soap he could find smelled of lilac, it felt good to wash yesterday away.

"So, what is plan?" called Marya Petrovna through the door as he towelled himself down.

"Not that it's any of yours, but I was gonna see my boss and straighten it out," he said.

"Boy. While you stay here, everything is Marya Petrovna's business."

Oyster grunted and looked down at the reeking pile of clothes.

"You got a phone?" he said, looking around.

"No," said Marya Petrovana, shaking her head with obvious disgust. "Shrinking voice to fit through wire makes telling lies too easy. So… running to the man who has had you beaten, this is your best plan?"

Oyster grunted again.

"This plan is shit plan," she said. Through a crack in the door, she placed a pair of pink, candy-striped pyjamas on the bathroom floor.

"Here. These belonged to friend of mine," she said.

Oyster thought about what Cécile had said concerning Lucas as he'd left the flat.

"Okay. So, I was thinking. You remember what you said the other day when you dropped me off?"

"About your father?" said Marya Petrovna.

Oyster nodded.

"Perhaps we talk about him tomorrow," she said.

"Why do you care?"

Marya Petrovna shook her head from side to side noncommittally.

He sighed and inspected the pyjamas before pulling them on. They smelled of mothballs and were folded into a tight rectangle, suggesting they'd been sat at the bottom of a drawer for a long time.

He examined himself in the steamed-up bathroom mirror. It had been a long time since he'd worn pyjamas. The ones he wore now were a size too small and monogrammed with the letters *BF* on the breast pocket. The bottoms clung to his calves and the sleeves reached his forearms.

"Not a word," he hissed as he opened the door.

Marya Petrovna looked at him expressionlessly.

"Hungry?" she said, changing the subject with a jaunty air.

"Not for anything that features yak as an active ingredient."

"Very well. It is middle of night. You must sleep."

Oyster was about to argue, but realised he was exhausted.

Marya Petrovna prodded him into a darkened room at the rear of the flat.

She flicked on a light switch and Oyster flinched. The room was about ten square feet, but seemed much smaller. Directly over his head hung a small, stuffed bat. To his right was a tall, wooden cabinet housing a collection of stuffed monkeys, some plastic dinosaurs and a pile of tattered books with their spines facing the wall.

Opposite him, in the far corner, was a glass-eyed chimpanzee wearing a dinner jacket, bow tie and top hat. The creature had a copy of Darwin's *Origin of Species* tucked under its left arm and a bunch of dresses on hangers hung from its outstretched right hand. Next to it was something tall and narrow, concealed under a grubby, floral bedspread. Between them both was a tatty leather chair.

"Welcome to the Lamasery," said Marya Petrovna.

"What evs," said Oyster. "What's with the stuffed monkey?"

"Pinker is a chimpanzee. Not a monkey," she replied.

"Well," said Oyster, "ignoring the fact that you are a pedantic old witch, why have you got a stuffed ape?"

"A monkey's hands, too small for hangers." Marya Petrovna mimed a clutching motion. "Now wait here, I fetch bedclothes."

Oyster rolled his eyes and slumped into the chair. It farted a cloud of tobacco smoke as he collapsed into it. *What to do? What to do? What to do?* The words orbited inside his head.

He tugged at the bedspread next to him, curious about what it concealed. It slid off with a hissing noise, kicking up a cloud of dust that made Oyster's nostrils itch.

Beneath stood a magician's cabinet made of ivory and inlaid with strips of mother of pearl that had been worked into long, looping hieroglyphics traced all around its surface. The front housed three doors of equal size. There were horizontal slots on one side, just above the bottom door and below the top one. He winced as his tattoo began to sting in way that it hadn't since he'd been with Nonesuch, and he massaged the inflamed skin of his torso. There was the distinct sense that he was missing something here, but he wasn't sure exactly what it might be.

Oyster hooked a fingertip under the bottommost door and pulled. The door swung open, revealing a velvet-lined interior. He tried the others, and they all swung open on well-oiled hinges.

He snorted. He vaguely remembered seeing this sort of nonsense on Saturday night telly programmes when he was a kid. The sort that featured high-kicking dancing girls and rows of orange-tanned twerps in bow ties doing jazz hands. Part of him yearned to be back there now, sitting in the dark, flicker-lit by the telly; listening to the slow bear-like shuffle of Lucas moving around the flat, the smell of takeaway and cigarette smoke settling into his clothes.

He leaned over and stuck his head into the bottom part of the cabinet. It smelled of wood-varnish and something else... something he couldn't quite put his finger on.

"What are you doing in there? Get out! Get out!" yelled Marya Petrovna, dropping the bundle of blankets and pillows she'd been carrying.

"Keep your wig on," said Oyster, delaying the removal of his head just long enough to communicate defiance.

Marya Petrovna took a deep breath and looked at the ceiling.

"Did not mean to shout, but this is very valuable. Easy to damage."

She pushed him out of the way and busied herself making a bed for him on the floor.

"What's this called?" he said.

"It is cabinet," she replied without looking up.

"No. I mean the trick you do with it," said Oyster. "I remember seeing it when I was a kid."

"Is Zig-Zag Girl," said Marya Petrovna, pulling the final blanket into place. "Invented by me. Is old trick these days. You would call it a cliché."

She stood up and looked at Oyster.

"But not the way Marya Petrovna used to do it." She gave a magician's flourish, then replaced the bedspread back over the cabinet.

"If you say so," he said.

"Right, I am going to bedroom over there," she said, pointing through the door, "and you will be here. You already know where is loo and kitchen."

With that she bustled out of the room.

Oyster rolled onto the makeshift bed and stretched. Pain rippled across his back and shoulders. He shut his eyes experimentally and then opened them again.

He couldn't shake the sense he was being watched, but when he got up and went to the window, flicking open the room's curtains and peering behind them, no one was out there. Pinker's eyes watched him glassily. Next to him on the wall was another old-style black-and-white print. Three people stood on the front steps of a large Victorian house. It might even have been this one, years ago. Two men and a woman faced the camera, all with the solemn look typical of early photographs. The woman, given the resemblance, had to be Marya Petrovna's grandmother.

Gently, he removed the photo from the wall and examined it. There was something mesmeric about it. As he stared at it, he realised there was a fourth figure in the shadow of the doorway behind the others. The figure was not much more than a silhouette, but it was hard not to sense that this figure was grinning. There was a familiarity about it, too, that he could not quite fathom. It was like having the name of someone on the tip of his tongue, but being unable to recall it.

The photograph was inscribed on a small brass plate at the bottom of the frame:

Madame Petrovna
Dozvhenko, Benjamin
Fauks and Jack Devlin

The Miracle Club
1882

25
SPRICHST DU DEUTSCH?

Oyster was sitting in the dark. He knew he was in Marya Petrovna's Zig-Zag cabinet because his cheek was pressed against its velvet interior. The doors were tight shut. He was curled inside and dozing peacefully.

He stirred and the space around him changed. He was no longer in the cabinet. It was still dark, but the darkness was a presence itself rather than simply the absence of light. He stumbled to his feet as something moved furtively towards him. He knew it was the same thing that had crept across the floor in his bedroom earlier that evening.

A voice whispered in his ear. He started, throwing up his hands and stumbling in the opposite direction.

"*Hat sie dich geschickt?*" it said.

Something brushed his cheek, and he fell onto his hands and knees.

"*Sprichst du Deutsch?*" the voice asked. Oyster's knowledge of languages was vague at best, but it sounded German.

He struck out blindly at the voice, which gave a girlish giggle. Something gripped his ankles and held him down.

Yelling, he tried to kick his assailant, but the invisible hands held him fast. He shut his eyes.

"*Sprichst du Englisch?*" said the voice.

Something crawled up his body. He didn't want to look down.

"Yeah. Yes, English," he yelled. "What do you want?"

"Ah, so it is you. I have something to show you," said the voice, and Oyster was back on the bridge, crouched behind an overturned car. The sky above was a sickly yellow. He was sweating profusely and the air was livid with staccato gunfire. He took in a breath of air and his lungs burned.

"Lousy Stick Men got us pinned down here."

It was Big Mickey. The man looked older, smaller.

"Hey, stay suited up!" he said, reaching to a respirator mask that hung limply around Oyster's neck, placing it over his mouth. Big Mickey had his own clamped over his face.

"Breathe," he ordered. "Need you full compos if we're gonna get out of this."

Oyster coughed, drawing the oxygen into his lungs. He looked around. He and Mickey were backed against the raw metal of the car's underside, which lay widthways across the road. His nose was full of the smell of smoke. His clothes reeked of petrol that had leaked from their makeshift barricade.

While he recognised the bridge, the buildings around it were an endless, unfamiliar wall of glass-and-steel skyscrapers; digital hoardings flickered with advertising for unrecognisable products. In the distance, the ruddy huddle of the Houses of Parliament was gutted and blackened, razed by fire. The Thames flowing beneath was a high black tide, stinking of shit and chemicals.

"Cover me," yelled Mickey. "I reckon I can make it across to the old bus back there. As long as the feds' drones don't make us as well."

Mickey heaved himself into a crouching position.

"Cover you?" said Oyster.

"Get your fucking head in the game, disciple!" Mickey slapped Oyster gently across the cheek. Oyster looked down. The weight in his hand was a revolver. A barrage of bullets thudded into the car.

Right. He needed to man up. Represent and all that. But he was terrified.

He cradled the gun in his hand and leaned onto his haunches.

There was another sizzle of gunfire that spattered into the tarmac around them.

"Aw. Fuck."

Oyster looked round. Big Mickey lay on his back. Blood stained the road around him. Oyster cried out and threw his weapon down, grabbing his captain's enormous paw in both his hands. Mickey's grip was weak and his dark eyes were glazing over. He smiled.

"Guess this is it, disciple," he said. "Big checkout. Big death scene."

Oyster couldn't speak. Even above the city's stench, he was overcome with the coppery scent of Mickey's blood.

"I'm sorry about what happened to your sister. To Cécile. I really am," he said.

More gunfire rattled around Oyster. He heard the murmur of police tannoys and what might have been helicopters.

"Wake wake! Rise and shine!"

It was Marya Petrovna.

Oyster snapped out of his dream. His heart was racing, and he felt sick. It had all been so real, this weird vision of a fucked-up future London. He peered down at his hands with sleepy eyes, half expecting them to be coated with Mickey's blood.

He groaned. As his body woke up, his face started to ache again. He could just make out Marya Petrovna sitting opposite in one of the room's leather armchairs, puffing away on a roll-up. The cigarette filled the room with planes of undulating smoke.

Oyster wasn't sure of the exact hour, but from the weak light that seeped around the lounge's thick curtains, he figured it was a lot earlier than he normally woke up.

The horrible dream had left him rattled. He couldn't let the images go. Mickey lying in a pool of his own blood. The enormous buildings crowding out the sun and the air. Plus, the underlying feeling that what he'd seen was for his benefit somehow.

"What do you want?" he grunted. His tongue was coated with something, and his left side throbbed from yesterday's beating.

Marya Petrovna took a long drag on her cigarette and held

the smoke in her lungs, before sending it out of her nostrils in a dragonesque torrent.

Her face, wrapped in shadow, looked stony and dispassionate.

"So how long have you had that?" she asked.

"Had what?" said Oyster, yawning and then rubbing his jaw as it throbbed with pain.

"Tattoo."

He looked down. His bedspread had worked its way off his top half in the night. He pulled the blankets up around himself.

"Brought you tea and sandwich." She nodded towards a plate and mug next to his makeshift bed. Oyster smelled bacon and his stomach grumbled. Early morning headlights strobed over the curtains and across the ceiling.

"Well?" she said.

"What's it to you, anyway?"

Marya Petrovna took another luxurious drag on her cigarette and levered herself out of the chair.

"Okay. Get up. Get showered. And eat breakfast. You need strength. We have work to do." She shuffled out of the room.

Oyster shook his head. The old woman's demeanour had changed markedly overnight. Last night she had seemed like a batty old eccentric; this morning, more like a drill sergeant.

He rolled out of bed, ate and showered as instructed. The warm water cleared the remnants of the nightmare from his head. He pulled on his clothes as quickly as he could, vaguely registering they'd been laundered. He scooped up his playing cards and shoved the snub blade of his knife into the front pocket of his jeans.

He had to admit, he felt a lot better than he had expected. Perhaps the old woman's peculiar tea had healed him more quickly after all. Grabbing his phone, he thumbed the power as he walked into the hallway. It lit up, issued an electronic burp, and promptly shut down. He shook his head and slipped it into his pocket. It still hadn't recovered from its dip into the Serpentine. But then perhaps he hadn't either.

He sighed. He was dislocated from everything he'd known up to this point. The gang, as dubious as his feelings about it were at times, had been his family. And now he was here, in this madwoman's flat. On the run. Without much of an idea what to do next. He sighed again. His tattoo twitched and his armpit had a sore lump under it. *Fuck it.* He was falling apart.

Marya Petrovna was seated at the kitchen table, next to an overflowing ashtray. A transistor radio was blaring out a mediocre pop ballad and the birdcage was now uncovered, revealing a large cockateel that eyed him suspiciously. Oyster realised from the cards scattered over the tabletop that she was engaged in a tarot reading.

"Ach. Here he comes," she said. She looked up and took him in, then pointed at the bird. "Meet Minnie, she is oldest, bestest friend. Now, sit. Sit."

There were three cards on the Formica table, the rightmost depicting a man hanging upside down from a tree.

"That can't be good, can it?" he said, pointing at the card.

Marya Petrovna looked up at him and shrugged.

"Cards not so straightforward," she said, waving at the chair opposite with her lit cigarette.

Oyster slumped into it with a sigh.

"Come on then," he said with a grin, "give us the full hocus-pocus." He pressed his hands to his forehead and grimaced, adopting the sort of voice he imagined a medium might use. *"You will meet a tall dark stranger. Wooooo-oooooo."*

Marya Petrovna took a slug of dark tea and regarded him, unimpressed.

"Please continue. Am pissing myself laughing here, really," she said.

She laid three more cards beneath the first row and overturned the one nearest to her left. It showed an upside-down stone tower. The middle card depicted a red-tongued demon, boiling some sinners in a vat. She looked up and squinted at him.

"I think, perhaps, you already have. Met a stranger, that is."

"What's that supposed to mean?" he replied.

She pointed to the table.

"Your cards suggest things already in motion. That you are in middle of upheaval."

Oyster rolled his eyes.

"Look, Marya Petrovna, Mrs Kaminsky, or whatever your name is – you can't kid a kidder. Running a short con is my day job. I know what a cold reading is, and when I walked in here with my face all fucked up looking for a place to crash, it doesn't take Derren Brown to suss any of this out, does it?"

Marya Petrovna exhaled a long stream of smoke. She nodded and collected the cards back into their pack.

"Fine," she said, stacking them next to the ashtray. "Let us talk about your father then, eh?"

"I'd rather not, if it's all the same to you," he replied.

"It isn't," she said.

"What I mean is *I don't want to*," he replied.

"I know exactly what you meant, I was just ignoring it." She pressed the tip of her roll-up into the ashtray. It fizzed for an instant and died. "But you seem conflicted as far as father is concerned."

Oyster mimed giving her a silent round of applause.

"Oh, well done, Doctor Freud. And why wouldn't I be? That dick ran off, leaving me, my sister and my mum high and dry. I fucking hate him. I can assure you I spend every day making sure I give fewer shits about him than he did about me. But still, there isn't a day that goes by that I don't wonder where he is. Or if he's ever coming back."

Oyster's voice faltered and he turned away.

Fuck this shit.

He gulped down air to calm himself.

"You need moment?" said Marya Petrovna, her voice softer.

He shook his head and steadied himself.

"Okay, if you are sure. What about tattoo, then?" she continued, pointing at his midriff.

Oyster shrugged. The collar of his clean T-shirt was rubbing and his skin prickled.

"Cost a lot of cheddar. I know that."

Marya Petrovna nodded and took another sip of tea.

"I think it's infected," he said finally. "It keeps aching. Seems to be getting worse."

Marya Petrovna pushed back her chair and stood.

"Let me show you something."

She shuffled out of the kitchen, beckoning him to follow, and led him back into the lounge.

Sunlight flooded in between the heavy velvet curtains now, but Marya Petrovna did not draw them. She stood in the centre of the room and, clearing her throat, slipped the covering from the Zig-Zag cabinet and opened its doors. As Oyster approached the lounge, he was filled with an unexpected sense of unease. He didn't want to get any closer, but he cleared his throat and stepped into the room anyway.

The mother-of-pearl inlay set into its frame glistened eerily in the grey light of the morning.

"Notice anything?" she said.

Oyster shook his head and remained where he was.

"This word, perhaps?" She pointed at the hieroglyphics that were part of the cabinet's frame.

Oyster's face ached and he was cold and sweaty.

"I don't feel so good," he said.

"Ach, ach," exclaimed Marya Petrovna, fussing him back into the corridor. "If you're going to throw up, do it in here please."

There was something about the lettering around the cabinet that was making him feel unwell; a sensation of woozy, familiarity as though he was slightly drunk. Then he realised.

"This," he pointed at the cabinet, which pulsed in the half-light, "this is the same writing as my tattoo."

PART THREE

INTERDIMENSIONAL TURF WAR BLUES

26

MINKOWSKI INVOCATION

"Ha! Now he has it!" Marya Petrovna clapped her hands together. "I knew you were not complete imbecile!"

Oyster's torso glimmered with intense pain, as though the tattoo was trying to tear itself free and take a fair proportion of his skin with it. He had a sense of being dragged towards the cabinet bodily, as though some force was pulling him into its yawning entrance.

"Make it stop!" he yelled, dropping to his knees and holding his side.

"Hold still." She kneeled next to him and pulled up his top. The tattoo was an angry red smear that encompassed his body. Her lips moved silently. She blew on her hands and placed them either side of this belly button. She muttered in a low voice. Within seconds the pain subsided, and the tattoo lost its livid quality. She winced, suddenly in severe discomfort herself.

Marya Petrovna leaned back, breathing heavily.

"Thanks," he whispered.

She nodded slowly. She looked ill.

"What did you just do?"

"Am able to share things, to help people," she said. "I just shared this pain. Reduced it for you. It will not last forever, but will do for now."

She regarded the tattoo with a frown.

"I need smoke and fresh cup of tea. But first, tell me: from where *exactly* did you get this design?"

Oyster grunted. His natural reticence to share anything welled up inside him. He looked away from Marya Petrovna's grey eyes.

"If you tell me nothing, then nothing is all I can do for you."

He nodded and swallowed. He sniffed, and then before he could stop himself, it all came out: the night Lucas left them, the papers that Oyster found and the way they had come together.

"This..." she pressed a fingertip to the spirals that covered his abdomen and he flinched, but the pain had gone. "This has meaning. Is part of a word, or conjuration or map, young man. Maybe all three."

She sat him back into one of the room's leather armchairs.

"Wait here," she said.

Oyster sat in the darkened room. He drew in breath after deep breath. Beads of cold sweat stippled his forehead. A bus braked with a hiss on the road outside. Could all this be real? Oyster had a strange feeling of bilocation. That these two things could not co-exist at the same time in the same place. There was London. *His* London. And then there was all this other shit that he couldn't explain. He felt dizzy and he wished he was ten years younger. To be curled up in bed; no decisions to make.

Marya Petrovna returned. She had lit another roll-up and its smoke curled around the room.

"If I am not wrong, this is Minkowski invocation." She was consulting an old paperback which she placed on the chair's armrest.

Oyster shivered. Now the pain had subsided, he was cold.

"And what exactly is that?" he asked, rubbing his eyes.

"It is type of hermeneutic worldline based on work by Hermann Minkowski. A good mathematician, but rotten kisser. He laid foundations for Einstein, and *he* was an even *worse* kisser, let me tell you. But Minkowski invocation is word of power. Rather than being spoken, it is position in time and space that invokes it. Being in close proximity with cabinet and, perhaps, other things has actuated it."

Oyster sniffed. *Why would Lucas have had something like this?* he wondered.

"If it's a word, can you read it?" he said.

"Hold still," said Marya Petrovna. Her eyes ran along his skin and her lips moved wordlessly again. She flipped up the rear of his shirt so that she could read the tattoo's other side. She breathed in suddenly and her eyes glittered. An odd expression, somewhere between fear and surprise, flitted across her face and was gone.

"Well. I cannot be sure, but this appears to be dedicated to one of the ancient Celtic pantheon. The one the Celts, and the Gauls before them, called Lugones." She fixed him with a gaze.

He shrugged. "And?"

"They are somewhat mysterious, a three-in-one god composed of Esus, Tuetates and Taranis. The Romans connected Lugones back to Mercury, their trickster and messenger, and through this relation he is connected to gambling and chance. In some interpretations Lugones is also associated with commerce. Really, this guy had more jobs than Tory MP."

"A game of chance is a sacred thing," said Oyster, echoing Deano's patter.

"What's that?" said Marya Petrovna, squinting at him.

"Nah, just something someone on my crew used to say. I always thought it was a random bit of patter, but maybe there was more to it than that."

Marya Petrovna nodded sagely.

"Almost certainly. So, Lugones is at the root of other legends in the Celtic realms, where he is conflated with Lleu Llaw Gyffes or Lugh of the Long Arm. Great warrior, general gobshite, sexist asshole. You know the sort."

Oyster shook his head. What had possessed him to go and get this thing attached to his skin? Cécile was right. Sometimes he was a massive donkey.

Marya Petrovna looked at his feet.

"Come on, what else?" he asked.

"Well, we are back where we started. If you got this from your father, perhaps he is not who you thought he was," she said. "If we are to find him, I need to know more about him."

Oyster's pulse quickened. This was all too close to home. He'd already had one tizzy on account of his feelings for Lucas, and he didn't feel much like having another in short succession.

"For a start, no one said anything about finding him. And for another, when you picked me up in the car you were all 'Let me drop some lore on you about your dad', and now you don't know anything? Which is it?"

Marya Petrovna shook her head from side to side. "You had air of lost boy about you. This much I could tell. But look. This thing you have on your skin. I think it is drawing you and your father together. Perhaps best way to help yourself is to find him."

Oyster tasted sweat on his upper lip. He didn't want to have anything to do with Lucas. But perhaps this old woman was right. Perhaps he needed him.

He inhaled deeply.

"So, assuming you're right. What do you want to know?"

"Well, how about exact circumstances of his disappearance."

Marya Petrovna drew on the cigarette and it sizzled. Oyster felt himself slipping sideways. He was unanchored, unmoored from something. The traffic outside became louder again. He walked to the window and pressed his fingertips to the wooden frame. It was thick with dust, but its solidity was good.

Outside, in the world beyond, a steady trickle of cars, taxis, motorbikes and mopeds chugged up the road. On the pavement opposite, some kids huddled in a bus shelter mock-punched each other and laughed, waiting for their school bus. The sky above was an unremarkable grey, but it pressed down on them like an unseen monster. People went about their business in the usual way, but Oyster knew now that he was marked somehow and that he would never be able to look at the city in the same way again.

He looked up. "Why does that matter to you?"

Marya Petrovna looked sympathetically at him.

"World is changing, so are you. It is a lot to take in at once."

She cleared her throat and released another jet of smoke. It rolled across the room.

"But this is old and powerful word. Alive in its own way. Your father kept it hidden amongst his effects and you, with *wisdom* of youth, have seen fit to write it on your skin and wander around with a blank look on your face. Now, I make more tea."

The tattoo niggled Oyster's side. It knew they were talking about it.

Marya Petrovna disappeared back into the kitchen and Oyster sat back down in the leather armchair. He looked at the open Zig-Zag cabinet. Again. Its red velvet lining gave him the distinct impression that he was looking into some sort of great vertical mouth. The word wrapped around its casing glittered now with a kind of malignant glee. He shuddered. Marya Petrovna returned with two steaming mugs of black tea and a fresh cigarette.

The lounge was now enveloped in a smoky fug.

"Fuck me, woman, have you not heard of secondary smoke? Could you not hit the gum for a bit?" said Oyster, trying to disperse the settling smoke with his hand.

"Ach, ach," said Marya Petrovna, waving at him with disdain. "With your generation it is always 'me, me, me'!" She hauled herself to her feet and cracked the nearest window. The morning air rushed in, adding the metallic zest of car exhaust to the heady cocktail of smells already in the room. She collapsed into a chair and stared at him.

"I am still waiting," she said. "How *did* your father disappear?"

Oyster took a breath and closed his eyes.

"Okay," he said, and he told Marya Petrovna of the night his dad had gone out and not come back, stopping short of describing the new memory of Primrose emerging from the shadows to spirit him away. He didn't want to tell her that. Telling someone else would make the whole thing too real.

Marya Petrovna listened intently, pausing only to take swigs from her tea. When he had finished, she frowned and asked him some more questions about Lucas. Where he was born. What their family was like. What his interests had been.

Oyster answered these questions as best he could. It pained him to realise, as he did so, how little he really knew about him. If Lucas had stayed put then maybe he would have had the chance to know more, he thought bitterly.

After he had finished, she patiently rolled yet another cigarette, taking the tobacco and papers from a braided bag that hung around her neck. Instead of lighting the roll-up, she placed it on the broad armrest of the leather chair. Oyster stared out of the window at the undifferentiated iron of the sky. He was relieved he didn't need to talk anymore. His stomach had been clenched all the while he had been speaking.

"Very well," she said at last. "Working assumption should be your father was priest of sorts. Affiliated to Lugones, by the looks of what you have on you."

Oyster frowned.

"My dad was a dickhead from South London who walked out on us."

"They are not mutually exclusive, these things," said Marya Petrovna.

She scooped up the remaining tobacco and unlit cigarette and placed them in her bag, then produced a mint humbug which she unwrapped and popped into her mouth.

"This is all connected," she said, sucking on the sweet. "Too much of coincidence that you are here. That you have *this*."

She pointed at his stomach. It responded with a flicker of pain. She slurped and swallowed.

"But I don't want it," said Oyster. "I don't want any of this. I just want to sort my shit out and get back in with my crew. How do I get rid of it?"

Marya Petrovna shrugged.

"I think, perhaps, die is cast, dear boy."

27

THE HORNED ONE

The next day came and went in a smoky fog. Marya Petrovna tried to send Oyster out of the house on errands, but he was reluctant to leave the relative safety of the Lamasery. He doubted the Urbans had eyes and ears this far north, but he didn't want to test it. There was no telling to what lengths Mickey might go to get even, plus there was the added complication of whatever skullduggery Deano had been up to with Primrose.

Against Marya Petrovna's protestations, he had managed to stick his dead phone in a bag of rice before having at it with her ancient hairdryer, all in a fruitless effort to revive it. He felt cut off and disorientated without his constant connection to the world outside. Cécile always told him that he spent too much time on the wretched thing, but if this was what life was like pre-digital then he was glad to have missed it.

Marya Petrovna bustled out of the flat at midday, muttering something about an appointment, and Oyster sat alone in the lounge surrounded by her ghoulish menagerie of dead animals. He wasn't so far from being one of these himself, he thought, trapped in some characteristic pose, glassy-eyed and frozen forever, embalmed and stuffed with rags.

Next to him sat the Zig-Zag cabinet. Oyster eyed it circumspectly. The sinister gleam its inlaid characters had possessed early in the morning seemingly extinguished in the grey glare of full daylight. Now it just looked like a slightly forlorn wooden box. He pressed his fingertips to it. There was no magic here, no evil presence, just wood, nails and the smell of ancient history.

He watched the city outside slip past the lounge window. His sense of time felt heightened, and he found himself thinking about Primrose's diatribe on the subject.

There are wonders and horrors that you are not capable of comprehending.

Rain came and the clouds whipped over the city. On the pavement below, people hurried about their everyday business, coats wrapped against the sudden squall. But just like yesterday, instead of being caught up and thrumming with the city's subterranean rhythms, he felt apart, as though under observation by the city itself.

Suddenly finding himself hungry, he gingerly picked through the carnage of Marya Petrovna's kitchen to make himself some beans on toast and a mug of black tea. Minnie the cockateel watched him as he ate in silence. He regarded the plates piled in the sink and row upon row of filthy teacups arranged like squaddies on the Formica worktop and sniffed. There was clearly something very old and dead in the fridge, and the bin was stuffed to overflowing. He shook his head. Minnie considered him stoically.

His family had their problems, but at least they weren't slobs. He wondered idly if he would ever go back home. Grief snaked its way up from his belly, sudden and unexpected, but he swallowed it; clenched his fists and pushed it back down and out of his body. Out of his head, his throat, his heart.

Shitnuts. I need to be busy.

He opened the cupboard beneath the sink, and among the piles of dishwasher tablets and bottles of washing-up liquid there was a roll of bin bags, some rubber gloves and an unopened bottle of kitchen cleaner. He took a deep breath and set to work.

It took him a couple of hours to empty the bins and clean the kitchen, top to bottom. As he cleaned, he turned things over in his mind. Everything had been such a jumble, one bizarre thing happening upon the heels of the next, making it impossible for him to tease them apart and look for how they hung together. What was the bigger pattern? Being a pickpocket, good at cards and patter. He knew how to look for distractions. See what he was being directed away from.

There was clearly a connection between Primrose and Deano. There was also a connection between the Mannish and Primrose. So, was he running them? It would make a certain sense if he was sending them off on his errands. But to what overall purpose he wasn't sure. Maybe Deano was working with him, trying to destabilise the Urbans for his own push at the big job?

But Primrose. Who even was he? He turned up at the oddest of times, seemingly at will, and that trick he pulled, jumping from the roof of the tower last night, suggested he wasn't someone to fuck about with. What's more, thought Oyster with a sinking sensation, he owed him, now, twice over.

And then there was Lucas. His father was even more complicated than he had realised. But maybe, at some level, he had always known that. The man cast a long shadow, although it was composed mostly of absence and questions. Could the things Marya Petrovna had said about him be true? If Lucas understood the tattoo, would he know how to get rid of it? Or at least what to do with it.

He sat back on his haunches and sucked in a lungful of air. Since this morning the ache in his tattoo had subsided, but the itch beneath his armpit had become more acute.

He stood and gathered the tarot cards scattered on the kitchen table so that he could wipe off the grease that had accumulated in its corners. His mum, Paris, had been bang into this crap when he had been little, and he wondered if that was at the root of Lucas and his mum's bond. Out of curiosity, he laid the first card. It was the Devil. He knew enough about the cards not to be literal in reading them. For example, this probably had fuck all to do with the actual Devil, even if there was such a thing.

But what bothered him most was the portrait itself. An enigmatic silhouette beckoned from the edge of a twisted wood, but rather than horror movie goat horns or a pointed tongue, this figure was stag-antlered with limbs that grew into clutching stick-fingers. A crow perched on its shoulder and a fox entwined itself around one leg. It was hard not to be reminded of the graffiti sprayed on the back of the Clip, or the strange ceremony in the wood he'd dreamed about.

On the card's left-hand side was a churchyard with an open grave, while on its opposite edge was a field of blossoming wheat. *The Horned One* was written beneath in gothic script. Oyster knew he had heard that somewhere recently, but couldn't quite place it. He shuddered and put the cards away with the cups.

He surveyed the kitchen. It was never going to win any home-maker of the year awards, but it was vastly improved. He had managed to scour geological layers of limescale from the taps, and washed, dried and put away all the teacups in the overhead cupboards. The aluminium tube of the bin sat empty, its black plastic lid gaping like a mouth and its body gleaming in a way that Oyster figured it had probably not done this century.

He made himself another cup of tea and returned to the lounge. He froze in the hallway, certain that he'd left the lounge door open, which was now shut. Taking another deep breath, he turned its handle. Then pushed the door open with his foot, remaining in the hallway.

For a second he got the distinct impression that something had been moving about in the room before the door opened. There was the merest hint of shadows dissolving into nothing. The cabinet doors were agape, too, the box's velvet interior looking wet and organic.

"Who's there?" he called out, but there was no reply.

He put his head around the doorframe. Pinker the Chimp scowled back at him, his hand outstretched as usual.

"Big up to you, bro," nodded Oyster. There was so much in this room, it was no wonder it freaked him out.

He seated himself in the armchair furthest from the cabinet and took a sip of tea. His thoughts were still a jumble, but he had understood a few things. Firstly, he really needed to get hold of his dad. Secondly, as much as he might be able to use the shady shit between Primrose and Deano to get back into Big M's good books, he didn't know for sure whether Mickey was in on it or not. So, for now, he should avoid it like an electric fence.

And all the Greater London business? He took another sip of tea and swilled the bitter liquid around his mouth before swallowing. Legit or not, maybe he should just assign that to the bucket marked *weird shit that happens when you are off your tits in a dumpster.*

If he could find the Mannish, somehow, get hold of some solid proof of their existence, then he might have a chance not to end up dumped in a canal or over a roof like Ed had attempted last night. But was that even feasible now? Could they be found? If he believed even half of the crazy talk Marya Petrovna had been spouting, were they even anywhere that he could locate?

Maybe or maybe not, but he had a plan now and at least some semi-coherent thoughts about what his next play should be. He brought his knees up to his chest and massaged his toes. His face was still swollen and his jaw hurt. He let his head loll back in the chair and shut his eyes.

Oyster jumped awake. There was an odd hollow feeling under his arm and the sound of something scuttling around behind the Zig-Zag cabinet.

He felt his armpit and was surprised to find his fingertips came away wet, but he didn't seem to have been bleeding. He worked his fingers under his T-shirt and found, to his horror, two loose flaps of skin with some sort of slit between them. His fingertips slipped through the laceration and his mouth was full of cotton wool, nausea swimming around his head. He removed his fingers and checked again. No blood, but they were wet with some sort of silvery mucus. He yelped and stood up. The room spun.

The scuttling behind the cabinet became louder, and nearby a velvet curtain gave a tremor as though something was climbing up it. *Fuck!* Did the old woman have rats too? This was too much.

His armpit, the noises. He stumbled to the bathroom, slamming the lounge door shut behind him. The last thing he wanted was rodents following him about.

Beads of sweat broke out on his brow, and he wasn't sure if he was going to throw up or pass out. He ran the cold tap, rinsing the goo from his fingers before splashing water on his face. Every second felt unnaturally extended and the colours buzzed as though they had been turned up to eleven. He dropped to his knees, flipped up the toilet seat and leaned over the bowl; at least the bathroom was much cooler than the rest of the flat. His knees ached from the slabbed flooring.

What was happening to him?

He was unable to tear his thoughts from the slick, disorienting feeling of his fingers slipping inside his own body. The stinging sensation had gone now, but another wave of nausea broke over him and he retched. Questions tumbled through his head. Was he dying? What sort of disease would produce something like this?

With increasing panic, Oyster heard scuttling in the hallway now. Whatever had been in the lounge had managed to get out of there. He twisted so he was facing up from the toilet bowl and kicked the bathroom door with his foot. The door banged shut, but not before a shining black beetle the size of his fist buzzed clumsily into the bathroom, bounced off the mirror and landed with a mewling sound next to him. It lay on its back, multiple legs waving in the air.

Oyster screamed, but realised almost immediately that the intruder was the nuajin that had climbed onto his chest in Greater London.

TESCO METRO

Oyster recoiled, jumping up onto the toilet, feet precariously planted on either side of the bowl. The ink beetle chittered, righting herself, and with a murmur of blue-black wings flew up into the air. Oyster had an instinctive fear of anything large and flying, and he flicked out at her with his hand, trying to swat the creature away, but she continued to buzz around him, taking long swooping dives at his head like an oversized moth.

Oyster reached down and grabbed the toilet brush, feinting and parrying the nuajin's efforts to get closer to him. He was terrified. What did this thing want with him? Eventually, the ink beetle took to hovering just out of range of his makeshift weapon, at head height. They regarded each other for a moment, and Oyster somehow knew that she wasn't going to hurt him. He raised one hand.

"Right, little one, I'm just going to put this down." He indicated the toilet brush in his other hand. The nuajin squeaked in reply.

Slowly, Oyster got down from his perch and, keeping the ink beetle in sight, shoved the brush back into its receptacle.

The nuajin hung in the air, wings fizzing into an oily blur of spectral colours. He couldn't believe he was thinking this, but if he disregarded her large-flying-thingness, she was sort of beautiful.

She settled onto the tiled floor in front of him and Oyster sat on the open toilet seat. He had the feeling they were looking at each other again.

"I sense you're trying to tell me something, girl," he said. "But I got no idea what."

The ink beetle gave a coo. Oyster could not quite believe what he was seeing. He leaned forward and offered her a finger. The nuajin nosed towards it and nipped it playfully.

"Woah!" said Oyster, sitting back up. She was really here. He wasn't hallucinating.

The nuajin. Nonesuch. It had all been real. All the crazy shit that had been driving him nuts for the last few days. It was all true. There really was a place called Greater London. Full of looüt and gebel and weird buildings made from bones. He shook his head and found himself smiling. He'd pushed the whole episode to the back of his mind, worried that he'd been losing it. The comfort he felt knowing that all those events had really happened was palpable.

He leaned down again and reached out a hand. The ink beetle scuttled onto it. Gently, he held her up to his face. Up close she was amazing. Her back was a muted spiral of rainbow colours, like sunlight reflected in an oily puddle. She was like some sort of goth ladybird. A ridiculous number of tiny legs protruded from beneath a delicate carapace. For a second, her wing cases flicked open and gossamer wings whirred in the light like intricate clockwork.

His armpit twinged, and he remembered the cavity he'd found under his arm.

"Holy fuck," he exclaimed to himself, "you've been under there all along, haven't you?"

So what had brought her out now?

The front door of the flat slammed and the nuajin squealed. She flew off his hand into the darkest corner of the bathroom, and curled into a ball, exactly like an oversized woodlouse.

"Honey, I am home!" came Marya Petrovna's voice from the hallway. Oyster heard his host bustle into the kitchen.

"By all that is holy! What has happened here!" she yelled.

Oyster jumped to his feet. It was probably best to leave the nuajin where she was right now, he figured. Taking a last look at her, he flicked off the light and closed the bathroom door. He poked his head into the kitchen. Marya Petrovna sat at the Formica table, surrounded by bags of shopping.

"I have brought provisions," she said. "It has been long time since Marya Petrovna Dozvhenko had house guest, but that does not mean she has forgotten how to host. Also, I was not so sure of what things you like to eat and drink, so I have brought many options. Most important, we have caviar. And good *nalyvka*. You know I always used to say to Geli Raubal, 'Don't waste good caviar on bad men.' For all it helped with the way things ended for her. But *you* are not bad man, I think. In fact, you are hardly a man at all. Merely from perspective of age, you understand." She paused for breath and looked around again. "But what *have* you done to my kitchen?"

Oyster rolled his eyes.

"Have you been on the cocoa-puffs?" he asked.

Marya Petrovna smiled, her teeth an uneven row of tombstones on a rainy hillside. It was an odd expression on her austere face. But it suited her, Oyster thought.

"I might have taken restorative nerve tonic on my way to Tesco Metro, but that is because I am in good mood. Let us make the most of, eh?"

She waved at her surroundings.

"But this, ach, this is confusing. You have moved everything."

"Don't tell me. You had it all just the way you liked it?" said Oyster, shaking his head.

Marya Petrovna grimaced and moved her head from side to side. "*Comme-ci, comme-ça*," she grumbled. Reaching into one of the bags, she extracted a colourful bottle labelled in what Oyster had to assume was Ukrainian, whose logo featured a semi-naked nymph clutching a pair of oversized cherries suggestively over her chest. Marya Petrovna placed the bottle on the table and winked.

"Now we must eat, yes!"

She stood and fussed round the kitchen looking for glasses, then sat and opened the bottle's flip-top cap with her thumb before pouring two ruby-coloured measures. Oyster regarded the booze with suspicion.

"Jesus, it's not even the afternoon yet," he said.

Marya Petrovna rolled her eyes and took a long sip.

"Always with your generation it is 'too much this' or 'not enough that'. Have you considered just how lucky you are just to be alive now? One hundred years ago, boys your age were dying screaming in mud. And all over again twenty years after that."

"Are you gonna tell me that I've squandered my inheritance on avocado toast?" said Oyster. "Cause if you are, I'll just leave now."

"Not at all, boy. You kids have it *really* shit right now. I am just asking you to consider, on balance, that in some ways things not so bad. When I consider my own case, I find appreciation of recent history can be beneficial to the outlook. Taking cosmic view, longer even than Marya Petrovna has been around, most humans who have lived on this planet spent their time throwing rocks at each other and grubbing around for beetles. We have it easy. *Relatively*."

She raised her glass, toasted Minnie, and then drained it, smacking her lips. The cockateel clucked in response. The thought of beetles reminded Oyster briefly of his unexpected guest, but that could wait. He took a slug of the booze. It was sweet and strong with a hint of berries and soft fruits.

"This stuff isn't half bad," he said.

"Exactly!" Marya Petrovna topped up both glasses. She looked briefly downcast. "A taste of home. A taste of long ago. But now we eat!"

She shuffled to the stove and rolled up her sleeves.

"Food is life," she muttered. "Now take that cabbage and slice it, and when you've done that, peel the mushrooms. No, in other bag, flapdoodle."

Oyster stood, woozily. It was early in the day for him to be drinking. By crew standards, Marya Petrovna was unexpectedly hardcore. Or at the very least, a high-functioning alcoholic.

He wasn't sure of the names of any of the food they prepared together that day. There were cabbage rolls stuffed with minced rice and meat in a rich tomato sauce, fried chicken filets filled with butter and mushroom sauce and, just when he thought he was going to burst, she produced a plastic tray of delicate, honeyed pastries dusted with poppy seeds.

Afterwards they sat at the table and drank thick, strong coffee that Marya Petrovna brewed on the stove in an aluminium pot and to which she added ladles of sugar. It was only then that Oyster remembered the nuajin.

He took a mouthful of the tooth-dissolving coffee and considered for a moment whether he should just find a way to bundle up the ink beetle and keep the whole thing secret. The more he turned it over in his head, though, the more likely it was that the whole Greater London situation was totally up this crazy old bat's alley.

He cleared his throat. She might be able to help him. Maybe it was the booze, but he sensed he could trust her.

"I got something to show you," he said.

Marya Petrovna helped herself to another shot of the liquor, swilled it round in her mouth, and swallowed.

"After such a feast, Marya Petrovna is ready for anything," she replied, clapping her hands together.

"Okay," said Oyster. "Well, grab your Zimmer and hold on to your hat, 'cos shit's about to get weird." He stood. After all the food, his belly was creaking.

"Weird is good," said Marya Petrovna with another flash of a half-smile.

"Yeah," replied Oyster, "I know you might *think* that, but I mean this is *proper* weird."

"Yes, yes," said Marya Petrovna, "so you keep saying. Come along, lay on, Macduff and all that."

"In here," Oyster said, leading Marya Petrovna to the bathroom. He opened the door slowly and peered into the corner, half-expecting the ink beetle to have disappeared. But sure enough, there she was. Exactly as he had left her. He turned and put his finger to his lips.

"Don't want to disturb 'em. They can get a bit antsy. How're you with creepy crawlies?

"Ach, enough of this," said Marya Petrovna impatiently, pushing past him and round the door to where the ink beetle lay.

"Don't say I didn't warn you."

Oyster readied himself for her reaction.

"My eyes, boy, not so good in the dark," said Marya Petrovna. "What am I looking at?"

Oyster spoke in hushed tones. "Over in the corner,"

Marya Petrovna leaned towards where the nuajin lay.

"Oh my. By all the saints."

She turned to Oyster with a look of wonder on her face.

"It is ink beetle. I never thought I'd see one of these again."

29
FLAPDOODLE

"You know about these things?" said Oyster, surprised.

"I had friend a long time ago. Engineer of sorts," she said with a sad smile. "Kept one as pet. Both long gone now."

Oyster was shocked and slightly disappointed at the same time. After all the woman's hocus-pocus, he'd been looking forward to weirding *her* out for a change.

Marya Petrovna knelt with a crackle of tendons. She stretched her hand out to the nuajin and issued the sort of cooing sound that people usually made when trying to attract a cat's attention.

The creature immediately unfurled. She chittered in response and moved towards Marya Petrovna's outstretched hand.

"Don't tell me you can talk to her too?" he said.

"Well now, aren't you a little beauty," said Marya Petrovna, ignoring him. She looked up. "I think there may be more things that you want to tell me, eh?"

"Um, yeah, maybe," said Oyster.

Marya Petrovna shook her head. She bustled to the kitchen to fetch a saucer of milk which she placed near the nuajin. She petted the creature's head and turned to face Oyster, standing with a staccato accompaniment as her bones clicked back into place. She led him back to the kitchen and collapsed into a chair. The nuajin followed behind them, flying up on the table and rolling into a ball next to the coffee pot.

"Now, tell Marya Petrovna all."

And so, Oyster talked.

Being in the crew had developed his pre-existing taciturn streak to mammoth proportions, so he was surprised how good it felt for him to unburden himself. He told Marya Petrovna about the drop and the Mannish Boys and the strange beach. He told her about Nonesuch and the clerks and the looüt (and here, to his satisfaction, she really did appear to be surprised). Then he went over the city and its vast dome with its painted sky, even telling her about Mr Primrose and his enigmatic job offers.

Marya Petrovna worked through a series of roll-ups while he spoke, drinking two more glasses of the cherry liquor, and offering Oyster top-ups which he refused. He wanted to keep this all straight in his head. By the time he had finished the room was choking in smoke.

"Well," she said, stubbing out her final cigarette. "That is that, then."

"What do you mean, 'that is that'? Is that good or bad?" said Oyster.

Marya Petrovna shrugged.

"Don't go doing the inscrutable shrug thing, either," said Oyster. "'That is that' is a definite thing. You've come to *some* conclusion. Come on, spill."

Marya Petrovna blew the remaining smoke through her nose and tossed back the last of her drink.

"Very well, flapdoodle. These are Marya Petrovna's conclusions. Firstly, Mannish Boys did nothing to you that you had not already done to yourself. You are simply a walker. Someone who can move between the worlds. Secondly, this Minkowski incantation you have on your skin, it is word of power, a symbolic code which is designed to pull you in a certain path through the world, to certain points in time and space. Imagine it as opinionated occult compass. It helps to open the way for you to go back and forth between our world and the place you call Greater London. Other places and even times too, theoretically, what with time and space being one thing. Thirdly, this ability is perhaps reason Primrose wants you. But there is bigger pattern here, too, I just cannot see it yet."

Oyster experienced a strange sense of satisfaction mixed with the dislocation that he'd felt earlier. At some level he knew what Marya Petrovna was saying was correct. He just didn't want to believe it.

"But I don't want any of this," he said finally. He thought again of his home and Cécile. Would he ever see them again?

"Hard cheese," said Marya Petrovna with a grimace. "From moment you saw fit to tattoo yourself with this word, your fate was set. Probably."

Something fell over in the lounge with a loud crash. The nuajin flitted up into the air and settled on Oyster's shoulder.

Marya Petrovna's long face knitted in concern. She motioned him to remain still.

"Is anyone else here?" she hissed.

Oyster shook his head.

"*Kurwa!*" she said.

She tiptoed to another of the kitchen cupboards and slipped open the door. Oyster was impressed by how the old lady was able to move so silently. Feeling around inside the cupboard, she removed a cricket bat. Oyster grabbed a knife from a rack in the kitchen.

She opened the door a crack and waved him behind her. They peered out into the empty corridor beyond. The lounge door was ajar.

Marya Petrovna halted. She counted to three on her fingers and then kicked the door open.

The three of them charged into the room.

Pinker lay face down on the floor, his outstretched arm keeping the ape's rigid body at an angle.

There appeared to be no one else in the room, but if that was the case, who had pushed over Marya Petrovna's coat-hanger?

"Look!" yelled Oyster. Scuttling across the top of the bookcases was a second nuajin, smaller than his but more brightly coloured, sporting a streak of yellow across its back. He recognised it immediately as the one belonging to Nonesuch, Bamyasi.

His own nuajin flew up from his shoulder to join the newcomer with a chittering noise. Nonesuch's creature answered with its own cackle and the two of them rolled over and round each other to form one larger conjoined ball.

Marya Petrovna hurried to the room's bureau, retrieved some sheets of yellowed paper, and lay them on the Turkish rug at the room's centre.

She looked up at the nuajin and cooed.

"I think you have mail," she said in answer to Oyster's unspoken question. "But let us see."

She made the cooing sound again and the ink beetles separated. Oyster's buzzed to the ground, landing on one of the sheets of paper. With a gurgle, she extended a tiny point from her tail and shimmied across the paper, leaving a scrawl of characters behind her on the page.

"*Blyat!* It worked," exclaimed Marya Petrovna.

Oyster watched as the creature scuttled back and forth, left to right and top to bottom. After a few lines, the ink beetle emitted a sort of exhausted cough and stopped. She flew back up to the bookshelf to join Bamyasi and the two of them emitted a stream of clacks and tweets.

He pressed a hand to his damp armpit, worrying at the flap of skin through his T-shirt as though it was a loose tooth. He was already becoming accustomed to it.

"Quick! Quick! What does this say?" Marya Petrovna asked.

Oyster grabbed the paper and squinted at it. The wet ink glistened, and up close the paper had a robust scent, like dust and libraries. He wasn't sure what he'd expected exactly, but the note was comprised of a couple of lines of characters that were inscribed in the neatest handwriting he'd ever seen. He read it aloud.

"'Dunno where you gots to, Dry Bob, but we got glaziers on your quarry. Shickle your arse. Get here quickest, N.'

"Get here quickest?" said Oyster. "Easy for her to say. How the hell do I do that?"

Marya Petrovna grinned at him.

"Ach, what do you think we do, moron? We train! We train!"

30

THE CRACK IN THE WORLD

Marya Petrovna was shin-deep in discarded books and manuscripts. She had already cleared one of the bookshelves in her search and now she was working her way through the next one down.

"I have it somewhere here, I am sure."

"Have what?" asked Oyster.

He had seated himself in a leather chair with the ink beetle he was beginning to regard as *his* on its headrest. Receiving the message from Nonesuch's nuajin had drained her.

Similarly, Bamyasi had buzzed against the dirty lounge window until Oyster had opened it onto the afternoon traffic and the creature had zoomed up into the grey sky like an oversized bumble bee.

How on earth had it ended up here?

Perhaps these ink beetles could do the walking thing that Marya Petrovna had been talking about? It would make it easier to get messages back and forth, he guessed.

Meanwhile, Marya Petrovna had busied herself wandering to and fro throughout the length of the flat, muttering. Then, she started pulling books from the shelves, flicking through them at a pace and emitting sounds that Oyster was sure were increasingly exotic swear words, before dumping the volumes unceremoniously on the floor.

"What are you after, lady, maybe I can help?" Oyster had said.

"Ha! Ha! Yes! Yes! You will help! But not this right now! Conserve your energies! Conserve! Conserve!"

Oyster wasn't sure if she was still under the influence of the "nerve tonic" she claimed to have knocked back earlier, but since the arrival of Nonesuch's note she was full of a manic energy that he hadn't seen before.

The paper lay on his lap. He read it and re-read it.

He was pretty certain that it meant Nonesuch had located the Mannish. And that meant he was in with a chance now; an opportunity to clear things up, to prove to Mickey and the rest of the Urbans that he was on the up and up. He shut his eyes. Until the crew had been taken away from him, he had never been sure if it was the right thing for him, but his sudden exile from their ranks affected him keenly.

It was as though he had been racing over some dark, empty plain, only to plunge over an unseen precipice. He was in freefall now. What happened next depended on where he landed, if he even landed at all.

Marya Petrovna had climbed a set of collapsible steps and was now running her hand over the top of the bookcases themselves. Clouds of dust mixed with the smoke that filled the room.

"Aha!" exclaimed Marya Petrovna. She was holding something small, red and rectangular.

"Is that it?" he asked, disappointed. He hadn't been sure what she was looking for, but he'd imagined that it would be something more spectacular and a bit more in keeping with her mystic-nutcase vibe, some sort of enormous leatherbound tome, or a magic staff.

"Not very Gandalf, is it?" he said.

Marya Petrovna dismissed his complaints with a flick of her hand.

"Look, look!" Her eyes were beaming.

She climbed down from the steps and handed it to him.

It was a foldout map of central Madrid.

Oyster took it from her and examined it. The creases were

worn, as though the map had been in and out of pockets, many, many times throughout its lifetime. There was nothing remarkable about it at all.

He shook his head.

"I don't get it."

"You want to return to where note came from? Yes?"

Oyster nodded.

"Then we must drift," she said.

He shrugged.

"Still not feeling you," he said. "*Drift* what, how, where?"

"To drift, or to give it true name, *dérive*, is elevated technique discovered by Arch-mages of the Situationist Order."

"And?" said Oyster.

"Ach. So obnoxious are you," she replied. She reached into her pocket and pulled out a tangerine and held it in front of him. Oyster noticed that the tips of her fingers were flat and stained yellow from her endless flow of roll-ups.

"Observe orange."

Oyster stared at it exaggeratedly.

"What do you see?"

"A pair of old fruits," he replied.

"Very good," said Marya Petrovna. "But you are not really seeing orange. The mind, if we can grace your atrophied organ with that description, is taking sensory input from eyes and matching it to concepts it already has. 'Ah, this is probably orange!' it says, then fills in the rest with things we know about oranges: orange has this colour, this size, this shape, this smell. What you see is *idea* of orange, not orange itself. Put in simplest way, you have no access to reality that does not come though senses and interpretation."

"I get it," he said. "So, it's like if I'm asleep and I hear a siren, I might dream about the police."

"Yes, and your dream will feel real, but siren might be ambulance, fire engine or so forth. Brain extrapolates reality from available inputs. So it is with everything. Even when you are awake, you dream the world into existence. Materiality is constructed from concepts and symbols in mind, but there is no fundamental connection between world outside and your internal reality. All meaning is mediated, constructed from labels in the mind. This is symbolic order. If reality is computer game, symbolic order is operating system it runs on. Mostly we all just play *Space Invaders*, so do not need to know where or how high scores are stored."

She tapped the side of her head, then dug a large thumb under the tangerine's soft skin, twisted her wrist a few times, and with a flourish removed its peel in a single piece.

"Arch-mages of Situationism realised this. Understood that since actuality is byproduct of language system, walking through a world deliberately mislabelled creates sensitivities to ur-structure underpinning it. Now you understand? Yes? Yes?"

She stabbed at his forehead with her forefinger and he winced.

"Hey! Still dooked in, remember?" He rubbed his temple.

She dropped the orange peel into his lap, its aroma tickled his nose.

He thought about the evening he'd got into it with the Mannish. One of them had been holding a map of Paris.

Marya Petrovna marched out of the room and reappeared moments later holding a freshly lit roll-up, wearing a trench coat and holding a blue plastic bag. She beckoned.

"Come, come," she said. "What are you waiting for? Put orange peel in bin and put on coat. As little Marie Curie used to say, 'Best way to learn is by doing'!"

The sky had brightened now, and Oyster and Marya Petrovna tramped across the grass of Primrose Hill towards the largest clump of trees they could find. Oyster had needed a lot of persuading to leave the relative safety of Marya Petrovna's flat, and even now he felt exposed, surrounded as he was by its flat grassy expanse. Parks had always seemed like anomalies in his natural environment, green blisters in the city's concrete skin; an easy place to get spotted. He pulled his hood up and looked down at his feet.

As he had readied himself to leave, his nuajin had squealed and chattered until he had relented and allowed her to climb back into the cavity under his armpit. She was nestling there now. It was more comfortable than he'd expected. To be honest, from the moment she'd crept back in there he felt whole in a way he hadn't since she'd emerged. It was odd, but on the scale of all the odd shit that had happened so far today, he was just going to let it slide.

Marya Petrovna had smoked three rollies between here and her flat. She huffed and puffed, navigating the scattered paths and Narnia-esque streetlamps that organised the park's green spaces. He could only imagine what the old woman's lungs must look like. He visualised a pair of leathery bellows that breathed smoke.

At last, they reached the sparse cover of a copse and Oyster's overwhelming sense of being under observation abated. He took a breath and glanced upward. The clouds overhead scudded restlessly, revealing an even greyer vault beyond them. From this vantage point he could see the city spread out all around. There was the pencil topper of the BT Tower and the brutal magnificence of Centre Point. It was late afternoon, and the darkening horizon already hinted at the evening to come. He was suddenly lonely, as though he had been cut off from some vital galvanising current.

Marya Petrovna stomped her final cigarette underfoot and unfolded the map. A sudden breeze flapped its edges back and forth.

"Very well," she said. "This is how it is done. You take map. You close the eyes and walk. You feel where map wants to go. When you are lost, the way is found. Typically, one also needs symbolic connection to destination. In this case, you have ink beetle."

"Very Yoda," said Oyster. "Is that it? Don't you got any other words of wisdom?"

Marya Petrovna handed him the map and clapped him on the back.

"Such travel is beyond words. Beyond signs and literal meanings. Is exciting, though, eh?" she said. "Can you feel it?"

Oyster wasn't so sure what he felt was excitement, but he was prepared to indulge her. He was out of any other options now, anyway.

"Right, let's give it a go," he said.

"So, first look at map and fix at point on it. Try to soak in deep information that map abstracts rather than detail of what is shown. Shut the eyes and try to lay map onto grass, trees, sky that surrounds. Laying one on top of other creates semiotic fissure. This is the crack that opens door."

Oyster peered at the jumble of lines and colours that he held. At the map's centre, Marya Petrovna had drawn a solid black circle from which multiple arrows flew. Beneath and around the symbol, unfamiliar place names leapt out at him: roads that were coloured in yellow and blue, patches of green with exotic names; the geometric sprawl of the metro system. He began to wish he'd paid more attention to the few Spanish lessons he'd had at school.

"Do not be distracted by words on map," said Marya Petrovna. "They are merely tool to get you into correct state of mind."

"That's easy for you to say," he replied.

Far overhead, a jet plane whined. He wondered what it must look like from up there. He remembered Cécile pointing out that when you got up above the clouds the sky was always blue. Where she'd gotten this titbit from was a mystery, since neither of them had ever been on a plane. At the time it had seemed liked a such silly observation that he'd teased her about it for a few days after she'd said it. But it suddenly felt profound.

He closed his eyes, felt the earth beneath his feet, and wondered how much mud was getting stuck to his trainers. How stupid must he look, standing here with this mad old bat and her map? He thought of the sky above and the plane slicing through the air over his head, being pushed up into the sky just by the shape of its wings.

The branches of the nearest tree rattled in the wind. Its wooden fingers reached towards him, their sound like waves crashing on a distant shore. For an instant, the world slipped beneath his feet, like plunging downward on a roller coaster. There was the distant, staccato report of a woodpecker and, beyond that, the dizzy, dirty thrum of the city. Car horns; the hiss and chunter of buses. He was on the edge of it all. Distant. Marginal. He was insubstantial, liable to just slide into the ground.

And then, the moment passed. All he could think of was how he was going to get his head handed to him, and that this was even more likely now he was standing in a field with just a demented OAP and a map of Spain for company. He opened his eyes one at time.

Marya Petrovna stood in front of him. She pulled the peeled tangerine out of her trench coat pulled off a few segments before handing them to him. He tossed them all into his mouth at once. The sweet juice ran down his throat.

"Working?" she asked.

"I dunno," he said. "I just feel like a dick."

"Of course, but anything else?"

Oyster didn't want to reply. Things had definitely gone a bit weird, but just for a second. And he didn't want to give her the satisfaction.

"Again! Again!" said Marya Petrovna, clapping her hands together in encouragement. "Next time you feel yourself within the dérive, the tide, you must take a step and see where she takes you. Let me see if I can help. Cultivate state of indifferent vacuity."

She emptied the contents of the plastic bag on the ground. It contained an incense holder and a small brass hand bell that was engraved with characters which resembled those on her cabinet. She pushed several joss sticks into the holder and lit them, then rang the bell. Its tone was delicate and clear.

"Very well," Marya Petrovna said. "Now we bring out big guns."

Even in the open air, the incense emitted a thick cloud of sandalwood and citrus. Oyster coughed.

"Begin!" ordered Marya Petrovna. She began to chant in a low voice, just as she had when calming his tattoo. Every now and then she would punctuate the chanting with a loud ring of the hand bell.

"How am I supposed to do anything with you raising a stink and making such a racket?" he said.

"Do not be distracted by materiality. Am invoking a state of gnosis to open path. Sounds and scent are one way. But any will do. You must *believe* that you can do what you need to. Belief is the tool that will open the crack in the world."

Oyster shook his head. This was impossible. He shut his eyes again, tried to block out the smell of the incense. He sensed movement and opened one eye only to be rewarded with the sight of Marya Petrovna, arms akimbo, shuffling backwards and forwards in front of him, while continuing to chant in her low monotone. She looked like a hippo trying to old-school bogle.

"For fuck's sake!" exclaimed Oyster. "Can you just take it down a notch?" With all the chanting and smells they must be attracting attention.

Marya Petrovna stopped and looked at Oyster, unimpressed.

"Do you want to catch Mannish and find your father?" she said.

"Yes, but isn't there some way we can do this that doesn't involve you doing the fucking sand dance?"

Marya Petrovna looked genuinely hurt.

"There is no need to be crass. This is not sand dance. Sand dance was dance hall routine performed by Wilson, Keppel and Betty in the 1930s."

"And why should I care?"

"Who do you think Betty was?" Marya Petrovna tapped her nose with a wink.

Oyster blew out his cheeks in frustration.

"Look, I'm sorry. Maybe I just can't do whatever it is I'm supposed to be able to do?"

"I, for one, am sure that you can, and Marya Petrovna is never wrong about such things. It is exactly as I used to say to Yellie, 'First step to being good at anything is to forgive yourself for being shit at it.'"

"Yellie?" said Oyster.

Marya Petrovna's demeanour changed. The maverick joy that

had animated her ever since the nuajin had emerged dissipated all at once.

"Ach. Nothing. She was old friend. Confidante. I will tell you all about her another day. Now is really not the time."

They spent the remaining hour practising. They tried with and without the chanting. They tried with and without the joss sticks. They tried with and without the bell, but nothing worked.

Eventually – frustrated, cold and tired – Oyster had had enough, and so they returned to the flat where he fixed them both fried egg sandwiches and cups of dark, sweet tea. He was disappointed in himself, and Marya Petrovna's spirits had crashed too. He wasn't sure if this was to do with his failure to accomplish anything, but her usual bullishness had collapsed into something more quiet, surly and coarse.

They drank more of the cherry liquor and she taught him how to make roll-ups, not that he had the least interest in smoking them, and then went their separate ways to their rooms.

31

THE DOOR

It was night. Oyster's back twinged. It was a little stiff from sleeping on the bedroll for the last two nights, but all in all, given that he was basically just dossing on Marya Petrovna's floor, it wasn't that bad.

Instinctively, he pressed his fingers under his armpit, still not accustomed to the new cavity that his body had developed. This was all just too strange. And then there was the note. He'd read it and re-read it a hundred times, and now it was folded up in the pocket of his jeans. Somehow, he needed to get back to Greater London, but given his progress so far that might not be anytime soon.

Images of Nonesuch's livid red hair and pulsating lights drifted through his mind. Although he had not been in Greater London for a long time, his memories of it had a quality that was both intense and vague simultaneously, the same sort of qualities as half-forgotten nightmares or bad trips. Oyster had done a bit of acid in his youth, and mushrooms too, as they were cheap and easy to get hold of, but none of his drug experiences possessed the same ferocity as the memories of his time in Greater London.

He realised the reason he'd woken up was because his ink beetle had left him again. That creeping unease he'd felt when they'd been apart yesterday had settled on him once more. His tattoo had started to ache as well. Nothing too painful right now, but enough that he'd need to get the old lady to do her mumbo-jumbo routine on it.

He sat up. From the kitchen, he heard a muffled buzzing. There she was, flying about: his new pet. His tattoo flared up angrily. *Fuck it*. He needed to see if there were any paracetamol left. He rolled out of bed and stood woozily. His thoughts spun through his head in a jumble. He wasn't sure what the time was. And he needed a new phone. He had the money, just hadn't had the time.

He stretched, his back ached and he stumbled into the corridor. Marya Petrovna's map lay on the floor, unfolded and face down. Perhaps the nuajin had been playing with it. Still half asleep, Oyster picked it up and refolded it flat. He stumbled into the bathroom, shut the door behind him and felt around for the light switch.

Locating it, he shaded his eyes with the map and flicked the switch. There was a flood of light and Oyster was suddenly cold.

"Dry Bob!" said Nonesuch. "So you made it."

32

O-LE-AN-DER GOS-WICK

Oyster opened his eyes. It was daylight. Or at least the weird green light that passed for daylight in Greater London. It was cold and he was standing in front of Nonesuch in his boxer shorts. The overpowering smell of fish hit the back of his throat.

"Neato on the garms front, kid," came a gruff voice Oyster had not heard before. "Strong look. Loving your lack of concern for the dress code."

Oyster's vision was still struggling to come to terms with the sudden increase in the amount of light. He could only really make out one figure.

"Like he says," said Nonesuch, "might want to cover your inconvenience with this. And park the buttocks. You're gonna gets us fingered."

Nonesuch slipped off her own grey coat and he pulled it on. It was too big for him, having been cut for Nonesuch's broader, more athletic frame. As his eyes adjusted, Nonesuch guided him into a cross-legged sitting position. He stowed the folded map of Madrid in a coat pocket.

Oyster squinted. They were sitting on a broad, flat, corrugated-iron roof. Nonesuch crouched in front of him. Her lights rippling with a low order magnesium glow. At her side sat a mid-size Jack Russell terrier.

His mind was spinning. Had it actually worked? He took the

opportunity to surreptitiously pinch himself. He was here again in Greater London.

"So what's the dealio?" said the gruff voice.

"I got your note," Oyster replied, rubbing his eyes.

"Wasn't talking to you, kiddo," said the dog with a wag of its tail. "Was speaking to the boss."

"What the fuck?" said Oyster.

"Go fuck *yourself*, kid," said the dog. Its nose wrinkled.

Oyster was unable to respond. What he had just seen was so weird that every single part of his brain was frozen, simply trying to understand what he had witnessed. He couldn't even shake his head.

"Oleander Goswick," continued the dog.

Oyster's mouth opened but no sound came out.

"My name is O-LE-AN-DER GOS-WICK," said the dog, enunciating each syllable.

Finally, the knot at the back of Oyster's head untied itself and words formed.

"You're a dog," he said.

"That is not in question," said Goswick, shaking his head. "What I am trying to ascertain is the appropriate nominative to apply to you, my slack-jawed chum. From what the boss has told me, I'm assuming that you're Royston?"

"Oyster," he corrected.

"Whatever. Pleased to meet you," said Goswick. He looked up at Nonesuch. "Are you sure about this? 'Cos I'm thinking, from the look of him, alpha-fuck here might have been damaged in transit."

"Enough," said Nonesuch. She fixed him with blood-red eyes. "Me and Goswick landed the skinny on the Mannish and we need to make use of your talents also. Think on this as your basic twofer situation."

Oyster was dizzy. He remembered Marya Petrovna calling him a walker back at the flat, so maybe it was true. He felt the map in his pocket. If he was going to get to the Mannish, and then somehow to Lucas too, he needed to try to take this in his stride. He took a breath, parked all the questions he had.

Nonesuch prodded him

"Hullo. You receiving?"

He took a breath.

"A twofer?"

"A two-for-the-price-of-one. As in, you help us acquire items that me, you and bow-wow here are all necessitating."

"*Bow-wow*?" muttered Goswick.

"Hush now, Mr Woofkin." Nonesuch reached out to stroke him.

Goswick growled and backed away.

"I need you to pull the whole light-fingered-jack routine; maybes use your *knack* to get in and out of somewhere with the valuables. And we'll need the help of your borrowed nuajin."

"Yeah, sure. You might need to be a bit more specific?" said Oyster.

"Not out here. Let's be getting you decent first, Dry Bob. You'll make more of an entrance than intended lacking breeches."

She shuffled along the roof, which was composed of mismatched sections of corrugated iron bolted together, swinging open a hatch and stepping into it.

"Don't you lot make anything yourself?" said Oyster.

"Us *lot*?" She laughed mirthlessly as she dropped, hand over hand. Oyster sat on his haunches, looking down into the darkness. Next to him Goswick yawned.

"Kid, this one I'm gonna give you gratis, on the understanding that you have not been in these parts much, but you'll soon become acquainted with the sad fact that gebel are pretty much the shits of the shits here under the Lid. Please don't annoy the boss."

Nonesuch was obviously nettled. Her lights pulsed brighter and redder, making the room below look like some sort of fiery pit.

"Master Gee is correct, Man-Friday. We're worked till we drop, drained of our glimmer and thrown overboard. All kinds of ironic since we were here long before your sort turned up and took all and everything for themselves. Even our speech is disallowed."

"We're talking now, aren't we?" said Oyster.

Goswick sighed and shook his head.

Nonesuch stopped and glared up at him. Oyster suddenly felt his semi-nakedness keenly.

"Shut your eyes, you fucking nik-ninny."

Oyster suppressed the urge to ask why. She was clearly nettled enough already. The edge to her voice was cold and terrifying.

"Do what she says," whispered Goswick. He lay on the roof and did his best to cover his eyes with his paw.

"Shut your eyes."

Oyster did so. Suddenly, an intense rainbow of light erupted from the hatchway. A blinding glare of strobing colours so deep and vivid that there were a few he wasn't sure he could entirely see properly. There were certainly some that he had no name for.

And they moved. They flickered and swelled and faded one on another in breathtaking succession. After seconds the display was gone, but his eyeballs ached from the intensity.

"That's how gebel communicate, Dry Bob. Not with this atrophied bit of gristle." She poked out her tongue and disappeared down the ladder.

Oyster was dizzy from the lightshow.

"Okay, okay. I get it. I'm sorry."

"Well, I'm glad that's over," said Goswick.

Oyster wrapped the coat around him followed Nonesuch down the ladder into the room below.

THE CITY AND THE COMPANY

The daylight from the hatch was faint, but it was enough to illuminate the room below a little. As he reached the bottom of the ladder, Oyster recognised it at once as the top floor of Nonesuch's crib. The ceiling they had descended through was decorated with rococo ripples of plaster. On the walls, ghosts of long-gone furniture had stained grandiose shadows onto the satin wallpaper. It had clearly all been ornately decorated once, but that had been long ago.

"Hey," called Goswick from above.

Oyster looked up.

"You any good at catch?" asked the dog.

"I'm pretty good with my hands," replied Oyster.

"Okay then, Geronimo!" The Jack Russell pitched himself over the opening and down into Oyster's outstretched arms.

"You better shut that, too," he said, nodding up to the trapdoor as Oyster dropped him to the floorboards.

Oyster complied with a shrug.

When he returned, Nonesuch was sitting in front of a long-dead fireplace on a makeshift beanbag made from a hessian sack. Goswick lay at her side. A gentle rosy glow emanated from Nonesuch, illuminating them both.

"What happened here?" he said, indicating the walls. "This whole place is made of crap that's stitched together."

Nonesuch looked around and glimmered a morose deep-sea blue.

"S'more to it than that, Dry Bob," she replied. "Long before my time, the city hereabouts was grander then grand, but for the longest it's been in a losing competition with the Most Honourable East India Company."

Oyster nodded. "You mean that stretch with the mahoosive blinged-up buildings in gold and marble?"

"That would be it," replied Nonesuch. "The looüt you saw leaving the Lid when we met? That would be one of theirs, all full-grown and crewed and profiteering. When she returns from the Outer Indies, she'll be laden with spices, finery and what have you."

"So, they get all the cheese and this place rots? Sounds depressingly familiar," said Oyster. Nonesuch shimmered in agreement.

"Before your sort arrived and started the Company, most gebel made a living combing the Beach of Lost Things for articles to re-use as the great Tree of Life decrees. And while fresh trappings turn up there with regularity, there's not as much as there used to be. Each time the city retreats a little, the Company advances somewhat, and versa-vice-a. And the Company is a strictly humans-only kind of rave."

Nonesuch peeled the gloves from her fingers, laying them next to her seat. Over the shirt was a black silk waistcoat decorated with tin badges that she must have pilfered from the beach.

"Me and my hive-sibling Motet are looking to even the score. That's why we keep our heads down low and why those clerks were beating on me on the beach."

The rolled-up sleeves of Nonesuch's shirt showed bruises on her forearms, presumably left by the clerks. Phantom muscles and tendons moved beneath her skin. It ought to have been gruesome, like a primary school anatomy aid, but it was fascinating, beautiful even.

Goswick gave a satisfied snort. Oyster's eyes travelled down Nonesuch's arms and rested on her hands. Folded flat against each palm was a second thumb. She rubbed the extra digits as though they'd gone to sleep. Nonesuch caught him looking and glared back. Fairground lights undulated across her neck.

"Rude to stare at the glidefins, Mr Nawpost," she said, brandishing the extra thumbs. Coloured light illuminated her hands from within, trickling up and down in delicate patterns.

"Now you're here again, let's see what your babby's got," said Nonesuch, pointing at Oyster's armpit before he could ask another question.

"Are you sure this is such a good idea?" said Goswick, sitting up. "Tweedledimmest here could be a Company stooge, for all we know. Could be playing the whole 'lost human' card. Getting us onside then calling in the jackdaws on our sorry asses. Subtle-like."

The dog and gebel regarded each other for a second, then began to laugh.

"Alright, alright," said Oyster, clapping his fingers on the palm of his hand sarcastically. "Very funny. But as payback, before you two get what you want, you need to find me some garms."

"Well, it's hardly our fault that you decided to rock up in your scanties, but lucky for you, you're about Motet's size and shape, and that gebel is a peacock. Lemme see what's to be done." She stood and walked to a tall wooden wardrobe that lurked at the back of the room, returning moments later with a black woollen skirt, a T-shirt and a blue tartan waistcoat similar to her own. The outfit was completed with some towelling socks and a pair of yellow-stitched Doc Martens that were so ancient the leather was cracking around the toes.

Nonesuch handed them to him.

"And before you start in, we're out of trews."

Oyster took the clothes. They were crumpled and smelled stale, but beggars couldn't be choosers in this situation. He walked to the bathroom to change.

Despite being open to the air, the bathroom still stank with the acrid smell of burned rubber. The lamp lay on the floor, surrounded by the scorch marks and ashes from his last visit. He looked out over the city in the bleak daylight, and as he dressed, he wondered about Primrose and how he figured in all of this, if at all.

The road overlooked by the house was quiet, but a few streets over there were smoke and smells that suggested people. In the far distance, across the river, he caught glimpses of the ruddy gold of the East India Company buildings. He yawned and stretched; his bones cracked and tingled. *Time to get a move on.*

He returned to the faded grandeur of the lounge. Nonesuch nodded in approval at his outfit.

"Right, now you've got your cooch all covered, we need to see Syzygy," she said.

"Who?" asked Oyster, fumbling with the tight buttons of the waistcoat.

"Motet's nuajin, the one that's taken such a shine to you. All kinds of strange, in fact. Ink beetles usually stick for life. Has she nested?"

"If that's what you call it," he replied. "I nearly shit a brick when it happened. You could've given me a heads up that she was gonna park in my armpit."

Nonesuch laughed. "Yeah, 'cos that would've helped your parlous 'tude, Mr Royston."

"It's Oyster," he corrected.

"Got it. Royston." Nonesuch flickered a peach colour.

Goswick coughed loudly.

"Hate to be the one that breaks up the hormone party, but this one already took freaking ages to get here. Ain't we on a clock or something, boss?"

Nonesuch's lights were a delicate purple for an instant and she nodded.

"Want to catch me up?" said Oyster.

"Cast that mind of yours back to when your sorry arse first washed up," Nonesuch replied. "Gave you a hit of glimmer to pacify you. So, there are sorts out there addicted to it. Thusly, there are crews who'll cater to that appetite by capturing my kind and draining us to the point of death. Shineheads can keep a gebel trussed in a basement for months till they finally return to the tree."

Nonesuch cooed and the nuajin slipped out from her hiding place, beneath Oyster's arm, climbing across his chest and rustling her wings beneath his chin. Nonesuch pulled a large scrap of crumpled paper from her breeches' pocket and shepherded the beetle onto it.

Syzygy turned around on the paper, like a cat trying to find the most comfortable spot on a cushion. After she settled, Nonesuch slipped one of her glidefins between the nuajin's translucent wings. Her fingertip pulsed with gentle blue light and the nuajin wriggled and purred. After a pause, Syzygy scuttled around the paper, scratching out inky letters with her abdomen.

"Is that what happened to Motet?" asked Oyster. "Caught and drained?"

"Unsure. He was onto one of the big shine-rings, trying to break them up. Run by none other than your friends, the Mannish. But pulling such larks makes you enemies."

Syzygy stopped her dance and Nonesuch brushed her gently from the page, grabbing the paper and waving it in the air to dry. The ink beetle scuttled back towards Oyster. He took a deep breath and raised his arm. She flew up into her nest once more. He grimaced, feeling a nip under his arm as though the cavity there had been caught by tiny teeth.

Nonesuch held up the paper.

"Ha! We got summat, dogsbreath!" said Nonesuch, her lights flaring with excitement.

"Nice," replied Goswick.

"So, what's next?" said Oyster.

"Fetch your coat, we'll fill you in on the way," answered Nonesuch, already at the door.

34

FLIMFLAMS

In the daylight, Nonesuch's crib was no longer covered in retired nuajin, revealing the pitted red brick of the building beneath. The sky overhead was a bluish-green and the air cold enough to turn Oyster's breath into vapour. He was warmer in the skirt than he had expected, but he was glad of the long grey coat that Nonesuch had lent him. It looked to be ex-Soviet-era military. Just another gift from the beach, no doubt.

Nonesuch had folded her red hair beneath a periwig as much as possible and wore a sweatshirt with a hood pulled over her face. Goswick padded along beside them, his tongue lolling from his mouth.

"Hey kids, just for the record, I am putting it out there that I am fricking hungry."

"Shhh," said Nonesuch, leading them to the house's rear and stepping around the foul-smelling mud beneath the toilet.

"Just saying, if I see a string of sausages anywhere, I'm not going to be able to overcome my own canine nature," he said. "It'll just be like an old-timey Tom and Jerry cartoon."

"Don't know what you're gabbing about," replied Nonesuch, "but do please stubble your muzzle."

"What's the deal with you two?" said Oyster. "Is he your pet?"

Goswick growled.

"Nah," replied Nonesuch, "four-legs is my friend. Helping me out. We goes way back." She winked at Goswick.

"Okay, then." Oyster shrugged. He clearly wasn't going to get any more out of her on the subject.

The air was tinged with its habitual briny smell as the sound of people and commerce grew louder. Nonesuch led them into a narrow alleyway and through a maze of tight-knit streets walled by houses and tracts of mud.

They finally stepped into a thoroughfare so wide by comparison that Oyster felt dizzy. The street was cobbled and thronged with people. Men in powdered wigs, topcoats and knee breeches swaggered purposefully up its length, bantering with each other ostentatiously. Street vendors in mud-spattered smocks and aprons advertised their wares at top volume.

Not everyone was on foot. Here and there were sedan chairs, some ornately gilded, constructed from leftover plastic. There were hand carts, too, trundling to and fro over the rutted street. All the vehicles he could see were hauled or carried by gebel.

Women in brocade dresses, with skirts so wide they blocked traffic, picked their way through the mud and filth littering the street. They stepped daintily around a sewer at its centre, while the sky overhead boiled with ink beetles carrying messages from one place to another.

The smell was overpowering. The city's fishy undertow was the base note in a stomach-churning medley of raw sewage, cooked food and smoke. He followed Nonesuch's lead, ducking into the flow of people and keeping his head down.

This was the first time he had seen the human denizens of Greater London, and they appeared, in most respects, to be the same as those in his home city. Every colour, size and shape was represented. The other gebel he saw, though, were poorly fed and ill-treated. They shambled along, none meeting his gaze with the same ferocity as Nonesuch. It was clear that whatever social order existed in Greater London, as Goswick had explained, they were at the bottom.

He turned to Nonesuch.

"So what's the play here?" he asked.

"Got to locate brother-mine. The deets from your ickle Syzygy said the shinehouse was somewhere in this vicinity. But a gebel and her best friend can't just rock up at such locations, if you know what I mean," said Nonesuch.

"What do we do?" said Oyster.

"Nuh-huh, not us. Just you, jack-jonesing. You'll reconnoitre. Locate brother-mine. Our kind can't get in there for obvious reasons. But the crew runnin' this house put word out they're in the market for a walker. That is to say, someone with your ickle knack. That furnishes you with an *in*, Dry Bob. So once you're on the inside, use your glaziers, scope the situation, spring my hive-bro if you can. If not, shickle out of there with the particulars and toot on this." She handed him an ancient dog whistle. "We'll find you."

Oyster nodded and pocketed it.

They pushed through a group of red-tunicked cavalry officers sporting shaved heads and gang tattoos. Oyster was accustomed to using other people's clothes as a way of measuring their mood, allegiances, and even how likely they were to give him a kicking, but he struggled to find some rule underlying the jumble of styles and periods on show here. It was as though clothes, people – even buildings – just washed up here from time to time and knitted themselves into the city's fabric.

"Ain't gonna be straightforward. But split it into three stages. One: an invite to enter. Most houses have flimflams running out front. Hook one of them and work your way in. Two: pretty mouth an excuse to check the place out. Three: get the deets and scram. Worst case, use your knack to do the flit out of there."

"Yeah, about that," he grunted. "I'm not so sure I can pull that off on command…"

He was distracted mid-sentence by a glimpse of the great ivory-boned palace he'd first seen on arrival, off in the distance. Then had to duck beneath the outstretched arm of a grubby footman who was using a dead tablet computer as a tea-tray and— *Shit*. He'd lost Nonesuch and Goswick.

A slippery feeling unwound in his stomach, reminding him that he had no idea how to get back to Nonesuch's safe house. He scrabbled around in the pocket of his coat for the dog whistle.

Suddenly, he was a kid again, letting go of Lucas's hand to tie his shoelaces on Streatham High Road and losing sight of his dad. Everything had ground to a halt in that moment: his breathing getting faster and faster, adrenaline making him tingle with the sickly realisation that he didn't know where Lucas was or how to get home.

The tears had welled up and burst out of him. Seconds later, Lucas had come running back out of a nearby bookies. Spotting Oyster, he'd swept him up, clutching the boy to his chest, cursing. He wiped away the boy's tears and told him to stop snivelling.

Where was Nonesuch?

"Come on, Dry Bob, can't keep losing you," said Nonesuch's voice. She stepped out from behind a sedan that had just been left stranded in the muddy street.

Relief flooded into Oyster.

"According to your nuajin, our destination's around here somewhere. Leastways their gaffles and games are all this side," she said, nodding at a scruffy kid at the edge of the road running cups with one of the cavalry types.

"Sausages," whispered Goswick from the roadside.

Nonesuch shook her head and put a glittering finger to her lips. "Fade time, let's allow our man here attend to his business."

Oyster was not at all sure that he could pull off half of what Nonesuch had mentioned, but he did know about short cons, and cups was one of the oldest in any universe. He looked around, but the dog and the gebel had already ghosted. No doubt they were watching him from somewhere, he just couldn't be sure where.

What had Marya Petrovna said earlier? *Belief is the tool.*

Oyster turned it over. If this game picked out by Nonesuch was attached to the shinehouse, then his best strategy was to play it coy, get on the inside and then escalate. Wouldn't do to be too keen. If they were anything like his crew, marching up to them and asking for a job probably wouldn't work. *One step at a time.* He idled up to the boy and stared up into the tinted sky. The clouds above might be artificial, but Oyster was struck that, handcrafted as they were, they were beautiful.

There was a tap on his leg. Oyster looked down.

The kid wore a scarlet brocade jacket and matching silk waistcoat. A pair of trackie bottoms had been cut off at the calf to reveal muddy stockings and a pair of Cuban-heeled shoes.

"Let us play, sirrah!" said the kid in reedy voice, noticing him for the first time. "You strike me as a gent of some fortune."

He waved at a low folding table and three upturned plastic cups.

"Forget it, young blood," said Oyster. "I ain't no mug."

The kid pulled a face.

Oyster considered it for a moment. Perhaps he could use this to his advantage.

"You wouldn't know a woman by the name of Ambidexter, would you kid?" he asked. "Runs with the Mannish. All inked up?"

"That name ain't immediately a familiar one, but then again," the kid shrugged, "fresh as I am, I ain't no peach."

"Okay. Okay," said Oyster. "I get it. How about we play. If I win, you tell me what I want to know."

The kid thought about it for a second and then nodded.

Oyster reached into the coat for his wallet, only to realise he didn't have one with him. *Shit*. No money.

"Throw me a bone, junior," he said. "I'm all out of folding."

The kid looked Oyster up and down, assessing his monetary worth. It rankled to be on the receiving end of that sort of glance for a change.

"Vamp us them creps, sir, that'll cover your stake," said the boy.

Oyster shook his head in confusion.

"Those," said the boy, pointing at his Doc Martens.

"Aw, come on," said Oyster. He'd already lost enough of his clothes over the last few days.

"Fair enough then, sir," he said. He shrugged and turned away.

Oyster rolled his eyes and tapped the kid on the shoulder.

"Okay," he grunted.

"Very well, sirrah," said the boy, indicating the plastic table. "Relinquish said creepers and place them thusly."

Oyster removed his shoes and stuffed his socks into his jacket.

The mud covering the road oozed between his toes. He tried not to think too much about what was in it.

"The best of three makes a win. Keep your glaziers fixed upon the ball and victory will be assured," the boy squeaked. He rolled a plastic ball not much bigger than a pea under the first cup.

The kid ran through his patter, shuffling the cups in a circular motion, giving his intended victim glimpses of the ball as it rolled between them, but Oyster was looking for the rest of the boy's crew. He clocked a man, slouched against a street corner, keeping an eye on him and the kid long distance. From his size and bearing, Oyster pegged him as muscle.

"And now, sirrah, the time has arrived to make your choice!"

Oyster picked the middle cup and lost. The kid mock-scolded him for not paying attention, then exchanged the briefest of glances with another man in a tall, white wig and a corn-yellow jacket further up the street. The man was pretending to clean a pince-nez with a dirty handkerchief; his face was powdered and rouged so much he resembled a clown.

Got you.

Sure that he'd located their bag man, Oyster watched the boy's routine. It was typical cup-and-ball schtick, he knew the drill. Like all short cons, the trick was to avoid listening to the charmer in front of you and consider what was actually going on.

The whole point of the gag was that when the shuffle ended, the ball wasn't under *any* of the cups; it was, in fact, in the kid's hand waiting to be tossed beneath whichever cup hadn't been chosen. And having lost the first shuffle, Oyster knew this kid was a lefty.

Here we go. The boy ran another shuffle, the ball flying from one cup to another.

"Second chance, the choice is yours!" said the kid.

Oyster reached towards the middle cup, but then grabbed the kid's left wrist and twisted it up with a jerk that opened their fingers.

"Unhand me, muffbuggler!" he squealed as the tiny ball rolled from his hand and plopped into the mud. *From here on in it was going to get messy.* With his other hand, Oyster knocked the cups from the table.

They hadn't even landed before the crew muscle was bounding across the street, dodging between pedestrians. Oyster grabbed his shoes from the table and released the boy's wrist.

"Sorry about this," said Oyster. "Admire your grift and all, but you've gotta do what you've gotta do."

He gave the boy a good shove, sending him backwards into the road.

The bag man in the makeup was on the move too, legging up the street at a pace that was as fast as he could go without drawing undue attention. Oyster stepped behind a passing sedan chair, hopping to slip on his muddy shoes while simultaneously keeping Mr Muscle at bay and his eyes on the bag man. If they were anything like his crew, Wiggy here would have standing orders to run back to base with their takings if things went south.

Luckily for Oyster, their muscle was more interested in rescuing his protégé from the mud than catching him. He had no difficulty dodging under one side of the sedan chair and emerging from the other. He flicked his hoodie up over his head and doubled his pace to catch up with the man in the wig, determined to follow him to their crib. This was all going to plan.

Oyster almost ran straight into a pair of clerks in ruby glasses, picking their way through the mud, their iron tongs swinging from their belts. He didn't think it likely they would be after him, but it wasn't worth taking any risks.

The bag man looked over his shoulder before hurrying down a side street next to a great, ridged slab of brutalist concrete protruding out of the ground at an angle. The building looked as though it had just grown there. At its foot were two men slumped on the kerb. Drunks or, just possibly, the addicts Nonesuch had told him about. Perhaps he was on the right track.

The street ran around the side of the concrete building and another team of clerks lurked at its far end. If this shine business was illegal, they either didn't seem to know about it or didn't care enough to intervene. Oyster scurried towards the building, tailgating two women in silk dresses who giggled to each other behind folding fans. He held his breath as he passed the clerks, itching distractedly at his tattoo, but they took no notice of him.

He was about as close to the bag man as he could get, so he dropped back a little and considered what he would do if and when he made it to their crib. *Just take it a stage at a time.* No doubt he'd have to improvise.

But then suddenly, pain flared in his forehead and he saw stars. He fell backwards and landed on his back, his temple throbbing. Mr Muscle loomed over him, and the kid he'd pushed into the mud aimed a kick at Oyster's legs.

"That's the fucker!" the boy said, pointing at him.

The pair went through his pockets, exchanging a glance when they unfolded his map.

Muscle dragged him to his feet and hustled him through the street. Oyster was too woozy to do anything but comply, and in any case, something *like* this had been part of the plan.

"Try to turn over Doctor Lazenby or her crew and we return the favour," said the kid. He addressed himself to the man. "This paper-skull here was after information. Could be a jackdaw incognito. If he makes a squeak, feel at liberty to give him a milling, Monsieur Patteepan."

They passed beneath canopies and over walkways that smelled of sewage and booze. pushing him towards a low metal door set into one of the windows of the building's rear. They knocked. Oyster pretended to be woozier than he was.

"Watchword?" came a muffled request from the other side of the door.

"Mind your beeswax," replied the one called Patteepan.

The door swung open, and they passed through a plastic beaded curtain and into the hall within.

Immediately, Oyster's nostrils were stung by clouds of tobacco smoke. He rubbed his eyes and coughed, waiting for them to adjust to the low light. When they'd recovered, he saw a row of people sitting on long benches, poring over steaming saucers of thick, black coffee. The building's high windows were covered with heavy curtains, transforming the greenish daylight into a sickly trickle.

They passed through another beaded curtain, up a narrow

flight of stairs, and into a cramped room dominated by plastic office furniture.

Behind the desk sat a woman of about Paris's age wearing a bowler hat and a linen suit. She was reading a well-thumbed copy of a book titled *Foucault's Pendulum* and smoking a tightly wrapped cigarillo. She ignored the new arrivals as they entered and continued reading, pausing only to take long drags from her tobacco. There was a tattoo over her right eye in the Celtic style that all the Mannish seemingly favoured. Nonesuch had been right, this lot were clearly connected to them somehow.

The kid cleared his throat and the woman looked up, apparently surprised to see them standing there.

"Why in the name of the Lid are you disturbing my philosophical time?" Her voice was much more refined than Oyster had expected.

"Apologies, Doctor Lazenby, ma'am. We apprehended this villain trying to turn over one of the games," Patteepan stuttered, surprisingly anxious for such a large man.

"So, cut the cull's throat, throw him in the river," said Lazenby without even glancing at Oyster.

"Would have done so already, Doctor Ma'am, but the roger here was carrying these upon their person."

Patteepan placed Oyster's map and Nonesuch's dog whistle on the desk.

The woman unfolded the map, looking long and hard at the symbol Marya Petrovna had drawn at its centre. Her cigarillo crackled as she took a long drag.

"He was sticking his nose in about the Mannish, too," squeaked the kid.

"Well, this is unexpected, however welcome," she said before licking her fingers and squeezing the cigarillo's tip until it was extinguished. She lay it in a ceramic ashtray and addressed herself to the boy.

"Master Finter, go bring in some padding for our guest's behind. And fetch up some saucers of the finest and freshest. We're going to have ourselves a little parlay."

35

PARLAY

"What is your name?" asked Doctor Lazenby. She smiled and her green eyes glittered.

"John, uh, Elton," Oyster replied.

"So, Mr Elton," continued Lazenby, placing a long, pale finger precisely on the centre of the map. "Do you have any idea what this might be?"

Oyster remembered what Nonesuch had told him about this crew needing a walker. But it might be best to play it dumb. Maybe by continuing to let them have the upper hand he could get some more info out of them yet.

"To be honest, doc, I haven't got the foggiest. I lifted it from this demented old lady." He was only half-lying, he figured.

Oyster watched Lazenby. He calculated that she was used to deference, so winding her up might force a misstep of some sort. But it was also a dangerous game. Push too far and he could easily end up with his throat cut.

"It's *Doctor* Lazenby," she corrected. "And that is a shame, since it means you are not useful to me."

"Ah," said Oyster.

"*Ah*, indeed," she replied.

"This is why it's always important to ask the right questions, your doctorship," Oyster said. "I might not know *what* it is exactly, but I have a pretty good grasp of how to use it."

"And?" asked Lazenby.

"It lets me, uh, *flit*," he said.

"Flit?"

"Move. From one place to another. Without passing through the intervening space," he replied.

Lazenby smiled like a shark.

There was a knock at the door. The boy returned with a chair and a friend who held two steaming saucers of black coffee. They placed the chair behind Oyster and the saucers on the table. Patteepan pressed Oyster into his seat with a grunt.

"Please, make yourself at home," said Lazenby.

"Don't take this the wrong way," he said, "but I have a condition. Can't drink caffeinated beverages. Bad for my anxiety."

"Is that so," she replied. "In which case, best to place all our cards upon the table, no?"

She nodded to Patteepan, who grabbed Oyster's arms and tugged them over his head.

The boy, Finter, probed under Oyster's armpits with a pair of the iron tongs that he had seen on the clerks. They gripped Syzygy and tugged. At the implement's touch she went limp, but squealed in protest. The pain was sudden and intense. She held onto some point under his arm with razor teeth. He yelped in agony.

"I've no wish to pull lumps from you," said Lazenby. "But trust that I will. Best to release your little friend here. Don't want to harm them."

"Leave off then!" he called out through gritted teeth.

Finter released the nuajin and seconds later she crept out from beneath Oyster's clothes. Finter scooped her up and stuffed her into a hessian drawstring bag along with the dog whistle, placing them on the desk next to the map.

"Hey! Be gentle with her," cried Oyster. The discomfort at being separated from Syzygy rose up in him again.

"Now, perhaps we can continue," said Lazenby. "Your appearance here, at this time, can only be a sign of the Great Providence at work. And if we're going to be working together, we will need to trust one another. That is a fundamental. So, let us drink to our joint enterprise." She took the nearest saucer and expertly sipped it without spilling a drop.

Oyster tried to do the same. The coffee lapped viscously as he lifted it to his lips. He took a mouthful of the liquid. It was thick and oily, and so full of grounds it was like drinking a cup of soot. Choking, he forced it down and returned the saucer to the table. He would never complain about Starbucks again.

He cleared his throat.

"Sorry, but I think I've skipped a track here. When did we say we were working together?"

Lazenby eyed him and swallowed another mouthful.

"Very well, Mr Elton, you clearly wish to hop, skip and jump directly to beating the bird from the bush. It is my professional opinion that you will find a partnership preferable to the other alternatives I have to offer."

Oyster nodded.

"To put it plain. A group of honest craftsfolk such as my own here have need of a fellow with your ingenious talents."

"So you want me to boost shit for you?" Why was it that everywhere he went people wanted him to work for them?

Lazenby waved his words away with another serpentine smile.

"By the great tree! A trapdoor like a thrice-damned beldam on this one, eh, gentlemen?" she said, addressing the comment to the rest of her crew. "Filch? Never! But there *is* a higher-up in my organisation who has demanded we secure some portable property for them."

Oyster nodded thoughtfully. He was out of options here, but that didn't mean he couldn't put some stakes in the ground.

"So if this is a partnership, what's in it for me?" he said.

Lazenby took another long sip of coffee and regarded him. Her green eyes looked deep into him, weighing him up. The smell of tobacco wafted up from the room below. He held her gaze.

"Well, for one thing, we will forget about the little contretemps betwixt you, Master Finter and Monsieur Patteepan, so you will get to retain your melon where it will do us all the most good."

She tightened the drawstring of the bag holding Syzygy.

"And secondly, you get your little pet here returned to you."

This had not at all gone the way that Oyster had expected, but perhaps he could still play the situation out. Whatever Motet had been onto here, his best bet was to follow the same trail.

"Alright, alright. Let's say I do help you out. I got a weak hand here. But I *do* want something for myself." He leaned forward, out of earshot of Lazenby's crew. "How about hooking a person up with some glimmer."

Lazenby tilted her head quizzically and pulled the brim of her bowler hat down.

"And what would make you think I'd know anything about that?" she replied.

"A person hears things," he said.

"You'll excuse me," she looked him up and down, "but you don't have the look of a shinehead."

"Just need a taste, that's all."

Lazenby shrugged. She folded the map back into a compact rectangle on the desk and tapped it.

"Very well. Your poison is your own account. I'll consider it if you help us. In any case, I shall be holding onto this for a little while longer, understand? Can't have you dashing hence unexpectedly."

She looked at Patteepan and Finter.

"Right, take brother beautrap here below till the hour arrives."

Oyster sat in a low-ceilinged cellar. The textured concrete walls were damp, and the moisture leeched into his borrowed coat and skirt. A cup of metallic-tasting water sat by his feet and his chin rested on his naked knees. He was unsure exactly what he'd landed himself in. He thought he'd known what he was doing when he'd gotten in here, but now, as he sat in the damp and the dark, he was a lot less sure of himself. Maybe Marya Petrovna had got into his head with all her talk about symbolic codes.

He could hear Lucas's voice admonishing him for not taking

control of the situation more. Cécile reminding him that he had been a complete donkey for having a plan to get in somewhere but not much more than the vaguest notion of how he might get back out.

The only light came from a slim, barred window set into its ceiling that opened onto the alley beyond at street level. The separation anxiety at being apart from Syzygy had its claws into him now, too. He hoped they were taking care of her.

In the opposite corner were sacks of coffee embossed with the letters E, I and C. He stood and hauled a pair of the sacks till they were beneath the window and climbed up on them to see out into the street beyond. He tested the bars. There was no escape route here.

The cloying stink of the city pressed in on Oyster as soon as he drew near. Dusk was already falling. The days here were much shorter than the ones in his London, he thought.

From his vantage point, Greater London's crimson sun was visible as it set over the eaves of one of the houses. Oyster shuddered. Again, he was struck by the sensation that it was looking at him as much as he was looking at it.

The traffic in the street had slackened by now. Men and women with powdered faces, silken topcoats, periwigs and assorted accessories from other centuries still strode up and down the streets, but they were fewer in number. There were hardly any hand-carried sedans, but Oyster saw a single, snoring human being conveyed in a gilt chair mounted on the shoulders of one unlucky gebel. A street cart carrying sweetly spiced food made its way past the window and Oyster's stomach grumbled. It was a while since he had eaten.

As the sun dipped below the buildings, a low bell tolled across the city and the mood of the traffic changed. People moved more quickly and with more purpose. There were suddenly more clerks visible, too.

A pair rattled though the street in the first wheeled vehicle Oyster had seen. Its passengers rode in two leather seats up front and open to the elements, while the rear comprised a padlocked compartment fitted with wire grilles. The overall impression it gave was of a jail cell mounted precariously on a pair of penny farthings.

The machine was steered via a brass yoke and a long metal handle protruded from the chassis on the side visible to Oyster. The enormous springs sprouting from its axles suggested the ride through the Greater London streets was probably an uncomfortable one.

The vehicle drew up with a clatter like the workings of an enormous clock. The clerks within dismounted and began to patrol, while the remaining street traffic made itself scarce. Curfew had begun.

Wind whipped down through the window and a low mist blew in. Sleet fell from the sky and some ice particles settled on Oyster's face. Just as on the beach, he could see that each one contained a tiny paper word, but this time he couldn't be arsed to read them.

With a sigh, he let himself down from the sacks and walked over to the door.

"Hello!" he called. Perhaps he could convince his captors to bring him something to eat.

"Oi!" he shouted again. "I'm hungry." But there was no reply.

He sat despondently and drank some of the water from his cup, realising he'd need to ration it as he wasn't sure how long he would be down here. In the corner opposite the coffee beans was an orange plastic bucket. Okay. No prizes for guessing what that was for. He rested his chin back on his knees, figuring he would just have to see what fresh indignity tomorrow might bring.

36
INTENTIONAL VACUITY

The cellar door swung wide open and Monsieur Patteepan stood in front of him. Wan daylight streamed in through the window. Oyster was groggy and had slept badly, mostly on his side, curled beneath his borrowed coat. All of his clothes were damp and musty. The compressed nature of Greater London's day–night cycle was really doing him in.

"Wake up, rantipole!" yelled Patteepan, aiming a kick at Oyster's buttocks with a booted foot.

"No need," groaned Oyster. "I'm awake."

"Who said anything about there being a 'need'?" replied Patteepan. "I just wanted to check if my boot fitted up your jacksie."

He dragged Oyster into a sitting position.

"Get your arse collected, beetle-pate. Your big day, so it is."

Oyster drained the remains of the water from his cup.

"Food?" said Oyster.

"You'll break your fast with the rest of us," said Patteepan, "no special favours here. And certainly not for you."

Without any further interaction, Patteepan marched him past a pair of heavy-looking cellar doors and upstairs, where he was served with a bowl of watery porridge at a communal metal bench. It was grim, but he forced it down.

As he finished eating, Dr Lazenby came down from her office. Today she was dressed in an expensive-looking, plum-coloured suit with matching tie and cream stack-heeled platform shoes. She was smoking a liquorice-scented cheroot.

She beckoned Oyster with a finger.

"We have plans for you today. Monsieur Patteepan, conduct our guest up to the derrick."

Oyster was guided upstairs, but instead of taking him to Lazenby's office they pushed through a door that opened out onto the building's roof.

"How's the fetch played, then?" she asked. "I'm cognisant all you walkers have differing gimmicks, foreign maps, pamphlets and symbols. Do we need to say 'ala-ka-zee-ala-kazam'? Must we anoint you with saint's breath and submerge you in the sap of the holy tree herself?" There was a mocking edge to her words.

Oyster blinked in the daylight. Plumes of ink beetles eddied overhead. The ruddy ball of the sun winked at him from low on the horizon. Odd as it was, there were similarities to his London. The rattle and hum from the streets as clockwork carriages dodged pedestrians. The constant assault of smells both alluring and nose-wrinkling. He was suddenly struck by the peculiar and specific beauty of this place. If he did end up stranded here, it might be a place he could come to love.

He breathed in a lungful of the fishy air. Right. *This was it.*

"Nah. None of that mumbo jumbo." He tried to think back to what Marya Petrovna had said. "It's all about… uh… intentional vacuity."

"Is it indeed? You don't sound terribly sure," said Lazenby. "But just so that we're both clear in our understanding, if you're unable to perform, Monsieur Patteepan here will cut you another smile. If the day denies us other wonders, then at least we shall see you swim to the bottom of the river."

"Yeah, I'm sure," said Oyster, affecting a nonchalant air he did not feel. "Before we get in to all that, though, you need to get me up to speed on what the gag is here? Can't be going anywhere if I don't know the destination."

Lazenby nodded and dragged on her cheroot. She exuded a stream of dark smoke that twisted up into the morning air. She turned her back on him and looked over the city, up to the Lid and the billowing clouds painted on its surface.

"As you'll remember from our exchange yesterday, collect and return is the name of today's game."

Reaching into her waistcoat, she produced a yellowed scrap of paper and handed it to Oyster. It was thick, marked with age and covered with scribbles and symbols that he did not understand. In its centre was a rough sketch of three coins.

The coins were marked on both sides. One showed an antlered, crossed-legged figure, holding a snake. On the other was a crude, hulking figure holding a spear. He drew in a breath in surprise. The coins, and the figures on them, reminded him of the nightmare he'd had the day before Primrose had fucked him over on the bridge.

"Not what you were expecting?" said Lazenby.

Oyster caught himself and waved her concerns away with a hand.

"Nah. S'all cool." But he felt far from it.

"Your task is simple. Lift these coins and restore them to me," she said.

He held out the sketch. "Is this all I've got to go on?"

"The boss says it should be easily located one you've arrived at your destination, but that last part is the trick," said Lazenby.

"Easy for you to say," replied Oyster.

"Indeed. And we had a much more involved infiltration plan before your arrival, but one has to take advantage of life's sudden opportunities."

He stared at the paper, trying to imprint the image of the coins on his memory, then slipped it into his pocket.

"You'll be needing this too, no doubt," said Lazenby, pulling his map from her jacket and handing it to him.

Oyster accepted it with a nod. *Now what?* His tattoo continued to tingle. It was reassuringly painful. He had come to the point now where he understood that the pain in his midriff was generally a message that he was on the right track. He took the map and unfolded it, trying to remember what Marya Petrovna had told him.

Belief is the tool that will open the crack in the world.

It was all about making his head empty of distractions. If the old lady had been there, she would've come up with some sort of crack about that, he thought ruefully.

He looked at the symbol Marya Petrovna had scrawled on the map and took a few deep breaths, blowing out his cheeks. He hummed a few times in a way that he hoped sounded appropriately mystical. Nothing happened.

Doctor Lazenby cleared her throat.

"No pressure. But we are waiting," she said. She removed the pocket watch from her waistcoat and consulted it.

"Yeah, yeah," he said. "I've just got to be in the right state of mind."

"No doubt," she replied. "But don't be too shy on it, Monsieur Patteepan and I are on a deadline."

In a jitter, he considered the other times he had been able to move between his world and Greater London. The first time he had been pummelled by the Mannish and out of his head with fear over the consequences of losing Mickey's cash. The second time was when he'd been pushed off the building by Primrose. Maybe what activated this ability was a sense of immediate threat?

This might be proper nuts, thought Oyster, *but you couldn't express your belief much more powerfully than by being in harm's way, could you?*

He swallowed and turned to Lazenby.

"Throw me," he said.

The woman's face creased in confusion.

"Please do not shit in our soup, whoreson."

"No, seriously," he replied, not quite believing that he was saying the words. "Throw me over the edge. It's the quickest way."

Patteepan grunted and cracked his knuckles with a smile.

"What angle are you playing here, Mr Elton?" Lazenby prodded his chest with the unlit end of her cheroot.

"None," said Oyster. "All part of the process, straight up."

Lazenby shrugged.

"Very well," she said, "do as he says."

With that, Patteepan grabbed Oyster by the shoulders and manhandled him to the building's edge. The muddy ground below whirled giddily. Faced with the sudden reality of his choice, an animal fear welled within him. He yelled out and tried to dig his feet into the slates to stop himself from toppling over, but Patteepan was twice his size and had him off-balance. The map flapped as Oyster windmilled his arms in an effort to stay put.

"Hey, wait a minute," he said. "I've got another—"

"Fly, you little prick," said Patteepan and tipped him over the edge. Oyster just had the opportunity to glance at the map before he and it were both tumbling through the air.

37
SOMETHING DIFFERENT

Oyster fell backwards. He saw the copper-tinted sky and its spiralling artificial clouds. The map fluttered in his hand like an ineffectual paper wing. He remembered that he'd left Nonesuch's coat in his cell, and then he wondered if he was going to die. Everything was happening very slowly. And he chuckled, realising what a commonplace that must be. *Is my life going to flash before my eyes?* he thought.

Instead, he remembered the last time he and Cécile had gone to Tooting Bec Lido, a couple of summers ago. Even though he couldn't swim, she'd insisted that he accompany her and get in the pool too. So, they'd spent the whole afternoon mucking about in the freezing water.

Later, he'd forked out for both of them to get ice creams and they'd sat on the pool's concrete lip, paddling their feet in the water under the blazing afternoon sun. He remembered the taste of that ice cream now, like velvet melting on his tongue.

Pain blossomed in his shoulder, and he realised he must have hit something on the way down. *This was a dick idea*, he thought, as the impact sent him spinning and then he hit the ground, and everything went black.

He opened his eyes. His shoulder ached like fuck. His outstretched tongue pressed into something furry and wet, and he couldn't smell fish anymore. His shoulder *really* hurt. Perhaps he'd dislocated it. He opened his eyes. He tried to move, but his body hurt all over.

"Well, look who it isn't," came a voice that Oyster recognised only too well. It was Mr Primrose. "To be honest, we were expecting something like this. We thought you'd have to come and find us sooner or later."

Primrose leaned over, bringing his strange mixture of scents with him, smells that triggered images in Oyster's head that he couldn't control. This time it was something like a field of wheat rippling in the summer sun, with undertones of something dead and putrefying in one of its far corners.

Primrose hoisted Oyster into a sitting position with his back against a crumbling plaster wall. Opposite him, at the other end of the room, was a high window with jagged cracks running top to bottom. He was in what once might have been an expensively furnished flat. Some sort of internal guidance mechanism told him that he wasn't in Greater London anymore. The fact that he could only see sky through the window suggested that wherever they were, it must be pretty high up.

The moment Primrose touched him, the pain in his shoulder evaporated.

"How'd you do that?" asked Oyster.

"Just one of our gifts," shrugged Primrose. He was dressed as usual in a long black trench coat that twitched as though it contained a flock of birds. Oyster had the distinct impression he was looking at someone composed of multiple parts all moving independently.

"We could instruct you, if you were with us. There are things we need to tell you. Things that would change everything you know."

Now the pain was gone, he could think straight. Of all the places he'd expected to end up, he hadn't expected to find Primrose here. He needed to think fast.

"That's why I'm here," said Oyster. "I want to know more. You told me you could help me, so here I am, like."

Primrose regarded him slyly. Oyster wasn't sure the man believed him, but it was worth a gamble. Primrose's mock-heroic features arranged themselves into a smile. They were even more peculiar than the first time Oyster had laid eyes on him. A collection of features that lacked any unifying principle. The eyes were too black and too widely spaced, the nose suspended in the middle of the face and the mouth too thin and lipless. The face they comprised was moving subtly, each of its features pulling away from every other. It was a face that only existed, thought Oyster, because Primrose's will held it together.

"So where am I, then?" said Oyster.

"Somewhere different," replied Primrose. "Neither where you were nor where you have been. Somewhere that existed before either."

"We'll that clears that up, then," he said with a sigh. "Sweet gaff. But didn't have you down for a yuppie. You always struck me more as a white-van-in-the-woods sort of a guy."

Primrose shrugged.

"We are everywhere. You know, 'beneath the paving stones, the beach!' and all that."

"Not really," said Oyster. "So come on then, 'fess up. I know you're dying to. You're the sort who just love to lay it all out. Who are you?"

Oyster put his hand in his pocket and fingered the sketch of the coins. He needed to find them and get back to Lazenby's gaff. The longer he could keep Primrose talking, the more time it gave him to work out where they were. He glanced around the room.

It had seen better days. The crimson luxury of the carpet was matted with moss; high ceilings were mottled with swathes of black mould. A plain wooden table hosted a pair of golden dice whose dots glittered like rubies. To his left was a doorway to a darkened room; to his right, the wall had been marked up with the same antlered figure sprayed on the rear walls of the Clip.

His brain lit up with recognition. Cécile was right, he was such a donkey: the horned creature on Marya Petrovna's tarot card. The graffiti. The figure on the coins. It was all the same person.

Or at least the same thing. So, his jump had brought him to the right place after all. The other coins had to be here. He needed to pick his moment.

"Actually, don't tell me." Oyster nodded at the wall. "I got this one. That's you, then, is it?"

"Finally," Primrose sighed.

"So, you're what, you're like, the Devil?"

Primrose laughed. It was a mirthless hollow sound, like rotten branches rattling on a broken windowpane. He shook his head.

"Guess again. Bit Judaeo-Christian, all that. Bit parochial. Bit twentieth century, frankly. Thought your generation were too post-modern; too sophisticated. But since you ask, we existed before all of this. Before what you call time. We were always here, watching and waiting."

"Boohoo," said Oyster, pretending to wipe his eyes. "Hang on, I'm tearing up here. Don't tell me, you never copped off at parties either."

For an instant, Primrose stopped his constant roiling. There was thunder in his eyes, and he looked at Oyster like prey. Oyster froze. The moment passed and the man smiled.

He pointed a blunt finger in Oyster's face and Oyster noticed for the first time how jerky the man's motions were, as though he were being animated, like some sort of full-size marionette.

"Allow us to expand your horizons. Time, as you laughingly perceive it, is not linear at all. Its deep, underlying structure is cyclical." Primrose's finger drew a circle in front of Oyster's nose. "And we are coming to the end of one of those cycles very, very shortly. Specifically, the one that started thousands of your years ago, during which you lot have had it exclusively your own way. Not to put too fine a point on it, but even the most casual observer would have to conclude that you have made a complete mess of everything you've touched. Your *civilisation*, if we can grace your people's way of organising themselves with that description, is quite royally fucked."

Oyster nodded. He couldn't really argue with Primrose on that one.

"So, what are you going to do, grampus? Are you joining the superglue-your-foreskin-to-the-Tube brigade?"

"Mock them all you like, sonny," said Primrose. "But at least those people intuit what is coming, however dimly. They see now for what it is: an inflection point. All the rest of you just want to get rich posting reaction clips online."

"Quite," said Oyster, "let me get back to you when this lecture concludes."

Primrose sighed.

"There are other ways, *more ancient* ways of being. Ones more rooted in the land. Over these millennia, the forces representing them have been rising, building upon what has come before. They are coalescing. At a certain point, very soon, they will confront the old guard and a choice will have to be made. One between much, much more of the same, accelerating what you have now. And something else, something *different*. You know what we mean. You can feel it too. *We know it.*" He jabbed a finger in Oyster's direction.

Primrose's words struck an unexpected chord within him. As much as he didn't want to admit it, ever since they had met on the bridge Oyster had felt that he'd been locked on a pathway that only led in one direction. That no matter what choices he made, there was something inevitable happening that involved him, and he could not change it.

Primrose's demeanour abruptly changed. He looked at Oyster in a way that seemed almost kind, concerned.

"There are other things we want to tell you. That we *need* to tell you. Believe me. But... they're difficult to say. Perhaps harder for you to hear. We need to get to know each other more first."

Primrose's peculiar expression and hesitant tone was more upsetting than when he was being intimidating. As Oyster looked around the room an unsettling feeling swept up from his stomach. Whatever Primrose wanted to tell him, he didn't want to hear it. He needed to change the subject.

He nodded at the dice on the table.

"So, let's start slow then, my dude. What's that all about, then?"

Primrose sniffed and nodded.

"*A game of chance is a sacred thing*," said Primrose. "With the right tools and words, the future, the past, the present. They're all one thing."

"Oh, that," said Oyster. "I hear that shit all over."

"Ever the joker, eh, young Mr McLellen?"

Oyster was shocked to hear his real name on the man's lips.

"Oh yes," said Primrose. "We know who you are."

Oyster scanned the room. Apart from the door to the left, there was nowhere the coins he was after could be stashed. He glanced at the doorway. For the first time, he realised he was being watched. Multiple pairs of animal eyes glinted in the darkness of the room beyond. He shuddered.

"What the heck?" said Oyster. "You keeping pets here?"

Primrose shrugged.

"These are our friends. Don't bother them and they won't bother you," he replied.

Oyster needed to shift the conversation's dynamic somehow, try to get Primrose off guard. Or at least off his home turf.

"I hope you let the landlord know. That looks like a fuck-ton of kitty litter."

"Yet more jokes," said Primrose.

"Speaking of jokers," replied Oyster, "what about Deano, eh? What you two up to there?"

Oyster was gratified to see shock appear on Primrose's mask of a face for an instant. He needed to lift what he'd come for and then skidoosh before the man could talk to him anymore. Even thinking about the secrets that the creep might be nursing made him feel nauseated.

"Oh, so the boy has some game after all," replied Primrose. "And what do you know about that?"

"Me and Broadsie know enough," blurted Oyster. "Seen you slipping round the Clip with Deano. Sure Mickey would be interested in that little titbit."

As soon as the words were out of his mouth, he realised his mistake. He'd been so encouraged at seeing Primrose thrown off his stride, he'd said too much. *Fuck! Fuck! Fuck!* How could he have been so stupid!

Primrose smiled again. He put his hand in his coat pocket and produced Oyster's map. He waved it at him.

"Oh dear me. Well, you'll excuse us. We suddenly have some business to attend to. Don't go anywhere now, will you?"

Primrose stepped past Oyster and was gone.

38
ANIMAL HOUSE

Oyster wanted to punch himself. How could he have been so cocky as to let Primrose in on what he and Broadsides knew? He needed to warn his friend that he'd have to lie even lower than he was already, but since Primrose had his map there was really nothing he could do about that now. He had better make the most of the man's absence.

One step at a time. He stood. His legs ached at being sat down for so long. At least with Primrose out of the way, he could look for the coins. Marya Petrovna's words rang in his head again. *Belief is the key.* Yet, here he was stranded again. He considered that perhaps her advice wasn't that useful.

He pulled out Lazenby's sketch and looked at it, asking it to show him where the coins might be hidden. He walked over to the window to see if he could get some sense of where he was, but the view was clogged with fog. Perhaps they were so high up that this was cloud cover.

There were no exits other than the door leading to the room on the left. *Shit.* He took a deep breath. From his vantage point by the window, the room looked pitch black. He gripped the coin tightly. It was slick with sweat. He took a deep breath and edged up to the doorway. The menagerie of eyes regarded him silently.

"Hey there," he called softly. "Good doggies. Or kitties. Or whatever you are. I don't mean you any harm. Just need to get my arse past you and out of this shithole."

He stepped through the door. There was no reaction from Primrose's private zoo. As Oyster waited for his own eyes to grow accustomed to the dark, he was aware he could hear the slow panting of the creatures surrounding him. Gradually, he was able to make out multiple shapes in the darkness. And although he had never been much of a nature boy, he saw specimens of every animal he might encounter out in the wider countryside: badgers and foxes, wildcats, ravens and other birds. There were some animals he didn't recognise that might have been weasels or polecats; even a couple of wolves. Yet, all were silent; all had their eyes fixed upon him. The only sound he heard was the sound of their breathing. He fought the overwhelming urge to turn tail and leave. *The only way out of here is through this room*, he told himself.

The ground crunched beneath his feet. He looked down. It wasn't solid, rather it was loose earth. *Weird.*

"Okay," he said, "I'm coming through. Don't eat me, please." He took another step and another and the darkness swallowed him. The smell was musky and foetid, reminding Oyster of the smell of London Zoo.

As he progressed, the creatures' eyes followed him, but none of them moved from their places. His fear abated and he was struck by the sensation that, as odd as it felt, he was welcome here. He was, after all, just an animal, here in the dark, amongst fellow animals.

Reaching the centre of the room, his heart jumped as he caught sight of a figure standing a few yards away.

It took Oyster an entire minute to realise that he was looking at just another portrait of Primrose, inked onto the rear wall. In the lowlight, he saw that unlike the one in the lounge, this portrait showed the phantom antlers Oyster had noticed on the bridge, either side of Primrose's head. One of his hands was outstretched, curving into a cross between a bony tusk and a branching horn; a curious combination of the human and the bestial.

As Oyster watched, its misshapen fingers writhed. He gulped in air, rubbed his eyes; his heart set off beating wildly again. Sweat tickled down his spine. He thought of the portrait on the coin. Of course! These weren't fingers at all, but snakes exiting through a hole in the wall.

This had to be it, then. He approached the picture, sidestepping a pair of squirrels that sat on their haunches watching him. It was odd how none of the animals in the room were upset by his presence.

"Sorry fellas," he said.

He examined the picture. The closer he got to it, the more his tattoo spasmed in pain. *Okay, I get it*, he thought. *This is important.* The drawing was much more detailed than the one in the lounge and had been completed in colour. It reminded him of a cave painting of some sort, and the Primrose figure formed only part of the composition. Off to its left was a rough figure holding a spear surrounded by wolves. Both stood either side of a great tree that blossomed in the darkness. In the trunk of the tree stood a figure holding three coins, surrounded by a loop of words that Oyster recognised immediately as the same as his tattoo and Marya Petrovna's Zig-Zag cabinet. The entire picture was dominated by a dark three-headed creature that loomed over everything.

Shit! This was exactly what he'd seen in his dream. Images tumbled through his head. The flashes of lightning. The freaky face of the young woman. His knees went weak. He forced himself to take a deep breath. He mustn't get distracted. Whatever fucked-up shit this was, he had to stay focused on the task at hand. He exhaled and drew closer to the painting.

The snakes were squeezing through a fist-sized hole in the mural, where Primrose's hand was located. Oyster took a breath. This seemed to be the most likely hiding place for the other coins. He knelt and tried to see what might be in there, but it gave up nothing. Counting to three, he slipped his hand into the hole in the wall. He forced himself not to yelp as the snakes slithered past his skin, but they were warmer and softer than he'd expected. There was nothing slimy or scaly about them at all.

"Don't get bit, don't get bit, don't get bit," he chanted in a low voice, as the reptiles glided past his arm and onto the floor. His arm slid into the wall up to his elbow. Finally, his probing fingers reached something soft and yielding. Pinching it between his index and middle fingers, he pulled it out of the hole little by little. He had to be quick, Primrose might return at any minute. The bag fell to the earthy floor with a thud. Yes!

It was a leather purse closed with a twine drawstring. He had to admit, it didn't look like much, but he grabbed it anyway. As he did so, he felt a sting and dropped the bag with a yelp. A snake wormed away from beneath it. *Fuck!* He tried to remember if there were any poisonous snakes in Britain, and then realised with a gulp that probably wasn't even where he was right now. What were you supposed to do exactly?

He was sure he'd seen people suck out venom in movies, but that must be total bullshit. Examining his hand, the back of his palm was marked with a pair of puncture wounds about half an inch apart. He pressed the back of his hand to his mouth and sucked anyway, spitting onto the earth beside him. Who knew if it would work, but it couldn't hurt, could it? He repeated the process a couple of times. The area around the tooth marks looked swollen already. He was okay, though. At least so far.

Taking more care, he picked up the bag and emptied it onto the floor. Three coins, identical to the ones in Lazenby's illustration, lay face up on the soil. *One step at a time. One step at a time.* He scooped them back up and tossed them into the bag. Adrenaline pulsed through his body, putting him on edge.

Something shifted subtly in the room's atmosphere, as one by one the animals all turned back to face the door behind him. There was a keening, expectant air.

"Where are you, boy?" called Primrose from the lounge.

Oyster jumped at the sound. He balled up the purse and pocketed it. Primrose was back.

One step at a time, so far, had got him into nothing but trouble. He needed a plan, and he needed his map. He turned and picked his way back through the room's furry sentinels, noting for the first time that the door jamb was host to an ant colony, whose members swarmed and boiled over the wood like a procession of exclamation marks.

Primrose stood in the centre of the lounge. Broodingly staring at the blank canvas of the sky.

"We thought we told you to stay put," he said, fixing him with a quizzical stare. "What have you been up to?"

"Nothing," said Oyster, keeping his bitten hand in his pocket. It was beginning to ache, and he felt light-headed.

"Somehow, we doubt that," replied Primrose. "*Nothing* doesn't appear to be in your nature."

Oyster shrugged. He needed to get his map back and then get gone. Time to use a different skill. If he remembered rightly, it was in Primrose's left pocket. He needed to keep him talking.

"In any case, your antics will have no effect. I've settled things on that side for now," Primrose said.

"What is?" replied Oyster. "What have you done, you creepy fucker?"

"Nothing that you need concern yourself with now, young gentleman."

Oyster pointed out the window into the blankness beyond. He needed to keep him off the scent of what he'd just lifted. The man loved the sound of his own voice. Maybe he could exploit that.

"Just admiring your artwork back there," he said. "Not at all disturbing. Or narcissistic. I suppose your bedroom is full of pictures of you in the nud, too?"

Primrose looked exasperated. After a long moment he continued.

"That is the Trian ritual. Through it, Lugones, the old gods of the three – Taranis, Esus and Tuetates – are conjoined. The bearer of the coins chooses a vessel and the triple godhead possesses them. Potent juju. With that power the vessel can do anything. They can change the future. Or the past. Do try and keep up. We did say a choice was coming."

Oyster swallowed. There was a buzzing in his ears now and he was sick to his stomach. He jabbed at the window with his left hand. The other one was hurting quite badly now, but he'd still need to use it. Once he'd manoeuvred Primrose so that he had a chance of getting to his nearest pocket.

"What's out there, then? And why do you have a bunch of animals holed up here?"

"Questions, questions and questions, eh? Well. Last things first," the man sighed. "It is in our nature to bring unlike things together, just as mischief is in yours. And as for where we are – well, let us merely say that things are not entirely what they seem here. What we see is merely an echo of what underlies, not so different from your city in a way, actually."

Primrose faced the window, sweeping an arm out with his stop-motion jerkiness. Oyster risked a glance down. Primrose's left pocket gaped invitingly. Oyster could even see one of the map's folded edges protruding. This was the moment.

He leaned forward and banged the windowpane with his good hand, while simultaneously slipping his swollen hand out of his own pocket and into Primrose's. His fingers were thick and inflamed, hard to manipulate. It felt like he was wearing gloves. But he had the map between his thumb and forefinger.

"Seems pretty real to me," he said to Primrose, thumping the glass once more for good measure.

And then he didn't have the map anymore.

"Do you really think we're that green?" Primrose grabbed Oyster's aching hand in his own with surprising dexterity. In his other hand he held the map, flicking it partially open. The top end of Marya Petrovna's sigil peered at him over a paper fold like a winking eye.

"What *do* we have here, we wonder? Ah. Of course. The hag's handiwork," said Primrose. "You know, you really are too trusting of that one. She has her own agenda. Has her own uses for you and your talents. Perhaps you should ask *her* about the Trian ritual."

The pressure on Oyster's swollen hand was unbearable and he cried out in pain, his knees buckling as the nausea from the snake bite took its toll. The buzzing in his ears was loud now.

Primrose registered the bite on Oyster's hand.

"Oh dear," he said, his black eyes glittering, "someone has been a very naughty boy, haven't they? Fancy that. Having the temerity to try stealing from us? Where are they, then? Our coins?"

Oyster looked up. He couldn't hear Primrose over the buzzing in his ears now and his vision was distorted. He looked up at the map and the symbol, and made a grab for it with his other hand. He caught its edge in his fingers. His tattoo twisted with pain as though it had been inked in fire. The only thought in his dizzy mind was that he needed to be somewhere else.

And then he was.

NOTHING IS TRUE. EVERYTHING IS PERMITTED.

Oyster spun end-over-end like a spoke in a slowly rotating wheel. It was dark. His mind winked on and off like a faulty light bulb. He didn't know how long he had been here, but he sensed it had been an age. It was the same exaggerated sense of time you got between successive blasts on the snooze button on cold winter mornings. Time enough for lifetimes to begin and end.

His floating body was alternately on fire and freezing and he was disassociated from what was going on around him. *This must be the fever brought on by the snake bite*, he thought, and then the buzzing sound rose in his ears and a wave of nausea swept over him and he retched. There was no gravity; no up; no down. He tried to remember how he had ended up here, because he thought he might never have been anywhere else. But that wasn't true. No. He had been with Primrose. Primrose had caught him and then he'd ended up here.

He was struck by the idea that he might never return to his own London, that this netherworld, or whatever it was, might be it. Maybe he'd live out what remained of his life here. He turned the thought over. It wasn't as terrifying as it he expected it to be. He'd just stay here indefinitely, no more problems with Big Mickey and Deano and the rest of his crew. No more running away from Primrose or being insulted by Marya Petrovna. No more weird shit. Just darkness and quiet forever.

No more Cécile?

And what about Broadsides?

Then the terror of being alone here, forever and ever, crept into him through a door left open at the back of his mind. An icy thought on spider legs, it crept and crept and grew and grew until he was shivering and scared, spinning alone in the depths of absolutely nothing, alone and forgotten in an empty universe devoid of life or love or meaning or anything at all.

A prickling at the back of his neck made Oyster realise that he wasn't alone. There was someone else here. Somewhere in the distance of this infinite nothing, someone was humming. It was the sort of absent-minded sound Oyster could imagine would be made by someone intent on some other task; a person doing some knitting or darning a sock.

And then the humming transformed into singing. The voice belonged to a woman, and Oyster recognised her immediately as the one from his dreams, that first night in Marya Petrovna's flat.

"*In stiller Nacht, zur ersten Wacht,
ein Stimm begunnt zu klagen...*"

The melody was both melancholically beautiful and chilling simultaneously. The singing came closer and so did the singer. He strained to see who it might be, but the darkness yielded nothing. And then he closed his eyes tight, suddenly overwhelmed by the fear of what he might see. As lonely as he had been seconds ago, he didn't want to attract attention.

The singing was strong and clear, suddenly darting to a point right in front of him as he cartwheeled in the black.

"*...ist mir das Herz zerflossen,
die Blümelein,
mit Tränen rein
hab ich sie all begossen.*"

Silence. It was cold, but his nausea retreated a little. In the quiet that followed, the noises of Oyster's body assumed titanic proportions: his breathing thundered in his ears, blood gurgled in his veins, his stomach grumbled tectonically. He felt dizzy.

"*Ich kann dich sehen*," the woman's voice whispered into his ear. The space around him was engulfed in a power so strong that it positively crackled. He swallowed, enveloped in a sense of wordless awe.

"*Ich kann dich sehen.*"

He yelled in surprise and his arms flailed and his rotation shifted, became quicker. He felt sick.

"For the last time. I don't speak fucking German!" he yelped, hiccupping bile into his mouth.

"Apologies, *liebling*, it is a force of habit. I have become very used to talking to myself," said the voice. "Now, move the arms away from the body and you will slow down."

Oyster did as she said, and was relieved to find that he did indeed turn more slowly. He swallowed the bitter taste.

"Why are you here in *der hinter*?" asked his visitor.

"The what?"

"*Der hinter*, the interval. *Intermezzo. L'entre-deux*. Call it what you like. This location. What you think of as now."

Oyster thought for a second. His natural reticence to spilling his guts about anything had not served him well so far. But where to even start? There was too much to even try to fill in. Maybe best to keep it simple. "I was trying to escape from someone. Protect my sister. Trying to find my dad—"

"Did she tell you about me?" interrupted the presence.

"Who?" said Oyster.

"I think you know."

"I really think I don't."

"Has she replaced me already?" The air suddenly tasted like ozone, as though he was in the centre of an electrical storm. His hair stood to attention. Whoever she was, he really didn't want to upset her.

"No, no, no," said Oyster, holding up his palms in appeasement. "Nothing like that. I'm sure I'm not. Absolutely. Listen, I'd love to be able to help you out, but I really don't know what you mean."

"Love," whispered the voice. "Love is such a numinous thing. One might even say it is the root of both the actualisation and abnegation of the self. The noblest paradox. We are such tiny beings in the cosmic scale. But love. The love that we create and which runs through us, which connects us all, is a thing of the utmost beauty. Simultaneously worth nothing, and yet the binding reason for everything. Consider the universe itself. Such an improbable a thing in the first place. But that it should become self-aware and come to love itself is a wonder of another magnitude altogether."

"Uh yeah. Cool… I guess I never thought of it like that," said Oyster. He wasn't sure that he followed what she was saying, but he didn't want to aggravate her. As terrifying as the presence was, she didn't seem to mean him any harm, at least yet.

"The love of the one for its other. The love of a parent for a child and a child for a parent. The love of a friend for a friend. The love of a friend that blossoms into something else. Silent and unspoken. Unacknowledged. But still there. All the greater, all the deeper for its lack of voice."

Oyster felt like a shepherd on a mountaintop crouching behind a burning bush. He was halfway between coming up on a tab of molly and wetting himself with fear.

"Do you need *meine hilfe*… my help?"

Oyster swallowed. He heard Cécile grumbling about his inability to ever ask for directions or let her help him talk through problems. *This isn't getting lost. I'm literally spinning arse-over-tit in the void*. He had to accept his inhibitions and then just ignore them.

"Yes," said Oyster. "Yes. I don't know where I am, and I need to get back to my friends."

"That is not where you arrived from, though, is it?" she asked.

"No," said Oyster. "I was trying to get away from there and I ended up here. Can you help me? I need to go back to Greater London. People are depending on me."

The power throbbed around Oyster. It was so strong now that he could almost see it. It pressed and probed him, and his tattoo needled him with a brief but intense flash of pain. Fever filled his head with fog.

"You are hurt. But it would also appear you have everything you need."

"He's got my map, though. Primrose. I mean, the man I was trying to escape from," he replied. "I need it to travel."

"As I have told you. You have everything you need."

"But I still need the map. The old lady showed me."

"Nothing is true. Everything is permitted," replied the presence. Oyster shut his eyes, but his mind bubbled with thoughts. All he could picture right now was Primrose's creepy animal house and he did not want to return there any time soon.

"Focus on the result. Do not think about how it is achieved," she said.

Oyster drew in a breath and fought through the fog in his head. He tried to imagine himself stepping into Lazenby's. His tattoo responded with a lick of agony that threaded around his torso. He cried out and the pain vanished. *Okay*, he thought, *maybe this was something.* He tried once more. This time the pain enveloped him for as long as he was able to keep the picture in his head.

"Do not flee the pain," said the presence. "For a woman, life *is* pain."

"Now you really do sound like the old lady," said Oyster.

"Hold onto that pain. Breathe your soul into it. Interrogate it. Be with it. Inhabit it."

Oyster took a breath and let the agony slip into him through the ink in his skin. His midriff was threaded with lightning.

"Are you sure that she did not tell you about me?" said the presence with a wistful air.

Oyster couldn't reply. He gritted his teeth and closed his eyes, grimacing as he surfed the spasms of agony rippling through him. A door drifted out of the black. It was wooden-framed, brass-handled and coated in heavy varnish. Other than the fact that it was hanging in the void, it was unremarkable.

"Yes, it is working! More! More!" cried the presence, unfazed by Oyster's suffering.

He careered towards the closed door. The pain and the emptiness around him made it hard to judge just how fast he was travelling. At the last moment, the door opened. There were shapes beyond it, but it was all too much of a blur for him to make anything out.

"Tell her about me, will you? When she asks you. Tell her not to worry, but that I am fine now. That I still love her. And that I will always love her. I know why she did what she did, and I forgive her. She must forgive herself. I have missed her so very much. *Sie war meine liebste.* I will always be hers. This is your stop, I believe."

And then he was flying across Lazenby's office.

40

A VALUABLE ASSET

Oyster was a few feet above the ground. He had just enough time to register that it was nighttime before his shins connected with Lazenby's desk, flicking him headlong into the wall behind it. He threw up his arms in time to cushion himself a little from the impact and he collapsed into a pile, upside down in a groaning heap. *I really need to work on my landings*, he thought.

He lay there for a few seconds, drinking in Greater London's smell. It was beginning to feel comforting. The fading pain in his tattoo was eclipsed by the biting ache from his skinned legs. But, he had actually made it.

Fuck, yeah!

Okay. So maybe he had had a bit of an assist from the Old Testament presence he'd encountered, but he was here now. All in one piece. Moving slowly, he twisted himself upright and felt in his pocket. Primrose's coins gave a subdued jangle, muffled in their leather purse, and Oyster suppressed a sickly smile. Maybe he could pull this off after all: this ridiculous string of one-step-at-a-times.

He pressed his back into the wall behind the desk. Breathing heavily, recovering his strength. Now that he had returned from *der hinter*, his bitten hand was swelling by the second. He counted to ten, listening for sounds that would indicate he had disturbed someone with his arrival, simultaneously waiting for the nausea to subside.

Beyond the concrete jigsaw of Lazenby's shinehouse there came the occasional clockwork staccato of the clerks on patrol. But there was no sound from within the building itself, nothing to indicate that the door might spring open to admit a bunch of oven-ready cutthroats.

First things first. Syzygy.

Cautiously, he called her name.

There was an answering chirrup from somewhere within the desk.

She was still there.

He checked each of the desk's drawers, but they were all locked. What he wouldn't give for Lucas's tools right about now. He stood woozily and made a quick circuit of the darkened room. At one end were a set of linen curtains suspended by hook-and-eye rings from long brass rods. *Perhaps these will do?*

As quietly as he could, he dragged Lazenby's chair beneath the curtains and, breathing hard, was able to free one curtain rod from the hooks that suspended it at each end. It was hard work and with his swollen hand it was like trying to tie a knot while wearing boxing gloves.

Shit! Shit! Shit!

The rod overbalanced and its far end hit the floor with a heavy *thunk*. The curtains slid off with a metallic ring. Slipping down from the chair, he took the metal bar in his hands, ready to use it as a bludgeon, but no one answered the sound. Adrenaline broke over him and was replaced with another wave of nausea. He dropped to the floor, crawling on his knees to the tin bucket Lazenby used as a wastepaper basket, and retched, cold sweat beading his forehead. After long minutes, the feeling moved on. He sighed and Syzygy mewled from inside the desk.

"Hang on, love," he said. "I'll have you out of there in a minute."

He picked up one of the curtain rings and examined it closely before slipping off the metal hook attached to it that held the curtain. It was steel, but no more than about twice the thickness of a very heavy-duty paper clip.

Without too much effort he was able to straighten the hook into a serviceable lock pick He took another ring and repeated the procedure, this time bending the hook roughly straight. He introduced a little hook at its tip by stepping on it.

"Hey there," he called, and Syzygy twittered in response. She was in the top drawer. Leaning against the desk, he slid his makeshift tensioner and pick into the lock. With a huff, he used the former to keep the lock still as he raked its pins with the pick he held in his good hand. There was a series of clicks as the mechanism slipped into place, and with a *pop* the drawer slid open.

"There we go, baby," he whispered.

Oyster allowed himself a smile of victory. He had the drawstring bag out on the desk and released Syzygy, pocketing Nonesuch's whistle. The nuajin purred as she scuttled out of the bag and flew straight to her nest under Oyster's arm. There was a moment of relief from the ill effects of the snake bite and Oyster slumped on the floor, resting his back against the desk.

He had his ink beetle. Now he needed a moment to catch his breath before moving on to what he'd come here to do in the first place: finding Motet. It was time to play a hunch.

There had been shineheads outside Lazenby's when he'd arrived, and the boss lady herself had been shady as fuck when he'd asked about getting some himself. These all pointed to there being some imprisoned gebel on the premises. Perhaps even Motet himself.

Taking the curtain rod in hand, he hauled himself to his feet and examined the office door. It was locked from the outside, but he was able to make short work of that with his improvised tools. He opened it and peered around. In the low light, he was just able to make out a short corridor and the door through which Patteepan had led him out onto the roof. At the end of the hallway was a flight of stairs that reached down into the guts of the building itself.

Oyster picked his way down the stairs and poked his head into the main room where he'd eaten breakfast. At its far end, wrapped in blankets and fast asleep, was one of Lazenby's crew. At least this guard was one hell of a sound sleeper.

Holding his breath, he stepped out of the stairwell and into the room, doing his best not to hit anything with the curtain rod. The floor was burnished concrete, cold underfoot, but at least he didn't have to worry about floorboards creaking. He traced his steps along the rear wall, keeping as far from the slumbering sentry as possible, and soon he was on the stairs that led down to the cellar.

Carefully, he made his way down the polished cement steps hovering in the stairwell, waiting for his vision to adjust to the darkness. He couldn't be sure there wasn't another guard down here. He felt sick and crouched on his haunches, waiting for the moment to pass. A slippery, dizzy feeling enveloped his head, but the buzzing in his ears didn't return.

The cellar was constructed from the same angular slabbed concrete as the rest of the building and embedded into the Greater London chalk. Redundant windows looked blindly into the earth itself. It was as if the building had just appeared here in the ground, thought Oyster. And perhaps it had.

Directly ahead of him was the room he had been held in; to his right, two more cement doors hung on great iron hinges, greased with oil as thick as treacle. He approached the nearest. They were both secured with serious-looking metal locks. There was no way he was going to be able to pick them. He prodded at them with the curtain rod, but they remained unmoving.

"Hey," he called as loud as he dared. "Anyone there? Motet?" No reply.

He called again. He was trapped between his need not to wake the guard and the need to let Motet know that help was at hand.

He called again. And again. Still no response. He tried knocking at the door. He got to his knees to see if there was any sort of gap between the base of the door and the floor, but they were flush to each other.

"Keep it down," came a voice from the cell next door, "you'll wake all and sundry, gift us a kicking into the bargain."

"Motet! Is that you?" hissed Oyster with glee. He sat up too quickly and things churned around his head drunkenly.

"And who wants to know?" came the response.

"Nonesuch sent me, I'm here to spring you," replied Oyster with a dry heave.

"Obliged. But 'less you've the key to this door or a ball of glycerine in your breeches, you're unlikely to get far."

"Okay, okay." Oyster thought for a second. "Can you kick off in there? Get Captain Sweatpants down here with us."

"You sure 'bout this?"

"Abso-fucking-lootles," replied Oyster.

There was a pause.

"Fire!" shouted Motet.

"Perfect," hissed Oyster, "keep it up till I say."

He crossed to the stairwell and hid by its exit. Gripping the curtain rod in both hands, he flattened himself against the ridges of the concrete wall. He wasn't feeling his best, but he would just have to make do. He waited.

Motet continued to yell, but the racket was setting Oyster off. The buzzing seeped back into his ears and he leaned against the wall, trying to remain standing, his knees wobbling. *Not now*, he thought. *Not now.*

Finally, steps came echoing down the stairwell. He gripped the curtain rod even more tightly and his knuckles whitened.

"Shut it, glowworm!" shouted the guard. "I'm coming!"

As Oyster had calculated, Lazenby's crew might not give much of a shit about Motet at a personal level, but he was still a valuable asset to them. This joker wouldn't want him burnt to a crisp on his watch. The man hit the bottom step and Oyster jumped at him, swinging the curtain rod down on his head with full force. The man just had time to turn before the blow cracked him across the temple. The ruby-tinted glasses he was wearing flew onto the floor and shattered as the man hit the deck in a heap.

Oyster just had time to register his success before the buzzing in his ears rose to a crescendo and he too collapsed onto the cement floor.

Oyster came to. His head ached. There was a roaring sound and there was too much light. For an instant, he wasn't sure exactly where he was. Instinctively, he felt for the weight of the coins in the leather bag. Still there. *Lazenby really could learn a thing or two about security from Big Mickey.*

"'Ceptional plan of yours," said Motet as Oyster rubbed his eyes. "Didn't grasp you wanted to escape *into* the cell with us. That'll really keep 'em off balance. *Very disruptive.*"

Oyster opened his eyes. He saw the family resemblance between Motet and his sister immediately. The man filled the cramped cell. Like Nonesuch, he was flame-haired and his skin was strung with pearls that glittered in the dark. He wore a skirt fashioned from a Union flag and a black donkey jacket. He stood with his hands on his hips regarding Oyster. Behind him in the cell were another handful of gebel, looking malnourished and ill-treated.

"Typical of my sistren she'd pick looks over utility. So, how did sibling-dearest snare you?" he asked, his expression suddenly becoming puzzled. "Wait a second, are those my clothes?"

"Long story," said Oyster, sitting up.

"Well, we gots nuthin' but time upon our hands," replied Motet with a sigh.

41

ESCAPE

"So, apart from the pleasing arrangement of your visog, do you have any other special features?" said Motet.

"I do, as it happens," said Oyster, reddening under the attention. "Now, if you strap your trap for long enough, perhaps I can have us out of here."

He thought about what the presence had said to him. He closed his eyes.

"Nothing is true. Everything is permitted," he mumbled.

"Quite the philosopher," snipped Motet.

"Listen, mate. Do you need a lie-down or a biscuit or something?" Oyster said. "Or perhaps it'd suit you better to hang around here and wait for a rescue that meets your demanding standards."

Motet's light flared up and then settled with a purple tinge.

"'Pologies," he said finally. "Your assist is appreciated. Bein' ill-used by the very crew I aimed to bring down has been a humbling experience. Not at my best."

He stretched out a hand.

"I'm Motet, by the way."

"Oyster," Oyster replied, clapping Motet's hand with his unbitten one. "S'gonna be okay, we'll think of something."

There was a chirrup from under Oyster's armpit. With a tickle, Syzygy emerged from beneath his armpit, crawled out from under his T-shirt and, with a crackle of wings, flew across to Motet, whose red eyes widened.

"By the holy excrement, is that my Syzygy! Is there anything of mine you haven't boosted?" he growled.

He held out his hand and the ink beetle settled there with a flicker. She crawled around his neck, chittering at him affectionately. In response, Motet coo-ed and stroked her.

"Yeah, that's a long story too," said Oyster. "Wasn't deliberate, I mean. I found her when I met your sis."

Motet ignored him, focused as he was on his reunion. This was about as uncomfortable as running into your ex after they'd hooked up with someone else.

"She's not well," said Motet in an accusatory manner.

Oyster raised his wounded mitt. "I got bit. Neither of us are a hundred per cent right now."

Motet tutted.

"Has he not been treating you properly, girl?" He tickled Syzygy on her belly.

Oyster shook his head and turned his back on them, ignoring the feeling of absence that crept up on him whenever he was apart from the ink beetle. He cracked his knuckles and closed his eyes. The ache in his swollen hand intensified. *Intentional vacuity, whatever that is, here I come.* He drew in a breath of dank cellar air and held it, trying to place himself away from the sounds and the smells here. *Okay. Okay.*

Motet and the nuajin drifted into the background. He found himself thinking of a day that he and Cécile had spent in town together with Paris. It was before Lucas had abandoned them. They had been on Tooting Common, in summer. A breeze had stirred amongst the trees, shaking the leaves.

"What are you doing?" said Motet, interrupting Oyster's reverie. Syzygy slipped under the gebel's collar to rest. Oyster tried to ignore it.

"Not very much, if you keep gassing," he replied. "Do us both a favour and shut it for ten, will you?"

Motet huffed.

Oyster shut his eyes. But the sense of Motet's silent annoyance was overwhelming.

"Can you not do *that* either?"

"What?"

"I can literally hear you sulking."

"Am not."

Oyster sighed. He had not tried this without the map, but the presence seemed like she knew what she was talking about. *You have everything that you need.* It was time to put what she had told him to the test.

He closed his eyes again. Picturing himself on the other side of the door, he tried to empty his head of any other thoughts, but it was hard. Closing his eyes made the symptoms from his snake bite more unpleasant. He still felt dizzy and the pain in his sore hand kept absorbing all his attention. Suddenly, his tattoo came alive with pain. Wincing, he rubbed at it. There was falling sensation as though he'd tripped up in a dream.

"What the—?" Motet's voice was muffled, suddenly coming from behind him.

Oyster's eyes snapped open. The light was low, but there was enough for him to see that he was now outside the cell, standing in front of the guard. The man had dragged a chair down here from upstairs to keep watch and then promptly fallen asleep on it. His old-timey pistol lay in his lap. The man's eyes opened.

Oyster was almost as surprised as the guard to find himself standing there, but he still had the jump on him. In the shocked instant before the guard realised what was happening, Oyster kicked the gun, propelling it from the man's lap and across the room.

The guard got to his feet, but Oyster smacked him backwards with a single blow. He yelped in agony, but the man connected with the angled ridges of concrete behind him and collapsed in a heap. Oyster's good hand hurt almost as much as the bitten one from the punch, and he rubbed his bruised knuckles. He was running out of hands.

Hurriedly, he grabbed the man's weapon and went through his

pockets, finding a brass key ring that hosted a handful of keys of varying shapes and sizes. Then he used the man's own belt to secure his wrists behind his back.

It was only then that he allowed himself to bask in the fact that he had been able to use his wild talent successfully for the first time. He wished the old lady had been here to see it.

He unlocked the door to Motet's cell. The gebel clapped theatrically and stepped through the door with an approving expression. The three other prisoners behind him followed blinking into the low light of the cellar. They regarded Oyster with suspicion and said nothing.

"Colour me impressed, Mr Oyster," said Motet with a whistle. "How, by the Great Tree, did you accomplish that?"

Oyster tapped the side of his nose. He was dizzy again. The sickness was on him, but there was something else, too: a sense that he had lost something, that somehow he was lighter on his feet.

"Don't mention it," said Oyster, bathing in the approval. "Look, dunno how long we've got before fuckwit here wakes up, but we should bust out of here sharpish. Make our way back to the safehouse."

They pulled the guard into the cell and locked him there, then picked their way up the stairs, relieved to find there were no more crew members. This lot really were way too over-confident. *They wouldn't last long in South London*, he thought ruefully. Another key on the key ring unlocked the side door and they emerged into the Greater London dawn.

The other gebel scattered, but Motet remained at his side, adopting a slouching, cowed air, and pulled a hood up over his head. Oyster had forgotten how badly the gebel were treated here.

The city was already awake. Traders wandered to and fro selling gin and clockwork parts. There was the smell of freshly baked bread. Oyster's stomach grumbled. He wasn't sure what passed for money here, but he knew without checking that he wouldn't have any of it.

"How did you get banged up?" he asked Motet.

"Too much smarts and not enough brain," he replied. "At least that's what sister-dearest would say. Dr Lazenby here is a small fish, hooked up with the Mannish Boys, who, it turns out, are the biggest shine traffickers in the city. Was on a reconnoitre, trying to map the full extent of the ring. Acquainting myself with where it starts and with whom it stops."

Oyster nodded. "I'm after them myself. That's why Nonesuch roped me in to spring you. Maybe we can exchange deets. I've met their boss, if that helps."

Motet's lights flared. Without meeting Oyster's gaze, he steered them into an alleyway and off the main thoroughfare.

"You know their captain?"

"Nasty motherfucker called Primrose," Oyster replied.

Motet's eyes narrowed and he glittered.

"Well, plan was to avenge all the downtrodden children of the hives. Cut the head from the serpent and the beast withers, that sort'a thing. There was a parlay between the lieutenants, 'cluding Lazenby, someone called Ambidexter and the Mannish's head jefe. Before I could act, got took into custody and chucked in that there cellar for my troubles."

"For what it's worth, I think Primrose is one tough arsehole to rub out," said Oyster, his mind racing at Ambidexter's name. Now he was getting somewhere.

Motet reached down and slipped a long finger into one of his boots.

"They may have laid hands on me before I could act," he said, "but I managed to sketch this likeness."

He handed Oyster a folded piece of notepaper from a child's writing set.

"This the Primrose you mentioned?"

Oyster opened the note and his stomach dropped. He looked at the drawing, blinked and looked again. He wanted to speak but his mouth wouldn't work. Staring back up at him from the grubby paper was Lucas.

42

GOODBYE

"This isn't him," said Oyster after he was able to form the words. "Can't be."

"There's no doubt," replied Motet. "This is who I saw at the meet. Sources were unimpeachable. This is the Mannish's captain."

Oyster shook his head numbly and handed the sketch back.

But he knew that Motet was correct. Oyster's head was about to explode. His stomach was cold. A heavy gust of wind blew down the alleyway, lacing the air with the smells of the city and tugging at his jacket. Oyster wrapped it more tightly around him. He had no idea what to do now. He had come here to find his father, but he'd never expected this. He felt frightened and suddenly very small.

"You ailing for something?" asked Motet.

"Nah, nah." Oyster swallowed, waving the gebel away. "I'm fine." He needed certainty; someone he could trust.

Marya Petrovna. He needed to talk to her.

Oyster halted. His feet felt as though they were not even touching the ground.

"Go on to the safe house," he said.

Motet looked confused.

"But—"

"Got my own shit to work through," Oyster said.

"Are you sure?" said Motet.

Oyster nodded. He handed Motet the dog whistle.

"Give this to Nonesuch," he said, "and say goodbye to her from me, for now at least."

Motet nodded and glittered a rainbow of colours. "A debt is owed to you, Mr Oyster."

"Pay me later," he replied. "Now, skidoosh."

Syzygy emerged from beneath Motet's clothes. She buzzed up into the green sky for an instant and settled on Oyster, slipping under his T-shirt before either of them could react.

Motet looked at him and nodded.

"She's chosen."

Oyster took a breath. Tried to place himself with Marya Petrovna. Wherever she was, that was where he needed to be now.

The pain flared in his torso. And he was gone.

43
WORKING MEN'S CLUB

One second Oyster had been in a street in Greater London and then suddenly he was standing in a dark, cramped, stale-smelling box of some sort. He sensed his confinement all around him. For a second, he panicked. He had never seriously considered the possibility that he might arrive inside a wall or halfway through the floor of a location when he flitted to it. *Had that happened now?*

Hold on. Hold on. He tried to calm himself. Surely he would just be dead on arrival if that occurred? He made a mental note to ask the old lady about it next time he had a chance.

There was a loud squawk, and something pecked at his ankles. There was something alive with him in here. Claustrophobia choked him and he drummed on the inside of the box.

"Oi! I'm in here! Let me out! Let me out!"

He continued to hammer on the surface in front of him, his swollen hand grumbling at the force of the impact.

"I'm here! Let me out!" he cried again. It rattled. The creature next to him joined in the chorus and pecked at him repeatedly. Whatever it was that he was standing in, it wasn't particularly sturdy.

There was a smattering of laughter from outside. Where the hell could he be?

Footsteps. And then the box opened.

A puzzled-looking Marya Petrovna was staring at him, her face gaudy with stage makeup. With a fluid motion she threw the other bolts on the doors and drew Oyster out.

"Well, I never!" she shouted theatrically, staring at him with raised eyebrows. "How unexpected! If it isn't my trusty assistants! Minnie and my nephew... *Enoch*. Ladies and gentlemen, big hand please for them both!"

There was another round of tepid applause. Oyster took a breath and stumbled forward, blinking into the light. He stood on a small stage in the centre of a wood-veneered function room. Silver streamers hung limply from the ceiling and a tatty purple curtain enveloped the stage to his left. There sat a gloomy man with a swept-over haircut, hunched behind a Casio keyboard.

The sparse audience sat at small, circular tables and the whole place reeked of stale beer and the sort of fossilised cigarette smoke that no amount of cleaning would ever remove. Marya Petrovna was resplendent in a white dress shirt and an evening suit. Her hair was platinum white and stowed beneath a brushed top hat.

Shit! He'd emerged in the middle of her crappy magic act.

She reached out an arm and Minnie the cockateel fluttered up from inside the cabinet. The old lady transferred her to a perch set next to the cabinet, where she was no worse for her experience.

There was another flatulent fanfare from keyboard guy and Marya Petrovna pulled Oyster forward, forcing him into an awkward bow.

"Better late than never, Enoch," she declared. "But you are just in time to help me with this!"

She thrust a small metal jug into his unwilling hands and with a flourish produced a glass pitcher filled with water. Oyster held the jug as she filled it splashily, his obvious reticence producing titters in the crowd.

"And now..." she said, dropping the pitcher and rolling a sheet of newspaper into a wide cone. She tipped the paper towards the audience to show it was empty. Taking the jug from him, she filled the cone with water.

"Let us place on heavy object!" With a flourish she slipped a piece of card over the cone's opening and turned it upside down, placing it on Oyster's head before he could refuse.

"Not the first time you have worn pointy hat, eh?" she said.

Oyster turned purple with embarrassment.

"Now, how brave are you, Enoch?" she said.

Oyster shrugged. His obvious discomfort fuelled another round of laughter from the audience.

"Well, you got to be pretty brave to be dressed like that," she said to the audience with a stage wink. There was another wave of laughter. The audience had warmed to them since he'd appeared on stage.

"Now, whatever you do, Enoch, do not remove card. You understand?"

Oyster shrugged.

"I said, whatever you do, do not remove card, yes?"

Oyster tried to nod, but the cone on his head made it hard.

"What did I say?" said Marya Petrovna, putting a finger to her ear.

"Not to remove the card?" Oyster squeaked.

"Exactly", she thundered. "I said, whatever you do, don't do this!"

And with that, she whipped the card out from between the cone and Oyster's head so quickly that no water escaped.

The audience laughed, thinking the liquid was trapped between his head and the paper. Oyster's scalp did not feel wet at all, though. *There was no water in his makeshift dunce's cap.* Marya Petrovna was pretty good at this, he'd give her that, but he'd had enough of being her stooge here. Fuck it, if he was going down in flames he might as well go the whole hog.

"Right! Enough!" he yelled. "I've been magicked up here and shouted at and now you're gonna get me wet."

In mock indignation, he whipped the cone from his head and threw its contents at the nearest table.

The four people seated there shunted backwards to avoid a soaking, but all they avoided was a flurry of tinsel. There was another tardy stab of cheesy keyboard.

Relieved laughter from the onlookers melted into applause.

"And that is all for tonight's show!" yelled Marya Petrovna, pulling him beside her and forcing him into taking several deep bows.

"Nice improvisation," said Marya Petrovna from the side of her mouth. "You see, boy, you are something of a natural for this line of work."

Then she led him behind the velvet curtain and down off the stage, waving at the man on the keyboard, who had already picked up a microphone and was heading for the stage himself. This was the sort of class establishment where the emcee also had to provide the musical accompaniment.

"A big hand, please, for Madame Kaminsky, Minnie and Enoch, and their mysteries of the East... *End*."

Now that the adrenaline of being on stage had ebbed away, the buzzing had returned to Oyster's ears.

He looked at Marya Petrovna.

"*Enoch?*" he said with a grimace. "Is that the best you could come up with?"

"Give me break, eh? You turned up out of nowhere. And well, I thought you would be pleased. He was ancient, biblical patriarch. And in apocryphal texts, Enoch is taught all the mysteries and wonders of heaven. Moves from one place to another *enigmatically*."

"I suppose you knew *him*, too," he said wearily and collapsed.

44
LOST THINGS

Oyster came to. There was a distant cluck and cackle from Minnie. For a second, he thought he was still trapped in Marya Petrovna's cabinet.

He was lying in a large ornate four-poster bed that had been crammed into a tiny bedroom at the back of Marya Petrovna's flat. Judging by the light that streamed through its grubby net curtains it was late afternoon. Syzygy was curled under his throat. As he stirred, she chittered excitedly.

"Take it easy," said Marya Petrovna. She sat at the end of the bed, wearing a blue winceyette dressing gown and encircled by smoke from her endless stream of roll-ups. Her hair was still pulled up into the silver bun that she had worn for the conjuring performance.

"That working men's club has not had many people collapse in it. You had old Happy Max and me properly worried."

Oyster tried to flex his swollen hand, but it was swaddled in several layers of bandages.

"If you'd left it too much longer, I think you would've lost that paw."

Oyster tried to speak, but his throat was dry. Marya Petrovna nodded towards a glass filled with water set on a bedside table. He sat up and took a few sips.

Lazenby, Nonesuch, Primrose. It felt like he had been away

from his London for a lifetime. Yet, that absolute sense of time that he possessed, rooted in the concrete of the capital itself, told him he had not been away for that long.

He lay back in the bed. The nausea he had experienced since being bitten had faded into a background tremor of queasiness, but there was an unease that lay beneath the physical sensations.

Then, with a sinking feeling, he remembered.

Motet. The Mannish. *Lucas*.

Lucas was in charge of the Mannish. What was he doing in Greater London? And how was he connected to everything that had been going on?

He needed to straighten events into some sort of order. He knew now that everything here was connected. Like one of those Magic Eye posters that had been all the rage in the nineties, he just had to stand at the right distance from events to glean what the underlying pattern was.

"I need to speak to you about something important. That's why I came here," he said.

The room spun and he groaned.

"As I said. Take it easy," replied Marya Petrovna. "I don't know how you managed to get bitten by snake, but you can tell me all about it later. Just rest now, eh? You are safe here. Lamasery has many symbolic protections woven around it. You are suffering from poisoning and the equivalent of arcane hangover. You have been using your talents, such as they are, overmuchly."

With a sigh she heaved herself into a standing position.

"Hungry?"

Oyster shook his head.

"Well, I am. Rest! Rest! And I will be back later and then you can tell me about where you have been!" Waddling out of the bedroom, she turned to look at him and her eyes twinkled as she closed the door.

Oyster allowed himself a smile. An odd feeling unfurled within him. It was pride. He was proud of himself at having been able to achieve what he had. And moreover, *she* was proud of him. It was a strange feeling, but he allowed himself to indulge it briefly. He looked down at his bandaged hand and felt the lumps on his head. All this had certainly cost him.

And then he thought of what Primrose had said about her. What had he called her? *The Hag*? Sounded less like shade and more like a title. He didn't want to let Primrose into his head, but it gave him pause. He'd said that she had her own agenda. Something to do with the Trian ritual. It all added to his sensation of queasiness and unsteadiness. A feeling that the bed was shifting beneath him. But fuck it. Everyone had their own agenda. Primrose most of all.

He lay back and tried to gather his jumbled thoughts. Images from his travels tumbled through his mind. As always, the time that he had spent in Greater London was dreamlike, as though his experiences hadn't really happened. He examined his bandaged hand again. His injuries were real enough.

Marya Petrovna returned, holding a plate piled high with blackened toast and a mug of tea. She took a bite then parked the plate and her drink on the floor. Reaching into her dressing gown, she pulled out the leather bag he had stolen from Primrose, emptying its contents onto the bed.

"I think you are in deep big-shit trouble. Deeper than you probably realise."

Oyster looked at the coins as they lay in a pile on the bed. He'd forgotten that he'd lifted them. Lazenby's sketch lay next to them.

Crap.

And then he recalled how he'd let slip to Primrose that he and Broadsides were onto him. He jumped out of bed in a second and was pulling on his old clothes, which had been stacked on the bedside table.

"What actual fuck are you up to now!" said Marya Petrovna as he hopped unsteadily into his jeans.

"I gotta split," he said. "I've landed Broadsie in it. Need to warn him." His head was aching and fizzing.

"Did you not understand anything I just said to you? You have been burning candle at both ends, monkey boy. You cannot just go marching out of here."

The burst of strength that had animated him ebbed. He sat back on the bed and pulled on his socks, before a cold sweat washed over him and he had to lie back on it.

"You have not recovered," she said. "Each leap of faith that you make takes something from you."

"But if anything happens to him it'll be on me," he said.

"Look, give me his details. I will go to wretched bloody phone box and leave him message, yes?"

"I don't know his number off the top of my head," said Oyster. "Who knows all the phone numbers of their mates off by heart?"

Marya Petrovna waved her hands sarcastically and rolled her eyes. "Oh yes, what kind of lunatic would have time for such *sorcery*?"

Oyster felt weak, almost insubstantial in a way he had never been before. He struggled to move but was tortured by the sense that he'd landed Broadsides in it.

"I've fucked up. I've got to get word to him as soon as I can."

"Okay, but not before you and I have discussion. It is important. Most important thing we can do right now. We have shilly-shallied around this for too long. I did some research after you did disappearing act the other day," she said, pointing at the coins on the bedspread. "From where did you get these?"

"I don't have time for this," he said.

"*Au contraire*, child. Time may be all that we have," she replied.

Oyster shrugged. He wanted to move, but he was still weak. Mad and maddening as she was, he had chosen to come back to talk to Marya Petrovna about all this stuff for a reason.

"Okay," he said, "here goes." He told her about his sojourn in Greater London and his jaunt to Primrose's gaff, and about Lucas and the Mannish.

"*Kurwa!* Perhaps some of this begins to make sense," she exclaimed.

"Alright, lay it on me, Super-Gran," he said. "I am literally your captive audience here."

"Quite. So, after reading your cards the other day, it becomes clear. This Mr Primrose that you tell me about. He is not what he seems at all."

"No shit," said Oyster. "Well, that solves that one then. What's our next case, Mr Holmes?"

Marya Petrovna rolled her eyes and made a pinching motion with her fingers.

"*Vybliadok!* Zip this hole, yes? My point is that I suspected he might be avatar in our world for other entity. Your little haul here proves my suspicions correct. I am thinking that this Primrose of yours is manifestation of *Cerunnos*."

"Okay. Okay," said Oyster. "So who or what is a Cerunnos?"

"They are deity associated with the old religions. Not much is known about them, but they are friend of nature. Lord of Wilderness. Fuck it, they *are* the wilderness. Sometimes a harbinger of death, sometimes of life. They are stag-antlered; carry bag of coins." She pointed at the drawstring bag's contents spread out on the bed.

It's in our nature to bring unlike things together. Oyster replayed Primrose's words to him in his head.

"*Fuckity-fuck*," he said.

"Fuckity-fuck, indeed," replied Marya Petrovna.

"What do they want?"

"That is where things become more complicated. Wait for second," she said and bustled off into the Lamasery. Oyster wanted to argue with her, to tell her what she had recounted to him was a load of old rhubarb, but he couldn't deny that, as crazy as it sounded, it felt right.

The sound of grunts and books being flung to the floor echoed up the hallway. Oyster shut his eyes; his tattoo was dancing with low level pain. He wondered if he'd ever be rid of it. Perhaps that just wasn't meant to be. Perhaps branding himself in this way had always been on the cards. They were part of each other now.

Marya Petrovna returned with an ancient laptop the size of a small suitcase. A dial-up cable trailed into the hallway and in the background came the staccato rattle of a modem connection. She placed the computer on the bed and pointed at its monochrome screen.

"This is Cerunnos," she said.

Oyster drew in a breath. The pixelated screen showed a woodcut resembling the ritual he had seen on Primrose's wall. He was cold. He looked up at Marya Petrovna.

"And?" he said.

"Well, little is known about them now. They are, for all intents and purposes, a lost god, partially forgotten. This might make them the worst sort in many ways. If not vengeful, then at least a bit petulant."

"He certainly acts like an arsehole if that's what you mean," replied Oyster.

Marya Petrovna gave a gallic shrug.

"There is one other thing," she said.

"Go on then," said Oyster.

She prodded the page with a nicotine-stained index finger.

"Little is known directly about old religions of the Gauls in these days. Caesar saw to that. But there is a cycle this entity is associated with; an ancient one, mentioned in the *Albrecht Dream Codex* and Galford's *Cosmonomicon*. In this cycle, Cerunnos as the Lord of the Wild stands in direct opposition to crafty old Lugones, the clever one, the toolmaker, the technologist. Remember him?"

Oyster's tattoo jangled. He nodded.

"He had something to do with Lucas?" said Oyster.

Marya Petrovna raised an eyebrow.

"Yes, indeed. So, these two are locked together in a cycle that rewrites history. *Fuck it.* Their conflict *is* history. Over millennia they grow in power: nature and Cerunnos on one side, Lugones and civilisation on the other. They skirmish over centuries, struggling with each other as their power grows, but at end of each cycle a point is reached—"

Oyster recalled Primrose's words; recalled the horrid sensation that there was something important that Primrose wanted him to know. Something that would hurt him. It was pulling at him, trying to suck him into the ground. He grabbed onto the pain in his tattoo and it focused him.

"Don't tell me. I know this one. I've seen it, believe it or not. They rock up under a tree and do some sort of weird ritual thing?"

Marya Petrovna nodded.

"Exactly so, they meet beneath the *Crann Bethadh*, the Tree of Life. For ritual to function, Cerunnos must have his coins and Lugones his spear. A choice is made for the next cycle of history and..."

Oyster thought back to his nightmare.

"The winner gets all levelled up," he interjected. "It's called the Trian ritual or something. Primrose told me."

"If Cerunnos is victorious," she continued, "then it is year zero, nature is in the ascendant. If Lugones wins, then *civilisation*, for want of a better word, gets rocket boost. Has been going on forever, this cycle. Last time round was six thousand years ago when money was invented. Perhaps is root of Atlantis myth and so on."

Talking about the ritual reminded Oyster of Primrose's warning. He pushed the thoughts away. His mouth was dry and he was giddy again.

But could all the rest of this be true? It all fitted together; all of Primrose's cryptic little comments and digs. Even his bizarre pet collection made sense now. And Lazenby. She had sent him after the coins for her boss. If what Motet had said was true, then her ultimate crew captain was Lucas.

"What has all this got to do with me?" said Oyster.

"Well," said Marya Petrovna, reaching down to take a slurp of tea from her mug. "Having been through all this with you, and knowing what I know, it is my considered opinion that far from being merely *associated* with Lugones, your father *is* Lugones."

45

THE MIRACLE CLUB

It was midday. Oyster was dressed in his own jeans and hoodie, but had pulled on Motet's jacket. He had seriously considered wearing the gebel's skirt too, he had really enjoyed its comfort, but figured it would probably attract too much attention. He needed to be invisible for what he wanted to do now.

A full night's sleep at Marya Petrovna's and some more of her patented tea had restored his strength. He looked at his injured hand. The old woman had bandaged it and applied a poultice of some sort. The swelling had come down and he had regained some feeling in his fingertips.

Syzygy had crawled back under his armpit in the night and she was there now, dozing fitfully. He felt different, slightly off, almost light-headed as though something that had been weighing him down had shifted. He felt more himself than he had for weeks, and perhaps more than that too. It was an odd sensation.

Marya Petrovna's bombshell about Lucas still bounced around the back of his head, but he didn't feel ready to think about the ramifications of any of that currently. That said, there was something else that was nagging at him, now he was back at the old lady's gaff: the photograph that he had seen the first night he had stayed here, the one of Marya Petrovna's grandmother and her old cronies back in the nineteenth century. The one with the shadowy figure that he thought he almost recognised.

From the kitchen came the sound of Marya Petrovna singing tunelessly to the radio as she made lunch. He strode down the hallway and into the living room, its crimson walls still hosting the legion of framed pictures of all shapes and sizes.

He stepped over Marya Petrovna's own bedroll and overflowing ashtray. The photo that had so struck him that evening was no longer there, but the space where it had hung was betrayed by a rectangular silhouette on the wallpaper.

He stormed into the kitchen.

"Where is it?" he yelled over the sound of the radio.

"And good morning to you," said Marya Petrovna without looking up, busying herself with a slice of cremated toast.

"That old picture you used to have hanging up?"

"What picture?" she said, turning to face him and taking a large mouthful of toast.

"The one of you and the other ultra-boomers standing around outside the house?"

"Apologies. I do not know of what you are talking?" Marya Petrovna replied unblinking and swallowing.

Oyster was having none of it.

"For a professional magician you are really shit at lying, you know that, don't you?" he said.

Marya Petrovna assumed a theatrically shocked air.

"*Moi?*" she said. "Would not know how."

"Come with me, then," said Oyster, grabbing her by the hand and marching her to the empty space on the wall.

"Ah," she nodded. "That one. Why did you not say so before? Is in cupboard under the sink. I took it down to clean it."

Oyster shook his head in disbelief and stormed into the kitchen, opening the appropriate cupboard and spilling its contents onto the floor.

Marya Petrovna sailed into the room behind him, leaned against the doorframe and lit a cigarette. She exhaled a stream of smoke.

"Do not mess this all up again, eh? Just got it back how I like it."

Oyster found the picture lying under a tea-towel. Retrieving it, he brushed the dusty glass and pulled open the curtains to look at the photograph in the grim daylight.

"What do you want with it?" Marya Petrovna took a long drag, releasing the smoke through her nostrils.

Oyster examined the photograph. There were the members of the Miracle Club outside the house. Marya Petrovna stood at the foot of the steps with the mysterious figure in the background. The sense of familiarity seized him again.

"If this was taken in 1882, how is it that *you* are in it?" he said.

"This is long story," said Marya Petrovna. "I do my cardio. Watch my micronutrients."

"Cute," said Oyster. "But really, how are you still around?"

She shrugged.

"You have your secrets. I have mine."

He peered at the picture, then flipped the frame over, unlatched it and drew the picture out so he could look at it more directly. He sucked in a breath. *Damn it.* However much he tried to shake off Primrose's warnings, his words about Marya Petrovna and the illustration of the Trian ritual were fresh in his mind.

"Come on. Throw me a bone. You know everything about me; I got squat on you. Who is that?" He pointed at the silhouette.

"Okay," said Marya Petrovna, taking another massive pull on her cigarette. "Am pretty sure now, that is your father. I mean, he called himself Luka Fillian back then, but since meeting you I had my suspicions. After all that has happened, is happening."

"What. The. Actual. Fuck," he heard himself say, but his mind was spinning, numb from what she had just said. His knees trembled and he steadied himself against the wall. Marya Petrovna stared at him intently.

"Tell me that again," he said.

"It is as I said," she replied. "I knew your father. Long time ago."

"Yes. But it's not like you just bumped into him at some rave in the nineties." He shook his head. "You're talking about over a hundred years ago. How is that even possible?"

A gurgling sound came from somewhere deep in the flat, interrupting the thousands of questions that crowded into Oyster's head. It was an electronic burble that was at once insistent and distant. Marya Petrovna pulled a face and bustled out of the kitchen. Oyster placed the photograph numbly on the table. This was so unexpected he wasn't even sure how to react.

"Hey!" he said, chasing after her. "How did you meet him? What was he up to?"

He gradually came to the realisation that the sound Marya Petrovna had reacted to was a telephone. He shook his head. So, the old woman had been lying to him about that, too. From the lounge came the sound of Marya Petrovna slinging books and ornaments around in an effort to find it. She returned some moments later holding an ancient landline in one hand and looking pale.

Oyster opened his mouth to speak, but she silenced him with a wave.

"That was Maxie from club. They had break-in last night. Some shitbags stole my cabinet."

Marya Petrovna bustled down the street ahead of Oyster. Wrapped in a long coat and army boots, she left a stream of smoke and the scent of lavender water in her wake. Over one shoulder she clutched a worn black leather bag that was secured with a sturdy brass zip. He observed once more that, for an old woman, she could really shift when it suited her.

He was still weaker than he was used to, and the buzz of the traffic on the road around him felt like an immediate threat. Every bus that passed or car that crawled near them might contain Deano, Mickey or another of the Urbans.

Despite being on the mend, Marya Petrovna's successive revelations were spinning him out. They were like depth charges dropped deep inside him, detonating in silence but overwhelming his sense of who he was and where he came from.

Back in the flat, she had shrugged off all his attempts to

engage her, seemingly preoccupied with the theft of her cabinet, but in the end had relented to his demand that they go and warn Broadsides.

"Hey! Hold up," he said. "You can't just stonewall me on this. We still need to talk about Lucas. Are you really telling me that you used to hang with my dad over a hundred years ago?"

"Yes, I am, and I am pretty sure I did," she said, over her shoulder.

"And you didn't think it was important to tell me any of that shit until *now*?"

Marya Petrovna stopped so suddenly Oyster nearly ran into her.

She turned on her heel deliberately and mechanically. Her face was grim. She took her cigarette and stomped it underfoot, giving the impression of holding in a great deal of anger.

"Firstly, was not completely sure. Secondly, you might recall that *I* have been trying to talk to *you* about your bloody father since our first meeting, but you have always wanted to avoid bloody subject! Thirdly, not everything in this world is about *you*!"

"Okay, I get it," said Oyster, "you're worried about your box. But you must be able to get a replacement. Can't you claim on the insurance or something? I mean, why would anyone want to nick it anyway?"

Marya Petrovna snorted and shook her head in disdain.

"Just forget about it. You see so little it is laughable. If we are to warn your friend, where are we going?"

He cast his mind back, combing through what he could remember.

"Well, Broadsie's got an aunt who works at the Salvation Army near Clapham somewhere. He said we can get a message to him there."

Marya Petrovna nodded.

"Very well. This is plan," she said. "You will need my help. You cannot very well go wandering in there with dick in hand, but I can."

"Right," replied Oyster. "Thanks for the visual, but yeah."

He took a couple of steps to draw up to her side.

"So, tell me about it then," he said.

"What?" said Marya Petrovna, burrowing her chin into her overcoat.

"This Miracle Club thing," he replied.

She nodded, crossing into the road, heading towards the nearest Tube station.

"Is ancient history," she said.

"May well be," he replied, "but seems like it might be very relevant."

Marya Petrovna looked at him and her eyes brightened.

"Well, well. Perhaps you are learning after all, flapdoodle."

She paused to roll another cigarette, and the sun passed behind a cloud. Oyster felt cold and vulnerable again, standing on the pavement, supremely visible to passersby. He shivered, pulled up his hoodie and looked at the concrete underfoot.

"Right. Where to begin," said Marya Petrovna once her cigarette was lit. She struck out towards the Tube station again.

"As you have seen, many years ago I was part of small society of occult practitioners. There were four of us. We went by rather pompous name of the Miracle Club, although there were precious few miracles, I can tell you."

They reached the Tube's entrance and took the metal-trimmed steps underground.

"To begin with, was just me and dear Benjamin Fauks. I met him and his wife Héloïse in Marsala when I was with Garibaldi."

"I hate them," said Oyster. "The dried fruit always gets stuck in my teeth."

Marya Petrovna sighed.

"You really cannot help yourself, can you?" she said, shaking her head. "He was great general, long before he was immortalised as a biscuit. I was naïve young thing back then, you see. I had taken it upon myself to travel east to study under the ascended masters: the eternal mystics who are secret rulers of our world."

She paused and held up her hand.

"Just don't say anything."

"I didn't," said Oyster.

"Really, this will be so much easier if you keep this hole in face shut."

She cleared her throat.

"Where were we? Ah, yes. So, Benjamin Fauks was very inventive engineer, you know. His war machines pretty much won battle of Calatafimi for Garibaldi, but Benjy was wounded in a skirmish at Volturno, so I loaned him money and he returned to England. He stayed at my house there, and when I came back, we toured illusionist act for little while. Ach, poor Benjy. He built me many wonderful stage gimmicks."

Marya Petrovna flicked the ash from her cigarette, stubbed it out and put it into her pocket. She insisted on buying tickets for them both from the machine and they stood on the escalator as it glided underground.

"He was dear friend," she continued. "When our act faltered, we formed Miracle Club. Later, we were joined by Jack Devlin, an American illusionist as well-known as Houdini at the time. These were the days when Spiritualism was all the rage. There were many crackpots and shysters, all taking advantage of people. Together, as the Miracle Club, we exposed fakirs and mediums who knew more about Dagenham than dharma. Our fame spread and we hosted crowned heads at our salons and counted the rich and powerful among our clients."

"And so, number four?" Oyster counted the members on his fingers. "Number four was Lucas, right?"

Marya Petrovna nodded.

"Yes. As you have guessed, our final recruit was young man named Luka Fillian, aka Lucas McLellen. He claimed to know about old religions: pagan practices Christianity had tried to wallpaper out of existence. You remind me of him in many ways."

Oyster scowled at the comparison as they emerged onto the platform, semi-deserted at mid-afternoon.

"Although we prided ourselves in seeking the truth and using stage magic to expose fraud, under Lucas and Jack's influence, we became more involved in occult ourselves. By this time, Benjy had built doorways into other worlds. So, you can thank him for the fact that I know what is ink beetle.

"During one adventure, Lucas came into possession of a book called the *Bur-cniht Codex*. He claimed it was assembled from writings so old, they pre-dated human civilisation, compiled by a eunuch in the service of Anglo-Saxon lord many, many years ago. Lucas became completely obsessed by it, guarding it jealousy and keeping it under lock and key."

They sat on a bench waiting for the next train.

"Between them, Lucas and Devlin pressured Fauks into building a device detailed in the book," continued Marya Petrovna. "An ancient machine composed of exotic materials. This thing, the *Mói Dórath*, channels and concentrates chaotic energies; allows contact with other worlds, perhaps even other times."

She sighed.

"Alas, I did little to stop them. I had filled Benjy's head with so much nonsense about ascended masters and Atlantis and what have you. I was just as much to blame for what happened next."

A train pulled into the station with a shudder of light and hiss of brakes. Marya Petrovna ignored it, so engrossed was she in recounting her story.

"One night in March, I think it was," she continued, "we used device, in combination with ancient summoning rituals I had learned, in attempt to contact other entities. Chaos beings whose power we thought to harness."

"And?" said Oyster.

"Well. We failed, horribly. Fire started in the device. It spread quickly. Fauks' wife, Héloïse, and his young daughter, Isobel, perished. As did others in the house."

Marya Petrovna was ashen faced. She looked on glassily as another train came and went, and another. She opened her mouth as if to speak and then stopped. Fumbling in her pocket for the unlit cigarette, she held it tightly, spinning it around thumb and forefinger.

"I never saw Lucas again. Devlin survived, although he was quite badly burned. He moved back to America as soon as he was able. Benjy, poor man, never stopped blaming himself. He left shortly after fire and went travelling. Although we remained in touch, I never saw him again."

"Brutal," said Oyster. "But how does this have anything to do with your cabinet?"

"Don't you see?" said Marya Petrovna. "This is why it matters so much that cabinet has been stolen. The *Mói Dórath*, Fauks' device – it *is* my cabinet."

46
ST JOHN'S WOOD

Another train rattled into the station and this time Oyster stood. Marya Petrovna had been drained by telling him the story.

"Come on," he said. "We're never gonna get anywhere sitting on our hands here. It's going to be alright."

She grunted and he helped her to her feet.

"I wish I shared your rosy assessment," she said.

"Chances are your gear's just been boosted by a rival. I mean, that sort of thing must happen, right?"

Marya Petrovna fixed him with a stare that could curdle milk.

"You are total pillock, you know this, don't you?" she said.

"Well, you're not the first person to say that." Oyster gave what he hoped was a winning smile.

"You know, I think I prefer it when you are being regular little-beam-of-sunshine self," she said and waved him away in disgust.

They boarded the southbound train, and as the carriages pulled out of the station Oyster glanced up.

There was a familiar figure lurking in the shadows across the tracks of the northbound platform. Wrapped in his great coat and standing behind the gates of a locked entrance was Primrose. The man smiled his graveyard smile and waved. Oyster's stomach lurched. He closed his eyes and looked again, and the man was gone. The sick feeling he had felt back at Primrose's gaff squeezed his insides and crawled up the back of his throat. What was it that he had said? "There are other things we want to tell you. That we *need* to tell you." Oyster shuddered. Whatever it was that Primrose wanted to tell him, he was pretty sure he wanted nothing to do with it.

"What is matter with you?" asked Marya Petrovna.

"Uh, nothing." Oyster looked at the floor and tried to steady himself. It was all going to be alright, he told himself. It had to be.

They hopped off at the next stop and Oyster's skin crawled as they ran up the stairs, their steps echoing on the station's tiled walls. Marya Petrovna huffed and puffed; she was weaker than she had been when they set off and they had to pause several times as they switched lines. Oyster kept his hood up, looking back and forth, suddenly feeling very conspicuous.

They reached the next platform and Oyster parked himself on a bench. He leant back, shrinking into his clothes. Directly opposite, on the far side of the tunnel, was an advertising hoarding: two beautiful people in oatmeal sweatpants lounged on a luxurious handmade sofa. Their smug, toothy grins annoyed the fuck out of him. If he'd had a pen handy, nothing would have given him more pleasure than to black out a few of their plutonium teeth.

The furniture in the ad was a million miles from the sort they'd had in his house. Furnishings and home luxuries had never been one of Lucas's priorities. Even when he had been around, it was the most Paris could do to troop them all to Ikea in Croydon once every few years to replace their tatty sofa, or the kitchen chairs that were falling apart. Once Lucas had left, they'd rarely had the spare cheddar to blow on the basics, let alone anything fancy.

And yet there were people all over the city – all over the world, in fact – who could afford that and much more besides. For all his hard graft, he had only ever been able to keep their collective heads above water. The inequity of the situation rankled. Despite all his obvious failings, maybe Primrose had a point. Humanity's current way of doing things left a lot to be desired. Maybe a new start wouldn't be so bad.

Oyster sniffed and leaned forward. The delays on the display above his head stacked up.

"What was he like, then, back in the day?" said Oyster.

Marya Petrovna cleared her throat and took to spinning her unlit cigarette once more.

"Lucas?"

Oyster grunted.

Marya Petrovna smiled as she recalled the memory.

"He was charm itself, that one. Could conjure the very birds down from the trees. Focused, yes, but always I had sense he was holding something back. They were good times, though."

Oyster found he was smiling despite himself. He pushed the feeling away. Marya Petrovna was lost in reverie. There was a satisfied look on her face that Oyster had not seen before.

"Oh my god," said Oyster, "don't tell me that you and him were—"

"*Ach!* No!" said Marya Petrovna, spluttering to respond. "Not with him! Not that dog!" She grimaced. "I am sorry. I mean, I know he is your father, but. Just. No."

Oyster blew out his cheeks in relief.

"What was his angle, then? He was always up to something. There had to be something that he wanted out of hanging with your crew."

"Well, we had wealth, relatively speaking. And he was instrumental in encouraging Benjy to build cabinet."

Oyster looked across the platform at the moronic advertisement once more. The wall beneath it was water damaged. There were great cancerous stains where the damp had leached its way into the brick beneath, rotting it away. But above it, the perfect couple sat in their perfect house, on their perfect fucking sofa, oblivious to the decay surrounding them.

47
SALVATION ARMY

They slogged up the tiled stairway and emerged from the Tube station into the light of the late afternoon. The sun crested the ragged concrete skyline, peering down from between a gap in the clouds, reminding Oyster of Greater London's cold red sunlight. It had taken them much longer than he'd hoped to get down to Balham. His probable sighting of Primrose had left him shaken, and meant he had wanted to take the most roundabout route possible.

It was late in the day and the city smelled like rain and despair.

Marya Petrovna had been deep in thought since they had discussed the cabinet. Every time he had tried to engage her in conversation, she had waved him away. The theft had plunged her deep into an internal world that he had no purchase on.

As soon as they hit the streets, she lit up her cigarette and puffed it down to a nubbin in a few lungfuls. Oyster hung back while the old lady asked people for directions. The entire process was just too awkward for him, and he was horrified by the way she just bowled up to random people and talked to them.

By the third attempt he had had enough.

"And your best idea is to, what? Walk around aimlessly until we find destination?" she hissed.

"I'm just trying to keep it on the DL," he said.

She met his comment with a derisive snort and continued ahead.

They crossed over the street and headed down Balham High Road. Opposite the station, Oyster spun around to glance at the building itself. Like much of the city's infrastructure, Oyster hardly even saw it, but he was able to appreciate that this station, with its squat concrete and slated glass, had a certain urban chic that he liked to think he might radiate on his better days.

The Salvation Army shop nestled between a pawnbroker's and a convenience store offering telephone repairs While-U-Wait. Much to Marya Petrovna's disdain, Oyster took the opportunity to duck in and pick up a cheap handset. As soon as the device burbled into life, he sighed with relief. He was connected back into the real world.

"What do you want this for?" she grunted.

"Might come in handy," he said, trying to remember Cécile's number.

The charity shop held rows of donated clothes and a wall of kids' games sat near the door. Fluorescent lights and fake plot plants hung from the ceiling.

"Right. Plan is, we get warning note to your friend and then across to Max's to discover what happened to cabinet," said Marya Petrovna, pushing open the door. Oyster nodded. The shop emitted the smell of mothballs and old clothes.

"Ugh," he said, wrinkling his nose, "I smell dead people's garms."

Marya Petrovna rolled her eyes and held out her hand. Oyster regarded her blankly until he realised she was waiting for the note he had scrawled for Broadsides. He had needed to borrow some of the old lady's stationery, and so it had been written on luxurious paper and sealed inside an envelope that felt as stiff as cardboard. There was a flicker of shame as he looked at his handwriting: Broadsides' name spelled out in childish block capitals. Marya Petrovna nodded and slipped the letter into her pocket before stepping into the shop.

Oyster spent the intervening time hovering outside with his hood up, trying to recall Cess's number. He wished he had taken to writing numbers down in a notebook the way he knew

Deano did. Thinking about his ex-crew captain made him feel very visible. He huddled inside his clothes and glanced around, his spider-sense tingling, but no one was eyeing him and Primrose had not reappeared.

Oyster jumped as the shop door swung open, accompanied by an electronic ringing. Marya Petrovna lurched onto the pavement with a surly expression on her face.

"People like you make me sick!" yelled the shop assistant as the door slammed shut.

Marya Petrovna looked shaken. Oyster was surprised. He had taken it as a point of perverse pride that nothing could rattle the old lady.

"What the hell happened in there?" he said.

There was a banging on the glass door and behind it stood the shop assistant, shooing them away. She had a phone to her ear, and she pointed to it and then at them.

"Never mind," said Marya Petrovna, stumbling back along the pavement in the direction of the station. She seemed shaken up.

"Did you try and lift something?" said Oyster, pocketing his new phone.

Marya Petrovna shook her head.

"Did you hand the note in?" he asked.

She looked past him and shook her head once more. He suddenly felt sick.

Oyster grabbed her arm and stopped her walking. Her turned her to face him.

"I don't understand," he said. "What happened?"

Marya Petrovna hustled to the nearest litter bin, peered in and extended a hand.

Oyster was totally mystified by her behaviour.

She stood, brandishing a free newspaper which she flicked through.

"*Kurwa*," she hissed, handing him the opened paper. "Pissing, fucking, shit-turds. Look."

Oyster looked down. There, beneath a headline about a gang murder, was an e-fit portrait of his own face.

A cold feeling crept up from the pit of his stomach, enveloping him. His eyes ran over the words of the article, and although he was reading them, their meaning refused to sink in.

The article described how a couple of kids fishing near the Thames had discovered the murder victim's disfigured remains. The victim had been knocked unconscious, strangled and then had their throat cut in what the paper described as a *vicious ritual killing*. Oyster had been named as the prime suspect.

The only lead the police had regarding the victim's identity was that he was a young male, and that one of their tattoos had read *Ida*. The story concluded with an off-the-record briefing from a police source suggesting the murder was the result of a drug-related turf war.

He looked up at Marya Petrovna.

"I recognise that ink," he said. His mouth worked on its own and his voice didn't sound like it belonged to him. He ditched the paper and turned to Marya Petrovna.

"They got him," he said.

She put a spade-like hand on his shoulder. He didn't shrug it off. Her eyes were greyer than they'd ever been.

"They're saying it was drug-related, but Broadsie would never have got himself mixed up in any of that. I know it."

She nodded, grabbed him by the hand, leading him away. He numbly relented.

"Come," she said. "We need to get away from here. Is too public."

Oyster's head was full to the brim. Things were moving too fast now. Everything was snowballing into some sort of climax and he was wound up in the middle of it all, unable to extricate himself. Like a kid coming down a slide that was too fast, too steep. He just wanted to go home. To forget about all of this. And then he thought about Broadsides, who would never be able to go home. *And it was all his fault.*

"Change of plan. As much as it pains me, we should forget cabinet for now. I think time really has come to find your father," said Marya Petrovna to his back. "This was ritual murder.

Sacrifice of some sort. And the struggle between Lugones and Cerunnos is at root of all of this. We need to find your father and warn him. As long as we have coins then Cerunnos cannot start ritual, but clock is ticking."

Oyster nodded. He was sick of being everybody's plaything. He needed to take control of the situation. And the old lady was right, he needed to get past himself on the subject. But the only way any of this made any sense was by finding Lucas and helping him. All that stuff Primrose had spouted about changes coming for everyone and everything: it couldn't be good.

Cobalt police car lights rippled on the far side of the road. Oyster closed his eyes and froze, but the car slid on past them.

"*Blyat*!" exclaimed Marya Petrovna. "Get head down. Idiotic bitch in shop has called out boys-in-blue."

The car pulled in across from the Salvation Army shop and a single copper emerged. Oyster mustered the swagger to look as though he belonged where he was. Marya Petrovna bustled off ahead of him, heading back towards the Tube station.

"Cool it," he said. "Don't move so fast. You'll attract attention."

He took a few steps and pulled abreast of her. With his face all over the papers he dared not look back.

"What they up to?" he said out of the side of his mouth. Marya Petrovna glanced over her shoulder.

"Mr Plod is going into shop."

"Great," said Oyster.

Up ahead, the Tube station seemed to recede into the distance. If they could get to it before these stiffs came out of the shop, he could fade into the background and anonymity. Up here, he was visible and vulnerable. It was just his bad luck that the Five-O had even answered the shopkeeper's call, but he guessed ruefully that a gang murder meant even they had to shift their lazy arses sometimes.

Oyster became very aware of the sound of his feet on the concrete in those long minutes. Next to him, Marya Petrovna's powered along, her breathing slow and laboured, all those cigarettes rattling around in her lungs.

"They have come out," said Marya Petrovna. "And are back in car. *Shits*. Head down."

Oyster imagined himself as being invisible. It was the way he and his gang tried to avoid feds on a stop-and-search kick. You looked at the floor and imagined that you were part of the city. The brutal colour of the grit and glass around you, transparent and beautiful at the same time.

He held his breath as the police car moved past, on their side of the road this time. Rolling to a stop halfway between them and the Tube station, at a parade of shops that ended in a kebab joint and a convenience store. It was dark now and they were bathed in the car's headlights as it pulled up ahead of them. Oyster's sore hand throbbed as adrenaline flooded his body. His fingers and toes tingled and went cold. Fuck. Had they been made?

Oyster wanted to turn tail and run.

"Hold it," said Marya Petrovna.

A cop emerged from the car as they were passing. He was laughing ostentatiously at some private joke. For a heart-stopping instant, he squinted at Oyster, but then continued into the kebab joint.

Marya Petrovna caught Oyster's eye, counted to three on one hand, and sped up, power walking towards the station.

"Come on, I am thinking we don't have much time before this one puts two and two together," she called over her shoulder.

She hurried into the darkened mouth of the station, clogged with rush-hour commuters, pulled a ticket from her bag and pushed her way through the gates. Close behind, Oyster took a running jump and galloped over the turnstiles.

"Why you did this? We already have tickets!" she yelled, waving them at him in exasperation.

"I thought we were in a hurry!"

"Oi, you there!" the police officer shouted after them.

Oyster caught sight of him as he ditched his kebab and broke into a run.

"Now, he wakes up," said Marya Petrovna with resignation.

48
THIS IS OOMPH!

They thundered down the escalator two steps at a time. Marya Petrovna staggered a little as she landed at the bottom. Oyster skidded, trainers squealing on the polished granite as he dodged around shocked commuters.

They sped through the brightly lit hallway and along to the end of the nearest platform. The acrid smell of electricity wafted from the tunnel's entrance.

"*Come on, come on,*" sang Oyster to himself. If they could make it onto a train they might be able to dodge the feds, but it wouldn't be long before they were down here, and it would all depend on timing. He bobbed over the platform edge, looking for the lights of the next train. Marya Petrovna tugged at Oyster's coat.

"Remove," she said, dumping her leather bag at her feet.

"Get off."

"Just do it, flapdoodle."

Reluctantly, he pulled it off and handed it to her. She lay it on the platform. Before he could protest, she whipped out a stick and scribbled some symbols on it in sap, then handed it back. He grimaced.

"What was that?" he said, trying to clean the marks off with his fingers.

"Guava twig," she said, slapping his hands away. "Leave marks, please." He was about to protest, but realised that most of the time she had good reason for the daft things she did.

Marya Petrovna dumped her leather bag and dropped to all fours. Grunting, she leaned out over the edge of the platform, peering at the tracks below.

Oyster didn't know much about the mechanics of the Tube, but he did know that at least one of the rails down there was carrying enough juice to kill them both.

"Please, hold legs," she said.

Oyster grabbed her boots, and the top half of her body plunged over the platform.

"I dunno what your game is, lady, but whatever it is, you better hurry," he said.

Marya Petrovna groped around the greasy concrete. The rails sang with the sound of an oncoming train. Light ran along the tiles of the tunnel wall opposite.

"Now. Pull!" yelled Marya Petrovna.

Oyster heaved.

It took all his strength to haul her back onto the platform, just before the train thrummed into the station riding a wave of warm air. They rolled backwards together across the floor and came to a stop just as the doors opened with a hydraulic hiss. Passengers stepped around them, eyeing them with a mixture of amusement and unease.

Marya Petrovna held a squirming rat.

"Ugh," said Oyster. "Is that hygienic?"

"Knife," she commanded.

"Mine?"

"No good. In my bag,"

"Don't we need to just get on board?" He nodded to the train, distinctly aware that the cops would be arriving any minute.

She shook her head.

"This time we are relying on your talent. You are powerful walker and you have this." She prodded his midriff. "But both of us need to drift. Are you ready?"

Oyster nodded, but his anxiety stepped up a notch. Could he

do this again on demand? Last time it had made him ill.

He grabbed her bag as commanded and peered inside. There was a cricket bat, a ring of blackened hair and some dice. He had the very odd feeling that however hard he tried, he couldn't see the entirety of the bag's contents. Shaking it, he found a small curved knife with a blade fashioned from black glass and a hilt carved into the likeness of a beetle.

It purred in his palm as he lifted it out and he almost dropped it in surprise. He sensed it was old and hungry for blood.

"Come, come! Throw me knife!" she yelled.

He tossed it to her, and she caught it without dropping the rat.

"What's all this in aid of?" he asked.

"Listen," she said, "we agree Lucas is answer to everything. But you are not practised, so, for both of us to make trip to Greater London requires little more *oomph*."

Marya Petrovna waved the rat.

"This is *oomph*. Are you ready?"

The other passengers had retreated and one or two were filming the odd ritual with their phones. The two police officers materialised at the end of the platform and closed on them slowly.

"*Suka!*" Marya Petrovna exclaimed. "Out of time. We go with Plan B."

"What's Plan B?" said Oyster.

"Just like stage act, *Enoch*, we improvise," she murmured. "Make yourself ready. When I say, you need to do that thing that you do."

Oyster raised his hands. Trusting the old lady or not, he didn't like the way this was looking. He took a step towards the train, but before he could jump aboard the doors closed.

"No closer, please! I have knife," Marya Petrovna yelled at the police officers, waving the blade in their direction.

"Yes, we see that, miss," said the nearest police officer in a northern accent. "Let's all just calm down, shall we? There's nothing to get upset about, ma'am."

"No closer!" she yelled.

She brought her hands together, decapitating the rat with a

single sweep. A jet of blood sprayed onto her face. Smiling and bloody, she tossed its body onto the tracks.

"Okay, okay!" said the other police officer, raising his hands palms towards them.

"Stay back, or me next!" she yelled, holding the knife to her own throat.

The dagger twisted itself in her grip as though it was trying to slit her open. She began to croon in a low, croaking tone. The song was rhythmic and guttural, composed of what seemed like one long word. Oyster looked at her: covered in blood as she was and rolling her eyes, she looked terrifying. Primrose's warning about her rose at the back of his mind. The cops eyed each other uneasily.

She looked across at Oyster.

"Do not stand there like dingleberry! Ready yourself."

Fuck. They were really going to do this.

"Votive object?" said Marya Petrovna to herself. She paused her song and addressed herself to Oyster. "Your phone, please?"

Oyster's hand went protectively to his pocket, but his new phone was no longer there.

"Apologies. No time to discuss," said Marya Petrovna and dropped something onto the granite platform, before bringing her foot down on it hard. Splinters of glass and plastic scattered across the platform.

"Was that my phone?" he said.

Marya Petrovna shrugged and kicked its remains onto the rails alongside the rat.

The policemen took advantage of the distraction and tried to charge her, but Marya Petrovna was too quick. She lunged at Oyster, grabbing him by the throat. She brought the blade to his face. The cops stopped in their tracks.

"What is the matter with you?" Oyster shouted. "Have you finally lost it?"

"Any more of that and I make this one into pin cushion," she said to the cops, her eyes flashing.

She backed against the wall nearest the tunnel entrance. Oyster smelled pachouli oil and breath mints. Mixed in amongst them was the high-pitched twang of brandy. The cops looked almost as frightened as he was. It was only now that he wondered whether she might be a proper nut job willing to stick him. It might be better if she did. He couldn't face getting collared again so soon, especially now that he was a murder suspect.

She resumed her song and Oyster's blood thrummed in his head. He struggled for breath as her forearm locked around his throat. The tip of the blade twisted in her grasp, gnawing at his still bruised temple.

"Now, now," said the northern cop as the other one called for backup on his squawking radio. "Let's all just relax a bit, ma'am, no one needs to be hurt."

"Then back off, patronising assholes," she yelled.

The soles of Oyster's feet throbbed as another train approached.

The rails rattled next to them and the police officers were bathed in yellow light.

"Do the thing!" she yelled.

"Hold on," he said, and her grip tightened.

He shut his eyes and let the ache that was wrapping around his torso rise up around him. But this time it felt different. Something wasn't working. Instead of getting to the place of emptiness that let him flit, all he could see was Broadsides' face. He imagined his friend's aunt getting the news that her nephew was dead. And then he imagined the same thing happening to Paris. He felt sick to his stomach and empty at the same time.

"Come on, go!" she yelled, leaping backwards and taking both of them into the path of the oncoming train.

PART FOUR

THE LIGHTHOUSE AT THE END OF THE WORLD

49
PERFORMANCE ANXIETY

Oyster saw the face of the train driver in the cabin windshield: a smudge of horror and shock. Pain flared up his spine as he and Marya Petrovna bounced off one of the tracks and tumbled into the recess between the rails.

Shit! Something was wrong. They were still in *his* London.

They rolled to a stop and Oyster lay flat and winded. His survival instincts reminded him that there should be enough space beneath the rails to let a train pass overhead, but Marya Petrovna grasped him by the feet and hauled him over them. He kicked and shouted, but she was still able to drag him out of the path of the hurtling train, just as it was about to hit him.

It hammered by an inch away from his head, wheels clattering and brakes squealing. He wriggled away and propped himself up on one elbow. Dazed and terrified, but in one piece.

"What the fuck happened there?" said Marya Petrovna, leaning over him. "I thought you were designated driver?"

Oyster was as surprised as she was to still be there. His back throbbed from his impact with the rails. He thought about Broadsides.

"I dunno," he said.

"Ach," said Marya Petrovna. "Now, you leave me to do the work."

She turned on all fours and disappeared into the blackness of a low tunnel that ran perpendicular to the tracks. Her head emerged from the dark and hissed at him to follow. Her expression looked demonic given the amount of blood on her face.

"Follow before cops see us."

He crawled in behind her. The bag with the cricket bat was slung over her shoulder and her overcoat was smeared with blood and oil. Oyster followed, choking a little from the dust and dirt that she kicked up as she moved ahead of him. Still smarting from his abject failure.

"Where are we going?" he called, only able to see the soles of her boots moving in front of him.

"Well, I am hoping that despite your inability to get it up we still have enough energy to make use of localised weak spot."

"If that means we're avoiding getting nicked, then I for one am all for it," he grunted. He plunged ahead, spluttering a little from a fresh mouthful of dust.

"Also: you are so buying me a new phone," he said.

Marya Petrovna nodded in a way that gave Oyster no confidence she would actually do so.

"You are," he murmured, trying to imbue his words with a sense of menace.

"But *of course*," she called back.

After about a hundred yards on their hands and knees, Marya Petrovna stopped and Oyster ran into her butt. She scrabbled in her bag and the next instant a flame danced from her lighter. Her feet brushed Oyster's face as she turned herself around within the tunnel's confines.

"Easy, lady," he yelled.

She muttered something long and low to herself.

"Here it is," she said. "You sense it, yes?"

Oyster shut his eyes. There was an odd pull, anchored just below his belly. It was drawing him forward.

Without waiting for a reply, she kicked out and there was the sound of wood splintering. A sickly yellow light flooded around them and then, with a sudden yell, she was gone.

"What the fuck!" exclaimed Oyster. Gravity had suddenly

gone wrong. He turned to crawl away from the opening, but it was too late, and instead he fell forward through the gap she had opened.

🎲 🎲 🎲

He landed in a heap next to Marya Petrovna, who had already stood up and was dusting herself down.

"You see," she said. "Up not always up and down is not always down."

Oyster rubbed his eyes and looked around. They were in the connecting concourse of another Underground station, but this was deserted and clad in tiles the colour of smokers' teeth.

Marya Petrovna led Oyster through a passage marked with a hand-painted *Way Out* sign. Pale light sputtered from a single gaslit globe overhead. All the background noises Oyster associated with Underground stations were absent. There was no automated chatter of announcements, no muffled slap of a thousand feet on concrete. Even the smell was unfamiliar. It was something old and decayed that took up residence in the back of the throat. Everything about it was familiar, yet wrong.

Marya Petrovna was ill at ease too, leading the way through the station with hardly a sound.

A sign read *Hollow Fleet*. Oyster didn't have an encyclopaedic knowledge of the Underground, but the name didn't ring any bells.

"Wait a second," said Oyster. "This is one of those old, dead stations? I read about them once. They're all over the place. Shut after the war or something."

Marya Petrovna nodded, noncommittally.

"What! You actually *read* something. Well done *you*. Would you like cookie and milk? Do you need lie down?"

Oyster gave her the finger.

"Come on," he said. "We need to shift, cops won't be far behind."

"No, they won't." Marya Petrovna shook her head. "Have you

not noticed the difference? We are not in your London anymore. I was able to move us both a little sideways, just not as far as Greater London. So, I do not think boys-in-blue will be here anytime soon. Nevertheless, let us keep schtum all the same."

Oyster nodded. At least that explained how odd he felt.

The tiled wall beneath the station sign was covered in meticulous graffiti written in sharpie, but it was unlike any tag that Oyster had ever seen before. It started out as a mathematical equation, but progressively became more and more baroque, using occult characters and others that he did not recognise.

"What do you make of this?" he asked. Marya Petrovna looked at it and sucked her breath through her teeth.

"Well. I am not economist. I mean, Hayek used to come to club I used to run in Soho, so one picks up little bit here and there, but—"

Oyster raised a hand.

"Can we just cut to the chase here? I don't need to see your entire Tinder history."

She swallowed.

"So... I think this starts defining basic cost/price relationship. Definition of profit, this sort of thing. But then it gets bloody *odd*."

"*You* think it's weird? Jeebus, lady, we must be fucked."

"Last section is binding spell, seal of protection, but trying to protect the caster, and this space, from something?"

She led them through the passage, climbing a set of deserted stairs. The unlit tunnels either side of Oyster gaped like hungry, toothless mouths. Next to one was a wall of similarly intricate graffiti over which the words **Fisher was right!** had been sprayed in red.

Finally, they reached the main concourse. A bank of some of the longest escalators Oyster had ever seen led up, until they were truncated by a rough wall of unpainted breeze blocks. While Oyster was normally at home in the Tube, suddenly the weight of the world above pressed down on him.

He remembered that Broadsides was dead; in the ground too,

perhaps. *Fuck.* Despair yawned within him. He let it take him for a second, but then he realised that, more than anything, he was angry. He swallowed the feeling.

"So, this is another world... like Greater London?" he said.

"Indeed," said Marya Petrovna, putting her index finger to her lips. "Now, quiet."

"How many are there?" he said. He walked onto the dead escalator and climbed up it a little way. Its metal steps were covered in dirt and unfamiliar litter.

Marya Petrovna shrugged.

"No one knows," she said. "Poor Benjamin Fauks had some theories. And from letters we exchanged after fire, he travelled to quite a few. But this does not resemble any he mentioned—"

"How're we supposed to get out of here, though?" interrupted Oyster. He continued to pick his way up, holding onto the handrail of the escalator and then releasing it when he realised how dirty it had made his hand. Nearer the wall, he saw that it too was covered top to bottom in the scrawl that they had seen elsewhere. *First Broadsides and now this.* His frustration boiled over and he aimed a casual kick at the escalator's metal siding. It rang like a gong.

"What are you doing?" shouted Mary Petrovna. "Idiot! Here I am trying *not* to attract any attention, and here you are kicking everything you come across like toddler!"

"But what are we gonna do?" he yelled.

"I know this is difficult for you, but this is not moment to have tantrum like spoilt *child*!" said Marya Petrovna, glaring at him. Something at the wall's far edge caught her attention.

"*Suka!*" she exclaimed, her anger suddenly forgotten. The change in her tone was disturbing.

Oyster turned and ran back down the steps. Marya Petrovna stood facing one of the concourse's darkened corners, which appeared to host a large mound of dirt. The sickly, cloying smell he had noticed when they first arrived became stronger and stronger. There was something organic about it.

It wasn't until he was standing next to Marya Petrovna that he was able to recognise that the leathery thing in the corner had once been people. He covered his nose and retched. It was a family. Two parents huddled together, arms raised protectively around a third, smaller figure nestling between them. Oyster didn't want to look, but couldn't take his eyes away from the sight. His stomach churned and he wanted to throw up. He held his breath and counted to ten.

"What the *fuck* happened here?"

"Am not sure," she said, turning to him. "But far from being built to keep these people in, I think wall here was erected to keep *something* out. These poor people were hiding."

She knelt for a second and closed her eyes. Her lips moved as she said a silent prayer for the dead. Oyster thought about all the other darkened corners they had passed on the way up to the concourse. *Were they full of dead people too?*

"Hiding from what?" said Oyster.

Marya Petrovna stood and cleared her throat.

"Judging by the spell back there, a concept that was suddenly alive and conscious and out of control?"

"What concept? *Economics?*" said Oyster.

"Maybe more specific. But whatever it is, I do not wish to meet it."

Oyster shook his head, but before he could speak, a tapping sound echoed across the concourse.

Marya Petrovna froze.

The sound came from the other side of the bricked-up escalators. It had a distinctly metallic tone, as though something skeletal was descending a long metal staircase. The tapping came again. And again. Each time its tempo more rapid and more insistent.

Oyster and Marya Petrovna looked at each other. For a second all he could hear was their breathing: his, quick and shallow; hers, slow and gurgling.

Suddenly, the wall bowed as though something enormous was pressing on it.

"Run!" she yelled and together they fled into the centre of the deserted concourse, dodging into one of the darkened tunnels that led off it.

There was another throb that Oyster felt in his chest rather than heard and the wall bulged as whatever he had attracted tried to find a way into the station. Chips of mortar and cement rained down onto the concrete floor, and bricks convulsed. He didn't want to be around to see what happened next.

He ducked ahead of Marya Petrovna, hurling himself down the stairs. Directly ahead was a wall covered with a Tube map for the Fleet Line, along with a catalogue of unfamiliar stations. Something that felt suspiciously like bones crunched beneath his feet, along with fragments of broken bottles and yellowing advertisements for products he didn't recognise.

"Left!" shouted Marya Petrovna, close behind him.

There was a crumbling sound as the wall above them finally collapsed, and suddenly the air was filled with an aggressive silence. Then the whispering started. It was the sound of graveyard leaves stirring under cold moonlight. Oyster swallowed and plunged on into the dark.

50

THE NARROWBOAT

Oyster's chest pounded as he ran through the archway and onto the platform. He skidded and his hand sank into something wet as he steadied himself. Flicking the filth from his fingers, he ran on, his eyes adjusting to the darkness as he went. There was a ringing sound as his foot connected with a glass bottle and sent it spinning across the platform, and from up above he heard the sound of something large moving around. The whispering had ceased, but he felt very much as though he was a little pig hiding in a house made of straw.

The tunnel was full of faintly glowing water, sending ripples of light along the stained ceramics of the station walls. Filling its far end was an old narrowboat, rocking on the glistening water.

It had been a thing of beauty once. Constructed from varnished wood, it was about twenty feet long and roughly rectangular, with broad windows and panels that alternated down its length. One boasted the words Eastern and Metropolitan Railway in ostentatiously hand-painted golden letters. Around its hull were a ring of semi-inflated leather buoyancy sacks. He realised that what he had thought was a purpose-built narrowboat was, in fact, an old, refitted Underground carriage which lay low in the water, listing slightly.

Oyster peered into the makeshift canal. The underground tunnel had been excavated at some point to accommodate narrowboat traffic and the resulting canal was much deeper than he'd expected.

"Are you sure about this?" he asked. "I don't know much about boats, but this doesn't look safe."

A squall of whispers from the passage interrupted him.

"Up you get," said Marya Petrovna, indicating a worm-eaten plank that led up to an open carriage window.

"How do you even steer it?" he asked.

Marya Petrovna pointed left. "Port." Then right. "Starboard. Beyond that, your guess as good as mine. Now, stop dithering."

Oyster hopped up onto the gangway. It bowed under his weight. With his free hand he grabbed the nearest windowsill, ducked his head into it and sniffed. It was ankle deep in stale water. Empty plastic bottles and bits of paper floated within it, and other shapes bobbed around just below the surface. He had an unsettling thought.

"Do rats like water?"

"Get in!" cried Marya Petrovna. "Do not be so dainty. We do not have time."

Oyster jumped in. A choking, peaty smell of rotten wood, stale water and mouldering fabric hit him. His feet immediately ached from the cold.

Marya Petrovna pushed the narrowboat free of its mooring and an unexpectedly strong current gripped it, sending it towards the tunnel's black mouth, and scraping the gangplank along the platform behind it.

"Hey," shouted Oyster, grabbing at the plank to stop it from dropping into the canal.

Marya Petrovna hopped onto it and ran up it as quickly as she could, with her arms outstretched. She was much heavier than Oyster and the plank bowed. He hung on to it with both hands.

"Hurry up!" he shouted.

The other end of the plank skipped along the platform, swinging the boat towards the edge of the tunnel mouth. The gangplank caught, twisted and tipped into the glowing water. Marya Petrovna yelled and pitched sideways, hitting the surface with a viscous *plop*.

Oyster was frantic. Could the old girl even swim?

He yelled out and something nearby whispered his name. He jumped at the sudden sound. The voice. It had been Paris's. How could she be here? For a second, the sense of urgency slipped away. He didn't want to move. He didn't want to do anything. He just wanted to stay here. It would be alright.

"Hey!"

Marya Petrovna's head emerged from the canal. The anaesthetising sensation was gone. Marya Petrovna spat out a mouthful of glowing water, swore loudly and paddled towards the plank's trailing end.

Oyster leaned on the makeshift gangplank, levering it towards her. She grabbed it and together they slewed into the tunnel's mouth. Panting, Marya Petrovna worked her way up the plank, hand over hand, until she was able to pull herself up to the window. The boat tipped to one side as she climbed aboard.

"Now, your hand please," she said.

Oyster eased her through the window, and she lowered herself fully into the boat. The vessel lurched to starboard, swinging deeper into the tunnel itself. The whispering sound echoed along the platform; whatever it was that Oyster had alerted to their presence, it was still following them. They had to keep moving.

Rusted cooking utensils, pieces of wood and cardboard bobbed up and down within the boat like shipwreck victims. Marya Petrovna leaned against the cabin, breathing heavily. They looked at each other for what seemed like an age.

"*Vybliadok*," she muttered.

"What is it now?"

"Well, between you and me, am sure this water is getting deeper."

Wordlessly, they both snatched up pots and pans and began bailing. Within a couple of minutes, sweat beaded Oyster's brow and he had to remove his jacket and hoodie to tie them around his waist. His feet remained resolutely freezing.

"Faster," said Marya Petrovna.

"I'm doing it as fast as I can," snapped Oyster. "If we had my phone, at least we'd have a light."

"Ah, fantastic. How I have missed you talking about your bloody phone," said Marya Petrovna.

"Do you *ever* think any of this shit through, lady?"

"If I did, when would you have opportunity to carp and whine about every inconvenience like little girl?"

"I'd like to see you say that to my sister," he replied. "She'd have your arse over the side in a second—"

"Then I obviously picked wrong member of your family to go on the run with, did I not?" Marya Petrovna tossed two pots of iridescent water out of the nearest window.

"Excuse me," said Oyster, "but in the last hour I've been chased by the Po-Po, chucked in front of a train, lost my new phone, and now I'm being pursued by the spirit of Jeff Bezos in a leaky boat! I was banging along at the top of my game before I met you."

Marya Petrovna raised her eyebrows. Oyster tried to hold her gaze, but he couldn't.

"Anyway," he continued, "we were supposed to be looking for Lucas and this is where I end up? Karking it in some shithole where no one will ever find us?" Primrose's words about her spiralled into the mix. "What even *is* your game? What are you up to?"

The words foundered on a rising note of hysteria. A black feeling swept up from his chest, closing his throat. Without warning, tears brimmed in his eyes. He wiped his face frantically with his sleeve. He glanced over at Marya Petrovna, but she was bailing water out of the nearest window. He hated her in that moment; that she had reduced him to this.

"Have you quite finished, Cinderella?" She turned to face him. "My game, as you call it, is helping you. Certainly, it is not way I wanted it, but we are where we are. So, we can either stand around and whine about it, or deal with situation as it exists. I did best I could, given your talent is not working."

Oyster sniffed.

They looked at each other in the half-light and burst into uneasy laughter.

"Look. I do not know how long we will be able to stay ahead of whatever it was back there, but we need to think of other plan, yes?"

There was a wriggle beneath Oyster's armpit.

"Syzygy," he said. He thought about how she was able to move between worlds. "I can use her to get a message to someone."

Marya Petrovna looked up from her bailing and nodded frantically.

With a chirrup, his ink beetle emerged from her nesting place and crawled onto his shoulder.

"Come on, girl," he whispered. She was clearly unhappy about where she was and nestled close to his throat, mewling pitifully.

He grabbed Marya Petrovna and nodded to Syzygy. "How does this work?"

"As I understand," said Marya Petrovna, "you just give them a message. This is long shot, but we are desperate, no?"

She stopped bailing and rifled through her bag, retrieving a bundle of yellowed letters, bound with a black ribbon.

"These are Fauks' letters to me. Always keep them to hand," she said, answering Oyster's unspoken question. The letters had not been in the bag back in the station, of that he was sure. Marya Petrovna slid the top one out of the bundle and replaced the rest.

The paper was covered in a florid inky scrawl and punctuated with incomprehensible diagrams of machines and mechanisms. In the watery glow, Oyster saw that the last sheet was dominated by a sketch of an enormous looüt, striding its way across a black ocean.

"This is imprecise, dangerous way of doing things. Have to know what you are doing for it be successful."

"You got anything better?" said Oyster.

Marya Petrovna shook her head and held up the page.

"Come here, girl," she called. The nuajin hovered in front of it, chirruping. "Find Benjamin Fauks. He wrote this. Tell him to come as soon as he can. Otherwise, it will be too late."

Before she'd even finished speaking, Syzygy flew up into the semi-darkness, her wings a golden blur, and then she was gone.

"Is that even gonna work?" he asked.

Marya Petrovna grimaced and gave a shrug.

"I hope so, Enoch. We are out of options. Nuajin have preternatural facility for finding people. And from last letter, I see Fauks was in Greater London. If anyone can find way to help, it is he. Now bail. Perhaps we only need to make it as far as next station."

Oyster emptied two saucepans over the side, glancing at what he could see of the tunnel as they drifted through it. Decayed arches of brick shimmered in the golden light. The only noise came from the *drip drip drip* of water from the ceiling into the canal below.

The presence that had pursued them back at Hollow Fleet might have diminished, but Oyster still had the eerie sense that it was not far behind them, sniffing them out like the Big Bad Wolf.

He threw another saucepan of water out of the boat. Despite their efforts, the boat was lying a lot lower in the water.

"How far do you think it is to the next stop?" he said ruefully.

"Not sure," replied Marya Petrovna. "Can you swim?"

Oyster shut his eyes and shook his head. What was it about being around the old woman that meant he always ended up in the water?

They bailed for what seemed like an age, developing a silent, nervous rhythm. It was hard to tell how long they had been down here in the damp and the dark. Hours? Days? Oyster was cold, thirsty and hungry. And then the boat shuddered.

Oyster looked at Marya Petrovna.

"You feel that?"

The boat shuddered again. It was swinging lengthwise. Marya Petrovna tensed at the sudden change, then she carried on bailing.

She coughed – a heavy, phlegmy convulsion that passed through her entire body – then leaned out and spat over the side. The narrowboat yawed.

Marya Petrovna held up a finger, her head cocked to one side. She hopped through the water to the other side of the boat, looking like an overfed flamingo. The rippled glow on the brick ceiling outside was moving faster.

"What is it?" asked Oyster.

The canalboat tipped suddenly as though it was trying to shake them off, rearing up in the water before plunging back down again.

An old wooden seat shot past Oyster, just missing his legs. Marya Petrovna grabbed the nearest windowsill and started to make her way towards him, hand over hand. The boat bucked wildly, and they were both knocked off their feet.

As he fell, Oyster caught a glance through the window. The mouldering brick of the tunnel had been replaced by bare rock walls. Beyond it, the canal had broadened into an underground lake. Water crested into great, roiling plumes that seethed down into an enormous sinkhole, disappearing to who knew where.

The narrowboat gave another convulsion and rolled over sideways like a collapsing fairground ride. Marya Petrovna was swallowed by glowing water as the boat completed its death roll. Oyster's nose and throat were flooded by a choking, stinging tide.

Fighting panic, he pulled himself through one of the windows beneath his feet. He clawed his way to the surface after what seemed like an endless lung-bursting instant and coughed and spluttered, drawing in the cold air. Marya Petrovna and the narrowboat were nowhere to be seen. Panic had him now, rising up from his stomach like a barely suppressed scream.

A wave crashed over Oyster, and he was sucked under. He thrashed to the surface again, just in time to see the prow of the submerged boat charging towards him like a juggernaut. He kicked out of its way, but its flat nose still smacked into his shoulder as the boat was drawn into the sinkhole's orbit.

Oyster re-emerged from the water coughing, his shoulder paralysed by pain. Marya Petrovna bobbed nearby. She was lying backwards in the water, her arms outstretched. Electrified with animal terror, Oyster was drawn into the water's roaring maw. He spun dizzyingly on a vertical wall of choking liquid, and when he looked again, Marya Petrovna had disappeared. The narrowboat was on the opposite side of the spinning typhoon.

He swallowed a lungful of water, then another. He was drowning. He knew that now, but was too numb to protest. His arms ached and he was suddenly very drowsy. Oyster wondered if he would see Broadsides, and found himself worrying about what he would say to him if he did.

He inhaled again, but his lungs were full of treacle. Oyster's ears buzzed with icy bees. Cécile would have no one to look after her now. Fat lot of good he'd done, coming here; but the time for regret was past. He was going somewhere else.

51

WORLD-KING

Oyster swirled in the water like an insect disappearing down a plughole. But that was okay. He was going now. None of this mattered anymore.

Suddenly, he stopped moving, vaguely aware that he must have snagged on something in the cavernous interior.

"Not yet," came a voice from far away.

The water rushed past Oyster. He was manhandled towards the rock face.

"Hold on!" shouted Marya Petrovna over the water's roar.

Oyster coughed and spluttered into consciousness, wind-milling his arms in shock and surprise.

"Grab side!" yelled Marya Petrovna. "I cannot hold us both for long."

He floundered, the tips of his fingers eventually finding purchase on the slick rock.

He pulled himself up, puking lungfuls of glowing water into the passing torrent. Marya Petrovna clung to an outcrop. She looked pale and insignificant compared to the waves that the sinkhole threw at them.

He was very aware this was just a temporary reprieve; that they would not be able to hang on for long. The cold was already seeping into his bones, and his fingers were becoming numb.

And then the thing from Hollow Fleet station found them.

It crept up the tunnel behind, reaching out. The cold in his fingers was matched by a dead feeling that grew from within. Little by little, bit by bit, his interior life was going out.

"Don't worry, Miles. Stay put, I'm coming." It was Paris's voice again. "It'll be alright."

He wanted to let go and drift away, and he lolled forward into the water. There was a long, suffocating moment. His body bucked and flailed. He was too young to die, he thought. But then, that must be what everyone thought. He was giving something up, flying away, but at the same time, not really going anywhere.

He saw Cécile at her desk at Deeside Secondary, tugging her dark hair back and fixing it into a ponytail with a yellow hairband. It was a habitual motion he'd seen uncounted times before without ever appreciating its natural grace and poise. He loved it now, because he loved everything that was alive. Cécile laughed with a drainpipe cackle and cussed out one of her classmates.

At the same time, Oyster watched Paris sashay down Streatham High Street, drawing the eyes of all the men. He had always hated this aspect of his mother and been oddly proud of it too. He saw now the beauty and strength in her. And the pride and the pain. Then she was gone.

Now, he saw himself sitting at the back of Captain Cluck's. He was in Mickey's seat right at the back, the area they called the office. Based on his viewpoint, Oyster figured he must be stuck to the ceiling. The version of him sitting below was older and dripping in gold. Older Oyster opened a drawer in Mickey's desk and slipped in his hand. He drew out a big-arse blammer and waved it around.

The gun was like something out of a movie. The office's lights glinted on its oily finish. He couldn't hear what he was saying, but Deano, sitting across from him, deferred to his every word. In the corner opposite sat Baby Ed. The boy was nodding at everything Oyster said with a big grin on his face, but from his vantage point he could see into the boy's heart; could sense that he was fingering the knife in his pocket and thinking about when he could make his move and, quite literally, stab Oyster in the back. And then he became aware that Deano was thinking exactly the same thing, too.

But so what? That's exactly how the world was made and unmade, wasn't it? Now, he could buy anything and anyone that he wanted. He was at the top of the heap. There was no guarantee that Ed's coup would be successful. Maybe he would break them instead and throw their bodies in the river. Survival of the fittest. It was the natural order of things.

"Wake up, flapdoodle!"

Marya Petrovna slapped him hard across the face, snapping him out of his dream state. He coughed and spluttered.

"The thing that was back there, it's here now." He waved back towards the tunnel.

"I know," she yelled over the torrent of water. "We must be on our guard."

"But I'd made it," he said groggily. "I had all the shit I could want."

"This is how it gets you," she nodded, "shows you what you want. What could be. We have to stay in moment."

Oyster flexed his freezing fingers as much as he could. A wave of tiredness washed over him. He looked across at Marya Petrovna. Her lips were blue and her teeth were chattering. He must look the same. It was pretty funny. He wanted to say something, but his words came out slurred, like he was drunk.

"Conserve energy," she said to him.

None of this mattered really, did it? If he released the rock with his fingers, the water would sweep him away. And why did that matter? He saw himself driving through the neighbourhood. He was in the back of Mickey's car. Without his old boss in it, the interior was much roomier than Oyster remembered. The car was warm. A crystal tumbler in his hand was filled with honey-coloured liquid. He peered out of the window. The estate slid past as he sipped at his drink. It tasted like rainbows. His gun pressed reassuringly against his chest. He might have to be strapped for the rest of his life, but he was the boss now.

He had the vague sense that someone might be shouting at

him, probably just some kids on the estate. There was no need for him to care. He was leaving something behind him, letting go of everything he no longer needed.

Something brushed his cheek, gentle as a kiss. There it was again, and again. It didn't matter. He yawned and stretched his legs. There was a delicious sense of drowsiness in his limbs. His eyelids were heavy. He could shut his eyes and no one would mind. He'd just be asleep for a moment. Oyster's lungs filled with honey.

Suddenly, the road up ahead twisted like a live thing, bulging and pregnant with menace. The tarmac liquified, bubbled before exploding, and the car reared up and flipped over. Oyster was sent spinning out of the window and was suddenly very cold. He was vaguely aware that something was emerging from the crater up ahead.

He heard yelps in the background, but could not be sure whether they were the result of fear or exultation. The thing slid out of the fissure in the tarmac, multiple limbs writhing, a beaked mouth clacking hungrily, and Oyster was too weak to resist as the creature picked him up with one of its many tentacles.

52
ADIONA

Oyster was hanging in the air, held so tightly around his midriff that it was hard to breathe. Around him everything was spray and foam. His head was still fogged with the images the entity had put in there – success, money and violence – but they were fading now.

As he emerged from its influence, he saw he was still in the cavern with torrents of water on every side. But the tentacled creature he'd thought was attacking them looked very different. If anything, it seemed to be trying to save them from the roiling water.

Its body was shaped like an enormous beetle, but parts of it were translucent like a jellyfish. Its underside was fringed with hundreds of pulsating tentacles that throbbed with rainbow colours, and which propelled it up and out of the water.

The creature's belly was a deep oily blue that reminded him of Syzygy's carapace, but its abdomen was transparent and arched into something like a dome. Gills running along its underside spouted jets of smoke or steam. The creature had used its tentacles to pluck both him and Marya Petrovna from the water, and they hung suspended above it.

Oyster had to rub his eyes to make sure he was seeing what he thought he was seeing, but there was no denying it. Inside the creature's translucent abdomen sat an old man wearing an ancient two-piece suit. He was laughing and waving, looking like he was having the time of his life. For once, someone looked pleased to see them.

With a gut-wrenching motion, the creature swooped Oyster towards a mouth that opened in its rainbow belly. He cried out, frightened for an instant that he was going to be the creature's breakfast. There was an uncomfortable instant as he passed along a dark sticky passage before being regurgitated inside the creature itself.

The smell within was damp and foetid, and he drew in a few heavy breaths of air. Next to him Marya Petrovna lay unmoving.

"Huzzah!" cried the old man. "Let us make our escape! All hands prepare for flux!"

Oyster saw that their pilot was connected to their vessel by long trails of translucent material which ran from his forehead and hands into the creature itself. Around his feet were a cluster of jellyfish flowers that he used as pedals to steer the craft.

Suddenly, the barge reared up out of the water on a direct collision course. Oyster braced himself as the wooden bow of the craft loomed, but with a cackle the old man pressed down one of the jellied flowers and the vessel rolled out of the narrow boat's path.

The man caught Oyster's eye and winked.

"Nothing to concern yourself about, young man!" he said, twisting the stems of another two of the controls. "Now, best make ready! Hold your breath, Adiona!"

Oyster realised that the man was addressing himself to their vessel. There was a popping sound, and the creature sank back into the centre of the sinkhole, the water raining onto the translucent cabin in a way that reminded Oyster of being on the inside of a carwash.

There was an instant where they seemed to be travelling down a long, dark throat, and Oyster felt a pressure change in his ears. The rainbow colours on the creature's belly pulsed throughout the craft and the entire vessel throbbed and contracted.

The cabin was flooded with greenish daylight. They were floating in a brown stretch of sea. On the horizon, Oyster saw a muddy beach and the low blackened skyline of Greater London. Had the old lady's crazy gamble with Syzygy worked?

Oyster took a deep breath. They might be safe, for now.

"Excuse me," he said, "but are you Benjamin Fauks?"

The man's face lit up and he nodded.

He leaned over, tending to Marya Petrovna, who opened her eyes and then closed them again.

"I dunno how exactly, but we're here," he said. Marya Petrovna shook her head groggily, unable to remain conscious. Her skin was pale, and her lips blue. Oyster removed his wet coat and draped it over her, though he wasn't sure how much it would help.

Fauks pulled at one of the controls and, with a shudder, the creature's rear carapace flitted apart to reveal four gossamer wings. There was a throaty buzz and they wobbled into the air.

"Holy shit," said Oyster. "This thing can fly as well?"

"But of course!" cried Fauks triumphantly.

The creature banked, skimming low over the murky water as they drew towards Greater London on the horizon. This was the first time Oyster had ever flown, and he wasn't keen on the sensation. It was all he could do to resist the primal urge to press himself to the cabin floor and close his eyes tight.

Fauks winked at Oyster again, but in doing so lost control of the craft which coughed, spluttered and plunged towards the sea. Oyster's stomach heaved and he squinted with discomfort.

"Apologies!" yelled Fauks airily, wrestling the controls to return them to a level flight path. "Still gettin' accustomed to this. Dashed tricky to fly is Adiona! Have to avoid distractions." He glanced at Marya Petrovna. His eyes widened and they yawed wildly.

"No, no, no! Not at all! Fault is all mine, dear girl," he said, patting the controls affectionately.

"How about you fly first, and we'll get to the questions bit later, eh?" said Oyster.

He busied himself by taking care of Marya Petrovna and sneaking surreptitious glances at Fauks to size up if they were in danger. The pair of them had been friends in the past, but it sounded like a lot of shit had hit the fan since then.

On the man's head was a periwig tied with a black velvet ribbon. His pointed features were accented by a waxed moustache and goatee beard. He was dressed in a dark blue topcoat, calf-length trousers that were trimmed with gold braid and white knee stockings. On his feet were low-heeled shoes adorned with large brass buckles and pointed toes. Lying on the cabin floor was a thin sword in an elaborate, though rusty, scabbard. To Oyster, he looked as though he might have fallen out of a nursery rhyme.

Marya Petrovna shivered and coughed. He didn't know much about first aid, but she was not rallying.

"I think we need to warm the lady up," Oyster shouted over the thrum of Adiona's wings.

"Indeed," replied Fauks. "Addie, dear girl, can you contrive to assist us?"

Oyster yelped in surprise as the cabin floor rose up like a welt around Marya Petrovna's prone figure and began to heat up. Soon enough colour had returned to Marya Petrovna's cheeks and her lips had lost their bluish tint. She stirred.

"Stay put for now," whispered Oyster. "Once we've arrived wherever we're going we'll sort you out, old girl."

Marya Petrovna grunted in agreement. Her eyes flickered.

"Need to tell you something, Enoch," she murmured. "Some *things*, actually."

"Whatever they are, they can wait," said Oyster. Unthinking, he reached out and squeezed her hand. It was as heavy and cold as a garden spade. A smile played across her face. He let her hand fall back to her side.

Adiona's wings vibrated at a lower frequency and she lost altitude, dropping towards the sea in a low arc. Oyster looked up. Through the transparent blister of the cabin, he saw the clouds painted onto the lid overhead. Even out here, over the sea, they were under the dome. Just how big was it?

"We're almost there," said Fauks out of the corner of his mouth. "Do you see her?"

Oyster looked down, expecting to see Greater London's cityscape below them. Instead, the city was way over to the right.

Then a trumpeting call rang out. It was a deep sub-bass throb, and with a sudden flash of recognition, he realised it was the same sound that he'd heard down on the beach when he'd met Nonesuch. Adiona yawed, and it was only then that their destination became visible.

"Woah," said Oyster.

A great, multi-legged looüt hove into view. It was steaming away from them, picking its way through the dark ocean below. Just like the one he had seen on the beach, this creature was an enormous mixture of animal and machine. He couldn't be sure, but this one might have been even larger than the one he'd seen before.

It looked as though someone had taken the biggest factory ever, mashed it up with a small city, and then erected the whole thing on gigantic insect legs. Fumes gushed from the pipes running the length of its body and it left a trail of black smoke in its wake. It reminded him of the daddy long legs that used to invade his bedroom on hot summer evenings.

With another foghorn blast the creature chugged to a halt, coming to rest in a cloud of smoke.

"Shit, we're not gonna land on that thing, are we?" asked Oyster.

"Of course," said Fauks, not looking at him, "where else would we be going?"

The looüt gave another elephantine hoot and raised its abdomen. As they circled, they were close enough for Oyster to get a whiff of its animal scent. He wrinkled his nose. Great sagging teats hung from its underside and there were translucent patches of skin through which he saw the silhouettes of people.

Oyster stared in disbelief.

"Is that thing carrying passengers?"

"Indeed, she does," Fauks replied. "The Spitalfields is my – or I should say, our – home."

Oyster steadied himself. It was only then that he noticed Marya Petrovna was mesmerised by Fauks rather than their destination.

Adiona adjusted her speed and dropped towards a flattened area on the looüt's rear in a final approach. Oyster clutched for handholds, trying not to lose what little food remained in his stomach.

They bounced onto the makeshift landing pad. Adiona's tentacles knotted around leathery loops that rose from the Spitalfields' surface, securing them tightly. Oyster exhaled loudly.

"A great landing, my boy!" cried Fauks, grinning at Oyster.

He jumped free of the pilot's harness, hurriedly fastening his scabbard around his waist. He sprang to Marya Petrovna's side and helped her to her feet.

"I hardly dared to hope when I received your missive! But it really is you! Marya Petrovna Dozvhenko-Kaminsky!"

He bowed low, grabbed Marya Petrovna's still icy paw and planted a kiss on it. His scabbard, belted too loose, fell around his ankles.

"It is a pleasure to see you again. It has been *too* long."

"Benjy, can it really be you?" Marya Petrovna's eyes watered with sudden warmth.

"The very one! The very same!" yelled the man with a flourish. "And you! Why, you look exactly the image of the day I last saw you. *Exquisita!*"

Marya Petrovna laughed. "Same flattery as always. You have not changed either, you old rogue."

"Indeed," he said. "Perhaps. But what is one hundred and thirty years *entre le meilleur des amis?*"

"Allow me to introduce my assistant, Oyster."

Fauks re-belted his sword around his waist and offered Oyster his hand.

"Benjamin Isaiah Fauks, Arch Mercator of the Spitalfields at your service."

Oyster nodded and Fauks pumped his arm warmly.

"A pleasure, sirrah! An absolute pleasure! Any confederate of Madame Dozvhenko is, *quod negotium poscebat*, a confederate of myself!"

"Well, now you two have quite finished tugging each other off, can we get on here?"

"But of course! Welcome aboard both of you. All our facilities are at your disposal."

Meeting Fauks had revived Marya Petrovna's spirits; she stood slowly, cracking her knuckles. Oyster noticed that, despite the entire episode with the whirlpool, her black leather bag had remained looped over her neck and shoulders. She removed it now and picked around in its contents, removing her beaded tobacco pouch.

Fauks addressed himself to their vessel.

"Adiona, we are ready for disembarkation."

At his words, an area in the rear of the cabin floor melted away, revealing a quivering, person-sized tube that led down into the bowels of the looüt itself. Undulations travelled up and down its visible length.

"Allow me to demonstrate," said Fauks, stepping to the lip of the tube and clutching his sword. "*Taille haut!*" he yelled and jumped, swallowed by the darkness below.

"Old boy certainly likes to make an entrance and an exit, doesn't he?" said Oyster.

"Indeed he does," she nodded. "Now, let us follow suit."

53
FAUKS

They followed him down the tube, landing on the organic equivalent of a bouncy castle, and clambered to their feet in a low-ceilinged, soft-walled corridor. There was the double ping of a bell and a lurch as the looüt set off again, sending Oyster and Marya Petrovna grabbing at each other for support. They stumbled their way up the tunnel until they reached a wrinkled membrane at the other end. Pushing through the slit, which closed with a *pop* behind them, they emerged blinking into the light beyond.

Oyster found himself in an antechamber decorated with red velour wallpaper. A pair of worn gilt chairs and a chaise longue were arranged around the walls. A thick, golden frame housing a mirror leaned opposite them. Oyster sniffed. A sickly, floral smell permeated everything like cheap perfume.

"Come! Come!" said Fauks, standing admiring himself in the mirror. "Greetings and *salutaciones*, once more."

He waved his hand and a nuajin swooped down from the ceiling. Oyster recognised her immediately.

"Syzygy!" he cried. She twittered in response and settled on his shoulder, butting up against his chin in a show of affection. With a chirrup, she slipped under his clothes and into her nest beneath the crook of his armpit. She was exhausted.

"A-ha! So, she is paired with you?" asked Fauks. "To tell

it plain, you have her to thank for your rescue. She arrived demanding assistance and would not stop badgering me until we despatched Adiona. She does, though, appear to be utterly spent after her flight between the worlds."

Marya Petrovna regarded the nuajin fondly.

"She is every bit as clever as I hoped," she replied "To be honest, old friend, I doubted it would work. It has been long time."

Fauks grinned broadly.

"Madame, *let us not question what providence in her wisdom hath wrought*. Tis enough that the Fates have seen fit to unite us once more."

"It is wonderful to see you, Benjy, but there are things we need to do. Something is coming. Something bad, I think. And we will need your help. We're looking for someone. An old colleague."

"Why you are in luck, then, for that is Benjamin Isiah Fauks' speciality." He turned and pulled a brass speaking tube from the nearest wall. He blew into it and was answered with a whistle.

"Midships, please proceed at full speed. And request that Madame La Pilota prepare the Brazen Head." He turned to Marya Petrovna. "As always, you may count upon me, unequivocally. Our bond was forged by peril and tempered by the heat of our own panache! *En garde!*"

With a cry, Fauks unsheathed his sword, thrusting it into the air at the exact moment that the Spitalfields lurched into motion. He went tumbling into the chaise longue.

Oyster looked on, not sure whether to be disturbed or amused by the man's antics.

Fauks stood, looking confused. He cleared his throat and fumbled to replace his sword.

"No doubt, you are both in need of rest and refreshment. The Spitalfields should amply provide in both respects. *Forward!*"

He indicated a membranous door which had opened at the far end of the hallway.

"Is he always like this?" muttered Oyster to Marya Petrovna, who studiously ignored him.

They followed into the Spitalfields and through a wood-panelled corridor whose floor was finished in chequer-pattern linoleum. The overall effect was of a suburban nightclub that had seen better days. Hanging at various points in the ceiling were what Oyster had thought were dim electric light bulbs. Another glance, though, revealed they were part of the market itself: larger, brighter versions of the lures grown by deep-sea angler fish. The lights throbbed in time with the Spitalfields' rolling movement. From all around, conducted through the floor and the walls, came the low murmur of people. Oyster's stomach swam.

They emerged through a low doorway and into a high arched chamber shimmering with chatter, so much so that Marya Petrovna had to raise her voice as she caught Fauks up on all they knew. There were stalls and small shops everywhere, thrown together in a ramshackle pattern. Shacks lounged against much larger and grander bazaars, coated in yellowing plaster. Their minarets and bulbous domes reminded Oyster of some of the posher Indian restaurants he'd seen. The sheer mixture of people, buildings and goods was dizzying. The air was alive with the smell of spices and food.

Most of the people were dressed in a similar style to Fauks: calf-length trousers, topcoats, powdered wigs and clubbed hair, and yet here and there were black-garbed gebel and people in regular street garms. All of this was too much to take in at once. The sensations hit Oyster like a wave.

"I ain't feeling tip-top," he said, leaning against a damp wall. His mouth was watering and his stomach was close to the back of his throat.

"Kinetosis is most common when one first boards, young sir," said Fauks. "Why, even I myself was stricken with it for some time when I made my home here. Naytheless, it will pass. In the meantime, this may help."

He pressed a perfumed handkerchief into Oyster's hand.

"If, as you seem, you are Marya Petrovna's *protégé*, I'll wager you are composed of sterner stuff than this. *Generalement*, the most efficacious manner to inure oneself to the market's motion is to pick a lofty point and fixate upon it, *thusly*."

Fauks stood still and stared at a point on the chamber roof myopically. Pale daylight shone down from a transparent patch in the chamber roof and Oyster stared up at it too, trying to tune in to the pulsating yellow light around him. He shut his eyes and inhaled, submitting to the Spitalfields' rhythm rather than anticipating it. He sniffed at the handkerchief and counted to ten.

"Onward!" cried Fauks. "If what Marya Petrovna says is true, we may have shilly-shallied enough already."

Oyster pushed himself away from the wall and the market chamber swayed around him. He lurched forward, Marya Petrovna at his side, feeling his way across the gently rolling floor like a drunk crossing a ship's deck.

54
MADAME LA PILOTA

Now that his stomach had settled, Oyster almost came to enjoy the market's rolling motion. The spaces they passed through within it had not so much been built or grown, but rather collected from other places. There were oak-panelled corridors, branching off into brick alleyways. There were tiled spaces and waiting rooms that looked as though they might have belonged to office blocks, libraries or even cruise liners. All were in constant motion as the looüt continued on its passage over the scudding waves.

One circular passage thronged with people. Here the skin of the great creature thinned to transparency. Oyster pressed his nose up against it and peered out. The backs of his knees tingled and his head swam.

When they'd first moved into Deeside, it had taken him months before he could look out of the windows without imagining himself tumbling downwards, end over end like a leaf in an autumn storm. But he'd made a point of doing it every day, steeling himself against the dizziness. It was a way of proving he wasn't scared of anything, although the knot in his gut never went away.

"Where are all these people from?" Oyster asked.

"Spitalfields is home to those who have fled the constraints placed upon them by the city or the East India Company. Or anywhere else, for that matter. They are, rather like myself, *inadaptés magnifiques*. Each one with a tale, oftentimes tragic. We are despised as outlaws and émigrés. As hated for our differences as we find ourselves bound by them. They leave us be, as long as we remain beyond their jurisdiction."

Fauks walked on, dancing with the undulating movement. Through the creature's skin, Oyster caught sight of the great stalactite-like formations he'd seen on his arrival. They hung in the distance from the dome of the lid near the horizon, reminding him of upended termite mounds.

"The hives," said Fauks, answering his unspoken question over his shoulder, "where the gebel are born."

As Oyster hurried to catch up, a fat, spider-like something crept into view around the stalactite's edge. The creature worked its way intently and methodically around the surface of the hive.

"Woah! What is that?" said Oyster.

"*Maiaguna kashaka*. It guards the hive," replied Fauks.

The creature's painstaking movements reminded Oyster of a worker tending a field.

"And what's it doing?" he said.

"Well, its primary crop is gebel," said Fauks.

Finally, they arrived at a large, jewelled sphincter door. Fauks removed a silver whistle and blew a few notes on it, and the door puckered open with a rush of cool air.

"The helm," said Fauks. "Madame La Pilota prefers a distinct *ambiance* compared to most of our crew and passengers."

Oyster took a breath and stepped into a darkened room.

"We have guests, Madame," said Fauks.

A horizontal slit appeared in the darkness, opening like an eyelid as the skin of the looüt altered to admit daylight. The room was braced with concrete joists arranged in a way that made it resemble the cabin of an old sailing ship. As Oyster's eyes adjusted to the sea-green light that dawned around the room, he saw it was crammed with every conceivable type of navigation aid.

There were maps of Greater London, his London, maps of England and maps of countries Oyster had never seen. There were globes that spun on brass hinges and cubes covered in silver dots that looked like maps too. Arrayed around the walls and in piles on the floor were yellowed rolls which, Oyster had no doubt, contained yet more maps. The air was heavy with the stale scent of old paper and dried seaweed.

At the end of the cabin was a figure in a ballgown that reminded Oyster of an old wedding cake. The person wore a netted veil, drawn tight around the throat and supported by branches of smoked glass that protruded from her head like antlers.

"Madame la Pilota," said Fauks with an elaborate bow. "Allow me to present our arrivals. Forgive me for this interruption, but events demand we plot a new course."

La Pilota glided towards them. It was only when she was close that Oyster realised she had no legs. Rather, she was supported by a pillar of grey muscle that snaked up from the cabin floor and under the lacy frills of her dress. Whether she was some sort of meat puppet or an integral part of the looüt wasn't immediately clear.

La Pilota's features were hard to distinguish beneath the veil, but her hair was long, shiny and of a black so intense and artificial that it was blue. Her features, too, bore only a passing approximation to a human face. There were doll's eyes and a sort of gap for a mouth. It was a face situated entirely in the uncanny valley.

Fauks introduced both Oyster and Marya Petrovna, but as soon as La Pilota clapped her glassy eyes on the latter, she stiffened.

"And what is this one's relation?" she said, addressing herself directly to Fauks.

"Why, we are merely old friends, *ma chérie*," said Fauks with a strangulated giggle.

La Pilota looked unconvinced.

"In any case, your message about the head preceded you, *mon chéri*," she said coldly. "That ghastly *truc* of yours is all prepared for use over there."

La Pilota waved behind her with a waxy hand. Over her shoulder stood a circular table with a metallic head in its centre. Around it were five black candles, giving off wreathes of sweet, fatty smoke.

Like everything Oyster had seen in Greater London, the

head's workings were constructed from repurposed components: clockwork cogs, pieces of an Etch-a-Sketch and some glass valves. The head itself, though, had been cast in brass from several pieces and its features were locked in a mocking leer.

Fauks advanced to the table and tapped the metal head in front of him with his index finger. He stepped back into the shadows, and returned holding a thick coil of grey sinew that connected back into the looüt herself.

"Do you have to use that *hateful* thing?" pleaded La Pilota.

"It is, alas, a necessary *accoutrement* upon occasion, Madame," replied Fauks with a wave of his hand. La Pilota grimaced.

"It's not so much what it says when you're talking to it; rather, I object to the way it mutters at the back of the cupboard after I've put it away."

Fauks plumbed the cable into a collar at the base of the head. Once attached, its valves fizzed and glowed with an orange light.

"So, Benjy," said Marya Petrovna, "we are trying to locate our old acquaintance Luka Fillian, who now goes by the name of Lucas McLellen, and whom I believe is avatar of Lugones."

Oyster had to hand it to the old man, he had a good game face; barely an eyebrow twitched. Without skipping a beat, he cleared his throat and busied himself with the head. Producing a piece of chalk from his waistcoat, he drew three concentric circles around it, then rapped on the head three times.

"Awake, please, good Doctor Magnus. I would converse with you a while."

There was a puff of steam from one of the head's ears, and to Oyster's surprise its eyelids flicked opened, its lips curled, and it yawned.

"SPEAK THY QUESTION AND IT SHALL BE ANSWERED WITH THE TRUTH AS BEST 'TIS KNOWN IN THE UNIVERSAL MIND."

There was an echoing, monotone aspect to its voice; something inhuman and buzzing that sounded like an insect in a bottle. More steam puffed from its neck.

Madame La Pilota hovered beyond the table's edge, her hands gripping the neck of her dress. Oyster wondered whether this device was what made Marya Petrovna so sure of Fauks' ability to locate people.

"I wish to know the situation in both time and space of a veteran *confrère*," said Fauks.

"PLACE BEFORE ME THY TOKEN AND PRONOUNCE UNTO ME THE TRUE NAME OF THY QUARRY."

"Ah," said Fauks, "but of course." He turned expectantly to Marya Petrovna, who gave a gallic shrug and turned to Oyster.

"Well?" she said.

Oyster frowned.

"Me? I got nothing. Aren't you supposed to be in charge?"

Marya Petrovna pinned him with a glance. He felt like the thin one from Laurel and Hardy.

"For fuck's sake!" he protested.

"Don't bring me into it, dear boy," retorted Fauks. "You do seem a tad scatter-brained for an apprentice."

"I said 'fucks', not 'Fauks'," said Oyster, exasperated. "And for the last time, I am not her bloody boy."

"Wait. We may have no token. But he is Fillian's son," said Marya Petrovna.

"Is he indeed?" Fauks peered at Oyster with renewed interest. "Well then. Let us make an assay. Approach the good doctor."

Oyster edged forward, intently aware of the head's twisted expression. Fauks leaned forward and muttered something in its ear. Its metal eyes rolled for several minutes; gears churned and its valves fizzed with an acrid smell. Oyster was coming to the conclusion that whatever scam the old boy was running, it had come to an end. Then the head spoke.

"ATTEND!" it said, steam flooding from its ears. **"THE PERSONAGE THOU SEEKETH IS BEYOND SKY AND EARTH. BEYOND SEA AND LAND. BETWIXT THE EMPYREAN AND THE PIT. THAT IS ALL."**

"Tell me something I don't know," muttered Oyster.

Fauks hushed him with a wave.

"Indeed, that is not very much to go on," he said. "Fillian would seem to be in existence, but that would be about the end of it."

The brazen head fixed Oyster with a lopsided gaze. It seemed very pleased with its failure to be useful. He bit his lip and thought, running through what had happened to him in the last few days. He thought of Syzygy, which was usually enough to rouse her, and he pressed gently under his armpit, but she refused to move. Then he thought of her previous owner.

"Wait up!" he yelled. "Tell it to find Motet! I'm wearing his jacket! Motet knows where Lucas is!"

Fauks nodded. "Very well. Let us try once more. Doctor Magnus, we seek the owner of this garment. Inform us of their co-ordinates in the terrestrial firmament?"

The head gurgled and twisted around to face Oyster.

"THY QUARRY IS WHERE YOU CANNOT TARRY," it hissed, **"HELD BETWIXT THE RED QUEEN'S BRIDGE AND CLERKS BELL TOWER..."**

The head wheezed to a stop, grinning horribly, its eyes half open. Fauks appeared unhappy with the answer and attempted to reanimate the device, but no matter how much he cajoled it, it remained frozen.

"Well, that's it," he said. "It would appear that we must take you where we are unable to go. We shall have to return you to that thrice-damned city."

55

TROJAN

Fauks led them across the market to a low chamber at the looüt's interior containing a scattering of rusted shipping containers. There was an instant of homesickness as Oyster was reminded of the Clip. Fauks pulled the bolt on one of them and swung its door wide, which squealed like raw metal.

"Please, make yourselves at home," he said, bowing low.

Within were two leather armchairs and a coffee table that had been made from the top of an aluminium barrel. In the container's centre, hanging a couple of feet from the floor, was a chandelier containing one of the Spitalfields' pulsing globes, which dappled Oyster and Marya Petrovna with diamond light.

"Allow me to bring you some refreshment."

Fauks produced a thimble-sized silver bell from his pocket and shook it. Within moments a man in a maid's uniform appeared bearing an enamel tray on which stood a dusty bottle of Black Tower Liebfraumilch, a pair of dustier-looking crystalline wine glasses, and a bottle opener.

Fauks motioned them to sit down and then laid the tray on the makeshift coffee table.

Marya Petrovna collapsed into a chair, sighing as though she had a slow puncture. Oyster joined her in the chair opposite. Fauks opened the wine then wished them good day and left, telling them that he would return when they had neared their destination. Marya Petrovna filled the glasses to the brim. The liquid shimmered in the golden light.

"Well," she said, raising a glass that sloshed with the Spitalfields' undulating motion. "We made it. No thanks to you, of course."

Oyster rolled his eyes and grabbed his own glass as Marya Petrovna made short work of hers.

"Lady, I have done trojan work keeping it together this far. Get off my case," replied Oyster. He felt his failure keenly. But his inability to flit was only part of it. Broadsides was dead, and it was his fault.

Marya Petrovna harrumphed and pulled a soggy bunch of tobacco from her pouch. She spread it on the barrel, where it resembled a patch of seaweed, and grimaced.

"This place is a lot to take in at once. I could really do with smoke right now, you know?"

Oyster regarded her as she slurped the remains of her drink and refilled her glass. He was surprised. He had thought she would have taken this all in her stride.

"You not in your element?"

Her nose twitched. "Well, there is knowing about something, and then there is practical knowledge. Here, it is fair to say, you have more field experience."

Oyster took an experimental pull of the wine. Its dense flowery taste flooded his mouth. He pulled a face and swallowed; the sour liquid tumbled down his throat. He'd never really enjoyed getting plastered. He remembered bunking off school once, and sneaking onto Tooting Common, where he'd sat with a plastic bottle of cider and some Frazzles. He could still taste the fizzy, sweet booze now. How it had tickled his tongue and bubbled up his nose; how he'd burped up apples and the weird fake bacon taste of the Frazzles. He'd ended up drinking the entire bottle and then, helicoptered out of his wits, had stumbled behind a bush to puke and pass out.

"What's the matter? Not to your palate's satisfaction, sir?" said Marya Petrovna mockingly. She drained her glass with a seismic glug.

Oyster pulled a face.

"It is, as a matter of fact, you shady old wotsit." He took a deliberate gulp and swallowed it. The liquid whirled into his stomach, lighting up parts of him on the way down.

"Apologies," she replied. "I am a little off-balance. Perhaps not my best self."

Oyster nodded. "There's a lot of that going around."

He toyed with his glass.

"I been thinking about Lucas and Cerunnos. This whole 'great confrontation' dealio." He reached into his pocket and placed the bag containing Primrose's coins on the slate-grey of the barrel with a clink. He reached into the bag with his injured hand. It shivered with pain as he pulled out one of the coins and turned it over in his fingers. Peering at it, he could just make out Primrose's faint figure on one side. There was an answering twinge of dread. *Fuck him. The horned twat.*

"I mean, originally, I was thinking that we find Lucas to help me. Help us. Assuming the slippery fucker would have been up for it. But things have gone so beyond that now. I think we need to help him against Primrose."

He thought of Broadsides again and his words trailed off. There was a sickly, black feeling in the pit of his stomach. If only he had been quicker to warn his friend, maybe he'd still be around. He bit his lip and looked down at the floor. There was a black wall across his thoughts, blocking his ability to think or even feel anything properly.

His tattoo itched and he scratched at it distractedly. *And what the fuck is going on with you? You've been a literal pain in my side since the moment I had you done, but now you won't let me flit.*

"Well, I am anxious about cabinet," said Marya Petrovna. She wiggled the empty wine glass in her hand and then refilled it. "I know we had to do what we had to do and all that. But still, it niggles. It is loose end."

She slurped at the glass, and her words were slurred. With a snort, she leaned back in the chair and closed her eyes. Within seconds she let out a snore that would have put a warthog to shame.

Oyster emptied the remains of the bottle into his own glass and sipped at it. He thought back over everything that had happened since he'd left home. Nonesuch, Primrose, Motet. It was hard not to feel like a complete failure. Marya Petrovna let out another crocodilian snore.

He studied the valleys and gullies of her face. It was odd to see her immobile. Strange, he thought, to have someone loom so large in your life and to know so little about them. That said, he thought he'd known Baby Ed and Deano, and look what had happened there.

The wine eddied around his head. He replaced the coin and shoved the bag back into his jacket. The rolling motion of the market combined with the pulsing chandelier were claustrophobic. He had to get out of here, so he skulled the remaining wine and stood. The Spitalfields lurched and he steadied himself against the table, heading for the door.

56

BAR FLY

Stepping out of the container, Oyster found himself in another of the Spitalfields' high-ceilinged chambers. The sounds and smells were overwhelming. Like the echoes of a thousand swimming pools combined with the noise from the Emirates Stadium.

If the sound was difficult to cope with, the smell was even worse. He snorted to clear his nostrils, but the air was filled with a heady mixture of blood, spicy food and wet offal. He couldn't tell what was native to the looüt and what was the result of her inhabitants.

He wrinkled his nose and leaned against the damp muscle of the chamber wall to steady himself. Beneath his feet at irregular intervals were large, pale ovals which shone with pearly light. Like the larger lights overhead, these things had grown in place. Looking up, the deep blue and crimson walls turned to black as they ascended. He didn't like to admit it, but this place stunned him. He took a deep breath and steadied himself. The wine was making it difficult for him to gather his thoughts.

He emerged through another sphincter-like doorway into an area dominated by bars. People nursed drinks, huddled around tables that emerged fungus-like from the floor, sitting on old sofas and mismatched chairs which Oyster guessed were yet more refugees from the beach.

He stumbled to an empty table and dropped into a chair. If what Fauks had said was true, they would have to head deep into

Greater London; but if he could get a message to Motet, then maybe Oyster could get him, Nonesuch and that mutt they hung out with out of the city's grasp entirely.

He put his hand beneath his armpit. There was a chirp and Syzygy stirred.

"You okay there?" he whispered. She responded with a twitch and a staccato crackle, before slipping out to peer over the neck of his T-shirt.

"S'okay, baby," he said. "Gonna be alright, I promise."

He thought about what Cécile would say if she could see him gurgling over a beetle. Actually, on second thought, she'd probably be down with it. She had always been smarter than him.

"'Fraid I'm gonna need you to haul my arse out of the fire again."

In response, Syzygy crept out of his clothes and flew to the table. He stroked her with his swollen fingers and she purred and nuzzled in response.

"You recovered enough to give it a shot?"

She chirruped in a way that he knew was a yes.

"Okay," he whispered, "I need you to find Nonesuch and her bro'. Get 'em to meet us at the beach, where we first met. If they can hang there, we'll pick 'em up."

With a flutter she was dancing on the air, flying up and into the heart of the chamber, where he lost sight of her. He felt anxious and empty to see her go. But things were coming to an end. He sensed that now. He would need everyone's help to get this done.

He stretched the fingers of his bitten hand and rubbed the knuckles, which ached deep in the bone somewhere. The snake's poison wasn't out of him yet. In a way, it might never be.

Oyster looked around him at the hubbub and life within the Spitalfields. He felt protected by his anonymity here and he liked it. He enjoyed not having to worry whether someone was going to bust out of the crowd and try to collar him, cut him, or even grass him up to Big Mickey. Why not just stick here? Drift away. No one need know that he was here. But what about his sis? If he didn't act, she might end up like Broadsides.

His thoughts were drawn to his lost friend. If he'd never started all of this then Broadsides would still be alive. He stamped on the train of thought. This wasn't helping. He needed to think of practical things. Why was he unable to flit? He formed a fist with his swollen hand and punched the tattoo. He winced at the pain. *Why aren't you working, you inky piece of shit?*

He took a few breaths and focused on a spot on the slowly rolling floor of the Spitalfields. *Let me see. Just an ickle jump.* He shut his eyes and cleared his mind. *Nothing is true. Everything is permitted.* He pictured himself there, and his tattoo flared with a pain so intense that it felt like the flesh was burning. The sensation rolled up from his torso and engulfed his body for an agonising instant. He bit his lips to stop himself from crying out. He opened his eyes expectantly, but he hadn't moved.

He swallowed his disappointment whole. *Enough.* He stared up at the ceiling, letting the pain radiate away from him. Above, the great canopy of muscle that was the Spitalfields rippled gently. The translucent sections showed darkness had come already. He shook his head. Up there, embedded into the looüt, a row of pale ovals shimmered. There was a twinkle and suddenly a shoal of stars swam like silver fish in the darkness overhead.

"Eggs."

Oyster spun around. Next to him was Fauks.

"This is an egg chamber," he continued. "Originally, they would have filled here, before she could lay them. Back in the great days of trade, marketeers would harvest them and grow them, mate them with a pilot."

"How many of these markets did there used to be, then?" Oyster asked.

"Oh, dear boy. Back before the East India Company ran everything? Countless. But these days our numbers are much reduced. If memory serves, still in operation there are," he raised a delicate hand and counted off with his fingers, "the Billingsgate, the Petticoatlane, the Borough and the Camden." He cleared his throat and lowered his voice. "And then there are others: the black markets, such as the Culduggan and the Sinecure."

"Black markets?" said Oyster.

"Inhabited by brigands, anthrophagists and worse. One really does not want to encounter them. Even talking about them is meant to bring bad luck. Rational as I am, I see no reason to tempt the Furies."

"Sound approach. So, what's the deal—" said Oyster.

A low-pitched siren interrupted him.

Oyster pulled a face.

"Come with me," replied Fauks, "we're nearing the city."

57
LEVIATHAN

The siren continued its mournful wail as Fauks led Oyster out of the egg chamber and to the nearest speaking tube. The mood inside the Spitalfields had shifted. There were fewer people visible, and those that were looked to be packing items up and closing stalls. Obviously, they were as happy about going near Greater London as Oyster was.

"One cannot blame them," said Fauks, noticing his gaze. "One of the ways we survive is by having as little to do with the city and its agents as possible. We trade with them when we must, but that is about the measure of it."

He lifted the speaker and was answered with the customary whistle.

"Madame La Pilota, it is I, Benjamin Isiah Fauks. Please may we request passage to the Hall of Egress?"

An opening puckered in the wall next to them.

Oyster regarded it suspiciously. It looked especially unpleasant.

"In you hop, dear boy! Nothing to be afraid of. *Taille haut* and so forth!"

"I ain't getting in that. Looks like an arsehole."

"Eh? What?" said Fauks.

He peered at Oyster blankly, then squinted at the opening for a second before doubling over, wracked with laughter.

"Why, indeed it does!" he said, wiping tears from the corners of his eyes. "Do you know, in all my years of living here I have never noticed the similarity before. Well, I never! What *drôlerie*! I can see why she works with you now. Yes, yes. Well, now. Let us both plunge into the fundament head first, as you have so eloquently put it."

And with that he stuck his head into the hole and was swallowed. Oyster took a deep breath and followed.

They were disgorged into a low-roofed compartment that housed Adiona. Marya Petrovna already sat within the creature's translucent abdomen, waving as they appeared.

This was the first time Oyster had really had the time to take the Adiona in. Her flanks were a beetle's golden-green that refracted rainbows in the Spitalfields' pulsing light. Her tentacles rippled with colour as they flexed to keep her horizontal as the market moved.

Fauks noted Oyster's admiration. "Isn't she something? One of a kind. A mixture of looüt and nuajin. My own and finest creation. Her unique parentage is why she can go anywhere, just like ink beetles do."

"Don't get me wrong, I'm loving the vibes," said Oyster, "but what are we doing here?" He reached out to touch the vessel's side and it throbbed with life beneath his fingertips.

"One cannot just wander into the city unannounced. Especially not in a free market such as the Spitalfields. We will use Adiona to achieve ingress incognito."

"Sweet." Oyster nodded approvingly. "On that subject, I'm hoping I got word to my people, we just have to hit the beach and lay low till they arrive."

"Huzzah!" cried Fauks, grasping at his sword and stumbling backward, off-balance. "This night we will write another chapter in the never-ending tale of the bravery of the Miracle Club! I cannot wait to stain my sword with the foul blood of the clerks and all their pernicious kind!"

"Hey! Hey!" said Oyster. "Chill, we're not there yet."

Fauks shrugged and recovered his composure.

"Indeed. Indeed. This body may be frail, but as you see, the blood still runs hot!"

Oyster smiled. He wished he had this man's confidence.

"And on that note…" Fauks fished around in his waistcoat and pulled out a small gun, which he handed to Oyster.

It was a low-calibre, ancient hand-weapon of a size and shape designed to be concealed. Its ornate ivory handle made it look like it might have been stuffed into the cleavage of a madam in a brothel.

"Just in case," said Fauks.

The man saluted and Oyster stowed the gun in his jacket. They stepped though the mouth in Adiona's belly. Marya Petrovna nodded at them.

"Finished your snore-fest, then, grandma?" said Oyster.

The old woman gave him a *fuck you* smile.

"I am much restored after my nap," she said. "You should try it sometime. It might restore your usefulness."

Oyster winced.

"That was low," he said.

Marya Petrovna shrugged and gave him the finger. The muted caterwauling of the siren continued throughout the Spitalfields.

Fauks sat at the console that Oyster had seen on their first journey. The thicket of polyps that circled Fauks' feet attached themselves to him as he sat.

"You see!" he said. "Nothing to it really. She is entirely sensitive to the pilot. One sits here and Adiona manages the rest; cogitating upon the required course of action enables her to perform it!"

A barrel of butterflies danced around Oyster's belly at the thought of flying in Adiona again. For a moment, he was struck by the oddness of his situation. That a dead-end kiddie like him from the wrong end of South London was sitting inside this remarkable creature. Weird shit like this must be going down all over, all the time, he thought. The world was a stranger, more wonderful place than he had ever realised.

Adiona's gossamer wings slipped from their casings and began to whirr. The sound was deafening in the confines of the chamber. They leapt up into the air, and, ahead, a knotted wall of muscle unlaced and they swooped though the opening and out into the copper-tinted dawn.

Heading out in a wide arc, they flew around the Spitalfields before swinging back towards the city. Adiona leaned into the turn, and beneath them the dark sea boiled. As Oyster looked down, he wondered what creatures, if any, might swim in its depths.

As if in answer, far below in the deep of the ocean an enormous eye opened and blinked. Oyster barely had time for the sight to register before it was gone, leaving him wondering if it had really been there at all.

"Observe! Our destination!" yelled Fauks over the din of Adiona's wings. Directly ahead, the city of Greater London hunched on the horizon like a sleeping animal. It was wreathed in an early morning mist that had risen from the sea, and sparsely stippled with artificial lights.

Oyster swallowed; his mouth was dry. He hoped that Syzygy had got his message to Nonesuch and co. He didn't really want to spend any more time than necessary in that city.

As he turned the thought over in his mind, he realised that it was the chance of seeing Nonesuch again, as much as the danger of Greater London, that was making his stomach do quiet backflips. He sighed. This kind of thinking wasn't helpful. He already had enough on his plate.

To distract himself, he looked back at the Spitalfields. She had changed course and was now steaming at ninety degrees to them, running parallel to the city's borders rather than encroaching on them. Oyster soon lost the looüt in the haze.

He leant over and told Fauks to head for the beach.

Marya Petrovna looked quizzically at him.

"Change of plan," said Oyster.

Adonia shuddered as they dropped in altitude and scudded just above the waves. Suddenly, a great swell rose up, and for a horrid sweaty instant Oyster thought they were going to be swallowed by the ocean.

Fauks emitted a high-pitched giggle as they dipped and yawed sickeningly, missing the wall of water by inches.

"Do we gotta be this low?" asked Oyster with a calmness he didn't feel. He looked over at Marya Petrovna. She was gripping her seat with white knuckles.

"Indubitably," said Fauks. "We need to maintain such an altitude in order that we are neither observed by the city nor the Company. Arriving without the mandatory *bona fides* would probably cause a diplomatic incident, or perhaps a small war."

Oyster nodded.

"Okay. Okay," he said. "Let's do it your way. I don't wanna cause undue ruckage. Although, we might have one of those coming up soon anyway."

Now it was Fauks' turn to look askance at Oyster, but he asked no questions and instead busied himself steering them over another massive wave.

"The tide is higher than predicted," squeaked Fauks as the water slapped Adiona's canopy. "But we are almost there!"

The waves dropped away. Beyond it, Oyster saw the flat grey mud of the Beach of Lost Things. Fauks was right, the sea was higher than when he'd arrived. Now, it stretched halfway to the city, lapping around the rusted underground trains that curled and twisted like a nest of giant tube worms.

Marya Petrovna looked at Oyster and winked at him.

"Fear not, Enoch. It is all going to be hunky and dory. Calm yourself."

Oyster eyed her.

"I *was* totes calm," he said. "Until you said that."

"And Pope shits in wood. When will you learn. Admitting weakness is not decrepitude. Is sign of strength."

"Yeah, good luck telling that to my boss."

With a final dive, Adiona settled on the beach, behind the mountain of abandoned office furniture Oyster had seen on his first visit there.

"And thus we arrive!" declared Fauks, disconnecting himself from the console. He faced Oyster. "I have fulfilled my part. Now, it is over to you and your friends."

"Yeah," he said. "I guess it is."

BENEATH THE PAVING STONES...

Oyster squatted out of sight behind the thicket of chair legs, tables and desk drawers. He scanned the uneven battlements of Greater London's dizzying sea wall.

"I do not see them, your friends," called Marya Petrovna from inside Adiona. He shivered and pulled Motet's jacket around him. The tide had started to come in and so his feet were both freezing and sopping wet. The early morning wind buffeted him with the city's fishy scent.

His sense of time was always out of whack when he was here, but he was sure they must have been on the beach for at least an hour. Long enough for the bloated red sun to crawl into the sky and bear down on him with its lurid glow.

"I said that I do not see your friends!"

Oyster jumped. He turned to see Marya Petrovna standing a few steps away from him, puffing on a roll-up.

"So this is Greater London," she said, pointing over his head with the lit cigarette. "You know, I have heard of this place and others like it for many years. But it is something else to be here. You have shown this old woman new tricks."

"How do you like it?" said Oyster.

She lifted a foot that had sunk ankle-deep in the muddy sand and grimaced.

"Frankly, it is bit shit. Too wet. Too cold."

Oyster guffawed.

"It is, innit? When you think about other dimensions and such, you think it's gonna be cool. Not mud and fish."

"So, when are they coming?" she said.

"Fuck me, old lady. Give it break, will you."

"So, you did not tell them when you would be here?"

Oyster shrugged.

Marya Petrovna took a lengthy drag as though she could not believe her ears.

"You *do* understand basic concept of rendezvous, yes?"

"Come on. I didn't know exactly when we were gonna arrive, so I just told them to get here as soon as possible."

Marya Petrovna's lips took a final gargantuan puff from the roll-up before slinging it fizzing into a pool of dark water.

"In which—"

The sound of a shot echoed across the beach, followed by the sound of barking.

At the noise, Oyster instinctively crouched down behind the cover afforded by the assorted furniture. He was scared. Everything was heightened. He looked down. His reflection stared back at him from the sea water around his shoes. He looked different. Maybe hanging around Marya Petrovna and her menagerie had aged him. He reached into his jacket and pulled out the gun. *Fuck it.* He was finally packing. The weapon sat uncomfortably in his hand. He didn't want to use the thing, but as Fauks had said, maybe it was good to have, just in case.

He imagined Cécile talking to her friends about her loser brother who'd got iced in a turf battle. That was assuming, of course, that she even found out what happened to him if he died in Greater London.

The shot was repeated. It was muffled, coming from the other side of the wall. Oyster exchanged a glance with Marya Petrovna, who had retrieved her obsidian knife from the shoulder bag.

"You never heard that old saying about bringing a knife to a gun fight?" he asked.

"Person who said that never saw this knife," she replied, and the blade glinted like blood in the muted sunlight. Oyster remembered how it had felt back at the Tube station; how it had shifted in his hand like it had a life of its own.

"Fair enough," he nodded. "I guess you know what you're doing."

He examined his weapon, and located and flicked off the ancient blammer's safety. He'd never carried before, but he'd seen enough movies and TV to avoid the obvious gaffes. He swallowed and cleared his throat. The stock was slippery in his palm. He wondered how many times it had been fired. How many times it might have snuffed out someone's life. And then he wondered whether the thing might not just blow up in his face when he pulled the trigger.

"I got a sister," he said, "if anything happens—"

"Quiet, Enoch, eh? Now is not time," she replied.

There was another shot and then something deeper throbbed though the mud, causing ripples in the water. The beach door opened with a slam.

Oyster bit his cheek and squinted. He could just make out shapes moving against the monolithic wall. There were three at first. His heart leapt in his chest when he recognised the fairy-lights and sure-step of Nonesuch. In front of her, galloping at full pelt, was the dappled streak of Goswick, and bringing up the rear was Motet. The ominous throb came again.

Oyster's friends moved out of the wall's shadow, dashing across the mudflats in a weaving pattern, but they were heading the wrong way. Oyster stood and waved, yelling Nonesuch's name into the salt wind.

Then came their pursuers. A troop of clerks streamed through the beach door, angry insects stirred from a nest. A few of them dropped to their knees and took aim. Another brace of shots rang out. The beach was so flat that it was only a matter of time before one of them would find their target. Oyster jumped up and shouted once more, trying to attract Nonesuch's attention, to no avail. The water jittered from another far-off, heavy impact. *What on earth was that?*

He had to do something. He steadied his arm over a tabletop and took aim at the nearest clerk. He couldn't be sure, but he thought it might be the one called Scudder. He breathed in the smell of wet wood and the briny squall of the sea. But when he tried to squeeze the trigger, his finger wouldn't budge.

All he could think of was Broadsides. Dead. Buried somewhere. A sickly feeling welled up at the base of his stomach. Even an industrial-grade shit like Scudder had a mother. Probably. Maybe even had friends. *Shit*. He shook his head, trying to clear it. He aimed at another of the clerks, but he couldn't shoot at them either. *Fuck it!*

Finally, he screamed in frustration and threw the gun into the mud, disgusted with himself.

"You missed," said Marya Petrovna evenly.

"Please, just leave it out for once," he yelled. "Right. Change of plan, where's the old boy? We need to get Adiona cranked up. Gonna have to leave in a hurry!"

She looked back at the Adiona's now deserted cockpit.

"No idea. Have *you* seen him?"

Oyster scanned the area. Far out, where the sea met the sand and the Underground trains, stood Fauks. The old twerp had taken his shoes off, swung them over his shoulder and was paddling. Oyster couldn't quite believe it.

"Shit!" Fauks was too far away to help, and everything was happening too quickly. It was up to him now.

"Move!" he called to Marya Petrovna, running back into Adiona and settling himself in front of the console. Marya Petrovna was close behind. Then the ground shook. *What now?* He glanced back. Marya Petrovna had felt it too. Something bad was coming. They all had to get gone.

Copying Fauks as best he could, he placed his feet amongst the stalks and petals that clustered around the console's base.

Fly, he thought. Nothing happened. Another shot rang out. Closer to them this time. *Fuck. This had better work.*

Take off, he thought. *Lift-off. Airborne.*

Nothing.

"Houston. Do we have problem?" said Marya Petrovna over his shoulder.

Oyster tried to hide his panic.

"What would the old boy do?" he said.

"Have you tried introducing yourself?

Of course. The old dude was as demented as a pigeon, but he was polite to a fault. Oyster took a breath.

Hey there, Adiona, he thought. *My name is Oyster. I'm shitting a brick here and I really need your help to save my friends. Can we, like, skidoosh?*

Instantly, his lower body was engulfed in a network of translucent vines and polyps. A handful rose up out of the floor like time-lapse flowers and stuck themselves to his face with jellied kisses. It wasn't an entirely unpleasant feeling.

Oyster was awestruck; his sense of himself dwindled and he became part of something greater. A composite being. His anxiety evaporated. While he couldn't exactly read Adiona's thoughts, he was overwhelmed by the benign sense of a presence, similar to what he had experienced in *der hinter*, but a more straight forward one. More generous.

He opened his wings, and they leapt up into the green sky.

59

OYSTER-ADIONA

Oyster-Adiona spun up into the sky like a drunken sycamore seed. The sense of freedom, of being able to move left to right, up and down was overwhelming. They just wanted to keep going up and up and up. They wondered briefly what would happen if they just kept climbing? At some point, they knew, they would collide with the lid. But even that would be worth it. *They could fucking fly!* Their tentacles, filopods, sang with rainbows in the brine-drenched air.

They became vaguely aware that inside their belly cavity, Marya Petrovna was yelling in distress. *Okay. We need to level out. We're seriously off our tits here.* Oyster-Adiona suddenly had a newfound respect for Fauks. No wonder the old man struggled to control things when he was flying. It was hard to keep it even remotely together. Fauks must be a lot more disciplined than he looked.

Something ricocheted off Oyster-Adiona's starboard skin, bee-sting sharp. They turned their attention back down to the beach far below. *Oh yeah, right, the clerks were still down there.*

Flicking their tail in the thick air, they swooped down in a dive-bombing arc. With a twist they righted, tasting the ground just out of the reach of their filopods. Ahead of them were the clerks, and beyond them, pinned down behind a cluster of skeletal, rusting pushchairs, were Nonesuch, Goswick and Motet.

The low-register vibrations that Oyster had heard on the beach were getting nearer. It was as though a giant was stepping over buildings, making their inexorable way towards them.

There was another dash of stings as the clerks fired at them as they thundered overhead. Through Oyster-Adiona's myriad senses, they knew the one called Scudder was down there, twisted in fear and perhaps disgust at the composite beauty of what they had become.

Opening their belly hatch, Oyster-Adiona dropped themselves between their friends and the clerks. Thickening their facing carapace to reduce the chance of a lucky shot hitting a vital organ, their filopods gathered up their friends with gossamer fingers and loaded them into the safety of their interior chamber.

For an instant, Oyster folded back into his body.

"Soz for the manhandling," his voice said. "Explain later. 'Kay?"

Oyster-Adiona was aware of their friends' fear (Motet), approval (Nonesuch) and copious swearing (Goswick), but they had to get out of here before anything else.

They had learned from their previous take-off. Using the gelatinous coating of their belly-chamber to cradle their passengers, they leapt back into the air at top speed, trailed all the way by waspish crackles of gunfire.

They headed back downward just long enough to pick up Fauks, who was charging the clerks' flank with only a hand pistol and his drawn sword for support.

"Not bad for an escape, eh?" said his voice, once they were all safe inside. "Those fuckers really didn't know what hit them!"

Motet raised a single thumb but remained resolutely on the floor of the craft.

"Got your message, innit?" said Nonesuch, throwing back a long leather coat to release Syzygy, who yelped joyfully, fluttering to Oyster's collar and nestling beneath his arm.

"Well, that *was* nicely done, I must say," said Fauks, who was dusting himself off, leaning against the cockpit wall. "You are something of a natural, dear boy." He reached into his jacket and pulled out a jewelled snuff box. But never got the chance to open it.

The low sound that had been pursuing them rose up though

the ground and burst into the open. Oyster realised that Adiona was afraid.

"What is that?" said Marya Petrovna, pointing back towards the city through the canopy. A thick cloud of smoke had engulfed the section of the wall that ran along the beach. Emerging through it, stepping over the sea wall and onto the beach like a great spider-crab, was another looüt.

It was as large as the Spitalfields, but squatter and blacker, its belly closer to the ground. It was decorated with silver streaks and each of its sturdy black legs was covered with spikes. It was an evil-looking thing.

"That's a military looüt, sweeties," said Nonesuch, recovering herself. Oyster tried not to notice how her red hair turned golden in the sparkling light from her face.

"Clerks set it on us to flush us out, back in the city," said Motet.

"I believe it is none other than the Merriweather," said Fauks.

As he spoke, a series of orange explosions blossomed along the creature's bridge.

"The cannonade has commenced! Evasive manoeuvres!" he yelled, throwing himself down onto the floor with his fingers in his ears.

Oyster was yanked back into Adiona. They dived down towards the water, swinging from side to side in an effort to avoid the Merriweather's bombardment. The looüt moved surprisingly quickly, heading across the beach and into the ocean in a monolithic scuttle. It fired again and again, unleashing a barrage that Adiona-Oyster managed to evade, sending it splashing into the sea in a cloud of steam and spray.

But the Merriweather was wily, peppering them with cannon that hemmed them in and drove them forward; some of the shots fizzed into the sea ahead of them, some behind, while others still landed to starboard and port. Adiona-Oyster knew each subsequent volley was drawing closer.

"Make for the Spitalfields!" cried Fauks. The man was up on his feet now, waving his sword about unsteadily. "We shall take this vermin and her scurvy crew."

"Hey! Watch it, grandpa, before you stick someone with that knitting needle," said Goswick. Fauks side-eyed the dog, but sheathed his weapon.

On the horizon, Adiona-Oyster could just make out the silhouette of the other looüt. The sight filled them with a sense of home and safety, and they darted up into the sky, spinning left and right in an attempt to avoid the latest salvo from their pursuers.

But the Merriweather had them in its sights now, and one of its cannons finally found its mark. There was an explosion of light and sound, and with a silent scream one of Adiona-Oyster's wings was ripped to shreds and her others were perforated with smoking holes.

They tumbled from the sky, shock and pain breaking the link between them. Oyster's eyes widened as the sea fell towards them in slow motion. Marya Petrovna's eyes were closed, and she seemed to be in some sort of trance. Goswick and Fauks were open mouthed with fear at their sudden fall. The sickly-sweet smell of Adiona's burning carapace was everywhere and the bitter perfume of the gunpowder stung his nostrils.

Nonesuch and Motet's lights both strobed like mobile discos, but of the two, Nonesuch looked more angry than afraid. With a gulp, Oyster took his pain and forged it into determination. They weren't all going to die here. He forced himself back into communion with Adiona. She was frightened and in agony, but he embraced the pain, shared it with her. Just as Marya Petrovna had shared his pain back at her Lamasery. With a sigh, they managed to bring themselves back under control, just a few feet above the swell of the wine-dark sea.

With a twist and a roll, they were heading towards the Spitalfields. For their part, Fauks' looüt had changed course, peeling away from the horizon and steaming full speed towards them. Adiona-Oyster cut their speed in an effort to confuse the Merriweather's guns, looping to starboard and port in a desperate attempt to avoid another hit.

The bombardment continued around them, but they were

out over the deep of the ocean now and the Merriweather's lower draught meant that it sank deeper into the water as it chased them. Despite their injuries, Adiona-Oyster were beginning to open up some distance between them and their pursuer.

They balled up their strength and put every ounce of it into making themselves a difficult target, flying buzzing sorties up into the sky, pulling back to aft then charging forward in an effort to perplex the Merriweather's artillery. Everything in the cabin was gunpowder and silence.

Oyster was beyond words now. He and Adiona were locked together in pain and concentration. He could feel the severity of their injuries. They were dying, and they only had a little bit of time left. They put everything they had into moving, into reaching their goal, and even though the Spitalfields loomed so close now, hanging over the waves like a walking oil rig, Oyster feared it might be too far for them to reach.

Another bombardment rocked them; a shell burst close by with a concussive whomp, peppering them with burning shot. They dropped low over the water, so low that spray dappled their flanks, kicking up a rainbow in the faint light from the sun. With a gasp, Adiona-Oyster fought to climb back into the iron sky, but it was too much. With an apology they came to rest on the water, cradled by the cold waves.

Oyster was bereft; hollowed out and empty, stunned as Adiona's presence slipped from his mind. He was aware that he was being gently levered from the pilot's harness and laid on the floor of the cabin.

"Is he alive?" said Motet.

Oyster grunted. He was weak and aching. He couldn't move.

"If he does die, can I eat him?" muttered the dog. "I haven't had a square meal since we've been on the run from those creeps."

"Hush," said Nonesuch. "He did good."

Oyster was aware of her cool, long fingers on his forehead.

Around them the Merriweather's guns thundered again and again, victoriously. He didn't know how much longer Adiona's skin could protect them.

And then there was silence.

"Clerks want us in one piece," Oyster heard Nonesuch say. "No point in dusting us proper now. They're needing information, and I for one shan't be turning peachy for anyone anytime soon. When they board, they're gonna pay dear." She brandished a snub-nosed pistol.

"I admire courage, but this is not the way," Marya Petrovna interjected. "If you are dead you cannot help anyone. I have been in worse scrapes, and waving guns around always makes things worse."

"I'm with my hive-sister here. Ain't going back to the cells," said Motet quietly. There was steel in his voice.

"And I, Benjamin Isiah Fauks, am with Marya Petrovna Dozvhenko," said Fauks.

"Well, I don't give a crap about who any of you are. Once that canopy pops open, this mutt is doggy-paddling for it."

Oyster tried to move but he was unable to do so. He was floating through the cabin, not bound to his body, existing ambiently in the gentle rocking-and-rolling motion of the Adiona on the sea. He remembered Broadsides and Cécile; his mum, Paris. Things hadn't always been so shit between them. How had they ended up there? Perhaps there was still time to repair things. To fix them. *Maybe it was never too late.*

"Here they come," said Motet.

And Oyster sensed, rather than saw, a small flotilla of boats heading their way from where the Merriweather hung above the water's surface; a giant, malignant crab filling the air with choking smoke. The silver streaks on its body reflected crimson in the sun, its cannon trained upon Adiona like lenses in a compound eye.

Oyster noticed that the boats, similar to Adiona, were possessed of flagella-like tentacles that propelled them across the water in a froth.

"On count of three we fight," murmured Nonesuch. "If we hang by the belly entrance we can take 'em *uno-por-uno* as they make way."

Motet nodded.

Oyster needed to say something, urgently. He tried locating himself in his body. It felt small and limited, disconnected, and for an instant he worried that perhaps he would never be himself again.

"I still insist we should *talk*," hissed Marya Petrovna. "They have us at disadvantage. We would spend our lives for nothing."

Oyster concentrated, forcing his body to move.

"Sorry, lady, but there really ain't no talkin' with these creeps," said Goswick. "Believe me, I know it. If you don't fit their worldview yer less than nuthin'. I've seen these fucks up close and more than personal."

"Enough," said Oyster finally, fully inhabiting his body again. He sat up and rubbed his aching head. His shoulders, where he had felt Adiona's wings, were especially sore. "We're not gonna need to do either."

As if in answer to his words, Adiona bucked in a massive swell of water that knocked all of them off-balance and threatened to capsize the little craft. There was a deafening hoot and the Spitalfields lurched into view.

"Our ride's here," he said.

60

RUCKAGE

"Huzzah!" shouted Fauks, going to draw his sword before Marya Petrovna calmed him. "We are rescued!"

Almost immediately, the Spitalfields dropped lower in the water and turned her flanks to face the Merriweather.

"Our fore battery will let them have it!" Fauks yelled. "If their forward cannons are destroyed, they will no longer have us at their mercy!" In answer, a fury of cannon-fire blossomed along the Spitalfields' hull as her artillery took aim at the Merriweather's boarding party. Their first volley blew the leading pair of boats to pieces. A second smashed into the Merriweather's forward cannonade.

Fauks clapped his hands together and danced a little jig as bits of the boarding vessel glanced off Adiona's hull. Another of the Spitalfields' shells undershot, missing their attackers and detonating close by in a deafening shriek that left Oyster's ears ringing with tinnitus.

"Are you sure your lot know what they're doing?" yelled Oyster, unable to hear his own words.

"What?" Fauks shook his head. "I cannot hear you."

"Hate to interrupt your Larry and Mo' routine," said Goswick, "but shouldn't we be getting out of here?"

The Spitalfields continued her approach, crouching over the Adiona like a mother hen, but the Merriweather had turned broadside-on now and let fly with its own heavy artillery. Explosions rippled along the larger looüt's flank and the Spitalfields staggered under the onslaught.

"Quickly," shouted Fauks at Oyster, "we must aboard!"

"Isn't that what I just said?" muttered Goswick. "Sheesh. Why is it no one ever listens to their best friend?"

"I am afraid I cannot hear you, Sir Dog," said Fauks.

Goswick rolled his eyes and looked over at Oyster. "Hey there, can you still hit it, kiddo?"

Oyster nodded. With what remained of their joint-consciousness, he opened Adiona's canopy, and for a second they stood in the smoke-choked air, before a tumble of pseudopods dropped from the Spitalfields. The tentacles were translucent and glittering in the sun like jellyfish. Grabbing each of them tenderly, the Spitalfields wound them up into the sky. Oyster's ears finally recovered, and he heard the slapping of the waves and the shouts and shots of the clerks in the remaining boats as they emptied their handguns at the escapees.

The Spitalfields drew them out of harm's way, delivering them into a body cavity that led into a loading chamber. Oyster looked down at Adiona, lolling sadly on the water. Her open canopy meant she was filling with water and listing badly. Her once proud filopods, which had vibrated with colour, were now a spectral grey.

Fauks lay a hand on his shoulder.

"I'm afraid there's not much we can do for her," he said. "She was magnificent in her moment."

"We were," said Oyster. It felt like part of himself was becoming waterlogged and being swallowed by the sea.

"Perhaps that is the most we can say for any of us," said Marya Petrovna, drawing herself to her feet amongst the tangle of pseudopods as they withdrew into the market.

"Onward!" yelled Fauks, leading the way up a corridor. "We have to repel these brigands and make our escape!" He grabbed a nearby speaking tube and blew into it. "We are aboard, Madame La Pilota. Let us arrange for these motherless sons to have our worst!"

At his words, the market lurched into her usual rolling motion.

Oyster was able to keep pace with Fauks this time as the old man led them up to La Pilota's chamber.

The mood within the Spitalfields had changed once more. All around them, the market's inhabitants were in motion; a single being with a single purpose. Amongst the stench of smoke, gunpowder and blood, they were tying things down, tending to the sick, carrying cannonballs and other weaponry to and fro with looks of grim determination.

"Benjy, I believe my talents for healing can help best here," said Marya Petrovna, heading for a group of injured who had been laid out on blankets in a makeshift field hospital. Fauks nodded and beckoned Motet, Nonesuch and Oyster onwards.

When they arrived at the chamber, Madame La Pilota was in a panic. A translucent patch in the looüt's skin showed a view of the sea below. As they sped away from the Merriweather it hunkered just above the waterline like a gigantic scorpion.

"*Mon cher*, we have been injured in multiple organs and some internal chambers have been breached. I fear for our locomotive facilities."

"Never fear, Madame!" he said, stooping to kiss her hand. "We shall prevail! Let us use our superior speed to head for the Lid's eastern boundary. Upwind we can take advantage of their leeward station. Keep them to port as best you can. And order the crews to switch the six-pounders from our starboard side. Perhaps we can marshal *une petite surprise* for our assailants." He snapped open a pocket watch. "At this time of day, the closer to the eastern boundary we travel, the more we place the sun in the eyes of our enemies! It will be just like Lepanto all over again!"

The market shuddered as she kept her flank facing the Merriweather, while continuing to pull away. Oyster was impressed by the man's rapidly restored confidence. He either knew exactly what he was doing, or he was a complete idiot and they would all be killed. Possibly both.

Fauks turned to Oyster.

"Make yourself useful, young friend," he said. "In the cabinet behind you, you'll find *Wennigram's Shipping Index*."

Oyster opened the doors. Rolls of yellowed paper rained on his head.

"Hurry," bellowed Fauks. "This is no time for tomfoolery."

"Keep your wig on," retorted Oyster.

At the bottom of the cabinet was a leatherbound book covered in a thick layer of dust. It reeked of mould. As soon as Oyster pulled it out, Fauks grabbed it. He blew the dust from its cover and flicked through the pages. Behind him, Motet tidied the maps away.

"That mess might be academic in a mo'," said Oyster.

"Strong agree. But this is the one thing under my control in the present circumstance," the gebel replied.

The rattling boom of cannons came from below.

"That thing is shooting at us again, oldster," said Nonesuch, her lights glittering with anxiety. "Hope you got something up that lace sleeve of yours."

"We had best take cover for now," said Fauks, "and order the port-side batteries to return fire as best they can, Madame—"

His words were cut off by the whomp of explosions rocking the Spitalfields. Oyster and Fauks were thrown to the floor. Dust flew from the rafters and Oyster heard muted screams from elsewhere on the market. His thoughts went to Marya Petrovna. The old girl was as tough as they came, but even she couldn't repel cannon fire.

"At least that last volley was wide of the mark." Fauks sat up and straightened his wig. The battle had rejuvenated the old man.

Oyster helped him back to his feet. With a flourish, he produced his lavender kerchief and sniffed it copiously.

"All in good time," said Fauks. "According to the *Index*, the Merriweather is fitted with double batteries, which means they will be able to fire more rapidly than we. By contrast, our six-pound guns are heavier ordinance than anything they may bring to bear upon us. However, those weapons are listed as comprising our *starboard* cannonade."

"Ha! And you got us to switch them over to the other side. You sneaky old sod." Oyster went in for a high five with the bemused-looking Fauks.

"For a grey-hair, you got some serious snike," said Nonesuch with a purple glimmer of approval.

"Indeed," said Fauks with a sly grin, "it will take a moment more, but assuming these villains are relying on the *Index* once we open fire, they should likely be taken aback."

"If we survive long enough, *mon cher*," said La Pilota.

"No use standing about. Lemme go help your crew out," said Nonesuch, and with some directions from Fauks the gebel was gone.

Oyster watched Nonesuch as she left, unable to move his eyes from her as she stepped into the dark, casting sparkling light wherever she went.

"Come on," she called to Goswick, who trotted up to her side.

"I'm only coming with you 'cos I want to," he said out of the side of his mouth, "not because you called me."

"And don't you fret, Dry Bob," she called over her shoulder to the onlooking Oyster. "I'm gonna be looking after *numero uno*."

Oyster reddened.

"Tough act to follow," said Motet. "Even tougher to have as a sibling. Always walking in the shadow, if you get my meaning."

Oyster thought of Cécile. "Got something of the same predicament myself."

"If we are to fully escape this situation we will need a heading," said Fauks. "Mr Motet, our young friend here says that you know the whereabouts of his father."

"Who?" said Motet.

"He's talking about the Mannish's head honcho," said Oyster. "You trued me up after I sprang you—"

Motet held up his hand, face twisted in consternation. Thanks to his interior lights, you could literally watch the revelation making its way through the gebel's head.

"It's complicated," said Oyster.

Motet turned, clearly about to cuss him out, but at that moment a second wave of roiling fire stippled the Merriweather's hull. All of them ducked, waiting for the detonation as the shells squealed past, narrowly missing their mark.

"You could've told me, fuckwit," said Motet.

"That's fair," said Oyster. "But didn't rightly know at the time."

Motet's light shimmered, unconvinced.

"I'm wise to the fact that I'm in your debt for this here getaway. But the price for spilling on his location is that we all ride along with you to his destination. Got business with that motherfucker."

There was a staccato burst of returning fire from the Spitalfields, and the looüt staggered under the recoil from her own battery.

"Sure, sure, abso-fucking-lootles," Oyster nodded. "Now, where we headed?"

Motet took a deep breath.

"You are not going to find this to your liking, but he's on the Outside."

Out of the corner of his eye, he saw Fauks and Madame La Pilota stiffen.

"What do you mean?" asked Oyster. "Outside what? Where?"

"He means outside of the Lid. In the black." Madame La Pilota's voice was edged with panic.

"Okay," said Oyster. "What's the deal with that?"

"We are not rated for traversing the Outside," said Fauks. "We lack the necessary navigation and steerage. Very likely the effort would destroy us, or at the very least fatally disable us and quite possible send Madame La Pilota insane. Possibly all three."

Oyster took all of them in. Each of them had helped him, risked themselves and their people for him, pretty much just on spec. Trust and friendship had been all they had asked in return. He was struck by the sense that it was just like the Urbans, but in reverse.

"That's the last thing I want. You've done more than enough for me and the old lady already. All of you," he said.

"That aside," said Madame La Pilota, so quietly that it was hard to hear above the sound of battle, "this close to the Lid's boundary, there is a gateway less than a nautical mile away. We will get you as close to it as we can."

"Set course, double speed!" said Fauks.

Immediately, the Spitalfields lurched to port, everything shaking as the market leaned into the altered course with renewed determination.

"My dear boy," said Fauks clapping him on the shoulder, "I would do it all again in an instant. This has been—"

Fauks was interrupted by the roar of cannon from below. This time the Merriweather's gunners found their target. The air erupted in flames and deafening sound. Fire passed in front of Oyster's eyes, and he was thrown back by the blast. For an instant, splinters stung his cheeks and the acrid smell of gunpowder and burning flesh was everywhere.

And then there was silence.

POUR L'AMOUR ET LA VAILLANCE!

Oyster lay stunned and still. His ears whistled. There was smoke everywhere and the cloying, coppery smell of blood. He knew he should get up, but the weight of the sea pressed down on his arms and legs.

He thought for a moment he was lying in bed long ago, waiting for Paris to wake him for school. A crow perched on the wardrobe in the corner of his room, regarding him mockingly. He heard the belching white noise of breakfast radio. He smelled the toast that Paris was burning in the kitchen as she stubbed out her third cigarette of the morning.

The pain from his tattoo slithered into his head and then he realised he was dreaming. He opened his eyes and Motet stood over him, shaking him gently. The gebel's light was a low red and he sported a large gash in his temple. His eyes were pleased to see Oyster, but there were other emotions deep within. Oyster would have to thank Lucas for that, he figured.

"Thinking you was gone there for an ickle minute," said Motet.

Oyster nodded. He took a breath, wiped his eyes and rolled onto his front. He licked his lips and tasted blood, but he didn't seem to be badly wounded. With a lurch he was up on his haunches. Everything ached, but he was in one piece.

The Spitalfields shuddered as its own six-pounders returned fire once more, singing a song of iron and death. Oyster swayed, still not quite believing he was alive, watching as a second round of grapeshot pounded the Merriweather, shattering one of its legs in an explosion of black splinters. Fauks' plan had worked, but he was too out of it to be jubilant.

Madame La Pilota's chamber was a wreck. All around them, the maps and atlases burned. Oily loops of sinew hung from the ruined ceiling, massive, scorched bones jutted from enormous gashes in the walls while black blood drenched everything. The wall behind him had been torn open to the sky and a chill salt-wind stirred the flames and the smoke.

Fauks himself lay at the far end of the cabin, face-up on a pile of smouldering furniture. He was in one piece, although his periwig was askew and a purplish bruise had risen on his forehead the size and shape of a plum.

Oyster shook him and he came round.

"Héloïse?" he said with a gentle smile, his eyes wide and unfocused. "Isobel?"

Oyster shook his head.

Fauks nodded and sighed. Oyster had never heard such a simple sound imbued with such sadness. His birdlike eyes remained soft.

"Upon occasion, I see them in my dreams. My family. My beautiful girls," he said wistfully. Oyster felt shame. He had forgotten how much this man had lost. Fauks' expression hardened.

The market lurched sideways.

"And where is Madame?" Fauks asked.

They found her sitting at the base of the ragged tear in the Spitalfields, as awkward and unmoving as a broken doll. Her unfinished sketch of a face was visible through the torn veil and her branched glass horns had been reduced to splintered stumps. The thick arm of muscle that she emerged from was lacerated in multiple places and there was black blood everywhere. She was in a bad way.

Her eyes clicked open and she looked around in a daze, taking in the smoking remains of the cabin.

"Oh dear. Mr Oyster, Mr Motet," she said. "This is quite the mess."

"Rest, *ma chérie*," said Fauks, elbowing Oyster and the gebel out of the way. "We will call a surgeon of physic and soon have you restored."

"Nonsense," she whispered. "It is imperative that we finish what we started here. What you and this young man can accomplish will bloody the nose of the city and the wretched Company. I will keep us on course for the gateway, but you must help them escape."

She coughed and Fauks cradled her to his chest. He closed his eyes. Tears ploughed tracks in his powdered face.

"Make haste. And I will be here when you return," she said.

Fauks kissed her forehead and released her gently. He stood, then unsheathed his sword. He saluted her and she smiled.

"For valour and for our love," he said quietly. "I shall make these brigands pay dearly for this cowardly act."

In the smoke and the chequered sunlight, Oyster saw for the first time that Fauks was totally kind of heroic.

"Assist our crew to the lifeboats. And get word and guidance to Marya Petrovna Dozvhenko and her companions," said Fauks, all business again. "They should meet us at the stables."

La Pilota nodded, closing her doll eyes once more. A low, keening moan emerged from all around them. "The lifeboats are ready. The evacuation has begun."

Fauks nodded and blew her a kiss.

"*Pour l'amour et la vaillance!*" he said.

"*Pour l'amour et la vaillance,*" she echoed weakly.

Fauks turned to Motet and Oyster. With a nod in their direction, he charged ahead of them, waving his sabre and pushing his way through the nearest exit.

Together, they made their way through the rocking, burning chaos the market had become. Oyster found Fauks' handkerchief and placed it over his face so he could breathe more easily. The old man led the way as best he could, stopping every now and then to lean against a wall and regain his strength. When the smoke obscured their way, Motet glimmered gently until they could find their route.

As Oyster surveyed the damage wrought by the Merriweather's attack, he found himself filled with a raw, incandescent anger. What had possessed the clerks and the city to unleash this sort of carnage on them?

He was angry at everything. He was angry with Lucas. If the man hadn't abandoned him then none of this would have happened. He was angry with Primrose. And now he was adding the clerks and the city to his never-ending shit list.

Eventually, they arrived two decks below. Fauks breathed onto a hatchway, which answered by swinging open. Climbing through, they found themselves in a high-ceilinged chamber that jittered with unsteady electric light.

In the centre of the room was a small metal craft shaped like a covered boat. A row of portholes ran down its centre and its rear flared to a fish-tail capped with a propeller. Above it hung a semi-inflated balloon. Opposite the vessel was an enormous sphincter door, clenched shut.

"*Et voilà*," said Fauks with a hint of his former panache. "My personal *montgolfière*, the Giuseppina."

He fussed around the balloon, tapping its sagging leather skin.

"Coal-gas," he said. "Only half-pressure. But should prove sufficient for your trip."

Nonesuch, Marya Petrovna and Goswick arrived at the hatch, each looking the worse for wear. Marya Petrovna had a spotty bandage over her forehead. She launched herself at Oyster, enveloping him in a sweaty bear hug.

"Great Yemama be praised! You are still living," she said, as Oyster extricated himself.

The gebel glimmered at each other, similarly grateful. Then Nonesuch and Oyster exchanged a glance.

"Good to see you all of a piece," she said. Oyster nodded, trying to downplay how pleased he was to see her.

"Hey, don't all rush. I'm okay too," muttered Goswick from the corner of the chamber.

"How far away is this gateway?" said Oyster.

"Less than a mile due east, I estimate," said Fauks, consulting his pocket watch and tenderly pressing the bruise on his head.

Then he hustled them into carrying a pair of heavy crates into the *montgolfière*.

"What the heck is in these, anyway?" said Oyster as he huffed and puffed to carry them.

"Boots, oilskins and such," said Fauks.

Oyster caught Nonesuch's gaze as she rolled her eyes.

"Maybe get us flying first. Worry about your shoe collection laters."

Fauks coughed.

"Temperatures beyond the protective shell of the Lid are arctical," he said tartly. "Your party will not last long without the appropriate *accoutrements*."

Nonesuch shrugged but stopped complaining.

"So, how're we gonna get this going, grandma?" she replied when the crates were on board.

Fauks pointed to a wooden track running along the floor of the chamber which ended at the closed hatchway of muscle. The *montgolfière* sat on a wheeled trolly mounted upon it. The whole thing was an enormous catapult.

"Please don't tell me you just ping this thing out into thin air," Oyster said.

"Exactly so," replied Fauks, looking far too pleased with himself. "A mechanism of my own design and based upon the ballistae of Ancient Rome."

"Okay," said Oyster, regarding the ring of muscle in the Spitalfields hull. "But how're we gonna do that with the back door shut?"

"That will be my job," said Fauks. "You are going where I, Benjamin Isiah Fauks, cannot."

"No, surely not Benjy," said Marya Petrovna. "Not so soon."

Fauks shook his head sadly.

"It has been such a pleasure to see you again, Madame Petrovna Dozvhenko. Thank you for the chance to play at the hero once more. If even for nothing more than a short while—"

In answer, the market staggered, throwing them off-balance. Rather than righting itself, the deck remained at an angle. The Spitalfields seemed to be on its last legs.

"Now, we must hurry. I need to tend to Madame La Pilota."

"But how will we know where to go?" Oyster asked.

"Fear not," replied the old man, "the gateway will be self-evident at this range."

Fauks hurried Motet, Goswick and Marya Petrovna aboard. Oyster and Nonesuch followed close behind. It was like being inside a low-ceilinged boat. There were two rows of three upholstered seats, each with leather seat belts. The smell of polish was a relief from the relentless stench of charred timber and burning meat outside.

At the fore of the cabin was a ship's wheel. Mounted on a dashboard next to it were brass dials, buttons and levers. So, they really were going to fly out into the sky in this thing. Oyster breathed in and closed his eyes. Well, it wasn't the weirdest thing he'd flown in today.

With a shiver somewhere between a thrill and a fright he recognised the long wooden handle next to the dashboard as the release mechanism. When pulled, it would free the pin on the catapult and the Giuseppina would bullet out of the landing bay. If they could open the hatchway door, that was.

Nonesuch belted herself in behind the controls and Oyster hurriedly followed suit. The leather straps on his seat had been tailored to fit a much larger passenger and he knotted them together to take up the extra slack.

"You know how to fly this?" asked Oyster.

Nonesuch shrugged and glimmered sulkily.

"Fair enough," he responded.

There was another sickening lurch from the Spitalfields and

Oyster was glad to be strapped in. The whole landing bay shifted, yawing wildly towards the ground at an angle of forty-five degrees. Oyster's stomach was in his mouth.

"We can delay no longer," shouted Fauks, reaching for the release handle. "Once free, you must fly into the gateway! Our presence has activated it, but the Giuseppina is not designed for such a voyage, so your transition to the Outside will likely be somewhat violent. Fare thee well and may fortune smile upon you!" He slammed the hatch shut.

"Hold up!" Oyster said. "Did you lot hear that?"

"Too late now. Hang on to your giblets," Nonesuch yelled, lighting up like a pinball machine. Marya Petrovna muttered behind him, deep in prayer.

Before anyone else could respond, Fauks pulled the release lever.

With a *pop*, the Giuseppina was hurled along its track towards the closed sphincter-door. Everyone in the cabin screamed. Oyster was blinded by the sudden acceleration. Through his fear he sensed the muscle wall, solid and unyielding ahead of them. Every part of him was screwed up, waiting for impact. He forced his eyes open and terror gurgled in his throat at the sight rushing towards him.

Through the porthole windows, Oyster caught sight of Fauks brandishing his vintage blammer. His tongue was sticking out of the side of his mouth and he was bracing his arm, squinting to take aim.

He pulled the trigger and there was a loud *crack*. Fauks' aim was true. The bullet hit the sphincter dead centre, and with a spasm the puckered circle of muscle dilated. An instant later, the *montgolfière* was thrown into the howling sky.

62

GATEWAY

There was a tearing sound as the Giuseppina flew into the clouds of smoke belching from the Spitalfields. Nonesuch struggled with the controls as the balloon plunged downwards. Oyster's stomach was in his mouth, but he was oddly calm. They were about three hundred feet up and arcing towards the sea at frightening speed. There was no doubt that, when they hit the water, the Giuseppina would be reduced to debris.

"Why are we dropping so fast?" yelled Oyster.

"Your guess is as good as mine," replied Nonesuch, looking at him with a wry smile. Was she actually enjoying this?

Oyster looked over the controls. Dials and gauges looked back at him blankly. Behind them was a network of copper piping whose functions he could only guess at. It reminded him of having to fix the boiler on winter mornings back home. His stomach writhed as they plummeted. He had to work fast. Working back from the biggest pipe he could see, he found a large valve that he hoped would feed more gas into the balloon.

He grabbed it with both hands and heaved, but it refused to budge. Time went very slowly. Each second inched past.

Oyster stood, twisting the brass handle with all his strength. Finally, it gave with a lurch and a hiss, but the balloon continued its descent.

"Shouldn't we be stopping?" he asked.

"Maybe gotta give it time, Royston," Nonesuch replied.

For an age, Oyster fought the sickening sensation in the pit of his stomach. Instinctively, he leaned into Nonesuch, bracing for impact, but she looked at him with such confusion that he froze; and then, suddenly, their plunge abruptly slowed.

"Thank fuck for that," said Goswick from the rear of the vessel.

"Indeed," said Marya Petrovna, already starting to roll a cigarette.

"Nice, now shift yourself and start the motive engine," said Nonesuch.

Oyster clambered to the rear of the cabin, feeling a sudden swagger in his step.

"Hey! This is a no-smoking flight," he said to Marya Petrovna. He had no idea how flammable coal-gas was, but he didn't want to find out the hard way. The old lady shrugged and packed the items away in her purse.

Oyster inspected the outboard motor connected to the propellor in the balloon's rear. It looked to have been salvaged from a dinghy. A nylon starter cord dangled from one end, and he pulled on it until it was taut before yanking it, hard. With a cough, the engine sprang into life. First time. He was on a roll.

Nonesuch turned the Giuseppina to port, facing back towards the smoking ruin that was the Spitalfields. The market was in a bad way. Two of her legs had collapsed and fires speckled her hull. Now that her assailant was vanquished, she was wading away from the Merriweather on buckled legs. Below, the wrecked husk of her attacker was engulfed in flame, giving off great clouds of black smoke.

Other passengers were making their way off the Spitalfields as best they could: some clambered down her legs, some abseiled, others escaped in balloons like theirs. A group of vessels had gathered around: paddle boats, steamers and trawlers. At first, Oyster was cheered that these people were aiding the rescue, but when he thought about it, it was just as likely they were preparing to salvage what they could of the Merriweather.

It made him sick and sad to see these wonderful beings reduced to smoking remains. Human beings, he reflected, made a fucking awful mess of everything they touched. Maybe Primrose had a point. But he was buoyed by the fact that the Spitalfields was still alive. Perhaps given enough time, Fauks could patch her up.

There was a creak, and the cabin darkened as they turned into the Spitalfields' smoking shadow. Nonesuch looked at the dashboard's compass and banked them through a cloud of smoke to swoop lower down over the water.

Oyster took in the looüt as they whistled past her speckled hide. He felt real sorrow for her as she fled. Grimly, he thought of Fauks and Madame La Pilota. He hoped they made it too. He peered over at Motet. Nonesuch's brother was smeared in soot. He looked exhausted.

"Been meaning to ask. Why'd they come after you so hard?"

Motet shrugged. "'Cos we're breakin' up their glimmer rackets. Sticking it to the city. And because they could. Any excuse to make an example of us."

Oyster nodded. It was basic gang dynamics, of course. Someone makes a move on you, and you slap them down hard. Big Mickey would've got it. Big Mickey who wanted him dead now, no doubt. Oyster sighed. He had a lot of payback that needed paying back.

He pulled Primrose's leather bag out of his pocket. It needed stashing. He turned to take in the Giuseppina's passengers. Marya Petrovna was wide-eyed, bracing herself against the metal walls of the balloon as it bucked and turned. She tried to smile at him, but, frightened as she was, it came out as a grimace.

Nonesuch was engrossed in steering the Giuseppina, her light sparkling as she concentrated and course-corrected. He threw the bag into her lap.

"Can you hold on to these for me?"

She didn't look at him but strobed a deep orange in response.

"Kinda busy right-here-right-now. But forly and surely."

She shuffled her legs and the coins jangled. Nonesuch pulled a knowing face. "We going steady now or summat?"

Oyster reddened.

"Um, uh. I mean. No, s'not like that. I mean, they're important, need someone to hold 'em for me."

Nonesuch turned to him and pressed a glittering finger to her lips.

"They do have jokes where you're from, yes?"

Oyster cleared his throat and nodded. He smiled weakly.

"Right-o. Where's this gate-thing that we need to…"

Nonesuch's eyes widened. As they pulled around the retreating hulk of the Spitalfields, a black tear opened up in the sky. A baying whirlwind gripped hold of the Giuseppina and sucked her spinning into the dark.

63
WHIRLWIND

The Giuseppina spun like a top. Oyster held on tight and tried not to lose the contents of his stomach. Events moved so fast they felt like slow-motion. Nonesuch was thrown into the air, as were Goswick and Motet. Marya Petrovna still held on to her seat, white-knuckled and grimacing.

No light came in though the portholes apart from occasional blue flashes of something like lightning. Inside the *montgolfière*, the only illumination came from the light of the gebel themselves. Of Goswick, Oyster had no sight.

With a gut-wrenching roll, the craft turned upside down as though swatted by a giant's hand. The crates in its rear were thrown to the ceiling, making the vessel shudder even more unstably.

Oyster tried to relax, to invoke his tattoo. He thought about himself moving through space, unfurling its spell like a banner. His body throbbed with a white-hot ache. But nothing happened. He couldn't escape his feeling of responsibility for Broadsides. All of this had started because of his bloody tattoo. And his stupid decisions. It was all his fault.

Then his temple was struck by something and he yelled in pain. His stomach leapt up into his throat as they went into freefall. This was it, then. They were going to hit the ground, wherever they might be, and smash into a million pieces.

"You owe us, Mr McLellen."

Primrose. Oyster's eyes were open, but he saw nothing. There was darkness all around.

"Get away from me. You murdered my friend."

"Sadly, we all played our part there."

Silence.

"So, have you asked her about the ritual?"

"Fuck off. I know what you're trying to do, Primrose or Cerunnos or whatever you are. Why don't you just kill me like you did Broadsides, and get it over with."

"That one was… what's that charming phrase you lot use? Collateral damage. Besides which, there are things we need to tell you."

"Fuck off, creep show," said Oyster.

"And *you* are a coward."

Oyster woke with a start. He was freezing cold and lying on a great plain of blue ice. He was surrounded by wreckage from the Giuseppina. There were the scattered remains of one of the crates and a chunk of fabric from the balloon's skin that flapped in the wind like a downed bird. What Oyster at first thought was a body turned out to be an oilskin coat, and he reached over, pulling the garment on and clambering to his feet. The coat was thick and heavy, and reeked of stale sweat. In its pockets he found a pair of gloves, mismatched, but he wasn't complaining.

Where was everyone else?

In the distance, it was difficult to say exactly how far, stood a tall lighthouse adorned with a thick band of dark paint around its centre. Its silent beams whipped across the desolate landscape every few minutes, bathing the horizon with a bleak electric glow.

Oyster squinted against the snow. The wind made his eyes water. He wasn't sure how this could be, but the horizon curved up towards the sky. How this fitted with the topography of the Lid he didn't understand, but it was the least of his problems now.

Flicking up the oilskin's broad collar as protection against the snow and wind, he followed the trail of wreckage over a ridge frosted by the beams of the lighthouse.

So, this was what it was like on the Outside.

The wind pummelled him as he trudged on, and Primrose's words turned over and over in his mind. The worst thing was that the man, if you could call him that, was right. Oyster was a coward, but not in the way that Primrose thought. He was a coward for not asking for help when he needed it.

Reaching the edge of the ridge, he leaned forward, stumbling up and over it. The force of the wind and the weight of the coat made him feel like he was an astronaut on the dark side of the moon.

He heard the others before he saw them.

"He's fucking dead! Let's just forget about the noisy little turd and focus on keepin' ourselves alive."

It was Goswick.

"Easy, Monsieur Four-legs," said Nonesuch. "More to him than appears. Hidden depths, innit."

"Can it, light bulb. Just 'cos you're hot to trot with the kid, don't mean we gotta follow your lead."

Marya Petrovna, Motet, Goswick and Nonesuch were sheltering from the storm in the cracked remains of the Giuseppina's cabin. They looked like chicks emerging from an unlikely egg, as they clustered around a small fire that twinkled in the darkness.

Oyster thought about hanging about a bit to hear what else they had to say about him, but thought better of it. Even he wasn't that much of a creep.

"Hey," he called out.

"Well, hello you too," replied Goswick. "We was just hoping you'd turn up."

Oyster left that one where it lay. Nonesuch tingled an imperial purple, before raising a gloved hand to beckon him, her expression serious.

He stumbled down the ridge into the caldera where the remains of the *montgolfière* had come to rest. The crater provided some natural protection from the constant howling wind and biting snow.

Marya Petrovna and Motet were nearest the fire. The old woman was laid out flat, unmoving. Her bandage was missing, revealing a dirty cut in her temple. Motet bent over, tending her. At the sight, Oyster's heart throbbed in his ears and he dropped to his knees. Marya Petrovna's long face was pale. He grabbed one of her hands but it was stiff and cold.

She couldn't be dead. He looked up at Motet, aghast.

"Made her as restful as feasible," said the gebel. "Flank's all lacerated, lost some of her animating principle. Fixed her as best I can…"

The sentence petered out.

"No. I am not dead, flapdoodle." Marya Petrovna's words were just audible above the wind. "But suffice to say I will not be running London Marathon as planned. Ach. Just think. All that training, wasted."

She smiled weakly. Oyster was so happy to hear her voice that he nearly jumped up and punched the air.

"Hang on in there," he whispered to her.

"Don't get sentimental, Enoch. You are still blockhead. Marya Petrovna will whup this and then she will return to kicking butts."

Every two minutes or so, the ghoulish light from the lighthouse swept the crater, fringing it with blue light. The seconds dragged past. Tears iced his cheeks.

Marya Petrovna grabbed his hands with her own, the fingers struggling to close around them.

"Listen, Enoch," she said. "Have not been completely honest with you. And it has weighed. You are good boy. Good man."

Oyster shook his head.

"Don't say anything, old lady," he replied. "S'all good. Save your strength." But he thought of what Primrose had said to him.

"Do not want to lose you like I did my *leibling*. My Yellie."

Leibling. Oyster had heard the word somewhere before. Recently.

"She was my companion at first," Marya Petrovna continued. "And we became much more than friends. I loved her. But back then, you understand, was harder to admit such things. I was foolish. Never told her true feelings. That night in cabinet. She went to her death without knowing."

"You don't need to tell me any of this," said Oyster. The old woman's grip on his fingers increased.

"I do," she replied. "Over the years, I have wished to be able to turn back clock."

Oyster swallowed. Primrose's words came to him: *With that power the vessel can do anything. They can change the future. Or the past.*

His lips were numb, and the words formed unbidden. He felt as though he was watching a movie of himself, knelt next to her. It was a betrayal to even think the question, and yet he still asked it.

"Has this got something to do with the Trian thing?" His lips were trembling as he spoke.

Marya Petrovna's mouth opened and closed. No words came out. She was ashen faced.

"With your abilities and tattoo, I could reach her in past, I think. It would be massive long shot, but perhaps I could contact her somehow. Warn her not to participate in *Mói Dórath* ritual. We would still be together, you see, if she had not died."

Marya Petrovna's words faded into the background din of the storm. Oyster was aware of dropping Marya Petrovna's hand and standing. People were speaking to him, this he knew, but their words passed him by. Goswick swore. Motet pleaded. Marya Petrovna was calling to him.

He ignored them all. Carefully he sifted through the Giuseppina's wreckage until he located one of the pairs of boots that Fauks had packed for them. They were only a little too big for him, with serrated cleats for moving through the snowscape.

Pulling them on, he flipped his collar even further up around his ears and walked out of the camp. As he crested the ridge, the full force of the storm battered him. He wasn't even sure where he wanted to go. But maybe he just needed to do what was right for *him* for once? The beams of the lighthouse swept over the ice in front of him, lighting the way. *If Lucas was going to be anywhere in this godforsaken place, he had to be there, right?*

64

BLUE ICE

Oyster's ears were frozen, and even in his boots he couldn't feel the ends of his toes. The wind pelted him with hardened snow that stung his eyes like powdered glass. He kept his head down, chin sunk into his coat. Thoughts danced around his head like loose leaves in a hurricane.

Primrose had been right all along. Marya Petrovna had been planning to use him and his abilities for her own ends. No wonder she had been so disappointed when he'd been unable to flit back at the Tube station.

Big Mickey. Deano. Lucas. Primrose. Marya Petrovna. He'd had enough of all of them. Everyone he knew and everyone he had looked up to for guidance. They had all dicked him around. Filled him with convenient lies and set him off like some sort of windup toy.

He leaned into the wind as it pushed him back. Far ahead on the upended horizon lay the lighthouse. He pulled the inner hood around him, against the cruel snow. Even under his two coats, the cold bit at him. He pulled the gloves further onto his hands.

The only way to make any progress at all was to stamp his feet down hard enough to engage the cleats and then lever them up as best he could. It was an arduous process, and his calves soon burned with the effort.

The clouds overhead writhed as though they were living things.

Occasionally, the lighthouse's beam picked out dark shapes within them, but they disappeared as quickly as he saw them.

The wind hissed all around. In his bleak mood, he preferred this desolate landscape, devoid as it was of any evidence of the effect of man. There was something honest about its desolation. Something engaging, even.

Oyster's rage was volcanic, too. Sealed beneath frozen ice, five fathoms deep. He was so angry with Marya Petrovna he didn't know what to do, but that rage was what powered him now. Drawing him on towards the lighthouse. He wasn't sure what he was doing exactly, but he knew that was where he had to go. It called to him.

Footsteps approached from behind and the ice around him rippled with light. He spun around to see Nonesuch closing on him. Wrapped in a sou'wester and a heavy woollen hat.

"Slow it, Dry Bob!" she hollered after him.

He turned back to his trudging, ignoring her.

"Hey!" she yelled, flicking out at his ears as she caught him up. "Know those face flaps are on. They're sure big enough."

"I ain't going back," Oyster glowered over his shoulder.

"An' I ain't asking," she said, igniting head-to-toe with an orange glow that painted their surroundings with autumn embers. She touched him on the shoulder. Oyster slogged ahead.

"Stands to reason you're hurt. Would be too in your place."

"She's been lying to me from the start."

Nonesuch nodded, and together they headed into a gulley that afforded them momentary respite from the constant wind.

"What even is this place?" said Oyster.

"Beats me," shrugged Nonesuch. "Beyond my ken. Where you headed?"

Oyster shook his head.

"Wherever will get me the furthest away from everyone. Get my shit. Get back home. I got no clue, to be honest."

Nonesuch laughed. It was a loud and hearty sound that rang bell-like in the darkness, accompanied by a glittering lightshow.

Oyster looked at her, unimpressed.

"Glad you find my predicament so funny," he said.

"We all are, ain't we, DB. Each of us wrapped in our vanities and such."

Oyster tested out the gully wall and then, realising it was too sheer to scale in his cleats, turned to walk along it.

"Everyone has been treating me like their personal butt-monkey."

"Think you might be jumping off the bridge while the river's a-boil. Consider this. Not saying you wasn't deceived and all, but croney-baloney back there was tryin' to let you on the inside. Courageous, kind of. Foolish, also."

"If she sent you after me, you can just turn back now," said Oyster.

"Nah, she didn't, but not like she could come after you herself anyways. 'Sides which, you got the only pair of boots we had left."

Oyster shrugged.

"Soz. Just count it as butt-monkey backpay," he said. With a huff, he found a route back up to the plain that was less steep and leaned into the wind as it shrieked across the ice sheet.

"None of us honest all the time, Dry Bob," said Nonesuch. "Leastways, you didn't come clean with me and Motet about your hive-daddy being Lucas, now did you?"

"That's different," said Oyster. "I didn't know when I met you. Plus, even if I had, I wouldn't have been planning on using you as some sort of messenger pigeon for my dead ex."

"Maybe. But you're still sayin' there's some occasions suitable for wriggling on the hook an' others that ain't," she said. "So, not everything's always black and white, eh?"

The righteous anger inside Oyster stuttered. He couldn't deny the truth of what Nonesuch was saying. It's not like there weren't things that he'd kept from Marya Petrovna. *Damn it!*

Being angry had made things so much simpler.

"Old Lady Warthog back there gave me the downlow on your situation. Told us how you lost a crew member in shady circumstance."

Oyster held her gaze. It was piercing. Like Primrose, she

possessed the ability of looking into him as though his skin was as transparent as hers. It was unnerving, suddenly being seen; being this vulnerable. But it was also exhilarating.

"You got to forgive yourself. Whatever song you been singing in that thick skull of yours. Take it from someone who's lost plenty. Family *and* friends. Easiest thing in the world is to point blame at yourself, and there are some who'll encourage you to, as it suits their purposes. But if you didn't wield the blade, then the fault ain't rightly yours to bear."

Oyster nodded, soaking in her words. There was sense in what she was saying. He closed his eyes and thought of Broadsie. And for a second, he could almost feel the man's presence. He just wished he'd had the chance to warn him, to say goodbye. Anything. But in that instant, he knew for the first time with certainty that she was right. *It wasn't his fault.* Primrose had been using this to keep him off-balance. For a second the dark sense of guilt shifted, and as if in answer his tattoo flickered with its familiar pain.

He opened his eyes. Nonesuch was smiling at him.

"Believe," she said. The word was carried up into the sky on the wind, taking the weight that had been pressing on him up and away with it. For the second time that day, tears trickled from his eyes, but he wasn't ashamed. He breathed in a lung of freezing air. Held it for a second and let out a shuddering breath. And in that moment of clarity, he knew.

"S'up," said Nonesuch.

"I have been such a donkey," he said.

"No doubts about that," said Nonesuch. The wind and snow dropped for a second and then blew at them from another direction.

"Been staring me in the face, but I just realised. That word the old lady used about her girlfriend. *Leibling*. German, innit. I've heard it before. The old lady's squeeze is still kicking about, after a fashion."

The sudden realisation was a thrill. He had good news. She'd be made up. But despite the excitement, he wasn't sure what he wanted to do with it. He knew that he should hot-foot it back to the camp. But he was still angry with Marya Petrovna.

"So, what's our play?" said Nonesuch.

He swallowed and looked at the gebel. Her hair whipped around her face from beneath the hat. She looked at him, appealing to his better instincts. *Fuck. How was it that she could do this?* Up until this point, he hadn't thought of himself as someone who even had better instincts. The lighthouse swept across the ice, lighting her up from behind. She reached out a gloved hand. Oyster paused for an instant before he took it.

"Let's get back to the camp and figure this shit out," he said before he was knocked onto his back, seeing stars in the clouded sky.

65
REDUX

Oyster hit the ice, his temple throbbing, and skidded on his side. He and Nonesuch had been so engrossed in their conversation that their attackers had been able to sneak up on them without warning. His ears rang from the blow; his eyes watered with the pain.

Before he heard the voice of his assailant, he knew from the swaggering figure they cut in the blue-limned dark that it was Ambidexter. Oyster's perimeter radar picked up that there were three of them altogether. The ones called Banbarra and Squeech were busying themselves trying to keep Nonesuch out of action.

"Stay put," said Ambidexter mockingly. "And none need get a haircut."

Oyster shook his head, rolling over onto his side and struggling to get to his feet. But Ambidexter was on him before he could move in his bulky clothes, bearing down on him and sitting across his chest.

"Well, well," said the woman, recognising him. "If it ain't my favourite whelp and wannabe scallywaggy. Might have known it was you coming down in that balloon back there."

Oyster was aware that in the background, Nonesuch had already recovered and was back on her feet, weapon drawn. Wordlessly she pirouetted into a sequence of vicious kicks and blows that had the other Mannish on the defensive immediately.

"Enough!" yelled Oyster. "I need to talk to your captain, you inked-up hoolie." He struggled as she held him fast.

Ambidexter grinned and leaned her face close to his. Her black eyes were like marbles that glittered in the little light that there was.

"Now, where would the fun in that be?" She breathed sour rum all over him.

"I'm serious," yelled Oyster, wriggling with frustration. But Ambidexter kept him in place. "Get me to Lucas. I got news for him. Gotta warn him. Something's coming."

Ambidexter just grinned her manic grin. Hawking up, she readied to gob on him.

Oyster shut his eyes and allowed his mind to empty. He thought of himself and Broadsides smoking cigarettes down by the bridge the day they met. He remembered the time he and Cécile had spent a whole day playing *Mario Kart* on the console he had bought from Big Mickey. *Intentional vacuity and all that*, he thought. Hot wires threaded through his body, and when the pain ebbed away, he was standing behind Ambidexter. His own bewilderment was nothing compared to the Mannish's, who was now up to her knees in snow. Nonesuch had fixed him!

He was back in action.

This would need to be quick. Grabbing a rock, he smacked Ambidexter across the back of the head. It was brutal, but he didn't have time for subtlety. He charged at Banbarra, who seemed to know he was coming without being able to see him. She side-stepped, dropping into a front flip. The move was full of a ragged street-style grace that dealt him a square one-two under the chin with her trailing feet. Oyster stumbled back. He'd forgotten how tricksy this lot were. Still, he had his own game now.

He took the pain from the blow and channelled it into his midriff, charging his tattoo as he blanked himself again. With a stutter he flitted behind Banbarra as she landed, and putting all his body weight into a right cross, he landed the blow on her temple, sending her spinning sideways. She recovered in time to pull out a vicious-looking blade and Oyster pulled his own. Banbarra grinned at him. The Celtic tattoo and pale skin gave her features an uncanny look in the blue light.

"Nice moves, Professor Chatty," she said. "Not seen the like of them before. D'you think fancy footwork will stop Sister Stabs here?"

She brandished the knife ostentatiously. Oyster held his own blade between his thumb and the flat of his palm and raised both hands. This was going south, big time. He had to end it quickly or one of them was liable to end up with hole in them.

"Look. Don't want no ructions here. Let's settle this peaceable."

"Seems you shoulda warned Ambi o' that afore you cracked her skull all egg-like, fucker-nuts. We're gonna gut you and drain your girlie of her glimmer."

She feinted. Oyster dodged.

Behind her, Squeech and Nonesuch were going at it full tilt, like a pair of characters from an arcade game. Although Nonesuch had lost her weapon, Oyster sensed that she was easily a match for the Mannish, who was ducking and weaving, flipping and spinning to avoid the gebel landing any blows. The snowscape shimmered with the fierce red and gold of Nonesuch's light.

While Oyster was distracted, Banbarra dived forward, flipping her feet up into something like an elbow freeze. The move caught Oyster off-guard, and her heel smacked him full in the face. He staggered back and his knife flew out of his hand.

She followed up with a vicious stab to his midriff, but Oyster was no longer there. Flitting behind her again, he barged her in the back, dropping her instantly.

Out of the corner of his eye, he saw Nonesuch flip backwards before diving and twisting towards her assailant, breaking into an arcing tumble that lit up like a floodlight. Even tangentially, her light was so bright that for an instant Oyster was blinded. There was no doubt that she'd had enough. Squeech yelled and dropped to her knees, shaking her head and rubbing her eyes.

"Gebel witch!" she squealed.

"Listen to me, all of you!" Oyster shouted. "I just want to talk to your boss-man!"

"Then talk," called a voice Oyster recognised from the top of the gulley. "Fucking here, aren't I?"

66

LUCAS

Lucas ambled towards them, stepping down from the ridge and into the dip in which they stood. He had the swagger of a man who owned every inch of the ground he walked upon.

"Down tools all," he commanded. "You're on Mannish territory now. No need to ruck it out. Your asses are mine." His voice carried easily over the constant scream of the wind. The Mannish Boys did as they were told. Ambidexter sat up groggily.

"What you done to my girl Ambi?" said Lucas. The man fixed Oyster with a glare, but he sounded impressed.

He was a physically imposing presence. Tall and broad, he wore a hooded leather coat, fur-lined. Snow crunched beneath his army boots as the wind dropped.

"No shit. Smallweed, is that you?" There was recognition in his voice as he took them all in.

Oyster had the sudden, distinct sensation of not being in his own body, and his knees trembled as the man approached. Lucas had never been big on hugs, but he opened his arms wide and beckoned Oyster towards him.

"Holy fuck, little man! So, you made it. Welcome to our turf. How's Cess and Paris?" he said without missing a beat.

Dizzy as he was from flitting, Oyster was overcome by a bow wave of familiar smells: stale cigarette smoke, Paco Rabanne and a faint hint of sweat. Lucas smiled, broadly, revealing a mouthful of teeth that a life of recreational drug use had whittled into grey pebbles.

Oyster swallowed. The pain in his torso throbbed so hard he had to steady himself and remind his lungs to suck in air. There *he* was. Lucas McLellen. His dad. A mess of feelings boiled inside him. A sudden ache combined with confusion and relief. He thought about the last time he'd seen Lucas, outside the tower block. It had been so long ago, the memories had begun to atrophy, turning into faded copies of themselves; reducing to an essence which was really only a feeling. An absence in the shape of a man.

The anger came swiftly, unexpectedly, igniting in the pit of his stomach and blazing into his head. The words he'd meant to say all arrived in his head at once, running into each other like broken train carriages.

Oyster sprung at Lucas, swinging wildly. All he wanted to do was wipe the smile off that stupid face. One of his blows connected with Lucas's chin and the man staggered backwards.

Squeech sprang to Lucas's defence, pinning Oyster's arms behind his back.

"Easy, man-child," she whispered. "Should I end him, boss?"

Lucas shook his head and rubbed this jaw.

Oyster's self-righteous anger fizzled out as quickly as it had appeared, leaving him feeling small and sad.

"So, you got some balls after all then, Smallweed," said Lucas. He smiled again. "Not bad. But it's time for you to get yourself together. Be a man."

"We were worried you might be hurt or worse. And all the time you were just dicking about here."

Lucas nodded.

"I'll spill soon enough. The Mannish here aren't your enemy, though. You and yours are welcome on my turf."

His eyes took in Nonesuch, who glimmered with sullen fire.

"Who's this one?"

"A friend," said Oyster.

"She don't seem to like me very much, kiddo."

"*I* don't like you very much," said Oyster.

Lucas nodded.

"That is your privilege. But in any case, you're coming with me. It's time. Things are moving into position."

"No way," Oyster replied. "I left crew, back there." He waved vaguely in the direction of the camp.

"You can see to them *after* what is necessary."

"And what is that?" said Oyster.

Lucas leaned towards him in a way that felt like both a threat and an invitation.

"Well, we've been sort expecting you, son."

Oyster looked at him blankly.

"The ritual, innit," Lucas continued. "That's the reason you came here, right? Bring me his coins and shit. Maybe give the old man a hand? Help me stick it to nature boy." He winked. "My girls here lifted your *Mói Dórath* to keep it safe and everything. Big C will be here soon enough to light the blue touch paper, and then…"

He made an expansive gesture with his hands. This was too much information for Oyster to take in. His head spun as he tried to fit it all together. *What a noob he'd been.* So wrapped up in his own bullshit that he couldn't see that Lucas had been mired neck deep in this thing the whole time.

Oyster sensed Nonesuch tense beside him. They exchanged a wary glance. He tried to empty his mind ready to flit, but he still felt drained after their fight with the Mannish and he wasn't sure how far he'd be able to go. In front of him, Lucas seemed to swell in size in the sweep of the lighthouse beam.

Three other Mannish slipped over the brow of the hill and stood expectantly, their tattooed faces glowering in the frozen light. Oyster looked at Nonesuch, who threw a *just say the word and we'll deck 'em* expression back. Oyster shook his head. They might have been able to take three Mannish, but now the odds were more than four to one.

"Look, I know you have reasons not to trust me, but I'm asking nicely here. Just give it some time and you'll get it. You'll see. We're blood, right?" said Lucas. "I mean, you could pull your whole Sonic the Hedgehog routine and escape, but that would still leave one of your crew here with us."

Oyster sighed. He was surprised by how much just being in the presence of Lucas made him feel like a little kid. Part of him, a big part of him, wanted to just let him take over; to allow Lucas to be the adult here. To trust his lead.

"Okay," murmured Oyster. "You got time. Make it count."

"Alright, son," said Lucas with a smile. He seemed to diminish in size as the threat of violence ebbed. "Let's split."

He turned, pointing towards the lighthouse on the edge of the upturned horizon. "I wanna show you our crib. You're gonna love it."

ACROSS THE ICE

Oyster and Nonesuch trudged across the ice sheet. Lightning split the sky, and in its sudden illumination Oyster saw the outlines of vast, frozen creatures embedded far below them. He shivered and pulled up his collar.

Lucas headed up the procession, seemingly unaffected by the cold. The Mannish Boys flanked them on either side with two crew members bringing up the rear. Progress was slow and Oyster felt the warmth leaching out of him. Perhaps it was a trick of the weird geometry of the place, but their destination seemed to be getting no nearer.

"No offence, but your daddy's an asshat," whispered Nonesuch.

Oyster nodded and shrugged. Being this close to Lucas stirred up so many memories. *Being this close to my dad*, he corrected himself, turning the word over in his head. He tested its shape; its heft. The idea was at the root of his identity. Whatever he was, however, much he might resent him, Lucas was a part of him. He couldn't deny it.

As he looked up, Lucas turned back to him and smiled that lopsided, slipshod grin of his that Oyster recognised so well.

"Hey, slow it up, will you?" Oyster said.

Lucas halted, waiting for them to catch up.

"Thought you wanted to talk?"

"Shoot," said Lucas.

Oyster rolled his eyes.

"Don't you have shit to tell *me*?"

"Language," Lucas winced.

"*Shit* isn't even a proper swear."

Lucas waggled a gloved hand in a maybe/maybe not gesture, and Oyster snorted derisively.

"Okay then, 'fess up. Why do you need the old lady's cabinet?" he said.

Lucas chuckled wryly.

"Ah, Marya Petrovna Dozvhenko. Haven't thought about that old witch in a long, long time."

"So it's true then, you did used to hang with her crew," Oyster replied, twinging at her mention. She was lying back at camp, injured and cold, and he'd legged it with the only set of gear they had between them. He swallowed his guilt. As she had told him once a long time ago: *one step at a time.*

"You mean you haven't worked it out yet? Figured you were smarter than that," said Lucas. The reprimand stung Oyster.

"Let me true you up. The cabinet that Fauks built. The *Mói Dórath*. It was made from the Tree of Life. It *is* the Tree of Life, or, at least, the only pieces left of it."

If Oyster could have slapped his forehead in the heavy gloves, he would have. It all made sense now. Lucas and Cerunnos had been hoovering up everything they needed for their ritual. Paying no attention to anyone else or the impact they had.

The party walked on, enveloped in the gulley's eerie silence, Nonesuch's ill-tempered light playing on the walls.

"Would you believe me if told you I was protecting you, Smallweed?" Lucas asked at last.

"Don't call me that." Oyster dredged up the words from deep within. "I watched you. The night you left. I saw him. Cerunnos, Primrose, whatever he is. Saw you both down in the car park."

Lucas nodded. They slipped into another broad fissure and the gale and sleet dropped away

"It's complicated, son. I thought… if I kept away from you, it would keep you safer for longer. I really thought it would keep him off your and Cess's back."

Oyster bristled at Cécile's name, but as they emerged from the icy furrow the lighthouse loomed above them, enormous and solitary, and his anger was forgotten.

Far above them, lighting split the clouds and the roiling shapes within became more solid, dropping towards them.

"Shit! Skyworms! Move!" yelled Lucas, sprinting across the remaining two hundred yards between them and the lighthouse. Oyster struggled to keep up, the cleats and his coat making it impossible to match Lucas's speed. Much surer of her footing, Nonesuch grabbed him by the hand and tried to pull him forward.

From behind them, the Mannish screamed. Oyster turned to look but all he got was the impression of one of the clouds hanging low over the ice, something shadowed and angry within.

Despite Nonesuch's help, his boots made running impossible. The lighthouse's brilliant beam wheeled overhead.

"Don't look back," said Lucas, turning tail and returning to help his beleaguered crew. "Get inside!"

With superhuman strength he picked up Oyster and threw him across the last stretch. With a thud, Oyster landed on his front and skidded up to the lighthouse's entrance. The impact knocked the air from his lungs, and he struggled to breathe.

The iron door swung open with a shriek of metal on metal. Primrose emerged and picked Oyster up, lifting him as if he were no more than a paperweight. He carried him inside before dropping him unceremoniously on the stone floor.

Nonesuch dived through the door next, followed by Lucas and the remainder of his crew, and there was an echoing *clang* as the metal door slammed shut behind them.

68
THE LANTERN ROOM

Oyster rolled over and lay on his back panting, filling his burning lungs with air. His legs were jelly from the effort of moving on the ice. Outside, thunder rumbled around the building as though looking for a way in. The rest of the party leaned against the lighthouse's thick walls, trying to recover their breath. Oyster counted them two Mannish down.

"We are no expert, but that would be *three* that you owe us now, Miles McLellen. And three is an ancient and powerful number."

"Leave him be," said Lucas. "There's a lot for him to get his head around, right now."

Primrose struck a match and a lantern painted the walls in yellow light. He dropped to his knees and Oyster was overwhelmed by the man's hallucinatory scent: dog shit and honey, lavender and black mould. The stag-antlers that Oyster had seen when Primrose had appeared on the bridge sprouted from his temples, gnarled and uneven as tree branches.

"You don't look too surprised to see us here. So it would seem that the penny has dropped in there somewhere." He tapped Oyster's forehead with a broad nailless forefinger. He nodded at Lucas. "Opposite sides of the same coin, him and us. Distinct, but part of the same mechanism."

Primrose stood. Oyster shook his head to free his nostrils of the odour. Nonesuch helped him to his feet.

"You know this stinky motherfucker?" she said, taking in Primrose with a measured glance.

"Only vaguely," said Oyster.

Primrose grinned his wax museum grin and bowed.

Oyster followed Primrose and Lucas up several flights of wide, granite stairs. He climbed them robotically, feeling the metal teeth on his boots grate the stone beneath, watching as their long shadows waxed and waned. Nonesuch was a few steps behind, Lucas and the Mannish bringing up the rear.

Whatever he had expected when he'd set off to help Lucas, he hadn't been prepared for this. Lucas being so tight with Primrose put him off-balance. He was glad that he was here with Nonesuch.

The stairs circled the outer wall, which was inset with windows so thin they were merely slits. Oyster buried himself within his coat, shuddering at the wind whistling outside.

Pushing through a wooden door, they arrived at a sparsely decorated room. Lucas removed his jacket and hung it on a nearby coat stand. He stationed Ambidexter and the remaining Mannish within.

The message was clear. There was no way Nonesuch or Oyster could make a getaway now.

A large four-poster bed and a chaise longue played host to piles of books and yellowing papers. These had all been woven into an enormous spider's web with wax and pieces of string. There were photographs, drawings, diagrams and sketches of every single size and shape. One looked suspiciously like the photo of the Miracle Club Marya Petrovna had back in her gaff. Oyster felt another pang of guilt at the thought. He really hoped the old girl was still in one piece.

"Worms nearly had you back there, didn't they? And that would've been an unfortunate end to a very, very long game," said Primrose, pointing at the crazy wall.

They passed through an adjoining door and up another set of steps to a smaller room, dominated by a broad column at its centre. On top of the column sat an enormous gear mechanism coated in thick grease. Its cogs and pinions slid and churned, creaking and moaning, driving the rotation of the lantern on the floor above them.

A wrought-iron staircase led up to a broad wooden hatch in the roof. Primrose climbed up through it fluidly, leaving the trapdoor open behind him. Oyster followed, clanking up the steps in his heavy boots to find himself in a glass-walled room at the top of the lighthouse.

In its centre sat the lens assembly, rotating glacially and sending out two perpendicular beams of light. Oyster shielded his eyes to avoid being blinded as one swept past him.

At the room's outer edge was an incongruous fireplace, harbouring a fire that had burnt down to its last few coals. In front of it were a pair of twill armchairs, a sofa and a Formica table. Next to the chairs stood a tall, rectangular shape covered in moth-eaten velvet. Oyster's tattoo recognised the cabinet before he did, erupting with a throbbing ache. He winced.

"S'up, son?" said Lucas. "D'you need something for the pain?"

Oyster waved him away.

Some mugs and a loaf of black bread sat on the table. Without invitation or ceremony, Nonesuch flopped into the nearest chair and began devouring the bread.

"Do make yourself at home, why don't you," said Lucas.

Nonesuch ignored him, pausing only to slurp the remaining water from the mugs.

"Tea, anyone?" Lucas asked, placing a red ceramic kettle over the fire.

Primrose stood at the edge of the lantern-room window, staring out into the whirlwind beyond. His outline, silhouetted in the glare from the lighthouse, vibrated even more than usual. Oyster found it hard to keep his eyes fixed on him. He slumped onto the armrest of the nearest chair. There was a pressure in his head. The light from the lens swept past Primrose again, making him briefly incandescent.

"Quite magnificent," muttered Primrose. He turned, fixing them all with an intense stare. "And now, if no one objects: to business."

He tugged at the velvet covering to reveal Marya Petrovna's cabinet. Nonesuch finished her meal and wiped her mouth with the back of her hand. She blazed with prismatic light.

"Not much to look at, is it?" said Primrose. "Despite being constructed from the Tree of Life itself."

The kettle whistled and Lucas busied himself making the tea. He handed a mug to Oyster, who accepted it, unthinkingly.

"You two seem awfully friendly, all holed-up here. I s'pose you've opened a cafe somewhere nearby, too."

Lucas banged a mug down in front of Nonesuch, who sniffed it and pushed it aside.

"I don't get it," said Oyster. "If you two have been working together all along, why the need for all this panto?"

Lucas cracked his knuckles and sighed.

"Don't be reading this wrong, son. We're still adversaries. Always have been, always will be. We try to fuck each other over. That's all part of the game. So, I try to get at his coins. He makes moves on my old crew. It's how we keep shit from getting dull. Really, we've got more in common with each than we do with anyone else."

"And then there's the hero's journey and all that piffle," said Primrose. "Besides which, *Cailleach*, the hag, had her claws into you. Messing everything up for her own filthy ends. But you had to feel like you were on a great quest in order to bring you to us. It all worked out in the end. If you hadn't, then the invocation on your body would not be triggered. Basic logomancy, of course. Although, we took the precaution of glamouring those little bits of paper you found just to be sure."

There was a crackle of lightning outside followed by a detonation of thunder that Oyster felt in the pit of his stomach.

"Taranis is here," said Primrose, pointing at the ceiling. "Esus and Tuetates will be along shortly."

Lucas drained his tea with a gulp.

"Storm's overhead. The sacrifice has been made. Time has come to make the choice," he said to Primrose.

"Sacrifice?" said Oyster.

"The enemy warrior," said Primrose.

Lucas cleared the table of its cups and lay a silver bracelet at its centre. Oyster could just make out the words *Brute Force* engraved on it. It was Broadsides'.

Oyster looked at Lucas, who was unable to meet his gaze. He swallowed and a cold sensation grew in the pit of his stomach.

"So, it was you that killed Broadsie, not Primrose," said Oyster.

Lucas shuffled his feet.

"I gave the word, but I didn't—"

"I don't wanna hear it," hissed Oyster.

All his rage froze into something stronger still: an immense, almost cosmic resolve. Whatever he could do to stop these jokers, he was going to do it. He was through with them moving everyone around like counters in an interdimensional game of tiddlywinks.

"I'm sorry," said Lucas. "It's just how it has to be. The ritual demands a sacrifice."

Oyster ignored him. He needed to stall them, long enough to work out a permanent way to bring all this shit to a close in his favour. He thought about how his patter worked on the bridge. How the arrangement of the words and phrases persuaded and cajoled people into doing what he wanted them to do. It was his own personal brand of magic. He had to do that now. With knobs on.

"So," he said evenly. He thought about the strange dream he'd had and the things that Marya Petrovna had told him. "Let me see if I've got this. It's the Trian ritual, right? My tattoo activates that thing and then you two dance the mystical hokey-cokey."

"In a manner of speaking, yes," Lucas nodded.

Primrose cleared his throat.

"Well, he has done his homework," he said, with something that sounded oddly like pride. "But you are wrong about it to one important degree. It's *you* who makes the choice."

Oyster sniffed. "Are you serious?"

The girl with the thousand-yard stare and the stained face – the girl from his dream – flashed into his head.

Lucas flexed his shoulders, and Oyster heard the sinews

cracking. The man had swollen. He was taller, broader. For the first time, even through his anger, Oyster saw that Lucas's humanity was something that he wore as lightly as his clothes.

"Yep," said Lucas. "A simple choice. It's more of our way, or it's his."

Oyster shook his head.

"Nuh, uh," he replied. "If it's down to that, I choose to go home."

"Not an option, son," said Lucas.

"We'll see about that." Oyster looked at Nonesuch. "C'mon, glow-stick, fetch your coat. We're gonna skidoosh."

"Was hopin' on that," she said, flicking them a rainbow-lit finger. "Laters, suckers."

Thunder burst; lightning crackled.

"Miles," said Primrose, "it gives me no pleasure to say this, but you have to stay. You have your part to play in the ceremony. You must make the choice."

"Where'd you get off using my name, you creepy-Halloween-mask-lookin' fuck-pig?" said Oyster.

The trapdoor banged open and up the steps came Ambidexter, leading a blindfolded Motet and Marya Petrovna. Both looked bedraggled and weak. Their wrists were bound with cable-ties, on top of which they had been roped together. Another Mannish brought up the rear, carrying a sack from which they emptied a prone Goswick.

"Thought this might happen, so sent my girls back to collect your crew. For leverage," said Lucas.

"You fucker," said Oyster. He turned to address the new arrivals. "Are you two alright?"

Motet nodded. Relieved as Oyster was to see Marya Petrovna, she was having trouble breathing.

"Enoch, I am so sorry. I did not mean to—"

"Stubble it," said Ambidexter, slapping the woman's face.

"Enough!" yelled Oyster. He took a breath.

"S'alright, MPD," he said quietly. "We're all fair and square. I've fucked it right up too. We're all good. Honest."

"Hag," said Primrose to Marya Petrovna with a nod of greeting.

Marya Petrovna ignored him.

"Best give her and her pet gebel the scenic view," said Primrose. Ambidexter ushered Marya Petrovna out of the lantern room and into the howling gale beyond.

Primrose cleared his throat.

"Okay. So. Our coins, then." He pointed at the table next to Broadsides' bracelet. "Here, now."

Oyster squared his shoulders.

"Well, that's where you two turd-blossoms have a problem, innit?" he said. "I don't got 'em."

"Wasn't asking you, Miles," said Lucas. "Was asking your girlfriend here."

Nonesuch ducked behind the chair, her dagger in one hand and a gun in the other. Her light flared.

"Hold it!" bellowed Lucas.

As Oyster's eyes cleared, he saw Primrose had squared up to her. The gebel crouched behind the furniture, the tip of her dagger an inch from his chest.

"As much fun as it would be to see you two go at each other right now..." He pointed to the figures of Marya Petrovna and Motet huddled against the lighthouse's low iron railings. "Think you're forgetting we've got your friends here. Any more clever shit and they're going for a cold-water swim."

Nonesuch poked out her tongue and made a feint at Primrose's chest. The man backhanded the weapon out of the way and held out his hand.

Nonesuch looked over at Oyster and tilted her head.

Oyster nodded.

She put away her weapons and drew the leather bag from her coat, throwing it across to Oyster, who caught it with a jangle.

"On the table, son," instructed Lucas. His face was twisted into something that was only superficially human now. His eyes gazed emptily over their heads, staring into an abyss that only he could see. "We're close now. The moment of possession is coming."

Oyster remembered his resolve. He had to switch things up. These two had had it their own way too long. He had to find a way to break the rhythm of the moment, control it himself; get these two at each other.

In any scam, pacing was important, but so was reading your mark. It was what let you into their head, let you use their own strengths against them. He bit his lip, thinking over what Marya Petrovna had said about Lugones, Cerunnos, whoever the fuck they were. These two were wildly overconfident. He could use that.

"So, tell me this," he said to Lucas. "You set up our crew originally, the Urbans. I mean, am I right? Set out the stall, made us a short-con outfit."

"Damn right," said Lucas. "I taught Mickey, Deano, all those OGs: I showed them a wager is a way of giving thanks to powers that be."

"Have a care," said Primrose. "We sense mischief here, Lugones."

He turned to Oyster and clicked his fingers, pointing at the table.

"I don't think so," said Oyster triumphantly. "I challenge you to play me for them. After all, a game of chance is a sacred thing."

"For fuck's sake," hissed Primrose. He turned to Lucas. "We told you to keep your bloody trap closed!"

Finally, thought Oyster, *I've got you on the back foot.*

Primrose sighed.

"And we are bound to accept. What are your terms?"

Oyster slipped his hand into his jacket pocket. His playing cards from the bridge were still there. He pulled them out.

"Best of three. I win, you let us all go and give up all the crazy shit. I lose, I help you. Willingly."

Primrose rolled his eyes.

"Are you a complete twerp? We bested you on the bridge. What do you think has changed since then?"

"All this chat," said Oyster, miming a flapping jaw with his hand. "Just tells me you're worried I can take you."

Primrose compressed his thin lips into a smile and drew up a chair in front of the table, indicating for Oyster to do the same.

"Let us get on with it. Time, ironically, is of the essence," he said.

Oyster took a deep breath. For a second, he remembered another London, an age ago, where he'd sat opposite Deano and learned how to deal. He flexed his fingers. A peal of thunder came from outside.

"Just listen to that! Esus, Tuetates and Taranis! My boys are in the fucking house!" yelled Lucas. His hands were raised and he was staring up into the sky.

"Okay," Oyster said, "just to be fair, let's warm you up with a few for free—"

"We can dispense with the formalities, don't you think?" said Primrose.

"How is it you're so eager to lose? Two freebies for you to get into the swing of things."

Oyster cleared space on the table, moving Broadsides' bracelet to its edge. It glittered as the light from the lantern swept past them. A voice at the back of his head told him to pocket it, but he couldn't while Primrose's attention was fixed on the table.

Instead, he dealt two straight hands, letting Primrose win each one. Oyster's confidence grew as his patter started to flow. It was good to have the cards moving. He could tune out the thunder and even the man's relentless smell.

"Come, along," said Primrose, picking up the queen of hearts and presenting it to Oyster. "Let's not trifle any longer. 'The play's the thing' and all that. Let's begin in earnest."

"I hear you," said Oyster. He stretched his back and swayed from side to side. He was enjoying having Primrose and Lucas under his control. Their impatience might create an opening. "Best of three. Winner takes all."

Oyster started the first hand. The cards were slick beneath his fingers.

"So, what's the angle then?" he said. "This choice malarkey. What are you offering?"

"It's very simple," said Primrose. "All of the worlds... but most specifically yours, have been following the pattern that was put in place during the last cycle. When Lugones had the upper hand."

"*Civilisation. Technology. Progress.*" The man put each of the words in air quotes. "Even you can't have failed to notice the state of things. You're destroying your world and others to make tea cosies and Happy Meals."

Oyster finished the first hand and made a perfect hype move, sliding the queen onto the right card instead of the centre one.

"That's *him*." He nodded at Lucas. "What's *your* play?"

Primrose rested his hand on his chin and Oyster got a waft of the man's scent.

"That experiment is done. Your lot fucked it. Humanity has failed."

"And?"

"Think of us as an avatar of nature."

Primrose sniffed and pointed at the cards.

"Are you finished here?"

Oyster felt sick. There was another peal of thunder.

"Yeah, do your worst," he replied, without meeting the man's gaze.

Primrose brought his index finger down on the rightmost card. Oyster flipped it over to reveal the queen.

"That is one to us, we believe, Mr Miles," he said.

Oyster nodded.

"You know, I just don't see the appeal," he said.

Primrose leaned back. A shimmer of lightning reflected in his stag antlers. There was a certain insane magnificence about him.

"What's the value of a blank slate to you, Miles? A fresh start? Isn't that what you've wanted all along? Running from this gang? Running after *him*." He nodded at Lucas. "We can wipe it *all* away. All the stress and pain between you and your mother, for example. You'd all still exist, of course. Everyone would still *be*. It's just that you wouldn't be quite so…"

"Civilised?" asked Oyster.

"Exactly. Instead, you would exist in a state of sanctified nature. A glorious state of unknowing; of unlearning all that 'being human' nonsense. We're offering you the hope of actual change. You know as well as we do that things can't continue as they have—"

"This sounds a lot like wearing loincloths and hopping round a fire worshipping you," said Oyster.

Primrose raised an eyebrow and tipped his head to one side.

"There might be the occasional element of ritual thanks involved, yes. But you are being *too* literal about this. *Too* arrogant. Are you so sure *he's* got all the answers? Try to think beyond the confines of what you know. There are other ways of being. You can *feel* it. You felt it when you visited our altar. That sense of yourself as an animal: a beautiful, wonderful animal. Nothing more, nothing less. Human history is basically the story of you denying your essential nature. That's half of your problems right there. We're offering you and everyone else the chance to transcend."

Oyster looked down as he dealt the cards. He wasn't sure whether it was the storm combined with the hypnotic intensity of Primrose's words, but what the man was saying did feel right.

Nonesuch caught his eye. How could he choose for her? Or for Cess? What right did he have to choose for anybody?

Out of the corner of his eye, the shapes of Marya Petrovna and Motet were silhouetted by distant lightning. He finished the deal.

"Nice speech. You almost had me there, too. Except for the fact that you got my fam by the throat, ready for a free diving lesson. So... pick."

The man nodded. He regarded the cards, frowned, and then brought his finger down on the leftmost. Oyster revealed the king, faking a commiserating expression.

"Soz, but that's one apiece. Next hand is the decider."

Oyster exhaled and waggled his head from side to side to loosen his shoulders. He dealt. He went for a straight deal this time, assuming that Primrose would be expecting something double-tricksy. The cards clattered onto the table and into place. The queen in the centre.

"Here we go, then," said Oyster.

"One here." He tapped the table in front of the rightmost card.

"One here." He did the same in front of the centre card.

"And last one here." He tapped next to the leftmost card. With any luck, Primrose would take his misdirection.

"So, what's it gonna be?" he said.

Primrose sniffed and looked at Oyster with narrowed eyes.

"Well," he said in a sing-song voice. "Let me see."

The lighthouse's beam rolled across the table, lighting up the cards like they were on fire.

Primrose reached out and chose the centre card.

Oyster swallowed his defeat. He had to think fast. There was one thing he could try. A move Deano had taught him to use against smart punters on the bridge. A switch-up. Keeping his hands steady, and moving as fluidly as possible, he reached across the table, palming the ace of clubs on the left. He was just about to switch it with the queen in the centre when Primrose grabbed him by the wrist. The man's fingers bit into his flesh.

"Drop it," said Primrose, nodding at Lucas. "Me and him were born a long time before yesterday. And he pulled better moves than this when he was half your age."

Primrose shook Oyster's hand to release the palmed card. It rocked back and forth on the table, face up. It looked as waxy and forlorn as Oyster felt.

"That's settled, then," said Lucas, breaking out of his trance. "The game's forfeit."

Oyster suddenly felt very small. Primrose sighed and rose to a standing position. Oyster picked up the bag of coins with shaking hands.

"Time has come," Primrose said.

THE THING YOU NEVER WANTED TO KNOW

Nonesuch was up on her feet in an instant, bounding over the chair and plunging towards Primrose, dagger drawn, blazing with light. He smacked her away with a flick of his hand. Oyster yelled out as she hit the floor of the lantern room with a heavy thud and rolled to a stop.

He kicked over the table and broke away from Primrose, but the man stuck out a foot and tripped him. Oyster hit the deck in a heap, Broadsides' bracelet glittered close by. Instinctively, he pocketed it as the man drew him to his feet.

"What have you done!" he yelled as he clapped eyes on Nonesuch's unmoving figure.

"Calm down. She'll be fine," he said. "We hardly touched her."

Lucas, looking even larger than he had before, walked over to Nonesuch, picked up her prone body and placed her on the leather sofa near the guttering fire.

"She's got some moxie, this one, I'll say that for her," he said.

"What is the fucking matter with you!" yelled Oyster in desperation. "Why are you doing this? You're my dad, you're supposed to be looking out for me. You're the one person here who's supposed to actually help me, and you're pulling all this bullshit!"

Lucas looked at Oyster and blinked. He swallowed and his golf-ball-sized Adam's apple bobbed. His mouth opened and closed wordlessly.

"Dad?" said Oyster. His voice sounded small. He was a kid again, watching him disappear behind the East Tower's stack of bins.

Lightning played patterns on Lucas's monolithic face. He knelt to right the table and picked up the bag containing the coins, placing them in its centre.

"You are a rotten sod," said Primrose. "Are you *never* going to tell him?"

And then Oyster knew this was the awful thing that he had not wanted to learn from Primrose. The sickly, sinking feeling that had pursued him across London and filled him with dread.

He held out his hands to Primrose.

"Don't tell me," he said. "I don't want to know."

"But you need to learn the truth," said Primrose quietly. "It really will set you free."

Oyster shook his head. He didn't want to hear it. But nothing could stop it now. He was at the top of a helter skelter. Dizzy. Ready to fall.

"Miles," said Primrose, releasing him from his grasp. "It's us. We're your *real* dad. Not this one."

There it was.

A cold wave of numbness swept up from his feet, swallowing him whole. He looked at Lucas. Begging for the man to make some sound, to deny what Primrose had said.

"We made you. *He* stole you when you were just a tiny thing. We wanted to find a better way to tell you this," Primrose continued, "but you just wouldn't listen to us." The words came from far away.

So, everything he had ever been told had been a complete lie. *He*, Miles McLellen, was a lie. The living embodiment of the long con that these two had been playing for years. Was Cess even his sister? She had been the one thing he'd been able to hold on to through all of this, and maybe she wasn't even his family.

He turned to Lucas. The man couldn't return his gaze.

"Miles, I'm sorry. I just—" he began.

"Quiet," said Oyster. His tongue felt unfamiliar in his mouth as it worked its way around the word.

Primrose led a dazed, unresisting Oyster towards the cabinet and opened the middle of its three doors. His tone was conciliatory.

"It's a lot to deal with, we know, but you need to understand it all before you make the choice."

With one move they had robbed him of everything. From here on in, perhaps, it was all inevitable. Perhaps this was how the girl with the stained face had felt all those years ago.

Tears welled up from within him. Tears for Broadsides, for Cécile and for himself. But he shuddered and swallowed them. He wasn't going to cry in front of these arseholes.

"So, what do I do?" he asked numbly, looking at the cabinet. Lucas produced one of the golden dice that Oyster had seen at Primrose's place and rolled it on the table. He took in the result and then went over to the fire, picking up a plastic kitchen timer that sat over the fireplace. He gave it a twist and slapped it on the table next to the bag containing the coins. It began to count down with a loud metallic tick.

"Three minutes," he said. Primrose's revelation had stripped Lucas of his bravado, his voice was small. Oyster couldn't even look at him.

Primrose reached into the bag and pulled out the dull, silver coins. He pressed each to his lips and muttered some words before replacing them in the leather bag. He drew the string and handed them to Oyster.

"Accept your role and it'll all be over and done with quickly," said Primrose softly.

Oyster shut his eyes.

"He powers it with his spear," Primrose continued. "You enter the *Mói Dó*rath. When the time comes, we empty my tokens, the coins, in the sacred circle. You pick them up and make your choice."

Oyster remembered what the girl had done in the wood.

"You choose the path. Place the coins on an avatar: me or him. Then the chosen one, the token bearer, gets a visitation from the three and is invested with their power."

Oyster nodded.

"What's to keep me from just holding on to them and screwing you all over?"

Primrose shook his head.

"We're sorry. But you wouldn't survive the moment of possession," he said. "Too much essence; too much power for a mortal to contain. You'd pop like a balloon."

"Miles," said Lucas over the thunder. "Before you choose. I never meant things to go this way. I know you're hurt, and I am sorry for that. But please, put that aside now, son. There's too much at stake here. Think of everything that will be lost if you choose his way."

Oyster grimaced at Lucas's use of the word *son*. Then, trembling, he shuffled towards the cabinet, disorientated and numb.

"Seems like you should have thought of that before you left me with nothing to lose," he replied. Stepping into the box, he shut its doors behind him.

Inside, there was an instant of disorientating darkness, and then the doors and slits were all ignited by the lighthouse's beam. Oyster looked around in the brief glow. The velvet lining was sticky beneath his fingers and there was a musty smell, like the cabinet hadn't ever been cleaned. Then the light died as quickly as it had appeared, leaving him in total darkness again. His tattoo was on fire in a way that it never had been before. His entire body throbbed with pain, but at least it was one that he had lived with, that he had become accustomed to. From outside came the sclerotic tick of Lucas's timer counting off the seconds.

He hauled in a breath to steady himself. Out of sight of everyone, suddenly alone, he was overwhelmed. What had just happened to him? He was dizzy with grief and shock. How could Primrose – that *thing* – be his real father?

They really had him on the ropes now. These fuckers. He thought of Cécile. But even the thought of her stuck him a little.

He sat with the pain for a second. He still loved her. No doubt she still loved him. How much did it matter really if she wasn't his actual sis?

What would she have said? Stop being such a donkey, probably. He sniffed and tried to straighten things in his head. They'd pulled all this shit to get him off his game. Make him manipulable. He was out of time now and he had to stop thinking about himself.

As Lucas's timer ticked off the seconds, he remembered Broadsides and his anger reignited. Everyone was fair game to them, he thought. They were like a pair of toddlers playing chess, but with his friends as the pieces. He had to think of Cess; of the rest of them.

He needed help, no question, but Marya Petrovna was a hostage and Nonesuch had been KO'd. What did he have that could help him out of this mess, to find another way? He touched his tattoo. He could still flit. Anywhere. He wasn't in the habit of running out on anything, but perhaps there was someone that could help.

He swallowed, made his mind blank. The lighthouse lit up the cabinet's interior once more, and then he was sitting in a garden having tea.

70

YELLIE

Oyster was blinded by sudden daylight. A bee buzzed past his ear and his nose was flooded with smells. There was the summery scent of freshly cut grass and the perfume of fabric conditioner. He made out the rich aroma of soft butter, warm scones, and even the dark, bitter notes of a pot of tea. Primrose's choking stink was nowhere to be found. A breeze ruffled Oyster's hair and in the distance he heard the faint chirrup and whirr of insects. This was very different from the last time he had been in *der hinter*.

His eyes adjusted. He was sitting at a table with a linen tablecloth set for afternoon tea. Across from him sat a young woman, not much older than he was. Her light brown hair was pulled into a pair of bunches. Her face had the pinched aspect of someone who had either grown up too quickly or, perhaps, tried to stay too young for too long.

The girl adopted a welcoming, if slightly amused expression. Her opalescent gaze was hard and intelligent. Penetrating.

Words arranged themselves into opening sentences in Oyster's mind several times, but each seemed too stupid to say. The girl was in no hurry to talk to him either, and so they sat and looked at each other for what seemed like a long time.

"Hallo again, Miles McLellen," she said finally in heavily accented English.

Oyster nodded.

"How'd you know my name?"

"I have been here long enough to get to know everyone. Do you know who I am?" she asked.

Oyster nodded.

"You're Yellie, the old lady's first assistant."

She smiled. It was the expression of a being infinitely older than the face wearing it, and for the first time Oyster wondered if he was in danger. The other thing he noticed was that his tattoo was no longer hurting.

"It is not awake here," said Yelena in answer to his thoughts. "You are outside of everything."

"How did you end up here?" asked Oyster.

Yellie leaned over and poured two cups of tea. Oyster waved his away.

"It is hard to remember all the details at such a remove. It feels like it all happened to somebody else. Perhaps it did. That night, I stepped into Fauks' *Mói Dórath*. And then I smelled fire. I tried to escape, but the bolts on the cabinet were drawn and the metal itself had become too hot to touch. I choked on great lungfuls of smoke. I think I died. But afterwards, I found myself in this place."

Oyster swatted away a wasp.

"I was terrified and alone. Can you imagine that? Just being totally alone and absolutely scared out of one's wits?"

Oyster opened his mouth, but he felt too bruised to want to speak.

Yellie tilted her head.

"Yes. You know, I think you do," she said. "For the longest time, I kept thinking that *she* would send someone for me. That she would try to rescue me. That was the worst thing, I think. Imagining that she had just forgotten about me."

"Marya Petrovna never forgot about you," said Oyster. "She was in love with you. She just needed other people. She needed me."

"I loved her too, you know." Yellie smiled sadly. "I went quite mad with the waiting, I think, several times over. Are you sure you don't want anything to eat? These are quite edible."

"I'm good," said Oyster. He leaned forward. "Look, we're on the clock here," he said. "And I'm all kinds of desperate."

Yellie waved regally at their surroundings.

"It is fine. As I said, we're outside everything here. Outside space. Outside time. Do you like what I've done with the place? I thought you'd appreciate it, being English and everything."

Oyster thought about it. This woman had been stuck here for longer than time itself. All along, she'd been waiting for someone to come and get her.

"I'm sorry you've been stranded here so long," he said. "And I'm not entirely sure if I can take you with me, but we can give it a shot, if you like."

Yellie laughed. It was a brittle tinkle.

"Oh my. That *is* a good one," she said. "*You* rescue *me*? I can see what Marya Petrovna sees in you. You have a good heart. Despite everything. She needs people like that around her. She's been alive *too* long."

For a second, there was a hint of the raw power that Yellie had radiated in *der hinter* before. The tea in Oyster's cup oscillated in sympathy to Yellie's laughter; energy rippled around her.

"She *still* loves you, you know," said Oyster.

Yellie looked at him and smiled.

"You came here looking for help, did you not?"

Oyster nodded.

"I can help you choose, if you like. Cast your mind back. I showed you what things might come to pass if you favour Lugones' path, the first time we met."

Oyster was confused. What was she talking about? And then he remembered. That first night at the old lady's gaff: the nightmare he'd had of the city all made of glass and steel. The air you couldn't breathe and the fighting, the fires. Big Mickey getting gunned down and Cécile. Something awful had happened to her.

Oyster gripped the table at the memory and forced himself to breathe slowly. His heart was yammering in his chest and the sweetness of the air made him dizzy.

"Now. Let me show you the world Cerunnos is offering…" She readied to click her fingers.

"No!" yelled Oyster. "No. No need. I get it."

Yellie nodded. "Very well. So, you must make a choice."

Oyster released the table and snorted.

"Some choice," he said. "Seems to me, having to pick between two options you can't control is no choice at all. This whole shitty game is rigged."

Yellie nodded indulgently.

"That seems a reasonable sentiment."

"So, am I fucked?"

Yellie smiled.

"No. You are not. Have faith in your talents and your family," she said.

Oyster's anger rose.

"They've just about eaten up my family and shat them out."

Yellie cleared her throat. "Well, there are the people you are related to and then there is family. You have everything you need. I am quite sure of it. *Nothing is true. Everything is permitted.*"

A wind started to whip across the meadow and the sky went from blue to a haunted, starless black.

"I can help things from this side, but you will still need to do your part on your own. Now. You really should be going," said Yellie. "Oh, and do send all my love to Marya Petrovna."

"Wait," said Oyster. "I still don't know what to do."

She looked around conspiratorially.

"Just use what you have to hand," she whispered. "Remember, mischief is in your nature."

She raised a hand to shoo him away.

With that Oyster was gone.

71

THE LIGHTHOUSE AT THE END OF THE WORLD

Oyster stood in the cabinet. Outside, the kitchen timer ratcheted off the seconds. He couldn't have much time left. His thoughts ran in circles around his head. What had Yellie meant? *Use what you have to hand?*

He slipped his fingers into his pocket. Broadsides' name tag nestled there. He thought for a second. *Wait a minute. Shit!* Perhaps he did have the makings of a play here, after all. Before he had time to work it all through, the alarm clattered, and the cabinet door sprang open.

Oyster stepped out. The whole building was vibrating to a single resonant note. The lantern-room floor was decorated with the interlocking spiral pattern he remembered from his dream of the ritual.

There were Lucas and Primrose, limned by the lighthouse's lantern. Both of them were larger and more alien than before. The ceremony was accentuating their inhuman essences. Oyster raised a hand to shield his eyes as the light slid past. Behind their silhouettes, Goswick's head twitched. The dog had come round and was trying to get his attention. *Okay, this he could use.*

"It's time, Miles," said Lucas. His voice was as bottomless as the storm outside.

Oyster took in a breath. The moment lasted forever. And in that second, he knew what he had to do, knew what Yellie had meant. The lightning was strobing furiously now and there was a pressure in his ears as though he was deep underwater.

He took a breath. *Yes.* He was going to screw over these fuckers and good. He dug his hand into his pocket, wrapping his fingers around the chain on Broadsides' bracelet. As the lighthouse beam swung into Lucas's eyes, Oyster motioned to Goswick in what he hoped was an appropriately *wait for it, doggie* manner.

"Lugones is right. Time has come," said Primrose.

"Okay," said Oyster. "But before I do this, you gotta stop holding my fam hostage." He pointed to the figures of Marya Petrovna and Motet out on the balcony.

Lucas nodded at Ambidexter, who opened the balcony door and shoved the pair through it with a scowl.

"Free them!" said Oyster. "Or I don't play ball."

"Come on," said Primrose, "we don't have time for this."

Lucas exchanged a glance with Ambidexter, who slit her prisoners' cable-ties with a flick of her dagger.

"Alright then," said Oyster. He wasn't as scared as he expected to be, suddenly feeling confident and sure of himself. He had these two in the palm of his hand now, despite all their scheming.

Lucas took his spear, stationing himself at the centre of one of the spiralling floor patterns while Primrose did the same, the leather bag at his feet. He nodded at Oyster, indicating where he should stand. Oyster walked across the concrete floor. As he did so, he winked at Goswick, indicating Primrose's leather purse with a surreptitious nod.

The dog raced across the floor in a flurry of fur.

"Don't do it, kid!" Goswick yelled. "Don't help these asshats!"

Goswick dived between Primrose's legs, snatching the bag in his jaws and scurrying away towards Oyster. Lucas was after him in a second, charging with spear in hand. Goswick dodged, evading Primrose, but running headlong into Oyster. They both crashed over in a mess of legs and fur. Oyster grabbed at the bag, sending its contents spinning across the concrete. He scrambled to pick them up.

"Enough with this sideshow bullshit!" yelled Lucas, enraged. He was glowering over the prone Nonesuch, his spearpoint at her throat.

"Alright," said Oyster, raising his hands to display the coins. "It's all good. You can have them. No need for anything fatal."

"Give," said Primrose. He licked his lips, aiming a kick at Goswick which drove him whimpering across the lighthouse and into a heap by the balcony door.

Oyster was breathing heavily. His tumble to the floor had winded him. He picked up the bag and theatrically dropped each of the coins into it, before pulling the drawstring tight. He approached Primrose. Ironically, this creature with its stag antlers and rippling mask of a face appeared more human than Lucas. He looked Oyster in the eye and nodded.

"That's it, my boy," he said. "You know what you have to do."

Oyster handed him the bag and walked to his appointed place while Lucas and Primrose took up their positions.

Lucas cleared his throat, and his spear rang as he struck the floor with it three times. Immediately, there was an answering rumble from outside. Lightning coruscated down through the ceiling to the spear's tip and into the symbol itself, which blazed with an angry energy.

He was taken aback by how strange Lucas looked in this moment. The huge figure in front of him resembled the man he'd thought of as his dad in only the most superficial of ways.

Primrose raised his arms and let loose a stream of rasping sounds that might have been words. Thunder rattled the windows. The wind bayed through the open balcony door. Lucas nodded. His eyes had glazed over again. He was in the grip of whatever cosmic currents the ceremony stirred up inside of him as it reached its final stage. The parts of him that had been Lucas receded and only Lugones remained.

Slowly, Primrose walked towards the centre of the spiral, pushing the cabinet out of his way with a brush of his hand. His face and body were a cascade of undulating movements that abandoned any pretence at humanity. Now, more than ever,

Oyster could see that this thing was an assemblage of competing elements all held together by Primrose's formidable determination. It was almost impressive.

With a victorious bark, Cerunnos took the leather bag and turned it upside down, emptying its contents onto the centre of the sacred circle. Then he held his arms aloft, just as he had in Oyster's dream, waiting for the ancient circuit to be completed. The moment of choice was here.

Oyster held his breath. They had tried to take his identity away from him, these two. But he still had all the things he had learned. He still had his skills. Mischief was in his nature.

Cerunnos stood for a second more. The ominous throb and the thunder ratcheted up and up, reaching a crescendo. But then nothing happened. Another second passed. Another. Finally, Cerunnos looked down at what he had emptied from the leather bag.

Broadsides' bracelet sat in the centre of the spiral pattern, glittering with reflected lightning. The coins were nowhere to be seen. There was a boom from outside. Cerunnos let out a heart-rending wail, low and keening like a lost dog.

"Now!" Oyster yelled.

Nonesuch sprang from the couch, lashing out with a kick aimed at the base of Lugones' spear. There was a *wump* as it broke contact and the symbol discharged. Nonesuch's body skidded across the floor, propelled by the force of the blast.

Lugones roared in frustration and banged the spear back down onto the floor, but it was too late. The ritual had been disrupted. The spell was broken. And already, Cerunnos and Lugones were less than they had been.

"Miles, you stupid, stupid little fucker," said Lugones. "You can't do this. You're just a person. You won't survive the transfiguration. It won't fix anything."

"Maybe not," replied Oyster. He produced the three coins from his pocket, where they'd been since he'd switched them up for the bracelet. "But if it fixes you two fuck-wombles then that's good enough for me."

There was an ear-splitting crash as lightning struck the top of the lighthouse and sparks flew from the metal window frames. With a blood-curdling yell, Marya Petrovna head-butted Ambidexter and the Mannish Boy staggered backwards, blood spattering her face and clothes. Motet dived at Lugones, picking up Ambidexter's weapon and driving it deep into the man's back, but he was already fading away into nothingness.

On the other side of the room, Nonesuch was up again, spinning and kicking like a Catherine wheel, taking out the other Mannish gang members in a whirlwind of blows. With another ghoulish wail, the thing called Cerunnos flew into a thousand constituent parts that smashed the glass panes of the lantern room as they left.

But it was too late for Oyster now. He looked at his hand. He tried to drop the coins, but they remained in place. The pressure in his head was unbearable. He put his other hand to his ear and his fingers came away sticky with blood. Primrose's words came back to him. He was the token-bearer now, which meant something was coming. He staggered and fell backwards. There was a sharp pain at the back of his head as he hit the floor, and someone was screaming as his tattoo wrapped his body in white-hot pain. Taranis, Tuetates and Esus were coming to squeeze him out of his own head. The coins in his hand were burning, but he couldn't let go of them.

Then Marya Petrovna had him in an embrace. He tried to move away from her, tried to tell her that touching him was dangerous, but his body wasn't his anymore. She whispered in his ears, gently prising his fingers apart, removing the coins and holding them tight. It was too late, though.

With a lurch, he was looking down on all of them. Marya Petrovna and Nonesuch were crouched over him, holding hands with Motet. Without understanding the words, he knew that the old lady was binding them all together. Soaking up his pain, sharing his burden with each of them, just as she had back at her flat. He knew she was taking the lion's share of the hurt, but she was so much weaker now.

She held him tight, whispered to him, sang him a lullaby. He didn't want her to go, but he knew this was her final song.

Lightning struck the tower again and again. He was being crushed under an enormous weight. He was a tiny fish lost at the bottom of the ocean, but he was not alone. And then he blinked out.

72

YOU HAVE TO BE LOST TO BE FOUND

"There he is. There's our boy."

It was Goswick's voice.

Oyster opened his eyes and groaned. His entire body ached. Every bone, ligament and piece of cartilage squealed in distress.

Nonesuch came into focus. She leant over him. She looked paler, if that were possible. Drained. Her lips brushed his forehead.

"Thought you'd gone for keeps, Dry Bob." She glimmered a weak purple.

He lay in the four-poster he'd seen on the way up to the lantern room. He shivered. Motet tucked the blankets around him tightly. Nonesuch's brother looked thinner. They all looked like they'd been through the wringer.

"You did good, after all," he said with a yellow flash of approval. "An apology is owed."

"Too right, kid." Goswick leapt on the bed, smothering Oyster's face with a succession of doggy licks.

"Hey! Hey! Not yet," said Nonesuch protectively, pushing Goswick back down onto the floor.

"Come on, we're tight now," said Goswick in protest. "After what we've been through."

Oyster's ears ached and his head throbbed.

Nonesuch nodded.

"Pooch's right. You're only breathing 'cos the old lady bound us together. All alone you wouldn't have made it, but as a unit…"

Oyster caught sight of the familiar figure of Marya Petrovna propped up on the chaise longue.

"How's she doing?" he said.

Nonesuch's expression saddened. She shook her head.

Nonesuch and Motet wrapped themselves in the bed's blankets and slept at the opposite end of the four-poster to Oyster. Goswick slept draped across the centre of the bed. Oyster woke in a sweat in the middle of the night, convinced someone had been creeping around the room, but the place was deserted. He felt much stronger, but the absence of pain from his tattoo made it difficult for him to get back to sleep. He rose silently and wrapped himself in his oilskin.

The fire had gone out and the cold wind whistled in through the broken windows of the lantern room. He shuffled to where Marya Petrovna lay. Her face was grey and unmoving. She looked as though she had just fallen asleep.

Wake up, he thought. *Wake up and cuss me out.*

He took her cold hand. She had been so much larger than life. Primrose had called her the Hag. Could someone like her even die? He knelt by her side, waiting till daybreak for her to wake up and call him a flapdoodle. But she didn't.

In the end, cold and numb, he trudged around the lighthouse. Gingerly at first, but with more confidence once it was evident that Lucas, Primrose and the Mannish were no longer there. A bloodstain on the floor of the lantern room was all that remained of where Lucas had been standing, but he doubted that something like Lugones could be killed so easily. If what he understood of their nature was true, they would have dissipated, everything reset for the next go round. Or perhaps what he had done had disrupted the cycle enough to stop it entirely. He hoped so.

At the very least, the ritual had been completed. Oyster had made a choice. It hadn't been the one that Lucas or Primrose had wanted. He'd refused their ultimatums. But that meant they were on their own now. The world was in a fucking state, but it would be up to humanity to fix it. He hoped he'd done the right thing.

He went through all the cupboards he could, looking for something to eat. Finally, he came across a variety pack of plastic-wrapped cereals, from who knew when.

He broke the cellophane and tore open the Coco Pops, throwing them into his mouth by the handful. He hadn't eaten anything with this much sugar in what seemed like a year, and as delicious as they were, they set his teeth on edge.

A quick search revealed a sink on the ground floor, complete with running water, which was freezing but drinkable. He spent a moment brushing his teeth with his finger. He peeled off his clothes and examined his tattoo. It hadn't spoken to him since he'd woken. As much as he wouldn't miss the constant nagging pain, its absence made him feel light-headed.

Syzygy was asleep beneath his arm like a balled-up woodlouse. She cooed but remained unmoving. He pulled at her gently, but she had attached herself so firmly it hurt to try to move her.

He shrugged and washed himself as best he could, using a cloth hanging over the side of the sink. He dressed and climbed back up into the lantern room, where a quick search revealed a pair of picks and a shovel. He woke the others and together they carried Marya Petrovna's body out onto the ice. It took them an hour to dig a suitable grave, and they worked in silence as the wind bit at them.

Tenderly, they placed her body into the hole they had dug. Oyster put Primrose's coins in one of her hands and her beaded tobacco pouch in the other. Wherever she was now, she would probably need a smoke. He climbed back up and they stood in a circle, looking down at her. Oyster wanted to say something but the words wouldn't come. There was nothing he could say that would make this right. In the end, they covered her body, the coins glowing strangely in the half-light, and then they trooped back up into the lantern room.

"Need a lift, glowworm?" said Oyster to Nonesuch.

"What 'zactly would you be proposing?" she said.

"Just trust me," he said.

He realised that he kept expecting to see Marya Petrovna there, ready with an insult or half-muttered swear word. *I never told her*, he thought mournfully. *I never told her that Yellie was still alive.*

Under Oyster's direction, they took the bedsheets and tore them into strips to make blindfolds. Nonesuch pulled hers on and tightened it. Her arms swung easily over her shoulder sockets in a graphic reminder that she and Oyster were not cut from the same cloth. Once her blindfold was on, he looked at her. She was taller than him, muscular and fearless. He couldn't look away.

"Can still see you, Dry Bob," she said. "Yer blindfolding skills are pants."

Oyster blushed and immediately began to fuss with Motet's blindfold. Nonesuch pulled hers down, letting it dangle round her throat. She strode over to him and touched his cheek. He flinched. The lights in her arms glittered in sequence.

"You're still so opaque," she said. For a second, he felt drawn to kiss her, but instead he swallowed and looked away.

"You could come with," he said.

"And for what? To be in a zoological garden in your London? Thank you, no," she replied. "An' besides, got unfinished business. Peeps need me."

Oyster nodded. She was right, of course. Feelings boiled around within him, but his tongue felt slow and stupid.

Motet cleared his throat theatrically.

"Unless…" she said, "you bein' a walker and all now. Why not stay here with us?"

She glittered with orange flame. Oyster swallowed. Part of him dearly wanted to, but he had to get home to Cécile.

"Tempting," he said. "But I got peeps too. Shit to sort."

"Offer's open, Dry Bob," she said with a smile. "If you change what passes for that mind of yours."

Oyster's face burned. He shook his head slowly and shrugged.

"Well, still gots Syzygy," she continued, nodding. "Make sure you keep in touch."

"Right. Let's get on with this then," said Oyster.

He wasn't sure exactly what he was doing, but he'd seen the Mannish do this sort of thing to travel to and from Greater London. Plus, even though his tattoo was powered down, Marya Petrovna had taught him well. *Sometimes you have to be lost to be found.*

"Right. Try not to think about where you're going. If anything, imagine that you're somewhere else. It's all about intentional vacuity."

"Some of us might find that easier than others," muttered Goswick.

Nonesuch took his hand and he marvelled at the feel of her six fingers in his. Motet held his sister's hand and he in turn carried Goswick.

"I hope you know what you're doing, kid," said the dog. "Or I for one am going to make sure that you never live this one down."

Oyster grunted and shut his eyes. He cleared his mind and took a few steps forward. He imagined himself sliding along the points between one place and the next, slipping into the gaps in between. He imagined Motet and Nonesuch back in Greater London and him in his own city. He took a few more steps forward, suddenly aware of the sound of his own breathing. Stretching out a hand, he touched the cold stone of the lighthouse wall with his fingertips.

He worked his way along the wall, suddenly aware that they weren't far from the trapdoor, and the last thing he wanted to do was fall through it.

Then he was on his own.

"Hey! Watch it, dickhead," said a man's voice a couple of centimetres from his face.

73
TOOTING

Oyster opened his eyes. The man he'd collided with was already walking away in the opposite direction, conspicuously checking his pockets for his wallet. Oyster was on the platform in a London Underground station. *His* London Underground. Nonesuch, Motet and Goswick were no longer with him, but he had a feeling in his gut that they'd arrived home too. A wave of nausea broke over him and he had to steady himself against the station's cold tiles while the feeling ebbed away. Jumping with everyone had done him in. He wouldn't be able to flit again for a while yet.

He shut his eyes and breathed it all in. The electric smell of the tunnels. The red, white and blue of the Tooting Bec Tube sign. Okay, he'd not made it all the way home, but close enough.

The shuffle of shoes on concrete. Coughs and shoves, shouts and phones. People pressed past him, their ears plugged with headphones. He wanted to run up and hug each and every one of them, declaring his return to the city that he loved and hated with equal measure. A wave of scorched air rode down the tunnel and washed over him, announcing a train. *Fuck me, it's hot down here.* He peeled off the oilskin. As he manoeuvred it over his arm, an envelope fell from its pockets. He turned it over. Written on it in ballpoint was the word:

Flapdoodle

He felt Marya Petrovna's absence keenly now; yearned for her reassuring presence by his side. It was as though he was missing a limb. Breathing heavily, he ran a nail under the flap and peeled it open. As he tipped it up, a brass key fell into his hand. Inside was a slip of paper and a folded note. On the paper, written in Marya Petrovna's hurried hand, was the address of a container storage company in Chelsea. Beneath it were six numbers – a PIN code, he figured – and the words *Unit 23A*. The paper was old, yellow and stained. *Yak's milk tea, probably*, thought Oyster with a smile that ached in his chest. But this was something for later. Right now, he needed to see Cécile. He stowed the envelope's contents and ran up and out of the station. He didn't stop running until he arrived at Deeside.

Oyster slipped into Deeside without being seen by anyone. The sun outside made the building's interior all the more gloomy. Skipping the unreliable lifts, he crept up the echoing stairs, hood up, shrinking into the shadows as much as possible.

He no longer felt too anxious about Mickey and the rest of the Urbans, but he didn't want any complications with the cops until he had a chance to fix things. He reached his flat without being made, opening the door as quietly as possible and tiptoeing inside.

It seemed an age since he had last been here. But everything seemed the same as it always had, as if he'd never been away.

And then Cécile was in his arms so quickly that it seemed like maybe she could flit too. "Where have you been, you idiot?" she said, words muffled by his chest, holding him tighter than he'd ever been held.

74
UNIT 23A

A few days later, Oyster was walking down the Kings Road. He'd forgotten how bright the sun was here, in his London. He'd always think of his home that way now. One of a smear of possibilities that were only a misread map apart.

At Cécile's insistence, he'd written up how things had gone down; how Deano had murdered Broadsides. He'd made two copies, marked one of them for the attention of Officer Peach and sent the second to Big Mickey. He still had a lot of explaining to do, but maybe this would start things turning his way.

For now, though, he was enjoying the rare feeling of the sun on his face and the wind rustling the trees in this moneyed part of town. Enormous houses stood in long white rows like a procession of perfect teeth. He couldn't quite get used to how high the sky felt, and its diamond hardness hurt his eyes.

Oyster arrived at the address. A concrete ramp led downwards to an automatic steel door with and number pad. CCTV cameras watched him from every angle. He sauntered down the ramp and punched in the PIN. After a pause, the door slid open, rattling like thunder, and Oyster ducked beneath it. The storage facility contained row upon row of metal units.

He shivered, suddenly cold. He hated these bloody places, with their damp corners and fluorescent lighting. Crossing to a stairwell, he pushed through the door. A pool of shadows lurked at the bottom of the next landing. He felt a sudden chill and thought about Primrose, but pressed ahead, lights flickering on as he descended. Emerging onto the second floor down, he found the container marked 23A.

The brass key was stiff in its padlock, but eventually the unit's doors swung open on rusty hinges. A musty smell rolled out of the container and Oyster stepped into it.

Inside were all manner of tables and furniture. There were cabinets painted with starred motifs, large glass tanks with ostentatious padlocks, and crates festooned with chains and velvet curtains. They were Marya Petrovna's stage illusions.

On a low wooden table was a thick leatherbound book. Oyster picked it up and opened it at random. The handwritten pages crackled as he turned them.

"'Instructions for the levitating cow: a stage effect by M. Benjamin Fauks & Mme Dozvhenko of the Miracle Club,'" he read out loud. He replaced it on the table before squatting on the ground amongst the assorted illusions. He found and unfolded Marya Petrovna's final note to him:

> I still think you would
> look good in leotard.
> P.S. Feed Minnie.

The laugh wormed its way up from his stomach, snaked around his face and forced itself out of his mouth. He laughed until he ached, until he was on his knees and his lungs burned from lack of air. Even then, he carried on laughing until he was lying on his back, kicking his feet in the air, the tears streaming down his face. And when he stopped, he realised there was one more thing to do.

It took him an hour to get back to Westminster Bridge from Chelsea. At first, he was a little surprised to see the gang still there, working their normal turf. But then, Deano's greed would never let them ignore their most profitable pitch for long.

Eventually, he picked out Baby Ed hanging about on the perimeter on lookout, but a crowd of punters obscured the game's dealer. The boy was almost unrecognisable, he was limping and his face was a tangle of yellowing bruises that still looked painful. Primrose had really done him over, up on the roof of Deeside West. When Ed spotted him, Oyster watched the emotions chase each other across the boy's ruined face.

He adjusted his baseball cap and, despite his discomfort, tried to swagger up to meet Oyster halfway, limbering up as though ready for a bout. *He's got balls, that's for sure*, thought Oyster.

"Well, well," wheedled Ed in his breaking voice. "Come back for another doofing?"

Adrenaline throbbed around Oyster's body. His first instinct was to head-butt the boy before he'd even finished the sentence. But he realised, in that moment, that Ed was just as much a victim of the gang's fucked-up priorities as he'd been.

Oyster feinted and Ed flinched. Then he raised his hands.

"Come in peace, brother," he said.

"Leave in pieces, more like," said Ed. "You're still a grass."

"Time to reassess your choices," said Oyster.

Ed stepped up to him and they butted foreheads. Oyster smelled the sickly-sweet mixture of Coca-Cola and burgers on his breath.

"Got nothing but pity for you," he said gently.

The boy continued to block his way.

"Where does a two-inch prick like you get off pitying me?" he grunted.

Oyster gave him his best have-you-looked-in-a-mirror-recently look and Ed's patience snapped. He went in to nut him, but Oyster flitted through him and the boy catapulted onto the concrete with a terrified grunt.

Oyster leaned over him as he struggled to get up.

"Who do you think did for Broadsides?" said Oyster with a nod towards Deano. "Truth'll set you free," he called over his shoulder as he walked over to the game.

Deano was hunched over his palette midway through a deal and didn't look up.

"Game is bent, ladies and gents," announced Oyster at the top of his voice. "Better bounce, cops are coming."

He took aim at Deano's palette and kicked it across the pavement, sending it skidding into the gutter. Deano looked up, in shock. He recovered himself and stood. Anyone else might have thought it was an easy-going stance, but Oyster knew there was nothing slow or lazy about it. The crowd melted away.

"You have an appointment with Big Mickey, *capitan*. I'm thinking he's gonna want to know how you've been working with Primrose to sneak his crew out from under him. And how you helped fuck over Broadsides."

Deano nodded. Oyster's only response was to stare at him with all the contempt he could muster. For a long second their eyes locked, and then Deano looked away. The man shrank before him. He knew the score had changed. Oyster was beyond his reach now. He picked up the palette and ambled into the crowd.

Behind Oyster there was a clattering sound and car horns blared. A vehicle was driving up the wrong side of the road on the bridge, careening up onto the pavement where it couldn't pass. It was an ancient, cream Volvo Amazon that had seen better days. Oyster broke into a smile.

There was only one old lady he knew who drove that badly.

ACKNOWLEDGEMENTS

Many thanks to my wonderful wife who has to hear all my daft ideas before anyone gets to read them, my daughter who has better ideas than me and never lets me forget it and my son who is, and always will be, an ideas man.

Thanks also to my agent Sam who saw the potential in Oyster before anyone else did and who is always in my corner. Likewise Michaela Roessner who encouraged the potential in me many years ago.

Also, a massive thank you to: Guy T. Martland (cacaw!) and Doug Howell who read early versions of this book and gave insightful and detailed feedback. The talented writers who run and attend the Milford SF Writers Conference. Toby Litt and the rest of the fantastic MFA Omnipeeps: Devin, Patrick, Sam, Finn, Mel, Aisling, Peggy, Anna, Brett and Hannah and my bass brother Warren 'Waz' Pleece, Sue and the boys.

Thanks to all the brilliant creative people at Titan: especially my editor Daniel who helped to ensure that each chapter closed with something other than people falling asleep; Bahar, Katharine, Caitlin and Kabriya for all your publicity smarts; and Miss Nat Mack and Richard Mason who ensured that both the outside and the inside of this book are equally gorgeous.

And lastly, a big thanks to Mum and Pops: look where lending me all those books ended up.

ABOUT THE AUTHOR

PHILIP A. SUGGARS has a single yellow eye in the middle of his forehead and a collection of vintage binoculars. His work has appeared in *Strange Horizons*, *The Guardian* and *Interzone* as well as being featured on many short-form podcasts. His writing has won the Ilkley short story prize, been long-listed for the BSFA short story award and been included in *The Best of British Science Fiction Anthology* series. When not writing words, he records music as one half of the post-punk electronica outfit, we are concrete. Born and raised in South London, he currently lives on the south coast with his family. *The Lighthouse at the End of the World* is his debut novel.

Also available from Titan Books

BASILISK

MATT WIXEY

Alex Webster is an ethical hacker who, like most hackers, prefers questions to answers. So when she and a colleague, Jay Morton, stumble across a mysterious game created by a shadowy figure known as The Helmsman, they are instantly hooked.

As they solve increasingly bizarre puzzles and uncover The Helmsman's deranged manifesto, they are pursued by a sinister group known only as XXX XXXXXXX XXXXXX, who will do anything to stop them uncovering the Basilisk, a cognitive weapon which makes anyone who understands it lose their mind.

When Jay disappears just as they close in on the truth, Alex is left trying to piece together what's happened to her friend, escape the awful smiling glitch people stalking her every move, and solve The Helmsman's final puzzle.

TITANBOOKS.COM

Also available from Titan Books

APPARENTLY, SIR CAMERON NEEDS TO DIE

GREER STOTHERS

In Which Many Dangerous and Homosexual Things Happen.

All his life, Sir Cameron has stayed as far away from danger as possible. He is, quite frankly, too handsome to die a pointless death in battle. But then the Church hands down a prophecy to his fellow knights: the only way to defeat their nemesis, the mad sorcerer Merulo, is to kill Sir Cameron. Short of ideas, Cameron throws himself on the mercy of the one person left who wants him to survive: the mad sorcerer.

Merulo isn't thrilled to be babysitting a spoilt, attention-seeking knight, but transmogrifying him into a vulture is at least entertaining. Cameron, meanwhile, is on a voyage of self-discovery. It turns out he's really, really into surly sorcerers who lock him up and tell him what to do. Who knew?

As a legion of knights surround their stronghold, Cameron finds he's still quite invested in not dying, but he's also invested in Merulo. And sometimes, supporting the sorcerer you care about means taking an interest in their hobbies. Even if that hobby is trying to kill God.

Even if it might get you killed, too.

TITANBOOKS.COM

Also available from Titan Books

STARTUP HELL

CAITLIN ROZAKIS

Morgan Blackwater is a junior salesperson at Zabloom, a tech startup that can't even decide what its product is. With magic dyslexia and a world-saving, demon-slaying Shadow Council wizard for a mother, Morgan is doing her best to carve out a niche for herself in the mundane world.

Until she discovers her boss dead in his office, along with the demon he summoned to trade his soul and make his quarterly target – the disturbingly-attractive Lucareoth (Luke for short), who is trapped on Earth until he finds someone to sell their soul.

With her mother hunting rumours of a rogue demon, Morgan struggles to protect Luke, help him get back home and navigate the dual corporate nightmares of the human world and the Infernal Plane. But one soul short of hitting their quota, the pair begin to realise that sacrificing their colleagues' souls – even the really annoying ones – isn't an option for them. What they need is something bigger…

TITANBOOKS.COM

For more fantastic fiction, author events,
exclusive excerpts, competitions, limited editions and more

VISIT OUR WEBSITE
titanbooks.com

LIKE US ON FACEBOOK
facebook.com/titanbooks

FOLLOW US ON TWITTER AND INSTAGRAM
@TitanBooks

EMAIL US
readerfeedback@titanemail.com